William Mumford Baker

A Year worth Living

A Story of a Place and of a People one cannot afford not to know

William Mumford Baker

A Year worth Living
A Story of a Place and of a People one cannot afford not to know

ISBN/EAN: 9783337218751

Printed in Europe, USA, Canada, Australia, Japan

Cover: Foto ©Andreas Hilbeck / pixelio.de

More available books at **www.hansebooks.com**

A YEAR WORTH LIVING:

A STORY

OF A PLACE AND OF A PEOPLE ONE CANNOT AFFORD NOT TO KNOW.

BY

WILLIAM M. BAKER,

Author of "Inside," "The New Timothy," "Mose Evans," "Carter Quarterman," etc.

———•———

BOSTON:

LEE AND SHEPARD, PUBLISHERS.

NEW YORK:

CHARLES T. DILLINGHAM.

1878.

I DEDICATE

THIS STORY

TO

MY SON D. B. B.,

AS AN EVIDENCE OF THE

ENTIRE CONFIDENCE, AS WELL AS HEARTY LOVE,

OF

HIS FATHER.

A PORTION of this book was published in "The Christian at Work," of New York. That, however, was but the germ out of which this volume has grown to such a degree as to deserve, as it has received, a new name.

CONTENTS.

4 CONTENTS.

CHAPTER XXIX.

CHAPTER XXX.

CHAPTER XXXI.

A YEAR WORTH LIVING.

A STORY OF A PLACE AND OF A PEOPLE ONE CANNOT AFFORD NOT TO KNOW.

CHAPTER I.

IN WHICH THE COLUMBUS OF THIS HISTORY SETS OUT FOR A NEW WORLD.

IT certainly seemed to Hartman Venable, the Wednesday afternoon he went aboard the steamship Nautilus, as if he were leaving an old and very dismal world. Earlier in the day he had sent his trunk to the boat, and nothing was left him but to follow. It proved, however, a good deal to do. The rain was pouring in torrents; and it took all his strength to keep his umbrella from wreck, as he strove along in the gusts of the storm. He was young, ardent, and full of an enthusiasm which bore him up like a kite against the wind, the harder it blew, so that the tempest was a welcome variety to his other and more sober enjoyments.

"Dame Nature," he said to himself, as he struggled down the street, "is having a washing-day of it, with a vengeance. What a vixen she is! The moment the black clouds stop pouring down, to rest a bit, she rushes at them as if they were lazy negroes, scolding and shrieking until they come back to their work with a sort of sullen fury." For the events to be herein recorded took place in the South, and before emancipation.

As he spoke, he wound his way at last through the merchandise heaped upon the wharves of the city from which he was departing, and which lined the shores of the great river for miles up and down. It was not easy to find his steamship among the scores of vessels of all sorts lying there. He knew it after a while by the black smoke from its chimneys, and climbed up the slippery gangway, very wet, and glad to be under shelter again. Pausing in the doorway of the cabin to fold his dripping umbrella, he cast a last look at the acres of cotton-bales, flour-barrels, sugar-hogsheads, and the like, each heap sheltered under tarpaulin.

"It is like so many corpses covered with sheets," he said to himself. "No wonder. You are all of you a dead world to me." As he spoke, the exasperated wind made one last rush at him, seized upon his umbrella, turned it inside out, snatched it from his wet hands, and cast it contemptuously into the river beyond.

"What do I care, old lady?" he said with a laugh. "I am going where people do not use umbrellas. Good-by." And he sought his stateroom.

By the time he had changed his clothes, supper was ready; an erect steward tapping at the door of his room, and telling him so in a certain military manner, which was acceptable, as signifying discipline on board, and consequent security. At the same moment the Nautilus backed from its wharf slowly and with many a groan. Heading down stream in an uncertain fashion, as if it had been aroused out of sound sleep, and was not quite awake, the boat began to settle itself to its work.

Possibly young Venable would not have gone to the supper-table with quite so much alacrity, had he known the opinions of old Steve, the rough and very tough negro hand, who made the morning fires in the wharf office of "The

Line," and was always on hand to cast off the cables of its boats when they left Wednesday nights. As the Nautilus drew itself painfully away from the landing, and as if out of clinging mire, Steve stood still for some time upon the shore, notwithstanding the down-pour, his wise old head upon one side, looking with a curiously solemn air at the boat, very much as if it were at a hearse departing from his door. At last, with a slow and sorrowful shake of his head, he sought his home in a dingy cellar near the wharf, and seated himself to his pork and grits. Even then he paused, knife and fork in hand, his face full of the same mournful thought.

"Dun gone?" asked his wife as sadly.

"Dun gone?" he replied. "Yes, old 'oman. De boat dun gone agin. I know I's said so for years; but dis time must be de last. Old 'oman, de Nautilus *can't* stand it. My Lor'! It's unpossible."

It was a singular coincidence. At the same moment the captain of the Nautilus was saying to his purser in the privacy of a glass or so of hot whiskey in the stateroom of the latter, which was also the " office," "Think the old tub will pull through this time, Jim?"

"My life's insured," the purser replied as coolly. "Insured for my wife, heavy. Best speculation I know. So is the Nautilus. Will she pull through? Can't say I do. Don't see how she *can*. You heard those stevedores, captain? They swore, only half in joke, they must have double pay for putting that tobacco aboard. The very rustabouts were afraid the weight would jar the old concern to flinders here at the wharf."

"Oh, well!" the other replied, as he drained his tumbler, and drew on his waterproofs for deck service, "I'll resk it. It's been a wonder to me for ten years how she stands it. Resk it this time, any way!"

Which was human nature. Even had Mr. Venable known

every thing, being actually on board, and the boat having started, his feeling, too, would have been, " Very well : I'll risk it." Women excepted, the sentiment is, in all like cases, spontaneous, universal, and of practical use.

Probably there were others who, knowing of the facts, had concluded not to risk it : certainly there were few passengers at the supper-table. The only one of these who seemed disposed — with such a roar of rain on the roof, and such a convulsive effort of the intermittent engine below — to conversation was an unusually large, florid, and genial-faced gentleman, whom our passenger hoped might possibly be a certain sugar-planter bearing a name familiar to him of late.

" This seat, Gen. Buttolph," the captain said, as they sat down, giving him the place of honor on his right.

" I am glad to know from your agent," the general replied, as they took their seats, — " glad to know," he repeated in a hearty way, — " that the Nautilus is thoroughly seaworthy. Especially as it is storming so. More especially still as I have my daughters with me : they are naturally timid, as well as unused to the sea."

" O papa ! how can you say so ? I adore the sea. You know I told you so." It was the elder of the two young ladies seated by their father who spoke. " It is Zeo you mean," she added.

The young passenger sitting opposite them had already glanced at the sister alluded to. While the one who spoke was tall and fair, and apparently the most energetic and talkative of the two, the other was low and dark, and yet somehow much more attractive by reason of a sort of meaning in the very repose of her silence. That might be mere fancy ; yet she held his attention to a singular degree.

" I am glad to hear it, miss. I think you said it was Miss Irene, general ? " And the captain hastened to add, " Have some hot steak, ladies. — Steward ! — You were speaking of the weather, general. It is merely a little rain. We always have it as the year goes out. Allow me to introduce Mr. — I believe you said your name was " —

"Venable, Hartman Venable," the person alluded to said, with a bow over his plate.

"I thought so, papa ! " the elder of the young ladies exclaimed, with an energy that brought the blood to the cheek of her sister. "You are, oh, so much younger than we expected ! but " —

"Irene ! " It was all her sister said, not looking up from her plate in her modesty. But it checked her impulsive sister as effectually as if she had placed her hand over her mouth.

"I am glad to know you, Mr. Venable," their father said at the moment. "I am Gen. Buttolph," shaking cordial hands with him across the table. "You may remember the name in the correspondence we have had with you. I am pleased to know you," and he evidently was.

To Mr. Venable, after the wetting he had got, and in his lonely estate, just separated from the entire world of his life up to date, it was a thing particularly welcome to find himself with so hearty and wholesome a companion. In the miserable little saloon tossing and tilting, the very presence of such a friend gave assurance of a substantial world yet.

"These are my daughters, sir," the general added, waving a large hand toward each. "My eldest, Irene ; my youngest, Zenobia, but we call her Zeo. Zeno would have been more natural as a pet name ; but he was a philosopher, somewhat sour I am told."

"Is it all of your family? " asked Mr. Venable, with deference, and merely to make a beginning.

"All except one, —our little boy in St. Jerome ; our spoiled baby," the general replied. "He is eight years old, and his name is Theodore."

"Would you like to know what we call him? " asked the elder of the sisters.

"Certainly, if you please," the young gentleman replied,
falling into her mood.

"Grit : shameful, isn't it?   Yes, Grit : in full, Clear Grit ;
he has been so self-willed ever since he was born.   He is the
shortest and fattest boy you ever saw ; at least, he was when
we left home for school.   He is going to be," Miss Irene
continued, "the living image of papa : he will lengthen out."

"Irene !"   It was all that her sister said ; but she again
yielded to the check, especially as the general began to speak
of St. Jerome, the city to which they were all bound.

The military steward smiled grimly as he helped the company to hot biscuit ; for the river down which they were sailing was soon to end in the sea, — a sea never more rough
than at this season.   He was a Prussian soldier, who had
deserted Germany and glory for America and the saucepan ;
but his drill stuck to him still, and he presented the uncorked
mouth of the ale-bottle to the glass held out to him by the
captain as if it was the point, instead, of his sword in salute.

"Come, captain," said Gen. Buttolph, rising up after a
meal which had been lengthened out by much pleasant talk,
"you long as I do for a cigar and for the deck, if it does
rain ; " and the two disappeared.   No one remained but the
young people and a sunburned seafaring man whom the
captain had introduced to them at table as Capt. Chaffin,
but who had eaten with mechanical movement of knife and
fork, taking no part in the conversation.   Seated with his
chest and head projected at a considerable angle with the
back of his chair and over the table, he had struck Mr.
Venable as being ridiculously like the figure-head, carved
out of walnut, — so very rigid and brown was he, — of a
vessel under full sail, silence being apparently part of his
very nature.

Mr. Venable had small trouble to keep up the conversation which followed after the steward had cleared the table ;
and they had seated themselves again around it under the

uncertain shining of the lamp swinging above, Miss Irene hastening to entertain him.

"If you want to know *all* about us," she said, "there is one more of our household to tell you of. We have got an old uncle Plenty at home, and a young Plenty, and a Mrs. Plenty, and all the rest; but there is one more of us on board."

"Irene," her sister said, "please don't. Mr. Venable can hardly care to hear about our " —

"Oh, yes, he does! you do, I'm sure. Besides, we have to become well acquainted some day, and why not at once?" demanded her lively sister. "Pa bought the one I mean in the city yesterday. I mention her because I am perplexed what to name her. Perhaps you can help me."

As she spoke she indicated by a motion of her thumb over her shoulder a mulatto girl who was standing behind her chair. Mr. Venable had already noticed her casually as the prettiest quadroon he had ever seen. She wore a good deal of brass jewelry about her neck, ears, and hands, and seemed of too slight a form to do much hard work. A crimson handkerchief of silk was wound about her black and abundant hair; but it was the stag-like eyes of the girl that struck him most, they were so large and so purely animal.

"I lay awake last night, running over all the names I could think of," her voluble young mistress continued, — "Flora, Cleopatra, Juno, Gloriana. How would Indiana do?"

"Very well," the gentleman said; "but, as you may know, I have been for the last six years in college and seminary, and have hardly seen one of your sex. How would Iphigenia do?" he added.

"Admirably. — Remember," the young lady said to her attendant, "your name is Iphigenia, — Iph-i-genia: don't forget."

"Yes'm," the servant replied with a ready smile, and showing her white teeth. Miss Irene changed the conversation, and Miss Zenobia seated by her was contented to listen while the other proceeded to tell Mr. Venable that they had not been in St. Jerome since their mother's death, two years ago; but she gave him a full description of the place and people up to that date. Then, in answer to a question which it required some swiftness on the young man's part to slip in, she gave an account of their school. Mr. Venable enjoyed the rapid talk of the eager girl, her hands and her fine eyes as incessantly in motion as her tongue. And a vast deal she had to tell about the principal of the school, "the hateful madame; the wretch, she painted so!" she said at last. At the word, Capt. Chaffin, reading near them, lowered his paper as by a spasm, but lifted it again as she added, "Her cheeks, I mean," and proceeded to speak of "the splendid drives" about the school, "the miserable cookery," "the awful meanness" of the school gardener, and of his "adorable flowers." Then, in reply to a question, she hoped they would have a real storm at sea, it was "so romantic," and a good deal to that effect. All the time their bronzed fellow-passenger had been seated with a newspaper, evidently absorbed in the slowly-read shipping intelligence, no more interested in her rapid talk than if it had been, instead, the whistling of a blackbird. And so for an hour. "But, O Mr. Venable! you ought to have seen our school gallery," she was saying at last. "We had, I do believe, some of the most glorious paintings." At the word the man laid down his paper with an, —

"Ahem!" There was such metallic sound in the exclamation, that the energetic speaker paused. "Ahem! Pardon me. You were speaking of paintings," Capt. Chaffin interposed, in dry accents. "My wife paints;" and he turned his eyes slowly and steadily upon his three companions, each in turn, to see the effect of the announcement.

There was dead silence for a moment; and then, with a sudden light breaking upon her face, the elder sister turned upon the younger, opening her eyes to their utmost while she slowly drew in her breath, — an expression of comic wonder on her face. But Mr. Venable's attention was drawn from every thing else by the prompt action of Miss Zenobia, who had hitherto sat so silent: there was quiet energy in it as she laid firm hold upon her sister's arm, as if to prevent some explosion, and said, —

"You are Mrs. Capt. Chaffingsby's husband; are you not, sir?"

"Chaffingsby, or Chaffin. Yes, miss," he answered: "I'm Capt. Chaffin. It's my wife who — *paints*," with stress on the last word. "You've seen her paintings, miss?" — with slow but proud expectation.

"Yes, sir," she replied, tightening her hold on her sister's arm, and coloring, but with great sweetness; "and I was much struck by them. Irene!" she added, and then, "please excuse us."

"It's the coming-on of sea-sickness, sir," Capt. Chaffin said, in low and solemn accents, to young Venable, as the ladies withdrew somewhat hastily.

"Why, hardly," his companion said: "we won't be out of the river for hours."

"No, not you and me," said Capt. Chaffin in a hollow whisper behind his hand. "It's their sex. We are nothing but men, you see," with a downward motion of his brown hand, and an odd contempt upon his stolid face. "Men! They are weemen! We are tough, very tough. They're as deelicate, now, as dreadful deelicate as — as —a—a—sea-shell. That's where they get their nice tastes and touches. That's how they come by their per-ception of beauty, their genius. There's my wife, now;" and the speaker paused at the word, and sat, his head projected forward, his eyes fastened upon the other side of the saloon, in rigid meditation concerning the lady alluded to.

"Have you any family besides?" his companion asked, at last, since there evidently was so much of interest left unsaid.

"Two children," Capt. Chaffin replied, — "one boy, one girl, twins, — Clara, Charles. But I was not speaking of *them*," he added, in such tones, that, although not knowing at all why he should do so, Mr. Venable said, "Ah! pray excuse me."

"I was speaking of my wife," the other continued, as if he were speaking of a city or an empire, — "my wife;" and he turned his face full upon his companion, and announced it as if it were a doctrine of theology or science. "She paints. Paints pictures. She is the slightest woman you ever saw. Pale. Thin. Deelicate. A breeze would blow her away. A bad smell hits her like a capstan bar. You might as well put a bullet in her stomach as a tough steak, — from a pistol, I mean. It is because she is all gone to soul. She paints pictures, — pictures almost as large as the side of a ship."

"Ah!" the other replied, greatly interested. "I will be glad to know her. I am fond of pictures. I presume she paints landscapes?"

"Landscapes!" Capt. Chaffin ejaculated, with contempt. "Not a bit of it. Nor seascapes either. She paints" — and very slowly he added, after a pause, and in words each to itself, — "she paints Prophets. Apostles. Kings. Martyrs. Evangelists. Seraphim. Cherubim. Archangels. She has painted" — and he looked steadily in the wondering eyes of his new friend, — "has painted our Lord himself, and on the Mount of Transfiguration at that. She wanted" — and the seaman looked so long, without adding any thing, into the eyes of the other, that Mr. Venable had to say, "She wanted — may I ask what?"

"She wanted to paint him on his throne in heaven, and surrounded by all his saints! That I would not allow. I said, No! I said," continued Capt. Chaffin, "'You are already as slim and frail, Angeline, as a bubble. You eat nothing. You never sleep. Your soul is grand, but your body has to have its rations too. As your husband, Angeline, you shall *not!* Apart from Charles and Clara, you have other duties. Better slacken down instead. Slow yourself down, if you must paint, by letting it be Phip Quatty, or me ; ease yourself down to a horse or a dog or a negro baby ; any thing.' I tell you, sir, — for she wouldn't, she screamed at the idea, — I tell you, sir "— and Capt. Chaffin leaned, in his kindling enthusiasm, nearer to the one addressed, lowering his tones to a whisper in the fervor of his feeling, "I tell you, sir "—

But, on the instant, Gen. Buttolph and the captain of the Nautilus returned from deck. With their return the light faded suddenly from the face of the admiring husband. He drew himself back from his companion, took up his newspaper again, and was nothing but a walnut figure-head as before. "It was well I did," he added, full ten minutes after, in a whisper to Mr. Venable, from behind cover of his paper, — "well I did ! It would have killed her, sir, — killed her dead."

CHAPTER II.

IN WHICH WE FIND THAT TO LEAVE AN OLD WORLD IS NOT
ALWAYS TO STEP ASHORE RIGHT AWAY UPON A NEW.

HARTMAN VENABLE went to his stateroom as Gen.
Buttolph and the captain of the vessel entered the
cabin. Entertaining as Miss Irene's talk was, and still more
attractive to him as was her silent sister, he had been
wishing to do so for some time. With the first day rapidly
approaching of the new year he would be twenty-one ; and
he intended, before he went to sleep, to make a new and
special consecration of himself to his work.

His history up to that moment can be put into a brief
compass. Born in a Southern State, his parents had died
as he left school, leaving him without brother or sister, and,
as he was quite poor, no relative to claim any interest in
him. By hard work he had contrived to scramble through
college, and, after that, through a training for the pulpit.
Owing to the stringency of his circumstances, he had been
compelled to devote himself to his studies to the neglect
of his bodily strength. He stood none the less at the head
of his class when he graduated at the Northern seminary
in which his course was completed. When, therefore, the
institution was written to for their best man, from the important South-western city of St. Jerome, he was immediately
selected and sent. Like the wheat-seed held so long in the
hand of the Egyptian mummy, his arrested health and vigor

needed but the opportunity to assert itself. Conscious that he had been too long shut up to books and from men, he was eager to give himself heartily in whatever direction his work should open to him; specially glad to get back to his native South, and into so fresh and promising a part thereof.

But he had not counted upon coming so soon in his career upon ladies like these, and especially upon one such as the younger of the two sisters. The older of them had told him, amid a good deal of other information, that Zeo was not yet eighteen; and he felt, that, being three years her senior, he had a right to admire her as the loveliest lady he had ever seen; to admire her so much, in fact, separated as he had been from the sex so long, as materially to interfere with the train of meditation he had intended to pursue.

As he strove to turn his mind from her, there was a knock at his door, and the captain of the steamer came in.

"I didn't like to mention it," he said mysteriously, "to Gen. Buttolph, seeing he has his daughters aboard."

"Sir?" the other said. "I do not understand"—

"I would rather you would not lock yourself in to-night," the captain said in a low tone, closing the door of the little room after him.

"Why not?" demanded the other, in surprise.

"I'm not the agent," the captain said, "and of course you'll be quiet about it. I don't sell the tickets, nor do any of the writing-out, any more than I do the sticking-up, of the steamship posters. It's very stormy, and the Nautilus wasn't launched yesterday."

"I do not understand you," the other repeated, understanding him perfectly none the less, more from the manner of the captain than from his words.

"Yes, you do," the seaman said. "And Gen. Buttolph, too; he ought to have known better than to bring his girls aboard. But she *may* stand it." With which words he withdrew.

Young and strong as he was, the passenger felt a numbness in his very fingers' ends as he shut his door; and then, drawing on his overcoat, but exchanging his boots for a pair of slippers from his trunk, — as a sort of gear he could more easily kick off in case there was any swimming to be done, — he stole out by way of the deserted cabin to the deck. The rain had ceased, as if blown out of existence by the furious wind. It was as dark as if the darkness was a solid something pinning them down upon the writhing sea for the wind to scourge. The lantern aloft and the light in the binnacle only made the night seem more dense and dreadful. Not merely the howling hatred, as it were, of the wind: the motion, too, of the vessel rendered it impossible to stand; and, staggering to one side, the youth laid hold upon what he took to be a mass of sail, very wet. "What pitiful insects we are!" he said, trying to adjust himself to a new and peculiar rise and fall of the steamship as it left the river for the sea. "Listen to the consumptive rattle of that engine below. Three wise men of Gotham went to sea in a bowl. If the bowl had been stronger, my song had been longer. One ought to have serious thoughts. It is strange I should be so foolish just now, and so glad too. But, yes, how weak is man" —

"Like being aboard an egg-shell," the roll of sail to which, as he supposed, he had been holding, remarked at this moment, in a lull of the wind.

"You don't think she is strong," he replied, letting go in his surprise, then laying hold of him again.

"Strong enough," his companion said, when another pause of the wind allowed, "for a pickerel pond, with weemin for a crew. Weemin ought never to go from shore: their sphere is on land, where things" — and the last words had to be spoken in a shout — "is tasty and deel-i-cate" — at the top of his voice, such was the fury of the wind; and Mr. Venable knew that the bundle of dripping sail was no other than Capt. Chaffin.

"Why did the captain start? Why didn't he anchor before we left the river?" the other shouted, as the storm lowered enough to allow of it. But the tempest was howling the same questions, with (as in the case of every thing when it is working itself into a passion) ascending inflections; and Capt. Chaffin had to wait, — to wait so long, that, absorbed in the grandeur of the occasion, young Venable had forgotten what he had asked, when, the uproar allowing of it, his companion shouted, —

"Instructions! Insured! Money! They stay a-*shore!*" the last syllable in competition with the blast rising again. The young man understood it as an allusion to the owners; yet, terrible as the hour was, he had no wish to be on shore with them. Although he was slightly built for his years, and pretty thoroughly exhausted by a course of hard study; and although the midnight lamp had been fed, in fact, by the fat (if such an impropriety may be allowed) of his body, — the marrow of his youthful bones having been fallen back upon when that was gone, — yet the over-culture of mind had resulted in the increase of that which is the very fat and marrow of the mind, will-power. Will, — the most splendid gift God gives, and that which most establishes our kinship to the Executive of the universe. It did its best, the will of this young man, to make up to and for the body what it had stolen from the body. It helped the eyes to see, where they would otherwise have been shut; it made the feet go, the hands work, the lips laugh, the heart beat as merrily as a kettle-drum; and all when, apart from such a will, the wearied body couldn't and wouldn't. At that instant the stomach of the man would have been deadly seasick; but the man himself, which means the man's will, would not hear of such a thing. Bodily speaking, he was in awful fear of being drowned, if it were not that this will of his, since it could not be drowned by all the water earth has, would not let him be afraid, — made him glad instead.

As Capt. Chaffin shouted the last words recorded, there
had been a general movement of the crew forward; one
could feel it was so, rather than see it in the darkness, or
hear it in the uproar. A yell from the seaman by his side
sounded like " pumps !" and, clinging to his companion, the
young man crowded a place for himself at the brakes, and
worked as he had never wrought before, even at the toughest
place in his Hebrew Bible. After some hours of this, and
when he could pump no more, another way of working came
into his mind. Staggering, tumbling, crawling, rolling from
side to side with the laboring vessel, aided by an opportune
pitch of the same in that direction, he descended the stairs
into the cabin. Gathering himself up, for he had fallen
head foremost, he worked his way to Gen. Buttolph's stateroom, and, after banging at the door in vain, opened it and
went in. To his astonishment the general had wedged himself tight into his berth by means of his carpet-bags and
valises, and was sound asleep. An unusually large man, in
full flesh, the power in this case lay on the side of the body.
It used its dead force in that direction, and slept; slept under
the inertia of his full weight down that line, slept like a big
babe being rocked by the ocean as if it were its mother, so
profoundly that his visitor had great difficulty in awakening
and then in explaining matters to him. On the instant of
entering the room, he had observed a strong smell of brandy, so strong that he had said to himself, " I suppose the
general brought a flask in case of sickness, and it has got
smashed. Whew ! It must have been a demijohn instead
of a flask."

" Miss Buttolph !" he cried, beating at the door of the
ladies' room while the father very slowly and stupidly arose
and dressed himself, "Miss Zenobia ! Miss Irene ! Don't be
alarmed. Please get up !"

He need not have slipped into his own room after doing
so, as hastily as he did : for, although Miss Zenobia came out

on the instant, she had been neither undressed nor asleep.
On returning he saw, by the dim shining of the lamp swinging violently to and fro, that the general and his daughters
had come into the saloon, and were holding to each other
and to the table. Hardly awake as yet, the father was explaining to them that there was no cause for alarm at all, no
actual danger. "At the same time," he repeated, "it is best
to be awake and prepared;" and he continued repeating
at intervals, "best to be prepared, best to be prepared," in a
somewhat sodden manner which surprised his new acquaintance.

As Venable looked at the general saying this, he saw that
there is a sort of strength in avoirdupois too; and in a
man on that account as well as in a pyramid. Evidently the
general felt in a dull sort of way the peril they were in;
knew there was nothing to do but to await the result, was
apathetic, and therefore calm. There was, however, both in
the general and his elder daughter, an air of deference to
the younger of the sisters, which perplexed their companion.
Both father and daughter seemed as children in a certain
indefinable bearing on their part toward her. And this was
the more striking by reason of the comparative quietness
and silence of the one they seemed so to lean upon. There
was nothing their fellow-passenger could do on deck until
he had rested a little; and, with the quickened eyes of his
great excitement, he could not but closely observe the two
sisters. He had heard the shriek of Irene, who had been
almost as sound asleep as her father, when her sister had first
awakened her, followed by outcries on her part, and lamen-
tations, shrill and unceasing. Her clothing had been hastily put on, more by her sister's hands than her own; and
now, with streaming hair, and hands clutching at and clinging
to every object and person around, she kept exclaiming, —

"O father! O Zeo! what shall we do? Why did you
make us come? Oh, how it rolls and tosses! Every dish on

board must be broken. How wet we will get! And there
is poor brother Grit. What will become of Grit if Zeo is
drowned? He is so bad, so very bad! Where is Mr. Venable? Oh, here you are! Can't you do something to stop it?
I am so wicked, I don't want to die. O Zeo, Zeo!" and it
was the firm grasp of her younger sister upon her which
seemed to hold her from greater violence. Even at that
moment, the wind coming and going like a charge of cavalry,
the sea surging over the deck with a hissing wash, now and
then the yell and jump of some one of the crew upon the
roof overhead, — amid it all Venable could not refrain from
wondering at the contrast of Zeo to the other. He had
casually admired her black hair and eyes, and the moulded
contour of cheek and lip and chin; but the repose of her
manner had seemed so full of strength, as in relief against
the unrest of her sister, that he had, during all their gay
talk the hours before, listened only less to her silence than
he had to her sister's incessant and amusing speech. In
some way the modest girl seemed to be taller and stronger
now. She had more to say, the authority of her words as
marked as their sweetness; the general as well as Irene giving an attention and value to them, the looker-on tried once
more, but in vain, to account for. And so the storm continued to rage; the elder daughter passing from one passionate appeal to another, struggling to rise, and held down more
by the hand and voice of her sister than of her father. It
was a curious study to their fellow-passenger, too, to see how
passive the portly general was, even at the worst assaults of
the tempest. Singularly lethargic, but with an occasional
hopeful word, he did not arise from his seat the night
through; his elder daughter weeping, praying, remonstrating
with her father for bringing them, subsiding into quiet not
until worn out or stilled, as a fractious child might be, by the
low-spoken girl to whom she clung. As to Venable, the night
fled fast enough, going to, and coming back when utterly ex-

hausted by hard work from, the pumps. There were rapid periods on his part, of prayer; the periods, however, of practical piety at the pumps, were much the longest. He could not but observe as he worked, crowded in among the crew, how their profanity, too, became, like his own supplications, terser and more thoroughly intended.

In going and returning to and from deck, he had observed a heap of what seemed woman's clothing lying in a corner of the cabin. It almost startled him to see, when the vessel was struck with a harder wave than usual, a pale face and a pair of terrified eyes looking out from the heap. It was the quadroon girl, deadly sick, and even more utterly helpless than the ladies; and in that condition she remained, with scarce a motion of life, during the three days of the tempest. She was a beautiful and terrified animal, nothing more either to the others or to herself than that.

As the young man was going back to the deck on one occasion, after resting a little in the saloon, the younger of the sisters accompanied him. The elder was lying worn out in her father's arms; and wrapping herself up, with merely a word of request to that effect, not heeding his remonstrances, she silently persisted in going outside. The instant they stepped on deck, she laid hold on the nearest rope, taut as a harp-string in the wet and strain on it, and abandoned his arm altogether. It was as if she wanted to face and see for herself the utmost of the peril. Not that any thing was really to be seen. So small a portion of the vessel itself was visible in the pitchy darkness, that it might have been a nutshell on which they stood; the smoke-stack beside them, and its whirl overhead of sparks, absurdly too large for the seeming size of the bit of boat writhing and rolling and pitching beneath. But the wind, the wind! It was as if the force of the universe had broken bounds, and was upon them; simply force, invisible, irresistible, — force pure and awful. It seemed to Venable as if it were sufficient to blow the earth from its orbit.

"As sure as I live," he said to himself, "this tremendous power and pressure upon me, as upon every one here, is intended to effect some commensurate result. What result?"

His companion remained beside him in the darkness as if she, too, enjoyed the storm. They stood side by side in silence, holding on only by firmest grasp upon rope and spar, until a shriek from her sister, for the first time missing her from the saloon, recalled the young girl below deck. Her companion assisted her down, and returned again; and so the hours wore by as if they were being slowly ground away in the mill of the tempest.

As day dawned Capt. Chaffin lowered himself down the companion-way. Irene lifted her head, her hair falling in disorder around it, for he struck violently against the table in taking a seat. She looked vacantly at him a moment, dazed with exhaustion after her excitement, and then, to the astonishment of Venable, burst into a peal of laughter which threatened to become hysterical.

" I understand," the captain said to Venable, seated beside him. "It's their nature. Excitable. That's where they ain't like us. Their pecooliar power lies just there;" and the seaman sat steadily in his seat, rigid as oak, except for an admiring deference in his manner to the ladies present.

"After what she has stood," he said in reply to a low question from Gen. Buttolph about the boat, "she cannot hold together. We must go down"— But, almost before the words were spoken, the other passenger anticipated the outcries of any there by saying, "Let us pray." It was hard to hold themselves in a kneeling posture around the table ; but there was deep silence during the short prayer, and when they arose a calmness deeper still had fallen upon all there.

"Ahem ! It's a miracle we're afloat," Capt. Chaffin said,

breaking in upon the silence. "After last night the Nautilus may hold together for ever and ever, for all I know. And it don't matter, any way. My wife's in St. Jerome. With this awful north-easter a-blowing, she might as well be aboard this old canoe. You know it, general: you live there. The wind has banked up the water of the bay, the rivers and such like pouring into the bay steady. St. Jerome's a good two to six feet under water now. A house is worse to go to sea in than even this old boat. If this wind holds, St. Jerome's gone under, sure's you're alive! We might as well be here;" and Gen. Buttolph gave Mr. Venable a slight nod of assent. The general had been thinking, doubtless, of nothing else, and it accounted perhaps for his passive condition.

"St. Jerome," he said at last, "is a beautiful city; but it is built on a reef of sand."

"And twenty feet of water piled up on it by this wind would melt it as if it was a lump of salt," Capt. Chaffin added sententiously. "Every now and then the yellow-fever pounces down on the island. Almost all who stay die: all the rest run away inland. They come back as soon as it's all over, and say, 'Pshaw! the yellow-fever may not come again for years.' So with an overflow: the city comes within an ace of destruction. There's a terrible to-do, — ships dashing against houses, sloops away up the streets. All at once the wind goes down; out goes the ocean. The island gives itself a shake like a Newfoundland dog coming out of water. 'Nonsense!' they say to strangers: 'it didn't drown us out at last, and it may not happen again for a century;' and at it we all go again, a-bargaining and a-building, and a-making fun of Chemaraw, the next city higher up inland."

No one denied the statements of the experienced mariner, and he continued, —

"We all have noticed how lively frogs are after a heavy

rain; the birds singing in the chapparal too, for that matter,
as chirky as you please. So it is with people on the island.
Things get to be flat and dull. Very well. A good overflow comes. The Chemaraw people sing out, 'Told you
so! You'd better give it up, and move your city up here.'
That and the storm stirs up St. Jerome. The town is never
so full of brag as when it is drying itself. They are as generous to the losers as you please, and full of life and fun.
Mr. Parsons flies around, and says, 'What do you think of
Hacamac now?' and plasters the town all over with his
posters, giving away his lots there to whoever will build. I
have noticed it makes Phip Quatty's very horses go faster,
to say nothing of *him* on Wednesday nights at prayer-meeting. And there's my wife," Capt. Chaffin added, after a
long silence, since no one else would cheer away the anxiety
of the hour: " she paints. She generally paints. Not like
she does after an overflow! ah, but how she goes to work
with her brush and things after that! I tell her to *paint* a
storm. But no. Then let it be a ship, I tell her, under all
sail; say a steamship under a full head of steam, plenty of
smoke, and in the trough of the sea while the gale is blowing. 'Let it be a bayou-boat exploding her boiler, my dear,'
I say to her, 'all hands a-flying through the air.' — 'Never!
A living being,' she says, 'in this world or the other, angel
or martyr, is the only thing.' Maybe she is right. She
never painted any thing but a conqueror, or an apostle of
some sort, in her life, — always the grandest people and
when they are doing their very best. Yes; and I can put my
hand on her Elymas, say, struck blind by Paul, or the man
that was healed in Jerusalem, shaking his fist at the council
of Jews, and say, 'That was painted after a storm, and I
know it.' She puts, you see, such an overflow-like into the
thing. Yes, sir. How a storm does stir her up, and start
her again!"

But the ladies had gone to their room at the captain's

first allusion to his wife, and even Mr. Venable was too tired to express much interest. After sitting a while in silence, Capt. Chaffin somewhat indignantly arose, and went on deck again,—went on deck to find that the morning had dawned, pale, haggard, and tremulous, after the excesses of the night.

CHAPTER III.

EXPLAINING HOW THIS COLUMBUS SETS HIS FOOT AT LAST UPON THE SHORES OF A NEW LAND.

AS day broke, Hartman Venable lay down in his state-room for a nap, exhausted almost as much by the agony of Irene Buttolph as by the violence of the wind and the toil at the pumps. Instead of a nap he slept the deep sleep, almost, of the dead, leaping up suddenly out of it to find, with surprise and shame, that during his slumber it was late the next morning, the wind still blowing as furiously as ever. It was the steward whose knock aroused him for the late breakfast ; and the military manner in which that individual did it, waiting at table afterwards as if going through the drill, was singularly re-assuring.

"We are glad to see you looking so fresh again," was Gen. Buttolph's salutation as each passenger held on to the table with one hand, and managed to eat with the other. There was still greater re-assurance in the inertia of the portly general, to say nothing of the glow in his broad and genial face.

"They are both asleep," he said, in reply to a question. "Irene was worn out with her terrors, and Zeo with comforting her. I hope they may sleep through it all." And the speaker proceeded to inform his friend that such storms always lasted three days, so that they had two days more of it yet to endure.

"That is," Capt. Chaffin, who had joined them, explained, "if the Nautilus holds together; and that is impossible. As the ladies are asleep, I might as well say it," he continued: "we are too tough, being men, to care. Yet I don't know," he corrected himself in a mechanical way, after a long pause. "You see, this old shell ought to have gone to flinders the moment the wind struck her. She's a living miracle, and she has been for years on years. When a miracle's on hand, no man can tell what'll happen." Having said which, he became grimly silent.

Young Venable found, during the day, that the captain of the boat, the engineers and firemen, the deck-hands and steerage-passengers, had all reached the same conclusion, — had found, in fact, considerable consolation in the very wonder of the thing; the comfort therein strengthening as the storm howled the day through, pitching and tossing the boat about upon the yeasty waves. Somehow, in virtue of its being but the biggest of the bubbles thereupon, it would not break; and so another night at the pumps came and went. When the next day came, the wonder of all on board had deepened into a superstition, a fanaticism. The passengers had crystallized, so to speak, into a dogmatic sect in regard to the endurance of their boat.

"Oh, blow away and be hanged!" Capt. Chaffin remarked contemptuously, at breakfast that day, as the wind shrieked overhead in a louder gust than usual. "That's why," he added, his mouth at the ear of Mr. Venable, seated beside him, "they call a ship a she. A boat may be as frail as — as — you please, and yet — capable of? Things a *he* can't even begin to try to do! St. Jerome's my fear."

"It is Mrs. Chaffingsby he means," Miss Zeo told Mr. Venable, when, the captain having left the table, he repeated the remark to her; and again her sister went off into a fit of laughter, only less violent, by reason of weariness, than on the occasion before.

"We sleep almost all the time," she informed Mr. Venable more than once; "and when I'm not in an agony of fear, I'm in a gale of fun. Zeo is kept busy being a mother to me, as she always was, dear little body."   But this phrase of endearment did not seem at all applicable to the lady spoken of.   She was seated at the table, her hands lying clasped together before her upon it ; and although she lifted her head, and smiled, there was that in her which reminded him of the repose of a lioness.   As he blushed to think such a thing of so modest a girl, her older sister exclaimed in continuation of her lively talk, "See, sir, if I'm not the first to wake you to-morrow."

And she was.   Before the sun rose on that Sunday morning, she was beating upon Mr. Venable's door, and calling, "St. Jerome, St. Jerome ! O Mr. Venable, come and see !"

Dressing himself as swiftly as he could, he hastened on deck to find the old world gone forever, and the new world arrived.   The last three days lay behind him like three years, rather, of trouble, a blessedness in its very darkness and storm now that it was gone.   For here was a new world indeed.   He could not speak at first, by reason of gladness. The very atmosphere seemed electric with new life.

"Oh ! is it not glorious?" she exclaimed.   "Look ! there is not a cloud in the sky, so blue and deep.   And the sea, too.   It lies, see, as blue and calm and pure as the sky, with not a ripple.   The air is as gentle as the breath of a babe.   Don't you see that long line of sand off to the right, and the houses and steeples, barely above the level of the water? That is St. Jerome.   And, oh ! the flowers there, and the fig-trees, and the glorious drives, and such nice people, not a bit like those anywhere else in the world. —You dear thing !" and in her joyousness the young lady startled her companion in the instant of her ejaculation, by putting her arms around the mast by which they were standing, and giving it a kiss as well as a hug.   "Won't

I do instead?" was what her companion asked her; but by no means aloud. That was one of the ten thousand things which he had habitually to keep himself from saying. "You dear, good old boat, to bring us so safely," she said, her arms still about the mast, "when all the people were abusing you so, calling you old!— Draw in the delicious air as I do, Mr. Venable;" and she inhaled with parted lips the fresh breeze, her bosom rising, her cheek glowing, her eyes radiant with joy. "That is the way it will be when I get to heaven," she said. "I will be so glad to be done with such a world! It isn't the storms I object to at all. I rather like a good rousing fuss of any kind, especially when it is over. What I hate is the everlasting propriety. One dare not do or say any thing now, but it is, 'O Irene, don't!' and 'O Irene, hush!' If I let myself go for one little moment, there are fifty people to hold up their hands with horror, and say, 'O Irene! are you not ashamed of yourself?' I hate such a world. I want to be where a girl can be as full of fun, and as free, as she feels like. I want to go where Miss Aurelia Jones will never shake her curls at me again forever. That's my idea of heaven," she added with enthusiasm: "to be and to do and to say, for ever and evermore, amen, exactly what I please. I am so glad we are done with school! St. Jerome's like heaven in that: people don't care a cent—

"And that, I suppose," her companion said, pointing to a pilot-yacht under full sail for them, "is like"—

"I know what you mean," she interrupted; "is like an angel—see its white sails! sent out from heaven to show a soul just arriving the way. I am so glad, I believe I could fly!" And the girl stretched out her arms, her hair falling back from her uplifted head, such high spirits in her tones, her complexion flushed so with light, that, turning to look at Mr. Venable, she could not but color at the smile in his face.

"And here is papa, and Zeo. Was ever any thing so beautiful?" she said, as the general and her sister joined them, and stood looking in silence upon the scene. "See," she continued, "yonder is the sun, just rising out of the ocean. It looks like a great bubble of gold. Did you ever see it appear so clean and sweet, as if it had been scrubbed and scoured by the wind and the water?" And as she gave words to her eagerness, her younger sister stood beside her very happy, and yet dark and silent, and even dull in comparison, not nearly as tall as the other, and much less as radiant ; miniature likeness, Mr. Venable said to himself, of her father, by whose side she stood.

"Why is it?" he asked of himself. "Why do I admire her so much the most?"

Meanwhile the pilot had reached them, and had climbed up the side, looking, as he did so, closely and inquiringly at the hull and deck and spars of the vessel. He fastened his eyes for a moment upon each person he saw, in the same way.

"And she pulled through it?" he demanded of the captain of the boat, not shaking hands as Mr. Venable had expected, but offering the other instead, and unasked, his plug of tobacco accompanied by his jack-knife.

The captain nodded his head as he took the plug, cut off a quid therefrom, and put it slowly and with a meditative manner in his mouth, a something too great for words in his way of doing it.

"And St. Jerome sailed it out too," he said at last.

"You bet," the pilot replied. "Our chances and yours were just even. Six of one, half a dozen of the other."

"You may tell me any sea-serpent story you please, now," Capt. Chaffin, who had joined the other two men, and taken his cut at the plug, remarked. "Don't stop at trifles : string his tail out six miles, if you want to, — six hundred, for that matter. I'm your man ; yes, sir, go ahead : I am ready for any thing."

But the firemen had thrown into the furnaces the last shovels of coal left in the bunks, and were engaged in pitching in the materials of the bunks themselves to add to the smoke and speed, and grandeur in general, of their arrival. The vessel did not steam straight for the city, which had now risen entirely above the water, as Mr. Venable had vainly hoped. Making a sweep completely around it, — the city being upon the side of the island looking toward the main land, — the boat reached the landing as rapidly as its disabled condition would allow. As they drew near he could not but agree with the rapture of Irene Buttolph, coming and going between her father and sister and himself.

"Is it not the most beautiful picture in the world? All the houses near the edge of the island are stone and brick, you see," she explained; "they look so strong along the side of the sea, — like bulwarks, you know. They are the warehouses, cotton-presses, and stores. Behind them are the long, broad streets of houses where the people live. See, every house is as white as white can be, except the blinds of the windows and verandas, and they are as green as the trees. You can't see half the city, it's all buried so in oleanders, orange-trees, and lemons. Oh, isn't it lovely! I was born there, you know."

"It may be all owing," Mr. Venable said, "to the storm we have been through, the danger and the darkness; and I have had years back of that, of pretty dark times and hard work. Perhaps it is this clear sky and brilliant light. The air is so crisp and fresh too. It may be because I am twenty-one years old to-day; it is Sunday, also, and that may be one reason. Whatever it is," he added, turning to the young girl, "this is by far the most glorious morning I ever knew. I'm entering on a new world; and I feel so fresh and strong! I will remember this day as long as I live: it is the first day of a new year, and I feel sure it will be a year worth living."

He was a comely young fellow, really as full of enthusiasm as the lady to whom he spoke, save that he had long ago deepened himself, so to speak, by severe study and small companionship with others, in such a degree as to hold within himself, and without too much overflow, all excess of feeling.

As they drew near, their vessel at least, to the landing, the bold front of the city rose higher and higher, and then towered protectingly above them. Upon the wharf there had gathered a large crowd of men and boys. They stood gazing at the boat as it approached, with silent but intense interest. Mr. Venable had observed among the throng a particularly tall and vigorous individual, dressed in black broadcloth as if for church. He was standing up on top of one of the piles which projected above the edge of the wharf.

"Yonder is Mr. Quatty, Zeo," said Gen. Buttolph, with placid amusement. "You certainly remember Mr. Quatty. That is the one on the top of the post, Mr. Venable," he continued. "He is one of our pillars. You will find him one of the most remarkable men," he added, with a smile upon his face which his friend could not fully understand.

"Fellow-citizens," the person alluded to called out at this moment, assuming, as he took off his hat, the attitude and the oratorical tone of a public speaker, "this is the holy sabbath day. To our unspeakable astonishment the old Nautilus has survived once more. In view of its being Sunday, and of this old Lazarus coming up again from a briny sepulchre, I wish, before proposing a few cheers, to make some appropriate remarks. Brethren — I mean fellow-citizens *and* brethren — ahem ! When we consider " — with a gesture. But, on the instant, a dozen voices called out, "Three cheers ! Yes, three cheers !" There was much movement and laughter. "In one moment, brethren — I mean fellow-citizens," Mr. Quatty continued, motioning eagerly, and by a suppressing movement of both his palms extended over their heads, for the crowd to be still. "I wish to offer a few remarks. When we reflect"— But the voice of the speaker was drowned in laughter and calls for cheers, a number of persons crying out, "Hold your horses, Quatty!" and the three cheers were given by the crowd with a will, the orator being ignominiously hustled from his perch at the moment by the striking of the boat against the landing, many jumping on and off long before the vessel was secured to the wharf or the gangways laid. In the confusion of the in-rushing and out-going crowds, Gen. Buttolph laid his cordial grasp upon his friend.

"Remember," he said, "you go with us. But I wonder where the carriage is ;" and he leaned over the side of the upper deck, looking up and down the streets running alongside the wharf.

"O papa!" exclaimed his eldest daughter, in a fever of excitement, "yonder is old Plenty and young Plenty, just the same, and I have not seen them for two years ; and see, Grit is with them. Grit!" she called, "Clear Grit!" but then yielded to her sister's silencing hand. By this time a very old, tall, and white-headed negro had followed a stout, thick-set man many shades blacker, who had forced his way to the edge of the landing below.

"Well, boys, where's the carriage?" cried the general.

"You hush. Shet your mouth," the older of the two men said, laying his long hand on the shoulder of the other. "Massa General's talkin' to me. — Yes, massa. No kerrige, massa. Kerrige-house swept away. Hain't had time to hunt for the kerrige yet. Somewhere in de prairie."

"That's a fact," his master said with emphasis. "I had forgotten. Is the house left, Plenty?"

"Shet up. Lemme talk," the old man replied. "Yes, Massa Harry, but wet, mighty wet," with an ominous shake of his venerable head.

"Oh, well!" said Gen. Buttolph, amid the exclamations of
Irene, "never mind. Get one of Mr. Quatty's hacks. Oh,
here is Mr. Quatty!— How are you, Mr. Quatty? These
are my daughters, from school. This is Mr. Venable. Can
you let us have a hack?" and the young gentleman last
named found his hand grasped, and heartily, by the orator
of the moment before. He was a large-limbed man, tough
and vigorous. His body seemed to be more loosely framed
than is usual; the arms being particularly long, with large
and sinewy hands thereto. His face, which was thoroughly
burned and roughened by the sun and rain and wind
of forty years, was one which the other thought he could
read at once. No traces of books, or society, or culture of
any kind, there; but, except for a restlessness of eyes and
manner, a kind, shrewd, and honest face. On the instant he
took a liking to him.

"We are going to get well acquainted, sir," Mr. Quatty
said, keeping the hand of the other in his own.

"I have no doubt of it," Gen. Buttolph said, with a sort
of comic·emphasis; "but you must get us home now, Mr.
Quatty."

And an amazing ride it was, to the stranger at least, after
the carriage had got behind the row of substantial warehouses which lined the wharves. "It's like the toy town of a
child, all scattered about," Irene said, as they drove through
the broad streets of sand white and wet. "Yonder is
another house washed into the centre of our way. Oh, look!
yonder is a sloop lying right in front of our church, the
mast almost as tall as the steeple! How can we ever get in
on next Sunday?" And so all the way. Mr. Quatty drove
them himself, and, from his seat on the box of the open
carriage, described the ravages of the tempest with great
pride. Wind and sea had invaded the city, washing the
streets and gardens into gullies and banks, tearing up the
trees, upsetting the smaller houses, floating the larger far

away, in many cases, from their foundations; yawls and
sailing-boats lay high and dry upon front yards. It was the
very chaos of a wrecked city. Grit, the brother to whom
Irene had so often referred, a plump boy of eight or ten, and
who had been devoured with kisses by her, pointed out the
various disasters as they rode along. Yet over and under
and through it all was the sparkling air and the brilliant day.
Evidently it was an atmosphere which was as much the
native element, in all its brightness, of the people, as the sea
is of its fish. As the hacks drove laboriously along, backing
and turning, winding in and out, and at times over the
scattered ruins of houses and fences, the inhabitants seemed
to be out in Sunday attire, as for a holiday. Not merely
men and women of the seafaring classes: everywhere, as
they drove with many a tortuous winding, there were gentlemen and ladies on foot, or in buggies, and in open convey-
ances of all kinds, with children swarming around, — all
curious to see what the storm had done. The multitude
were climbing over the drift, were clustered in groups about
some particularly ridiculous upheaval: on the face of all,
the same air of hilarity. Mr. Venable, looking up at the
sound of a bleating, laughed to see a ram with patriarchal
horns summoning assistance from the observatory of a tall
house into which it had managed to climb. The next
moment Mr. Quatty, from his seat, called their attention to
a cow which stood calmly chewing its cud, and gazing upon
the passing crowds, its motherly face thrust through the
window of a handsome residence in which it had taken
refuge. As their carriage turned in and out among the
wrecks, there would come, now from down one street or
alley, and then up from another, a peal of laughter at something very amusing which had just been observed.

"No lives have been lost, that I have heard of," Mr.
Quatty informed them as they rolled along. "They are all
frame houses, you see, and it will not get up into millions —

the damage.   I know it is not the first storm of the sort we
have had here in St. Jerome ; but then, as likely as not, it
will never happen again, you know."

It was thus Mr. Venable easily fell, that bright Sunday, into
the mood of Miss Irene Buttolph.   And she seemed to
express but more volubly what appeared to be the opinion
of all; which was, that, upon the whole, the storm and
overflow was one of the best practical jokes in the world.

The most venerable clergyman could not have been more
guarded as to his outer bearing than was this new-comer.
In comparison with the tropic region into which he had
been so suddenly introduced, he was as coldly correct as
Iceland ; but, like Iceland, he hid under the snows of his
propriety a good deal that was ready to break out.

"I do truly and sincerely prefer my work to every thing
else," he reasoned with himself, after he had been shown to
his room at Gen. Buttolph's house : " why is it, then, that,
from before my arriving here, I have been thrown with one
who threatens to divert my mind from it?   If this is the
way I am to begin, I had better give up at once, and go
back to my old cloisters.   Please Heaven, I will try and
absorb myself in my new duties so thoroughly as to forget
every thing else."

CHAPTER IV.

MR. VENABLE BEGINS TO KNOW THE INHABITANTS OF ST. JEROME,
AND THEY TO KNOW HIM.

DR. BURROWS, the pastor of the church of St. Jerome,
had left under peculiar circumstances, to be explained
by and by. At the suggestion of Miss Aurelia Jones, the
wealthiest as well as the most active, certainly the most
devoted, member of the church, the officers thereof had
written, a few weeks before our story opens, to the institution
at which young men were trained for the ministry. Commodore Thomas William Grandheur, long superintendent of
the sabbath school, had opposed such a plan from the instant of its suggestion by Miss Aurelia. But there was a
certain fervor in the lady which gave her an influence beyond that of the commodore himself. The application was
made, that gentleman protesting with all the emphasis of
his gold-headed cane, and voice ; and Mr. Venable was the
result. Although he had arrived on Sunday, as recorded, it
was impossible for him to preach. When he had stepped
ashore, it was cautiously, and as if he had expected the island
to tilt under him ; and it was many days before he was rid of
the roll and lurch and pitch of the Nautilus, which lingered
like a physical memory of his trip. The membership also
were too busy collecting their scattered fences, and, in some
cases, houses, to think of any thing else. Early on Monday
morning Gen. Buttolph took his guest to the spot to see the

vessel hauled away which had been washed up in front of
the church.   It was an easy thing to do at last; and the same
process was being at the same hour, and for weeks after,
applied to boats beached, and houses washed from their
foundations, over the whole city.   Logs were laid under, and
continually renewed in front as they were done with in the
rear of the moving mass, the whole island being a dead
level.   Twelve yoke of oxen it took to move the vessel from
the church; the oxen headed, as they always are in such
emergencies, by a mule of unusual size and solemn aspect.
The attention of Mr. Venable was arrested by the amount
of profanity applied, — one driver to each yoke of oxen, and
a commander-in-chief in charge of the mule.   Beginning
with the driver of the yoke next to the vessel, the blasphe-
my increased in volume and violence with each teamster in
order, until it culminated through the lips of its master, and
broke in thunder upon the head of the mule with a vehemence of wickedness the hearer had never before imagined.
Such suggestions in reference to its eternal hereafter were
urged upon the animal, that it would have been rock rather
than mule not to have heeded them.   With head moving up
and down, as it tugged steadily at its load, its long ears were
in perpetual motion, as if it said, "Oh, yes! certainly; yes,
yes, yes : I understand."   As Gen. Buttolph's guest meditated
on the possible recoil upon the swearers of such verbal violence, the vessel moved off, literally cursed away inch by inch,
driven seaward by a gale of at least intenser moral power
than that which had lodged it there.   And the young man
was struck, too, by the joyous indifference on the part of his
host to the profanity.   It was in keeping with his placid
unconcern during the storm at sea.   Not unconcern : the
same childlike recklessness was observed by the new-comer
every moment and in all he met, — a recklessness more or
less hilarious as to whatever might befall.

The richer people of St. Jerome seemed to be least in-

jured by the overflow; their houses being generally upon
higher points in the city, and of more substantial materials,
than the small frame buildings of the poorer of the population, — buildings all porch and window and green blinds,
and the only ceiling and lath and plaster of which was canvas, — canvas well stretched and whitewashed. Things were
being rapidly balanced, too, before the storm was well ended,
by negroes loaned, and money cheerfully given, on the part
of the wealthier citizens. There was a breezy, out-of-door,
picnic gladness and generosity and genial fellow-feeling, in it
all, which was, to the new arrival, in delightful contrast to the
rigors of the region from which he had just departed. As
if it had all been a mere mistake of wind and sea, to be
borne with and laughed at, fences and houses were being
replaced, streets regraded, turf and trees replanted, — the
whole city set to rights again. St. Jerome was barely above
the level of the sea surrounding it on all sides; and young
Venable could not rid himself of the idea that in landing
he had but stepped from the Nautilus upon the deck of
a vessel vastly larger, but fully as frail and as much exposed
to the perils of wind and water, yet all the better for that.
Very soon the big ship would be trimmed, the sails set again,
and all hands confident of a prosperous voyage henceforth.
There was something to him, fresh from scholastic shades,
in the sailor-like boyishness of the people, which was more
attractive than the transparent air, and sparkling blue of sea
and sky, and vivid hues of grass and flowers; a something
in every person he met, in strict sympathy and keeping with
nature, which seemed to be so wide open to him all around,
above too, and below.

Commodore Thomas William Grandheur excepted. Mr.
Venable speedily acknowledged that. On the Monday after-
noon following upon his arrival, the commodore called.
Gen. Buttolph's household were seated upon the veranda.
From the moment he slowly ascended the steps, the heart

of the minister sank within him. The commodore was
a large man of commanding presence, who had not been
so long in the navy and in supreme command of men
for nothing. The instant he stepped as upon the quarter-
deck of the general's veranda, the new-comer felt what a
green hand he was in such a presence. The commodore
had the same feeling evidently. Young Venable saw it in
the amplitude of the white vest of this his superior officer,
in the exuberance of the gold chain across his breast, in the
white hair, heavy moustache, and authoritative brow, especially in the manner of the man, as well as in his gold-
headed cane with which, as with the mace of office, he took
Mr. Venable in charge.

There was silence when the commodore, after saluting all
present, had taken his seat. Then leaning his hands, one
placed on the other, upon the top of his cane, which was
between his knees, he proceeded to examine the new recruit.
Where had he been born? When? What were his views
upon this mode of conducting worship, and that? How in
reference to the sabbath school? also the prayer-meeting?
pastoral visitation likewise? Not that there was any thing
offensive in the words, nor in the manner, except that the
speaker had long been commodore, in his own estimation,
of the First Church, and intended remaining so. His
assumption aroused within the other a counter assumption.
With his eye full in his, the young man replied to the questions respectfully, as to one so much older, but in an independent as well as off-hand way, which, he smiled to himself
to think, he had caught already, as by infection, from the
people about him.

"Our church, sir," the commodore said at last, "is the
First Church of St. Jerome, — in every sense the *First*
Church."

He was a noble-looking old soul ; his bronze complexion
well contrasted with moustache and hair and overhanging

eyebrows, which were very white. There was authority in
the "ahem" with which he began every new remark. Yet
the young man had an intuition from the first that his visitor
lacked substance to his size. He was ashamed to feel that
the commodore reminded him of a big bass-drum,—he
could not get rid of an idea of hollowness. In spite of
himself, the idea grew, the longer his visitor talked.

At last there was the dull roll of wheels in the sandy
street. In the instant of the utterance of an exclamation
by Irene, the visitor arose. His face was from the street;
but it was evident he had an instinct as to who was coming,
and wished to avoid a meeting. There was almost a sacri-
fice of dignity in the abruptness of his leave-taking, as, after
bidding all adieu, and lifting his hat to a lady ascending the
steps, he took his departure.

Mr. Venable bowed to her as he did so, regarding her
with keen interest. She was plainly dressed, had very black
hair and eyes, a fresh-colored and eager face, and a manner as full of emotion as that of the visitor before her had
been cold and magisterial. She greeted the young man with
an effusion which brought the color to his cheeks.

"I am so glad you are come, Mr. Venable!" she said at
last, in continuance of a good deal of welcome going before,
"and out of a terrible tempest too. And we, too, are just
out of a storm,—a storm following, as far as the First
Church is concerned, upon a calm which was worse still.
How plainly Providence was preparing us for each other!
Do you know, Mr. Venable, it was I who insisted upon your
being sent for? Miss Aurelia Jones,—I dare say they have
told you about me. Not that I can do any thing. I am
only a woman,—a very weak and cold-hearted woman, I
fear. But I *do* desire to do all I can." And she was so
childlike and overflowing, that Mr. Venable was charmed;
the more so, the longer she talked. She had little to say to
Gen. Buttolph, or even to his daughters just returned after
years of absence, in her eagerness about the church.

"I know," she finally added after quite a long visit, "that it is often worse than nothing; yet we *do* have the youth, the wealth, the fashion and culture and intellect, of St. Jerome, in our society. Yours is a serious charge, Mr. Venable; but you will have," she continued, with her heart in her eyes, "earnest, praying, confidential, devoted friends. I will not make a long call now," she added: "we will see a good deal of each other, I assure you. — And you are as grave as ever, Zeo," she said, turning to the sisters. "You, I am afraid, Irene, are as full of your mischief. How you are both grown ! You must take classes in the Sunday school. The commodore is a good, good man. But oh, me ! *me!*" with a laugh and a shrug of her shoulders. "Good-by ; " and she shook hands cordially with all as she departed. "I have a thousand things to talk over with you," she said to Mr. Venable after he had helped her into her carriage at the gate. "We must establish a mission-school out near Mr. Parson's place. He will be glad to manage it as he does his terraqueous machine. Have you seen it yet? He has dozens of inventions, and he is the most wonderful of them all himself. Then we should have the market-house for a Bethel. I have already worked a magnificent flag of silk, a white cross on a blue ground. Capt. Chaffin would help in that. Have you seen Mrs. Chaffingsby yet? Be on your guard, Mr. Venable: it is sometimes wicked to laugh. Oh, if it please Heaven ! " she said with fervor, holding his hand, and her eyes moistening, "we may have a blessing on our church. It was such a pity about Dr. Burrows, — such a *pity !* " And it was after a deal of further conversation on her part, that the lady was driven off.

Mr. Venable could not help, on his return to the veranda on which the family were seated, remarking on the impression Miss Aurelia Jones had made upon him. He refrained, however, from acknowledging even to himself a vague uneasiness in regard to her. There was a fervor which was fever; a something of strain too great to be either natural or lasting.

"She is the life and soul of our church," Gen. Buttolph said. "You see what a handsome lady she is. They say she is forty; but she has such a fresh color, and is so warm-hearted, that she does not seem to be thirty. She is rich, and is exceedingly active in church matters. I wish she and Commodore Grandheur agreed better. He is our superintendent, but she is vastly better fitted for it. Her infant class is well worth seeing."

"She is so far beyond me," Irene Buttolph had impatiently waited till now to say, "that I am as still as a mouse when I am with her: I am as cold then and wicked as a lump of ice; she is so ardent and loving and good. Zeo thinks the world of her."

"It is two years since we saw her last," her sister said, after a little while. She looked up from her embroidery as she said it, for she always had some work in hand; Irene being too eager with eyes and tongue, indulging in too much movement of her hands in company, to lend herself steadily to any thing else. "Miss Aurelia was very kind indeed when our mother was ill," Zeo added. "She used to write us long and beautiful letters when we were off at school. I wish," the young lady began to say, "that we could all be as good as she is; that is "—

"We will be," her sister added for her, "when we get to be angels. But I am not pious now, one bit. I love fun and flowers, and like to laugh, and to ride, and to talk, too much for that. Wait, sir, until Miss Aurelia begins to send you slippers and things. Wait! Tell us what you think of Commodore Grandheur, Mr. Venable."

"He seems to be a very stately, I dare say a most excellent gentleman," Mr. Venable replied with some difficulty, hesitating a little.

"As if you could deceive us!" the more voluble of the
young ladies said. "I won't hush, Zeo. He is exactly as
he was when we left. He has been superintendent of our
Sunday school for years. Ever since we can remember, he
wore that white waistcoat, and carried his gold-headed cane
and pompous manner, as if he were monarch of all creation." But here she yielded to the eyes, and hand on her
arm, of her sister. "Dear me! bless my soul! I'm always
doing something bad; but I only say what other people
hide," she added. "The commodore *is*" — But, under the
authoritative eyes of her sister, she stopped.

The young minister reddened as he caught the malicious
eyes of Irene fastened upon him: he had taken such a dislike to the individual, resenting the solemn superiority of
manner and air with which the commodore had taken charge
of him with his portentous cane. In virtue of an old and
bad habit of his, formed in college and seminary days, the
young man sank into deep thought, while Irene talked on
upon a hundred topics, her sister and father as silent beside
them as usual.

"Excuse me, Miss Irene," Mr. Venable said at last, and
recalling himself to the matter of which she was speaking:
"you need not defend yourself as being too full of life.
How could you help it, born and growing up in such an
atmosphere? So far as I can see, everybody seems" —

"As if he or she had been taking a little too much
brandy," his companion interrupted, as she always did;
"everybody except Zeo. She is an owl. It is because Grit
and I give her so much trouble. But no two people in St.
Jerome are the least bit alike. Everybody is a peculiar
person, but each in his own way. We are thrown together
here, you know, from every State in the Union, as well as
from all over the world. I haven't forgotten a soul of them;
they are people you can't forget, to save your life. There's
Father Fethero, he plainly perceives a gloom; never mind,

Mr. Venable, you'll understand what I mean by that as soon
as you know him.   Then, there is Farce Fanthorp, and Phip
Quatty; but you have met him.   Wait until you have heard
him !   Then there is — I liked to have forgotten him : we
always forget him — Mr. Nogens; and, yes, there is — let
me see " —

"You have forgotten Ezra Micajah Parsons," Gen. Buttolph said, folding and unfolding his hands as he sat in his
easy-chair.

"So I have," his daughter exclaimed.   "And there is
Col. Roland, editor, poet, and lover ; the youngest man you
ever knew, Mr. Venable, and the oldest."

"And Clara Chaffingsby, and Charles," Zeo said softly in
the moment of silence which followed.   There was a hush
upon all as she said it, as if she had mentioned the dead.

"For shame, Zeo !" her sister broke in again, adding, —

"And there is Mrs. Chaffingsby.   O Mr. Venable !   The
richest treat is before you in Mrs. Chaffingsby.   You have
no idea !" and the eyes of the young lady were so full of
fun as she spoke with uplifted hands, that, not caring particularly as yet about Mrs. Chaffingsby, the young divinity-
student carried a pleasing impression of the lively girl with
him to his room when he withdrew ; but his last thoughts as
he fell asleep, and his first upon awakening, were not of her.
She might compel his attention while he was with them, but
his expectation, so to speak, even then was fastened rather
upon her quiet sister than herself; and, as soon as he got
away, he reverted wholly to Miss Zeo.   He was beginning to
thrive wonderfully in health and spirits ; and somehow his
health had lodged itself in and was growing most vigorous
in the region of his heart.   But why should it turn, like the
witch-hazel in his hands, toward treasure out of sight ?   For
he could not understand her.

CHAPTER V.

IN WHICH MR. VENABLE BEGINS TO SEE THAT ST. JEROME IS
AS TROPICAL IN ITS PEOPLE AS IN ITS CLIMATE.

FOR the present Mr. Venable had yielded to the cordial
wish of Gen. Buttolph, and made himself at home in
his ample mansion. The building was two-storied, with a
broad veranda, two-storied also, upon every side, and supplied with Venetian blinds. Around the house, which was in
the suburbs of the city, were a dozen acres. Besides the
luxuriant kitchen-gardens behind the house, and the flower-
gardens on either side, there were orchards of fig, orange,
and lemon trees. These had to be helped with axe and
grubbing-hoe against the oleander, china, and ailanthus
trees, which, environing the place outside, crowded into the
front yard, and struggled like an army with banners, for the
possession, too, of garden and orchard. In one corner,
sheltered from the terrible northers, a few olive-trees and
almonds, guava-plants and bananas, clustered together like
foreigners not quite at home.

"How did your trees manage to stand the storm?" the
guest asked of a thick-set, vigorous, and very black negro,
whom he found working in the grounds a few days after his
coming.

"You hold your tongue, boy," replied a tall, thin, old
white-headed negro, hidden by the foliage, winter as it was,
off to one side. "You shet up, an' lemme talk," the old

man said, coming up and laying a long but feeble arm upon
the shoulder of the other; Mr. Venable recognizing them as
the two servants of Gen. Buttolph who had greeted their
landing. It was a wonder that he could stand up, much
less walk abroad, he was such a skeleton, such a mummy of
a man.

"He don't know nuffin," the speaker explained. "We
stood de storm," he added, " bekase we're on de highest
point ob de whole island;" and the old soul waved his hand
toward the expanse of land and sea around as if their twenty
feet of elevation was that of the Alps instead.

"But why don't you let this man speak?" asked Mr. Venable, turning to look again at the other negro, who, besides
being as stout as he was black, had a large head, no senator
possessing more dignity as by the majesty of his very silence.

"Him! *dis* child!" the old man ejaculated, looking at
the other as if at a weed. "Him! why, massa, he my
grandchild, an' born here in St. Jerome. I'm from ole Firginny, Prince Edward Curtus " (meaning " court-house ").
"He don't know much, but he do know not to talk when I'm
around." The aged aristocrat drew himself up with dignity,
as he said it; and the visitor recognized the source from
which the grandson had derived his majestic proportions.

But at this juncture the dinner-bell rang, and Venable
had to leave them, by no means unwillingly. After the
scanty herbage and close-cut hedges of the institution from
which he came, Gen. Buttolph's place seemed as glorious as
Eden. The fact that he had left the North in mid-winter, to
find what was comparatively summer again, made his new
home almost marvellous. Direct, also, from the Spartan fare
of his seminary, the table of his host seemed to him laden
with Oriental abundance. Such bread, for whiteness and
lightness, he had rarely seen. The beef was the tenderest,
the poultry the juiciest, the vegetables the largest and most
enjoyable, in all his knowledge. Not a sweet potato but

exceeded in sweetness his ideal of pudding, or would have done so if it had not been surpassed by a peculiar sort of corn-bread at breakfast, of which it was impossible to eat enough. The young man blushed at his keenness of appetite. The coffee alone, yellowed with richest cream, was a coffee before unheard of.

Every morning there would be a knock upon his door a good hour before the breakfast-bell rang; and, Mr. Venable awakened enough to say, "Come in," the younger Plenty would enter, and silently place a cup of this coffee on its silver waiter, with sugar and cream-jug, upon the little table at the head of his bed, and as silently withdraw. The heat and fragrance was as if a richer morning than that without had dawned within his room, and one could arise and dress so much more deliberately after draining the cup. Grit, the fat son of his host, sat next him at table, eating with a long and slow enjoyment of his food, which alarmed the visitor for the intellectual development of that youth. And a silent and yellow-complexioned boy of ten or so, Grit was; more like an extremely plump Cupid devoid of wings and weapons, and carved out of butter, than any thing else. He seemed to be so wholly flesh and blood, — so unlike the studious children, pale and crammed with learning, and always on edge, of his previous experience, — that the guest of the house took a liking to the boy as a charming variety of the species.

"I like to see him and talk to him," he said to Irene: "he is so fresh and childlike, and free from care. He does not say much as yet, but he seems to me as innocent as a babe."

Upon which, to his surprise, she exclaimed, "O Mr. Venable! I had no idea you could be so sarcastic. Is it possible you have not found Grit out yet?" with a look of genuine astonishment.

That very evening her sister drew Gen. Buttolph aside, as the supper-bell rang, to tell him something in a low voice, evidently about her brother. But Grit was at table afterward, partaking largely of preserved figs and cream, a cherub in serenity and sweetness, turning upon his father the gaze of innocence as the general held up his hand, upon his leaving table, saying to the boy in ominous accents, " Remember ! "

It was to relieve any embarrassment following on this, that their guest said, a few moments after, of his eating, " I suppose it is travel, change of scene and air, but really I am ashamed of myself."

" Not at all," his host replied. " Old aunt Plenty is the best cook in St. Jerome. I bought her in Old Virginia for that. Young Plenty — Okra is his real name — and old Plenty were thrown in : into one trade, I mean. I like to see our guests enjoy themselves. Enjoyment is, in my opinion," the general added, his broad face as genial as the rising sun, " a solemn duty."

" I am doing my duty, then," the young man said to himself that night, as he undressed for bed. " It is such a sudden change in my life ! Was there ever such a luxurious home? And what delightful people ! Then, I am twenty-one. There is the responsibility of this important church too. It is like Paradise. I wonder who or what is the serpent. It cannot be Commodore Thomas William Grandheur. Strange that an old gentleman of such fine presence and all should seem so empty. And how remarkable that he never dreams of it himself ! Yet he is. And, pray, who and what are *you* ? " he turned sharply and rebukingly upon himself with the demand.

He would have been more puzzled to answer this demand after the sabbath which followed his first in St. Jerome. The church was a large one. In virtue of being of a high pitch also, from floor to ceiling, and being, by reason of the climate, almost all windows and green blinds, there was a broad and airy effect within the edifice, wonderfully like that out of doors. Every seat below, as well as in the gallery above, at the end, and on either side, was filled. Morning and night the young man preached. The sermons had been prepared long before, with cruel care. He had been astonished at being able to prepare such remarkable sermons; and, being in his own estimation his very best, they were his very worst. Agonizing doubts, however, darkened his soul when he went home after the benediction at night. As to the market value of his efforts, no Hindoo at that moment in India could have been more profoundly ignorant: more than a million or less than a mill, he would have instantly adopted the opinion of the least hearer there, could he have known it, — eagerly adopted it as the only opinion a sane person could hold. If, however, you think, dear reader, that this man is to be the hero of this narrative, you are greatly mistaken. This is neither a religious biography nor a theological treatise: it is a true story of an actual world.

Upon his return with the family from church on Sunday night, the young people ascended, at the suggestion of Miss Irene, to the observatory, — not a house in St. Jerome without its little turret and flag-staff, — and gazed from their elevation upon the scene open on every side. Around them lay the city, buried in masses of foliage, the white houses standing out in strong contrast under a moonlight brilliant enough to read by. There were calm and silence to where sky and sea met in every direction around, and a light which was to that of the day as romance is to fact. The young ladies were more richly dressed than he had been used to see; and both seemed at once older and more beautiful in consequence, but in very different ways.

" The sky has never seemed so boundless above me," the young man said at last; "nor my life as boundless before me," he added slowly, regretting the words as soon as spoken.

"I do not wonder," the elder of the ladies replied.

Something in her tones smote him with apprehension; the fact being, that he was hesitating between two certainties. "To-morrow," he had stated them to himself, "the officers of the First Church will come in a body to tell me, with enthusiasm, that I am the most eloquent orator, the most desirable pastor, St. Jerome has ever imagined. Or, and more likely, I will have a call from Commodore Grandheur, deputed for the purpose, to tell me that I am a dead failure, and that, if I will take the Nautilus back on its next trip, they will be greatly obliged. And, now, what did Miss Irene mean?" he thought.

"Who was that dark and silent gentleman," he asked, staving off a decision of the matter which would be to him paradise, but much more probably perdition, "who introduced himself after morning service?"

"The one in the snuff-colored suit? Oh, that!" Miss Irene said, "was Mr. Nogens. He is an officer of the church because he is so good; that is, he never did any thing in his life, nor ever said any thing. Ever since I can remember, he was the same. He comes to every meeting, you know, and sits there. Nobody has ever found any thing to say about, much less against, him. He is such a good man! The instant you don't see him, you forget all about him. He is Mr. Nogens, and that is all; except that he wears a wig, and he thinks nobody knows it. Hush, Zeo! You see, he has a little curl of it pasted down on his forehead, and he can tell by feeling that whether it is on right. That makes Mr. Nogens so quiet: he is afraid of deranging his wig. He always feels for that little curl when anybody is saying any thing earnest to him. He keeps his finger upon it all the time when Miss Aurelia Jones is talking. Never mind about him, Mr. Venable; nobody ever does mind. But I wanted to tell you how exceedingly" —

"Pardon me," her companion interrupted with some haste. "I wanted to ask about a gentleman I met on Saturday. I was standing on the street, when he came along very rapidly. He is quite a tall man, very shabbily dressed, with a singularly narrow but high forehead. He had (I beg his pardon) an unusually long nose. I never saw a person drive along at such a swift pace, his head bent forward, his eyes on the ground. He caught sight of me in passing, but was under such headway, that he was a rod beyond me before he could turn and come back. Then he was in an extreme hurry. I could not keep up with him in what he said, at all. He shook me by the hand very cordially indeed, welcomed me to St. Jerome, asked me how I liked it, where I was staying, how old I was, where I was born, at what college I was educated, — a dozen questions without giving me time to answer one. Who is he? for he forgot to tell me his name."

"It couldn't be Mr. Phip Quatty," Irene Buttolph replied. "Did he say any thing about his having been an oysterman? We have been absent two years, you know."

"It was not Mr. Quatty: I know him," the young man said, "for we met him on our landing. Besides, Mr. Quatty told me at church to-day that he would certainly be at our Wednesday-night prayer-meeting."

"He did! I do wish," Irene said with energy, "that his horses would run away with him, and never stop until they got to China. And there is not a better man alive. Oh, bother!" she added violently.

"Irene," her sister said, laughing in spite of herself, and merrily, but laying her hand, in the moonlight, on her arm. "For shame, sister!"

"The gentleman on the street," Mr. Venable continued, "said he was glad to see me, because he had got an idea. He was full of enthusiasm about it. He said that it was a glorious idea; that he had hit upon a good many things, but that this was the best idea he had ever had: speaking as rapidly as he had walked. While speaking, he held up the palm of his left hand, and began, with the forefinger of his right hand, to draw his plan on it like a diagram. 'I thank God,' he said, 'that I ever thought of it. It is wonderful it was never thought of before.' But just then," continued Mr. Venable, "Capt. Chaffin came up, and shook hands with both of us, and asked me when I was coming to see her, — I understood him to say, — Mrs. Chaffingsby. The instant he spoke, the other said, 'Bah! Pshaw! Stuff and nonsense! Fiddlesticks!' and was off like a shot."

"I think I know who he is," Zeo made sober reply, her sister being unusually silent. "We knew him before we went to school, Irene. It must be Mr. Parsons, — Mr. Ezra Micajah Parsons."

"Of course!" Irene replied. "Did he say any thing else, Mr. Venable?" The young girl asked the question, looking archly at their companion, who colored.

The fact was, Mr. Parsons, having learned, in the course of his rapid questioning, that the new minister was staying for the present at Gen. Buttolph's, had said promptly, "Miserable business! This is all wrong! That will never do! There are two decided reasons against it;" with such emphasis on the word "two" that the guest shrank from telling the sisters of it. Yet they seemed to know.

"Why is it," Mr. Venable asked, to turn the conversation, "that every thing here in St. Jerome is so positive? The sky is so blue, the foliage so green, this moonlight is so unusually brilliant! This pomegranate, for instance," holding up one which he had brought down from the fruit-basket in his room: "its seeds are of such a vivid crimson; the skin is as bitter, too, as each seed is pungent. It is the same of the people. Almost every person I have met has a marked individuality. Even your Mr. Nogens is and does and says nothing, as you say, in a positive way."

"That is St. Jerome," Miss Irene said; "and O Mr. Venable! I am so glad you have come! I have been wanting to tell you how much we liked your sermons." And she did tell him, at some length too.　Although he made an attempt to deprecate, and arrest the enthusiastic young lady, she would have her say.　Nor was it immodestly done ; she seemed sincerely pleased.　"You know what an outspoken person I am," she added.　"If I don't like any thing, I speak just as freely."

He thanked her, not without pain, too, mingled with the pleasure, he knew not why.

"Irene," her sister interposed at last, " it is near midnight. Mr. Venable must be tired."　She had leaned, all the time, like a mere listener, upon the side of the observatory window farthest from the young man.　Somehow the authority of her words lay in their sweetness ; but their companion wished, as he undressed for bed, that she had said at least something.

Mr. Venable had been already called upon by the leading men of his church ; and the next day he set out upon his visits in return.　At first Commodore Grandheur went with him ; and the new minister was made to feel as if he were not merely a very young man, but as if he were an inexperienced young lady rather, needing assistance at every step.　It was as if his stately companion had said at each house, " You see I have brought this youth.　Be as forbearing with him as possible."　And then the old hero would plant his cane more firmly between his knees, smooth his white moustache, and patiently allow the other to vindicate himself as well as he could for daring to undertake so important a charge. After a few experiences of this kind, Mr. Venable insisted, although with all deference, upon going alone.　Occasionally, which was about the same thing, he took Mr. Nogens with him.　As Mr. Nogens never ventured beyond rubbing his hands together, and saying "yes" in emergencies, the new minister had uninterrupted opportunity of becoming acquainted with his people.

It was a large church, and the membership was as varied as

it was numerous. There were heavy wholesale merchants, as well as retail dealers, in dry goods and hardware ; doctors, fishermen, retired sea-captains, mechanics, milliners, provision-dealers, clerks, superintendents or workmen in the warehouses in which cotton-bales were compressed for shipping. Quite a number were families who had left their plantations to the care of overseers in the interior, and lived upon the island for the education of their children, and the marrying of their daughters. There were numbers of young men, also, whose connection with the church was hereditary, but whose personal interest lay in quite other directions. Behind St. Jerome was the magnificent State, an empire in itself. The city was like the hand which the State had reached out, open and cordial, to greet the coming world ; and the more the new arrival experienced of, so to speak, the pulse and pressure thereof, the more delighted he was that it had become his home. You can almost always awaken love in men as well as women by yourself falling in love with them ; and, just coming up as Mr. Venable was from the charnel-house of books, he was so much pleased with such a people, so un-bookish and in harmony with their beautiful climate and with Nature were they, that it was impossible but they also should be pleased with him.

CHAPTER VI.

IN WHICH, FOR THE FIRST TIME IN HIS LIFE, MR. VENABLE
SEES ONE OF HIS IDEALS ALIVE AND BREATHING.

ALMOST from the hour of his landing, Mr. Venable
had been both amazed and amused at the effect produced in him by having landed upon an island; especially
as he found that the twenty thousand people of St. Jerome
felt about it as he did. With him and with them there was
a feeling, in virtue of being surrounded by the sea, as if one
were done forever with the rest of the world.

"I am completely quit of the past," was his continual
thought. "I am to live here till I die, and I am glad of it."
Like everybody else, he felt as if he had a personal acquaintance with all he met. Being housed together by the
surf sounding all around them, they were at last but one
family. The climate being so delicious, they were there together upon the sand and among the oleanders and orange-
trees for a picnic, with splendid weather for it, under the
cloudless sky, or the almost as brilliant light of moon and
stars. It was not merely the fellow feeling of sailors on ship
and out of sight of land, but rather as of passengers on a
day's frolic together upon a coral island in mid-sea. In such
circumstances Commodore Thomas William Grandheur was
to be taken as a matter of course. His idea was plainly this:
"No crew afloat need a commander more than do the people
of this island, and no man is so admirably qualified for that

office as myself." He was not superintendent of the Sunday school of the First Church for nothing. The children were to be held firmly; but that was merely good practice, enabling him to keep steady hold upon the rest. Mr. Venable had been called to be pastor, against his wishes. That the people had defied his awful authority, was proof that he must stand firm and save them from themselves. The old man was so stately, so thoroughly satisfied with himself, so sincerely good at heart, that it seemed to Mr. Venable a sin, the unanimity with which everybody, from the least child up, laughed at their solemn custodian, glancing at each other in the midst of his most impressive assumptions, with lips pursed up and irreverent winks, as if it were the best joke going. If the commodore had not been near-sighted, a little hard of hearing, and so convinced of his own supremacy, he must have seen it. So it had been for many years. For weeks after Mr. Venable's arrival, Commodore Grandheur waited. Amid the general enthusiasm of the people for their new pastor, all he wanted to know was the final decision of Miss Aurelia Jones. But that lady grew the more fervid in her admiration with every passing sabbath. She was speaking about it in her infant-class room to a group of teachers one afternoon when Sunday school was over.

"No," she said, " you are all wrong. You like Mr. Venable because he is young; because he gets pale in the pulpit as he grows more in earnest. All wrong. I do not care for his beautiful periods, gestures, illustrations, pathetic prayers and appeals. All I care for in the world is fervor. Give me pure, humble ardor, yes, fervor, and I would be satisfied if he had nothing else." And the lady was so glowing, was so rich and useful too, that her words gave a sanction to the new minister. The fact must be added, that Miss Aurelia had, even thus early in their acquaintance, sent Mr. Venable a beautifully-worked bookmark or two. Miss Irene had been the one who had made a point to hand him the enclosure when it came, adding the mystical words, "Wait, Mr. Venable, you only wait," with a somewhat malicious smile on her lips.

Commodore Grandheur heard all the praise of the new pastor, — heard it often and warmly expressed by Miss Aurelia Jones. It decided him. The lady and himself had never agreed. They had come into collision upon a hundred points connected with church and Sunday school, and it was always the same. The colder the one was, that much the warmer the other. The ardor of the lady was turning the commodore from an iceberg into a rock. "I never say any thing," he said one day to good Mr. Nogens. "It is not wise to do so. It is beneath my dignity. But I never had but one opinion. This young man is more sophomorical than I had feared. He seems to be modest and sincere; but there is no fibre in him. What he may grow to be, I cannot tell; but his sermons are all froth and flowers. The enthusiasm will soon subside. I can wait. I have a good edition of *Blair* at home. You have read Blair's sermons, Mr. Nogens?"

No, Mr. Nogens had not. Mr. Nogens had nothing to say about it, one way or the other. Mrs. Nogens was deaf as a post, and her husband had exhausted himself for life in trying to make her hear. But no man, even the vilest scoffer, could find any thing against Mr. Nogens. He never did any thing wrong, never said a syllable out of the way. The commodore could unburden his opposition to him. Mr. Nogens was as safe as a man can be in such a case. He was like sawdust to stamping feet, like sand to running water: no fear of any thing doing any harm or making any noise through him. He was very sallow-faced, had no beard, and wore, as has been said, a wig. He sat and listened, but that was all. With his head a little on one side while you spoke, no friend could give you more attention, — slowly closing his eyes and compressing his lips as you became more and more excited in your statement, relaxing and slowly opening them again when your burst of feeling was over; and nothing beyond that, except to feel with the forefinger of his slow left hand, upon his temple, if the little curl plastered thereupon was all right, and then remark, "Yes," but in a way which was but the continuance of his interrupted calm. It relieved you to know that you had said your say to so good a man; that he must know that you were in the right, even if he never said so.

Not an hour after parting with the commodore on the occasion of the remarks just quoted, Mr. Nogens entertained his pastor, who had just called. Mrs. Nogens came in to do honor to their visitor, with her old-fashioned face, and such a cheerful readiness to hear and assent to any thing, if anybody could only succeed (which was impossible) in making her hear it!

"I am very well, I thank you," their caller said, full of enthusiasm, anxious to please where he was himself delighted. "What a glorious climate it is! Nothing can be more beautiful than sea and sky and this town. The streets are so broad and white, and full of trees! I have been making visits. I was in at his office to see Col. Roland just now. They tell me he was secretary of state to the governor. Why do you call your governor 'Old Ugly,' Mr. Nogens? The colonel has been an editor and writer of poems, I am told, for many years; yet he looks so young, a very pleasant gentleman indeed. And I dropped in at Squire Clarke's provision-store. I was delighted when I heard that he had broken his whiskey-bottles and poured out his brandy after joining our church the other day. Ought we not to buy our groceries there, Mr. Nogens?"

Mr. Nogens listened attentively; his face yellow, worn, and settled, in contrast with that of the other, which was bright with hope and eagerness. Mr. Venable paused at last, from very shame at having taken up so much of the conversation,

—paused for a considerable time. He was just beginning again, when Mr. Nogens, after weighing well all that had been advanced, replied very deliberately, "Yes."

"I have just been to see Capt. Chaffin also," the visitor began again, — "or Mrs. Chaffingsby : I do not know which it is. What a nice large place they have near the sea ! I never saw a more beautiful yard ; so full of sea-shells in heaps and lining the walks. I did not know there was such a variety in sizes, shapes, and colors, before. I rang, but the lady was out. A young girl, I mean a child, came to the door. I wanted to ask," — Mr. Venable hesitated and stammered, — "I mean, I wanted to inquire of you " — But the visitor colored as Mr. Nogens settled himself into a deeper attention, beginning to close his eyes and compress his lips as if for a confidence upon the part of the speaker. The silence of Mr. Nogens was so ominous, however, that, as soon as Mr. Venable could recover himself, he changed the conversation to church matters. In leaving, he tried to make Mrs. Nogens understand, by his smiling and the pressure of his hand, what he could not by his voice. She was very willing to hear, if one would but speak loud enough. Little less than a cannon, however, would have been sufficient. And yet Mrs. Nogens was far from being unhappy in her enforced seclusion from the world. There was a calmness in her face, which recalled to the mind the fact that "beyond these voices there is peace ; " and it seemed a coming-down on her part, as from serene summits, when she endeavored to hear what was said to her.

It was no wonder that Mr. Venable was perplexed as he walked away from Mr. Nogens, in the direction of Mr. Ezra Micajah Parsons's place, out in the suburbs. Ever since his coming, people had said, " Do you know Mrs. Chaffingsby ? " "What ! have you not seen *her* yet? You ought by all means to see her," and the like. There was something so peculiar in the way in which people mentioned her, that he was desirous, and yet almost afraid, to find her in. During his rapid rounds of visitations, as the weeks passed, he had called more than once, to find the front gate locked, and the house, a large two-storied mansion, apparently deserted. To-day, just before visiting Mr. Nogens, he had called again upon Mrs. Chaffingsby; and the door of the house had been opened by the person concerning whom he had tried, as we have seen, to question that gentleman. It was a girl who might have been eighteen years old, but was probably not more than fourteen. The visitor had met many surprises in his strange new world, but none so great as this. The blessing and the curse upon him was his keen sensitiveness. It was his nature, and it had been unduly cultivated during years of seclusion from the world, and hard study. But he was almost as deaf to music as Mrs. Nogens, in comparison to his passion for color and form. He had felt, ever since arriving, as if he had walked into the glowing painting of some great master. It was because he was of so tropical a nature himself; because he had been repressed so long; because, in the sudden enjoyment of the best health he had ever known, he had reached the tropical period of his manhood, and had entered upon it with new zest of body, of mind, and of soul. But who had supposed that such a person ever lived, except on canvas, as this girl who stood in the half light, half shadow, of the partially-opened door at Capt. Chaffin's that day? There was a subtle contrast between the exquisite white and red of her complexion, and the soft brown of her abundant hair, which he had never before seen; the purity of the perfect face was illumined by eyes, large, blue, deep in their childlike innocence. Sculpture had not revealed to him curve and form like this, nor had painting hinted of such blending hues. The girl stood looking at him, her lips parted like a rosebud beginning to bloom, her eyes suddenly yet steadily in his. The words in which she told him that no one was at home were nothing in themselves, yet they were in harmony as to their tones with the smile with which they were spoken. In fact, he had one of the few grand surprises of his life; and it was but for an instant. Opening the door with her left hand, she was with difficulty keeping some one back and out of view with her right arm extended behind her; and the meeting was ended almost in a moment. He hardly observed in his dazed condition, as he walked away, the loud and merry yet jarring laugh of some one from within, as the door closed behind him. And this explained his eagerness, and yet his unwillingness, to speak to Mr. Nogens about it, during his call upon him.

As he left that silent gentleman, it quickened his walk toward Mr. Parsons's house, the hope that he might learn something from him; for, that there was something singular in the case, some mystery behind the loveliness of the girl, he felt assured.

His destination proved to be farther away in the suburbs than he had supposed. Once he stopped a sailor at a corner, to ask the way. He had not observed, in his hurry, that he was drunk,—so very drunk that he was highly flattered at being questioned, was overflowing with information, and both dignified and effusive in the manner in which, at great length, and holding firmly to Mr. Venable, he told him the way; but told him so entirely wrong, that it was an hour before he found himself at last at the front gate of Mr. Parsons's place. And a magnificent place it was, containing about ten acres closed within a plank fence close and high. He could see, over the top of this, a profusion of trees, the house with its observatory and flagstaff on the roof in the midst. As he came to the gate, Mr. Parsons walked rapidly out, recognized his pastor, turned around after passing him in his haste, and came back.

"I am glad to see you," he said; "but I am in a terrible hurry just now: sorry to see you, in fact. How are you?

The fact is, I have just thought that the storm when you came must have washed out the channel of Hacamac. It is at the other end of the island, and ought to be the only city on it. I am the owner of Hacamac, you know. It is weeks ago since that storm, but I never thought about it. Ten minutes ago the idea struck me like a shot. How is Gen. Buttolph? You ought not to be stopping there. I will show you how and why." And the old man, tall and thin and eager, began in almost breathless haste to draw a diagram in the sand. "Here, you see, is St. Jerome. Miserable place! wretched channel. This is the arm of the sea. Now," making marks deep and sweeping, with the end of a stalk of sugar-cane picked up from the ground, "this point of the island projecting into the ocean is Hacamac, my property. Channel on this side," and he made a mark; "still deeper channel on this side," — mark yet more vigorous. "See? Why, sir, the navies of the universe could lie at my wharves there. Plenty of water, plenty, — oceans! And it struck me this instant, that the last storm must have washed my bars clean away. I am going to get Capt. Chaffin to take me out in his schooner right off. Next time you come, I will show you round. From four to six fathoms, I feel confident. And you like St. Jerome? It is because you know nothing whatever about it. I cannot see how a man can be such a fool. Ten years from to-day, there will not be a house here. Look at my town, Hacamac. Look! an idiot could understand;" and Mr. Parsons proceeded, sugar-cane in hand, to lay off upon the loose earth the points of compass, bearings, bars, channels, islands, and all, talking swiftly and eagerly.

"But, bless my soul," he suddenly said, "I cannot fool away any more time. And it reminds me that your sermons are too long. Good-by. Come and see me soon. I have five hundred things in there to show you. You have heard of my terraqueous machine? No: I walk too fast to be bothered with you. Thank you. Sorry you came to-day.

Glad to see you." And the speaker was off, only to turn around and come back again, a change in his manner. "All I do, sir," he said solemnly, "is for the Master. The entire world lies in wickedness and woe. A good part of the fiddlesticks and nonsense of Christians to-day is in thinking that the world can be converted with a few thousands, or a few hundreds of thousands. It will take millions on millions of money to build churches and send missionaries. I am trying to make money chiefly for that." There was a sincerity in the tones of the gaunt old man, a sudden lowering and sweetening as well as slackening of his speech, which confirmed Mr. Venable in all he had heard of the excellent individual, whose eyes brightened as he added, "As I told you before, I have an idea. It is, how to convert the Roman Catholics. A splendid idea! I have made accurate calculation. It can be done in fifteen years. It is a glorious plan, the best I ever made. My idea of Essential Fruit, even my great invention of Focussed Flesh, is nothing to it. It is sure to succeed. But good-by. Not now. Next time — Look here," he added: "has Miss Aurelia Jones sent you any thing special as yet? Ah, well, never mind! Just wait. But good-by, good-by!" and with his head bent forward he made up for lost time as he hurried away.

CHAPTER VII.

IN WHICH WE COME TO KNOW COL. ROLAND, MR. FARCE FAN-
THORP, AND BEGIN TO BECOME ACQUAINTED WITH MISS ZEO.

ONE morning, about a week after parting so abruptly
from Mr. Parsons, Mr. Venable was taking a walk before breakfast, upon the beach, which was so near to Gen.
Buttolph's that the last sound he heard at night, as well as
the first in the morning, was the dash of its waves. It had
a soothing influence when, pretty tired after his day's work,
he fell asleep to its rhythmic roar, and he yielded himself
pleasurably to its billows, as, lifting and lowering him, it
bore him at last, unconscious and far away, upon the ocean
of dreams. It was the sea which slowly awoke him in the
morning, as if its surges were bearing him back again from
darkness and sleep to light and labor; and he was forming
that passion for it which would forever make an inland life
dull and tame in comparison.

Upon the morning in question, he was strolling slowly
along the white sand, enjoying the cool air and the waves
lapsing into lines of crisp foam at his feet. So absorbed was
he in thought, his head upon his bosom as he walked, that
he did not observe a tall pedestrian who had come from
behind the heaps of drifted sand in the distance, and was
rapidly approaching him along the beach.

"Good-morning," the other called to him while some
yards away. "I am glad to see that there are two men

sensible enough to be abroad so early ; " and Mr. Venable saw that it was Mr. Parsons. "I spent last night at Hacamac, and am in a hurry to get home," he continued without waiting for a reply : "if you will turn, and walk fast enough, I will be glad to have you go with me. Col. Roland had a wretched editorial in his 'Standard' yesterday, in regard to Hacamac ; and I've been out to take fresh measurements in order to refute him. But what can you expect of a man who is a politician as well as a — Heaven help him ! — a lawyer and a poet ? Met Roland yet ? "

Mr. Venable had met him once or twice.

"Ever read in history about the Earl of Warwick ? " Mr. Parsons went on in his hurried manner ; and his companion turned and accompanied him, saying, "Do you mean the king-maker in the English War of the Roses ? "

"Yes, the man that made kings out of any thing he could lay his hands on, and who tried to make them work, which they didn't. Well," Mr. Parsons continued, "Col. Roland did that very thing. I'm an inventor. Some day I intend giving you a ride along this very beach, in a machine I have patented. But the colonel beats me. He invented a governor."

"A governor ? You mean, of a steam-engine. It consists of two iron balls " —

"Stuff and nonsense ! " the other interrupted Mr. Venable brusquely. "He invented Gov. Magruder, Old Ugly, the governor of our State. You've heard of *him* ? Very good. The way of it was this : Roland is a smart fellow, and very ambitious. He is a fine speaker, a splendid writer, has the smoothest manners for ladies of any man I know, but somehow he can't get the people to vote for him ; or, if they ever did, they swore they never would again. Very well. When the colonel saw that, he looked about him, as a man does for a lump of clay when he is going to make a jug. D'you see ? That's the way he picked up Magruder. He had just

come into his father's big sugar-plantation, — Magruder, I
mean, — and no more thought of being a governor than of
being a saint, and he's far enough from *that!* Well, Roland went to work, first on him and then for him. He had
him nominated in caucus, and then in the convention. Of
course Magruder gave his money like water. Roland wrote
him up in dozens of papers, paid young lawyers and old
ones too to stump the State for him, got up a cry about his
being born on our new soil, worked for him like a beaver
and a fox rolled into one. Magruder is not able to make
a speech, but he more than made up for that by his popular manners, and by shaking everybody's hand. Never saw
him?" To this abrupt question Mr. Venable was compelled to reply in the negative.

"Well, I want you to see him. Do you know what a
magnet is?" Mr. Parsons asked.

"Certainly, sir."

"No, you never saw one in good earnest. Wait till you
see Magruder. I wish every preacher, every Christian, was
like him; in *that*, I mean, not in any thing else. You'll
understand what I mean when you see him. Oh, well! before Magruder knew where he was, his popular manners and
his money had made him governor of the State, — under
Col. Roland's engineering, you observe. Of course Roland
was his secretary of state. He wrote all his speeches and
state papers. His Excellency's term was out not long ago ;
and now the colonel is working to make him a United-
States senator, all for his own ends. Time for you to go
back, is it? Better go on with me, and get some breakfast.
I want you to see my wife and our little girl, — our little
Owny we call her. But no," Mr. Parsons added, in the same
rapid breath, "you had better not, on the whole : they might
not expect you so early, might not like it. But you must
come soon. Good-by. I doubt whether either one of them
will do. But," and Mr. Parsons closed his irrelevant remark

with such emphasis as to bring color to the cheeks of his
perplexed companion, as once before, " I am sure *that* one
won't do at all, at all ! "

Old and weather-beaten, odd, even grotesque, as Mr. Parsons was, there was such sincerity in his headlong manner,
such a kindly look in his deep-set eyes, that it was impossible not to like him.   But Mr. Venable was not afraid, as
he walked homeward, of being late for breakfast.   Things
proceeded in too leisurely a manner for that at the luxurious
table of his indolent host.

That very evening he was called down from his room to
see Col. Roland.   He found him an unusually good-looking
gentleman, closely shaved, fresh-colored, carefully dressed,
with hands which were very soft and white.   He spoke also
in low and persuasive tones, using a good deal of gesture
and adjective.   Mr. Venable took the more interest in him,
having been told that he was a literary man.   As a general
thing, people in St. Jerome read little, he had found, beyond
the papers.   Gen. Buttolph cared little even for them, and
beyond his genial manner was rather a dull companion when
sugar-planting was not the topic.

When Col. Roland had shaken hands with Mr. Venable,
and said a few things in a polished manner, he turned away
to the young ladies, whom he had also asked to see.   In
contrast with Mr. Parsons, and in a lesser sense with everybody else unless it was Gen. Buttolph, the colonel was not
in the slightest hurry.   Although a partisan editor, he generally said his severest things in such flowing language that he
had been engaged in but one duel, and not once in a street-
fight.

The success of the man evidently lay in his social qualities and in his youthful appearance, which, although his hair
had been silvered for twenty years, left you in doubt whether
he was sixty or thirty ; most of all in his devotion to the
ladies, especially to those, like the daughters of Gen. But-

tolph, just making their entrance into society. And this last was the most remarkable thing about the colonel. From his earliest youth he had been a devoted admirer of the ladies; had always been in love; had been engaged scores of times, it was said, to many girls when they first came out; yet, somehow, was a bachelor still. All this would be incomplete, if it were not added that the colonel was far more popular with the ladies and the little girls than he was with the boys and the men; and all were quite prepared for it now when he drew from his breast-pocket, and read, a copy of verses in honor of the young ladies and of their return to their native city; the poetry, and the reading of it, being wonderfully good.

Mr. Venable had a really delightful evening, although only as a listener and looker-on, for the colonel had small reference to him in comparison with the ladies. But it was not so much in what the colonel said, as he reclined somewhat languidly in an easy-chair, toying with Miss Irene's cologne-bottle which happened to be on the table. He had many anecdotes to tell of the storm and of the overflow, of the leading men and women of the city, of books and events of all kinds, social, political; but it was the extraordinary way he drew out Miss Irene herself, which interested Mr. Venable most. "How charmingly you are dressed, and how very charmingly you are looking!" had been one of the visitor's earliest remarks to the lady. He had said the same many thousand times in other parlors, but it was a fact in this case. Since her return home, Miss Irene had slipped the chrysalis of the school for the butterfly attire of a young lady of wealth and position, with an energy which marked all of her ways. She was really a beautiful blonde; but her beauty lay chiefly in her brilliancy, and the sparkle of her eye was exceeded by the incessant speech of her frank lips.

The minister felt himself thrown very much into the shade as the colonel, by the subtle flattery of his deference and

admiring attentions, as well as by ever-varying suggestions,
urged the young lady on. He had flavored one of his remarks
with a proverb from the French ; and she, as if unconsciously, had passed from her own language into that, and chatted
on so swiftly and smilingly that her visitor, holding up a dep-
recating hand as he sat, had to acknowledge his comparative
ignorance of the language. Then, at the request of Mr.
Venable, watching his opportunity, she had seated herself
at the piano, and played and sung in a way which no doubt
astonished the excited girl herself only less than it did the
gentlemen. Italian opera was no more familiar to her than
were German Rhine songs. One or two of Beranger's mel-
odies were rendered in the original, with as much grace as
a little song of the colonel's last composition, and dedicated
to herself. Once or twice Mr. Venable winced a little at her
energy when conversation was resumed, she was so very
decided in her opinions about people and things.

" I am afraid we will not see Miss Zeo," the colonel said
at last.

" She said she would come in directly," Irene answered.
" Excuse me, and I will see."

"You are highly favored, Mr. Venable," Col. Roland
said, as she left the room, "to be the general's guest. Miss
Irene will be, I may say is already, the belle of St. Jerome.
One rarely meets a more beautiful and brilliant woman.
With Miss Zenobia I have less acquaintance. An excellent
young lady, I am told. Although younger, she seems to be
older than her sister."

At this moment there was a ring at the door, and soon
after a laugh which rang more loudly ; for Miss Irene, in
returning, had found Mr. Fanthorp in the hall, and they
entered the room together. Mr. Venable was introduced to
that gentleman, and received him with more trepidation than
curiosity ; for of Mr. Farce Fanthorp he had heard a good
deal.

He was a small, thick-set, swarthy-faced man, whom you would not look at a second time if you did not know him, and whom you would not fail to watch closely and curiously if you did. The minister's eyes had happened to be on him the first time Mr. Fanthorp attended church after his arrival. Commodore Grandheur was in the act of passing, with his peculiar stateliness, the contribution-box to that gentleman, who was seated in a conspicuous pew. As the solemn official held the box before him, Mr. Fanthorp held up his left hand as if for him to wait, while with the right hand he searched every pocket, first upon one side and then upon the other, apparently for his purse. When every face in the congregation was turned that way, the commodore coloring high at the detention, Mr. Fanthorp gravely produced, as the result of his search, a bar of tobacco, and bit out a quid, looking up at the commodore with the face of a babe.

Col. Roland was too perfect a man of the world to show it, or he would have exhibited his aversion for Mr. Fanthorp. If there was any object for which the colonel had both hatred and apprehension, it was this small, solemn-visaged young man. When it is added that Mr. Fanthorp was neatly but plainly dressed, and had dark eyes and hair and scanty moustache, all has been said that a photograph, even, could convey. Beyond a perfect ease of manner, amounting to assurance, there was nothing to object to in this inoffensive gentleman. Nor did he obtrude himself into the conversation, beyond a humorous remark or two, the fun of which was increased by his peculiar solemnity. And so the conversation flowed again as fluently as before, except that Col. Roland had straightened himself up in his chair, did not refer to himself as freely as he did before, and seemed to be more guarded in his manner. Leaving the others to themselves, Mr. Venable engaged in conversation with Mr. Fanthorp. As they did so he became, on account of the interest the other evidently took in all he said, more interested him-

self in the account he gave of his first impressions in regard
to St. Jerome, the people, the island generally; especially of
a fishing-expedition upon which he had gone in the morning
with old Judge Sefton.

"I confess I enjoyed it," he continued at last. "You
know that the judge has nothing else to do since he left the
bench, but fish. He fishes every day, I believe, and all day.
He had often asked me before; but we went after breakfast
to-day for the first time. We had long fishing-poles; and
the judge showed me how, after we had waded out into the
sea up to our waists, to bait, and throw out my line. Almost
as soon as I did so, I had a bite. I had not fished since I
was a boy, and was greatly excited. As it was in the ocean,
I expected to catch something enormous. Acting on the
judge's instructions, I put my pole on my shoulder, and hastened ashore as fast as I could. You may imagine how
eagerly I drew out my line; and, when I did, it was only a
little minnow *that* long!"

With some gesticulations Mr. Venable tells the story.
Miss Irene and the colonel are listening by this time, and
they all laugh. But why is it that they laugh with their eyes
rather upon Mr. Fanthorp, to whom he is speaking, than
upon himself? And why do they listen so eagerly, and
with such a covert exchange of glances, as Mr. Fanthorp
proceeds, warming into it as he goes on, and with, at last, a
good deal of gesture, to tell also of one of his fishing-ex-
cursions? Mr. Venable cannot wholly understand it. As
Mr. Fanthorp proceeds, Col. Roland and Irene Buttolph
give way to a measure of laughter beyond the fun of the
story, — so far as the minister can see, very much so.

But he is himself greatly amused soon after. The colonel
had turned aside to the lady to tell her of a caucus meeting
he had lately attended; and Mr. Fanthorp, addressing himself to the colonel the instant the other is through, told of
his experiences (and very amusing they are) at the same

meeting. With a wonderful facility, the serious-faced man has somehow changed himself, as he speaks, into the person he speaks to! His attitude in his chair, his tones, his manner of toying with a book as he speaks, the slightest movement of hands and head and foot, — to a hair's breadth Mr. Fanthorp has become Col. Roland, and all with the unaffected sincerity, seemingly, of a child. There is something exceedingly impudent, yet ludicrous, in it. The seriousness of the speaker, and the annoyance of the colonel, make it the more amusing.

Col. Roland is dampened beyond his power of recovery, and turns somewhat abruptly to Mr. Venable, while Mr. Fanthorp devotes himself to the lady. But neither the clergyman nor the colonel can enter fully into their own conversation, for watching, however furtively, the lively talk which ensues between the mimic and his hostess. Miss Irene was never more reckless, as if in defiance. And she is evidently as unconscious as Mr. Venable was himself: yet this audacious visitor is imitating to her face her every gesture and inflection, every word, exclamation, tone, and peculiarity. The insolence of the thing is almost forgotten in the subtle excellence of the mimicry.

" His imitation of me was not the least like, so far as I could see," Mr. Venable remarks to the colonel, in the end, as they go to the window to look out on the moonlight : " yet it is remarkable in this case."

" Nor does he ever succeed with me," his companion added. " Scoundrel ! And he said he was at that caucus. It is a falsehood. He tells such lies every day with the same audacity. It is because he is of good family, that he is endured. As to quarrelling or fighting with him, one would as soon have a difficulty with a monkey. It amazes me that such a puppy is tolerated. If Gen. Buttolph had seen it just now, he would have horsewhipped him."

But at this moment the general and Miss Zeo came in, and

the conversation changed. Who, however, looking upon the father, so genial and cordial in his placid hospitality ; looking upon the modest brunette who enters the room with him, simply a dark, quiet, low-spoken girl, — who, merely seeing these as they took their share of entertaining their company, could have imagined all that lay outside of that parlor and that presence? Something immeasurably beyond any mimicry of Mr. Farce Fanthorp, in that !

Take as a specimen the events of that very day, only one of many. Mr. Venable had been greatly pleased, as we have said, with the almost cherubic innocence of Theodore, who went, however, by no other name than that of Grit, — the plump and quiet-mannered little son of his host. A more beautiful child of ten or thereabout, gentle, soft in eye and voice and rounded cheek, you never saw. Yet was this angel really and truly of the infernal sort instead. It was an old story of similar circumstances. His mother had died two years before. As soon as his sisters had gone to their school in another State, the boy had passed almost exclusively into the care of the negroes at the sugar-plantation up country, and on the place of his father in St. Jerome. True, when in the city he was a favorite scholar of Miss Aurelia Jones in sabbath school. That warm-hearted lady loved, fondled, and made much of her " darling little dumpling," as she called him. Nor was he without due teaching during the week. But, in city and country, almost all of his life was spent with the slaves. From his birth his will was law among these. It was impossible he should not have grown up the abominable little Nero he was, — self-willed, passionate, cruel, lying, impure, foul in word and inmost heart, beyond license of description in these pages.

That day, merely as an instance, his pony had been locked up from him, by order of his father, for some one of his many offences. The moment the general had left the place, he had seized an axe, and began to hew at the door of the stable. In vain old Plenty and young Plenty and aunt Plenty had tried to persuade, to threaten, to bribe. They dared not lay hands on the boy. He would have struck them with the axe, bitten them, killed them if he could. Some devil seemed to enter him as he chopped furiously away. His sister Irene had tried her powers, but he had turned upon her with such a torrent of foul language that she had fled to the house; and she as well as the rest gave it up until "Miss Zeo" should return from market, to which she had been driven in the buggy by one of the negro men; having, for excellent reasons, taken that duty on herself since she had come back. As she drove into the yard, the young savage had forced an entrance into the stable, and was in the act of leading his pony out. It was far from being the first occasion of the kind, and the whole aspect of the girl altered as she advanced upon him. No one suggested that she should wait until the general came back. There were, alas! reasons why the boy should *not* be left until then. She must master him, and as rapidly as possible, before the arrival of her father.

"Theodore, dear Theo, please," she began as she went up to him. But her approach was repaid with a scowl and a vicious kick. "Grit, Gritty, Clear Grit," she endeavored, "you will for me, for Zeo;" and nothing could be more winning, humble even, than the attitude and persuasions of the girl, her eyes seeking, but in vain, to catch those of the infant desperado, as he stood with one foot in the stirrup of his pony's saddle. "*Dear* brother!" and she laid her hand on his shoulder. But he had planned in reference to her as well as the others, knowing her by this time fully as well as he knew the remainder of the household. On the instant he struck her full in the face with his whip, and opened upon her a torrent of the language heard from infancy on the sugar-plantation. The poor girl turned pale, and glanced up. Suppose Mr. Venable should hear? But no; his room was on the other side of the house. Besides, he was oblivious just then, in the preparation of the closing sentences of his next Sunday's sermon. She understood the emergency better than any one. Irene is taller and stronger; but on the instant she has taken the young savage in her arms, torn him from his pony, and, one hand upon his mouth, summoning the servants to her assistance, she bore him, kicking and struggling, into the stable, through the demolished door, into an inner room there, tied her veil firmly over his mouth to stop his paroxysm of foul language, and held him there, with a white face but a grasp of iron, until he subsides from sheer exhaustion. It takes a long time to conquer him, and she does it alone; but at last, hours after, she has the thoroughly spoiled boy in bed in her own room, asleep, the door locked upon them. Her task has been a terrible one; but, alas! bad as her brother is, he is the smallest part of her troubles.

She rises from his bedside at last, bathes her face, arranges her dress, smoothes her disordered hair, eats a little of the meal that has been brought to the room for her brother — the scraps that he has left. Then she looks around, pulls down the curtain a little more, sees that the door is indeed locked, reads mechanically a verse or two from her little Bible, and sinks upon her knees beside her brother, utterly worn out.

"Help!" she murmurs in disconnected prayer. "I am — but as a child — Help! — for the things that are so much — *worse* — so much worse than my brother! O my Saviour! — It is more than — a girl — can do. Oh, my poor, poor — father! Lord — I don't understand — money — only a girl as yet. And — a *woman* too — Lord, is it what a woman — a *girl* should know?" and, as she murmured it, her face rested on the bed, her neck, her very hands, clasped in supplication, crimson with shame, — a shame that burns and hurts, a fire rather which scorches. "O my Saviour! — oh

my poor papa ! — O Christ, it is so terrible — and so horrible !" She shudders as she kneels ; her head sinks, from
sheer exhaustion, upon the bed ; for her contest with Grit
began early in the day, and it is now late in the afternoon.

It was her weariness from this which had detained her
from coming that evening into the parlor to aid in entertaining Col. Roland and Mr. Fanthorp. But she had not
mentioned the matter to her father when he returned to the
house. As to Miss Irene, when she had fled from the violence of her brother it had been to her piano, at which she
had played long and loud in order to drown any sounds of
the strife ; when she tired of that, she had read a novel, taken
a nap, and then dressed for the evening : so that she was
quite ready to entertain and be entertained.

"Is it not remarkable," Col. Roland demanded of Mr.
Venable that evening, when the two had gone to the other
side of the parlor to examine a painting upon the walls,
leaving Mr. Fanthorp for the moment in conversation with
the ladies, — "is it not really wonderful that these sisters
should be so unlike? Miss Irene is full of life and soul.
As you say, she is as intelligent as she is beautiful, and how
accomplished she is ! It is a pity that Miss Zeo is so quiet.
Did you observe it? she seems to have hurt her face in some
way."

Irene Buttolph had made a deep impression upon both
of them. "She is a splendid girl," Col. Roland said to
himself as he drew off his coat that night on going to bed ;
"and really I must marry some day. I will engage myself
to her as soon as it is possible to do so, and *this* time I *will*
marry. Especially as the governor agrees with me, that he
cannot possibly do better than to take Miss Zenobia. She
is extremely quiet, and will gladly accept him. If he *is* a
fool, she will never know it. An alliance with a man like
Gen. Buttolph will help us in regard to the senate ; and, being brothers-in-law, Old Ugly will be an amazing help to me

when he gets there. It is the best plan I have ever laid."
By a remarkable coincidence Mr. Venable was saying to
himself in his room at the same moment, "It is a wonder
I could have thought of comparing the two sisters. Miss
Irene may be a charming lady in her dashing way, but how
inferior, although I wish I thoroughly knew why, to Miss Zeo !
What could Mr. Parsons have meant when he said, ' Not *that*
one particularly ? ' My health must be growing vigorous very
rapidly ; or is it this impulsive climate ? What a beautiful
girl it was who opened the door to me at Mrs. Chaffingsby's !
I wish I had gone in. Such beauty is too great to be real.
As soon as I can I will go there again, purely from curiosity,
though I am a fool to think of such things so soon. But next
to my work, I'll try to know that dark and silent girl. I
wish I could see as much of her as I do of her sister ; and
I wish she would say more to me, or that I could say more
to her. Above all, I wish I could find out in what her power
lies. There is one comfort : neither Col. Roland, even if
he were young enough, much less Mr. Fanthorp, — nobody,
in fact, — would dare to make love to *her*. Some day —
some day " — At the same hour the lady spoken of was
bending over her brother. He had eaten a hearty supper,
and had gone to sleep again, a slumbering St. John in
childhood as he lay, so innocent he seemed. She stooped
down and kissed him, though not upon the lips.

"As God shall help me, I *will*," she said.

CHAPTER VIII.

IN WHICH WE BID GOOD-BY FOR A TIME, TO THINGS INFERIOR,
AND ASCEND INTO THE REALM OF ART.

TO insure access next time at Capt. Chaffin's house, Mr. Venable had written to say how much he had regretted not finding the family at home before, and begging to know when it would be convenient to them to see him. A prompt reply came in the person of the captain himself. Mr. Venable went down into the parlor to find that seaman seated, very uncomfortably, in one of the chairs, his head seeming all the harder by reason of the closely-cropped hair, the beard and moustache as wooden as the rest of the walnut-hued countenance. The captain preferred to retain his low-crowned and glazed hat; and it lay, crown uppermost, upon his knees, which were drawn close together, his hands resting upon the top of his hat, the balls of his lumpy thumbs pressed together as if in argument.

"She begs me to present her compliments," he said, projecting the upper part of his person farther forward as he sat, and as if repeating a message committed to memory. "Also she will be pleased to see Mr. Venable — of course she means you — at four o'clock to-morrow afternoon, if the hour be agreeable to Mr. Venable — you she means."

"I will come with pleasure," said the other.

"I would come and show you the way," the captain added less mechanically, and as if with a load off his mind; "but I leave by light with Mr. Parsons, — Ezra Micajah."

"For Hacamac?" Mr. Venable inquired.

"No, not this time," the other replied, each sentence to itself, as if it were a rope given out from his hand coil by coil. "Hacamac is only one. He has one thousand things on hand. This is a steamboat. No paddle-boxes. Nary screw. It has a belt with paddle-boards on it all along, one to every two feet. The belt is driven along deck from the stern, over the bow into the water, all along under the keel, up out of the water at the helm, up and along the deck and down over the bow again, and so on for ever and ever. It's Mr. Parsons's idea. He invents: I apply. A dead failure. Not the first. Nor the last. I know it now. He will know it by night. Not a better man alive. If his smartness," Capt. Chaffin added after consideration, "could get down the companion-way into his hold, — his heart I mean, — and his goodness could climb up from his heart into his head, you see. But it is a singular world. Here on the island especially. I'm a silent man, myself; that is, away from St. Jerome. It's in the air, which is like brandy. You talk just *to* talk. There's my wife. Before she came here she no more dreamed she had any talent than you do. Nor then, until that long-haired artist man, that taught her how to paint, died at our house. Be gentle-like when you call," he added, rising to go. "She is all nerves. All over her they are, like ropes to a ship. Don't express your admiration too strong." And the captain departed the instant his errand was done, having the mechanical precision of an engine in that as in every thing else.

When Mrs. Chaffingsby opened the door to Mr. Venable at the set time, she was the very person he had expected to see, from the much that had been said to him of her; only, if the phrase may be allowed, more so. He had not supposed that a woman could be so small and light and slight, and yet be a wife and a mother. She had an old and care-worn face; and yet it was one which was singularly childish and almost sweet, with an unusual abundance of light-colored hair disposed in curls about her head, before and behind.

" I mentioned four o'clock," she said, as she welcomed him into the house, and took his hat by the edges of its brim with only the points of the fingers of a hand on either side, and as if it were full of water, and stood it on a table, " because you would then have had your nap." She alluded to the custom, as universal in that latitude as dinner, of the siesta after that meal. " I hoped to have had mine, but I could not sleep. The least excitement, you know " — And she lifted a hand, which he saw had more than one diamond upon it, to her forehead. In her dress, as in her voice and movement, there was something as of a large doll ; no, rather of a good little girl dressed for a child's party, — a perplexing blending of the two with the woman of forty years or more, which puzzled her visitor. There was a curious intermixture in her, not merely of woman and child, but of the natural and the artificial also, which was, however, not more bewildering to any other than it was to herself.

" Capt. Chaffin called," began her visitor, as she went before him with a springing step, opening a door leading to one side from the hall, and motioning him to enter.

" Capt. Chaffingsby, if you please," she corrected him, with a smile. " We always prefer that appellation. Walk in, if you will be so good ; " and he did so, avoiding any steady look at certain pictures with which the hall was adorned. For the same reason he confined his eyes to the face of the lady during the opening conversation which ensued.

" I have had the great pleasure," she said at last, disposing her arms across each other on her lap, as she sat, apparently, on the extreme edge of her chair, " of hearing you several times. I dare not adventure myself too often. Any

sentiment heard from the pulpit too striking, or too strongly.
expressed, seriously affects me. I bear it home like a blow,
and it prevents my sleeping. The same of the singing, if
there should be any discord, or if it should be too emo-
tional. So of the supplications. Too great a degree of
fervor is what I am compelled to avoid exposure to, as I
would typhoid-fever, so sensitive am I to all contagion, so
exceedingly sensitive," she added with a shiver, and continued, "My nerves are tense, because of the unceasing strain
upon them of my art. Yes, I am very, very sympathetic.
I regret about the Wednesday-evening meetings. Once,
when there, Mr. Quatty succeeded in speaking. As you
may suppose, I could neither sleep, nor partake of my food,
for many days. It is very, very foolish, but can I help it?"
And through all her affectation as of a smiling Frenchwo-
man, there was none the less the sincerity of a child.

"Capt. Chaf— Your husband seems of a vigorous constitution. I envy him his strength," her guest replied.

"You are right. He is as the rugged oak braving, in this
case literally, the elemental strife," she said; "as the sturdy
oak to which I am the frail and clinging vine. I am exces-
sively nervous, and he is very considerate. Nature, which so
wonderfully harmonizes its colors in earth and sea and sky,
has attuned us also, each to the other. My husband is a
noble man," she added, all affectation gone from the wife
for the moment. "Like all seamen, he is fond of tobacco:
yet has he wholly ceased to smoke, and is daily reducing his
quid. No man more fond of his grog; in moderation, I
mean. For my sake he never tastes liquor now, even when
most exposed. The least odor," and the lady closed her
eyes with a shudder, "*kills* me."

Upon this, Mr. Venable, postponing his amusement until
he has left the house, tells her of the like sensitiveness as
related of Queen Elizabeth; does so at some length, to get
himself the readier for what he knows is coming. The lady
listens, pleased, but a little impatient.

"'These are a few of my poor endeavors," she says at last, lifting a hand toward the wall. "Possibly you may have heard of them."

Mr. Venable had heard of them. Not from her husband alone : every person he had met had spoken to him about Mrs. Chaffingsby, and in the same way, Mr. Nogens excepted. He had experimented upon Mr. Nogens with the name of the lady. Listening seriously to all that he had asked about Mrs. Chaffingsby, Mr. Nogens had felt with his finger to see if the curl on his forehead was all right, and said, "Yes?" but that was all.

The visitor drew in a long breath as for a dive, or rather for an ascent into regions too ethereal for common breathing, and looked up. The other arose, and explained before a life-size painting upon the wall, in which yellow drapery largely predominated, —

"Judas, as you will perceive. You will observe the bag of money. I flatter myself on the firmness of his clutch upon it. Please remark how rapidly he is moving; as also how his mantle flies away from him behind as he leans eagerly forward. He is on his way, having just received his money. I pride myself somewhat upon his desperate hurry. I derived ideas of that from Mr. Parsons; also upon the gluttonous greed of his eyes; " and the artist stepped aside to allow her guest a full view, her eager gaze fastened upon his countenance. "I gave him," she added, "all the yellow I could, his garments as well as his hair and beard, because it is the color I detest. A horrible object, is he not?" she asked proudly.

"He is, indeed!" her visitor said; for all the warning he had received hardly prepared him for the shock. A more abominable daub, a more absurd caricature upon Judas, could not be imagined. But in every wreck there is some splinter to which we can cling. The other laid hold, so to speak, upon the eyes of the wretched piece of work, and sustained himself for the moment.

"The eyes are wonderfully well done," he said, as soon as he could : "wonderfully well," he repeated after a while, and more composedly ; and he told the truth. Every law of outline, anatomy, light, shade, color, every thing, had been outraged in the painting ; but amid the chaos, the eyes were admirable.

"Every one says the same," Mrs. Chaffingsby replied somewhat peevishly. "My husband may have told you," she added, while the other gazed silently upon the traitor, "of the artist who was with us. He came here, a consumptive, for the sake of our climate. It happened that he sailed over with my husband on the same steamer, and was so low that they refused to take him at the hotels, on the plea that they did not have (which was true) a fireplace in the house except in the kitchen. They knew that he would die on their hands. I was not so nervous then. In fact, I was not nervous at all, until I began to paint ; and I consented to take him in. He grew better, and remained in our house for many months. He was poor, and we would take no compensation. To gratify him, I took lessons instead. He objected, but I insisted on beginning with learning how to paint the eyes. When a girl, I was told that the little transparent bulb in the egg was the rudiment of the eye of the future chicken ; and I insisted," Mrs. Chaffingsby said with increasing eagerness, "in beginning where nature began. We gave months to it. Before we had fairly begun at any thing else, he died ; but he left us his sketches, his paints, and implements and books. Moreover, I had acquired a passion for art, for high art. I painted from morning until night. I often arose during the silent hours of darkness, to resume my brush. Could I sleep, think you, with a picture like this of the vile betrayer upon my mind? No, sir. I poured my abhorrence and hatred of the wretch upon the canvas. Every nerve was strung. I could not eat. My husband was far away upon the deep. If I could but render Judas

more an object of scorn and contempt than mortal had
ever imagined him, I would be satisfied. My religion con-
spired with my talent: true, my digestion was destroyed, I
fear forever; but no one," the little woman added with
fervor, "can, I flatter myself, look upon this picture without
emotion. You despise Judas, Mr. Venable, *despise* the
wretch more from this hour than you ever did before ! But
we have merely begun ; be so good as to accompany me."
And his hostess had wrought herself into such a state of
excitement as to be almost oblivious to any thing the other
might say, or fail to say — happily for him.

The whole house was crowded with Mrs. Chaffingsby's
productions. Hardly a hero or a heroine of Scripture had
been neglected ; and every one was but a renewal of the
false apostle, with small alteration, each worse than the one
before, of attitude, drapery, color, and the like. There
was a certain earnest purpose in all, a violence with which
Peter drew his net and Paul preached, which betrayed the
ardent soul of the artist. It was as if the dumb were
struggling desperately to speak. The visitor felt at each step
that if Irene Buttolph had been with him she would have
screamed with laughter ; and it was all he could do to control himself as his attention was called to a Magdalen
weeping, a Pharisee denouncing, a Sadducee ridiculing, a
Herod scowling, a Pilate protesting, and a Peter denying, each
with his garment falling off, his hair blowing away, his legs,
arms, and fingers extended in a hurricane of vehemence.
Once the visitor thought he must yield to the energy with
which an angel was singing, its head thrown back, its mouth
open, the hands smiting the wires of a harp as if for life ;
but the enthusiasm of the excited creator of the abortions,
as she explained each in turn, so satisfied him of at least
the purity and intensity of her purpose, that the smile died
in his heart as well as upon his lips. One thing he had
shrunk from, but Mrs. Chaffingsby had anticipated him, her

piety being stronger even than her art; and the face of Christ was invariably hidden by some object or person, in whatever scene he appeared. Moreover, in every case, the eyes were spots of excellence, the more striking amid a wilderness of absurdity.

"And that, as you observe," she said, after they had gone through room after room, up stairs and down, "that is Mary lamenting over Lazarus. See how bitter is her anguish. When I was at work on that, my tears were streaming day and night; I was utterly exhausted with weeping, myself. My art, sir, is *consuming* me!" She turned as she spoke; and her visitor looked at her with new respect, she was so, so frail, with a hectic glow in her cheeks. All the affectation of her manner had disappeared, melted away in the fervor of her enthusiasm. "The artist," she said, "told me that I really had talent. But he always added, 'You will have to study hard for many years, and see other works of art.' I do not think so," she continued with energy; "when one is determined to create, when you give your whole soul to your effort, it supersedes all else. You think so, do you not Mr. Venable?"

"Excuse me, but I do not see Martha," was his polite evasion. "Mary and Martha, you know," with a bow.

"I have a profound contempt for Martha," she hastened to explain. "Of course it is not the detestation I have scorched upon the canvas of Judas; yet, while Mary was full of feeling, her sister was totally devoid of it. You recall her remark to Christ in reference to the decomposition of her dead brother. She was a coarse woman, low and sordid in her occupations. "I have left unpainted," she added. "hardly an heroic character in my knowledge. Martha, however, I have placed where she belongs, in my kitchen. Since you insist upon seeing her, please follow me;" and the artist led the way, walking in a delicate manner upon her tiptoes, her usual gait, as if in danger of disturbing some sleeping invalid. Down stairs they went, and through rooms and passages lined with her productions, which she merely indicated with a wave of her hand as she passed, and a word.

"St. John in Patmos, you observe. Alexander and Clitus. Solomon in the plenitude of his glory. Judith and Holofernes. This is Pilate; and I would like to point out to you the Roman arrogance of his aspect, if we had time. David, you observe: I would dearly love to have you conjecture which of his psalms he wäs singing, but I am nearly exhausted."

Mr. Venable glanced at the royal singer tearing openmouthed at his harp with vigor, and, with a polite but inarticulate murmur, hastened after his guide.

"This is our kitchen," she said at last, throwing a door open. "O Clara!" she added, in the same breath: "my poor nerves! I had utterly forgotten!" For there stood the young girl whom the visitor had seen before, in kitchen undress, evidently taken by surprise. The instant she saw him, she had turned, and, as with a movement familiarized to her by long use, had placed her hands upon the shoulders of a boy larger than herself, and had pushed him before her, and out of a side door. Mr. Venable had lingered politely upon the threshold before entering; but one glance at the boy was enough. There was the negligent dress, the conical head, the loose lips, the unmeaning stare, of an idiot. The shrill laugh from the other side of the door, as it closed, was not needed to confirm that.

As she shut the door, the girl turned and came back. Her dress, though plain to the last degree, was clean. The disorder of her hair but added to the charm of her perfect face and heavenly eyes.

"Clara, my dear, this is Mr. Venable; and now go to Charlie," her mother said; and the girl acknowledged their visitor with a hand extended like that of a little child, and,

as on the former occasion, the brightest and sweetest smile
he had ever imagined. "How is it possible," he kept saying to himself, as she left the room, "that, with such a model
of all loveliness continually before her, this woman could
paint these atrocious daubs? Ah! but here is the secret of
those wonderful eyes;" and he saw nothing of the Martha
upon the wall, except that the artist had succeeded in making it, in her aversion, almost as bad as the Judas. He
hardly heard any thing of all that she said. The contrast of
every thing with this miracle of beauty was too great and
sudden, although he had been hoping and listening in expectation of meeting her, from the moment he entered the
house.

Nor did he breathe freely until, after parting with the
artist, he had left the building, and was unlatching the front
gate. As he did so, Mrs. Chaffingsby opened her door, and
called to him, beckoning with her hand.

"I am exhausted," she said, when he returned to find her
sunk into a sofa in the parlor, Judas clutching his bag and
flying with insane speed over her head. "Please hand me
that fan; as also that smelling-bottle. Wait until I recover
myself. In the instant of your leaving," she said at last, "I
have had an inspiration. They always come in my moments of almost death. I will not be able to eat nor sleep
for, it may be, days. But," added she, in a quiver of excitement, "I find I am too agitated to tell you now. It *is*
an inspiration. You may be able to prepare yourself for
what I intend, when I mention to you, as a clew, the names
of Rubens and Titian. But I am unable to explain to you
now. The conception shakes me like an ague. Besides, it
will astonish you greatly. I will let you know in time.
Good-by." And, once more taking a respectful leave of
her, Mr. Venable departed.

CHAPTER IX.

MR. VENABLE MAKES THE ACQUAINTANCE OF HIS EXCELLENCY
"OLD UGLY."

ONE morning some weeks after his visit to Mrs. Chaf-fingsby's, Mr. Venable came landward again from the boundlessness of sleep, upon the sound, as usual, of the inroll-ing surf. As he opened his eyes it was to see young Plenty standing beside his bed, in an aroma, also as usual, of smok-ing coffee. Although it was early it was impossible, after drinking a cup, yellow and sweet and hot, to remain in his room ; and he went out, as he often did, for a walk along the beach. On his return, breakfast not being yet ready, he sat down upon a bench under a trellis in the grounds, unwilling, by going into the house, to lose a breath of the beautiful morning breaking in glory upon land and sea. As he did so he saw that old Plenty was standing near by with his back to him, leaning upon the handle of a hoe with which the poor soul deluded himself into the belief he had been working. Having lived all his life, except when at college, at the South, and among negroes, he was not surprised to hear the aged black talking aloud although to himself.

"An' dere is Mars Grit," he heard him say, as he contem-plated the distant horizon. "Did ebber Ole Marster make such a debbil ob a boy as dat? My Lord ! He's de wust imp ebber lived. You lie, you fool ! I 'members his fader well when he was a shaver, an' he was wus.

"An' den dere's dat trubble wid my mars general. Ebbry night! It wa'n't dat way in ole Firginny. How you lie, you ole nigger! My marster his fader was dat same way, an' you know it!" and following this was a groan.

"Uncle Plenty," Mr. Venable said, fearing to hear any more, "who are you talking to?"

"An' dere is dat yaller piece, — dat Ifferginny dey calls her," the old man continued aloud, too deaf to hear the question: "O my hebbenly Marster, dat is *too* bad, too bad!" and he shook his white head mournfully. As he did so, the other remembered that he had lately missed the mulatto girl Iphigenia, who had come with them on the Nautilus, from the table at which she had waited. Nor had he heard her singing of late as she hung out the clothes in the back-yard. He knew that she was still on the place, however, for he had seen her about the stables and kitchen-garden when young Plenty had led out his horse for him to ride.

"I 'member his brudders an' his fader, an' dey was just as weeked. But oh, my Miss Zeo, my Miss Zeo!" The old man said it so loud, and with such a wail in his voice, that the listener walked rapidly away. Was it possible that under the flowers and fruits of this Eden there were indeed serpents, as he had asked himself before, venomous and hidden, of which he in his ignorance had not dreamed?

He ate his breakfast with less appetite and more silently than usual. Then he went, as was at times his habit, to the vestry of the church, and gave himself up till dinner-hour, to hard study. He had been accustomed, in college and seminary, to devote to his meals as little time as possible; but, with Gen. Buttolph, dinner especially was the event of the day. The courses succeeded each other like parts in music; and, with his napkin under his double chin, no one could be more leisurely than his host in the carving and conversation. His guest looked at him with new interest to-day. Gen. Buttolph always wore the best broadcloth

and the finest and whitest linen; a massive gold chain
across his ample vest, a large red seal upon a ring on his
little finger. His broad and almost purple face beamed
with perfect content; his voice deep and slow and soft, and
his whole manner that of a wealthy gentleman who enjoyed
himself thoroughly.

Miss Zeo sat at the other end of the table, as quiet as usual,
only lifting her dark eyes with a smile and a pleasant remark
when spoken to; or, as was more frequently the case, to
check with a glance or a low-spoken word, some misconduct
of Grit, seated on her left hand, or a remark too impulsive
and independent, of her sister upon her right, for, by common agreement, Miss Irene did most of the talking. But
on this day their guest, seated beside Grit and opposite Miss
Irene, did not laugh as readily as usual at her bright and
amusing remarks. Excusing himself as soon as possible, he
went to his room up-stairs, and got through the nap to which
he had come to yield as to a half-sin, as speedily as he could.
Then, stealing softly down stairs, so as to awaken no one
from their siesta, he hastened out to complete the last calls
of his pastoral round among the families of his church.

As usual, no two of the households were alike; and, in
his inexperience, he had to adjust himself cautiously to each
case. But, rich or poor, cultivated or ignorant, they were
alike in the cordiality of their welcome: that was as much a
part of St. Jerome as the surf or the orange-trees. He had
promised to call on Mr. Parsons next day; but with that
exception he had made, when he found himself back at
Gen. Buttolph's at night, a finish of his first round of visits.

Miss Zenobia did not come into the parlor immediately
after tea.

"Zeo has taken charge of the housekeeping," Irene said
to him, "and I am very glad of it. She is so good, you
know, and I am not."

As was usual, the general was smoking upon the front

porch, in his favorite chair. "You have never told me," she said to Mr. Venable, after playing for some time at the instrument, "how you enjoyed Mrs. Chaffingsby and her pictures. You are as prudent as Mr. Nogens. I am glad *I'm* not at all afraid of Miss Aurelia Jones, nor of Commodore Grandheur. I told him so last Sunday. I must tell you how it happened. You see " —

Mr. Venable seemed to be listening, as she gave an amusing account of her audacity; but all the while he was saying to himself, —

"How I wish it were Miss Zeo instead! I would like to ask her in regard to that beautiful girl at Capt. Chaffin's. It is strange she has never spoken of her; but I don't intend Miss Irene shall draw me into any fun over her poor mother;" and it was a relief when a servant ushered a gentleman into the room. At the sound, however, of his steps in the hall, and before he had shown himself, Miss Irene, with a hasty hand to her hair, and a still hastier expression upon her lips, fled through another door. As Mr. Venable arose to meet the visitor, he saw that he was a man of mark, although he did not know his name. The new-comer, who was unusually tall, but well-proportioned, came immediately across the parlor, and extended his hand to him, as if he had been in search of him, and was glad to find him at last. There was a certain willowy grace in his manner, which had a singular charm for the other, whose tastes had been cultivated in schools of art; and his hair and beard, black and silken, made a framing for the oval face with its regular features and eyebrows arched and clearly defined. His smile disclosed beautiful teeth, but the power of the visitor lay in his eyes. It was not that they were large and dark; but there was in them a something Mr. Venable had never seen in the eyes of any man. "I am glad to make your acquaintance, Mr. Venable, very glad," the visitor said. "Although I am not in St. Jerome often, I heard of you as soon as you came. Before we are interrupted, you must allow me to thank you for your admirable discourse last Sunday." But the fascination of the man was not in the complimentary things he proceeded to say, any more than it was in the cordial grasp which retained its hold upon the minister's hand. There was, in harmony with his words, his tones, his entire manner, a grasp also of the eyes of the visitor upon his own, such as Mr. Venable had not observed in the case of any other. During the conversation which followed, he was listened to as if he were saying that which was of the greatest personal interest to the one just arrived. It was more than attention on the part of the handsome stranger: it seemed to be the sincerity of genuine sympathy.

"I have heard of personal magnetism," Mr. Venable said to himself at last, "but I have never before experienced it. Magnetism? Yes, this must be Gov. Magruder, of whom Mr. Parsons spoke."

Sure enough: Col. Roland, who accompanied the governor, had tarried upon the porch to say a word to Gen. Buttolph; and, both now entering the room, the colonel proceeded to introduce him.

"It is not at all necessary," he said: "Mr. Venable and myself are already acquainted, — well acquainted, I hope."

But Miss Zenobia and her sister came in as he said it; and, except with more deference in his manner, Col. Roland's companion greeted them as cordially as he had done the minister. The habit of study was so strong upon this last, that, taking occasional part in the conversation which followed, he could not refrain from considering, contrasting even, the persons present. As to the portly host, he settled himself deep in the plush of a large chair, and beamed upon all present, his large hands clasped together or playing with his watch-chain; saying almost nothing, but ready with a reply or a hearty laugh. The utter enjoyment of the general was now, as always, something wholly new to one fresh from among people who were under the stress of religious principle, moral purpose, at the least, anxious energy in business; and there was relaxation in looking at him.

As the conversation became more general and animated, Mr. Venable observed that Col. Roland had been taken possession of by Miss Irene, while the governor was devoting himself to her sister. The habit of observation, of analysis, had been too long and thoroughly developed in the student for him to help noticing the difference between the two men. Col. Roland was listening to Miss Irene's lively and varied talk, as a polished man of the world would do, but took also as much part in it as he possibly could; eager to slip in a quotation, an incident, an anecdote in regard to himself. Not so with the other: Gov. Magruder made no allusion to himself, and, after the first salutations, had evidently devolved upon the lady the burden of conversation, listening intently to what Miss Zeo had to say. In fact, he hung upon her words as if he feared she would cease speaking: whenever she did, he was silent, even embarrassed, and plainly becoming more so. This was so evident at last, that Col. Roland came to his help, and both Miss Zeo and the governor sat comparatively silent, while Miss Irene and the colonel absorbed between them almost the entire conversation.

As Gov. Magruder became with every passing moment, if possible, more hopelessly silent, Col. Roland asked Miss Irene for music; and her execution was as brilliant, her songs as varied and as spirited, as usual. At a covert gesture from the colonel, his friend, when she ceased, led her sister to the instrument. Mr. Venable enjoyed the music more than ever. It was neither as loud, as rapid, nor as striking, as in the case of the other. Had the parlor been crowded, it would not have seemed unnatural for conversation to have accompanied the music of the elder sister, to have been stimulated by it, even; but Miss Zeo's performance was of a kind during which it would have seemed, even in the most crowded room, disreputable to converse. Yet this discord ran through the impression of subdued power it conveyed, this dissonance, to Mr. Venable at least, that Gov. Magruder was listening with an attention which was more than mere enjoyment, — so much so, that, as she arose the minister left the room and the house, and stood to one side of the front gate, under the oleanders. It was a fear too sharp and sudden to be endured shut up in a parlor. If only for a few moments, he wanted to be out in the cool air, to hear the roar of the surf, to be under the clouded light of the moon ; supposing when he left that conversation would follow the music. To his surprise the gentlemen made their adieux, and came away almost as soon as she arose from the instrument. It was a walk of some little distance from the porch to the gate beside which Mr. Venable stood in the shadows of the foliage, grasping the paling and looking out upon the sea ; and the gentlemen were talking in a low voice as they came. Col. Roland found some difficulty in unfastening the latch of the gate ; and the listener could not help hearing him curse it, and add in an irritated way, —

"Confound it, Magruder ! don't be a fool ! Why didn't you talk to her, man ? "

" I said all I could think of," the governor replied.

" Hang it, man, I kept Miss Irene off to give you a chance to talk ; and," his companion added, " you sat so mum at last, I had to propose music ; and then to come away the instant it was over ! You can't possibly do better, Magruder. She will make you a splendid wife. *Don't* be a fool ! "

"Suppose I don't know that? But," the other added, " it is a cursed shame, Roland. A fellow like *me* ! "

At this instant the latch yielded ; and with another exclamation at it, or at his companion, Col. Roland passed out, the governor undergoing what to the unwilling listener seemed to be almost a scolding as they walked away.

Mr. Venable returned to the parlor, but not for some time after, and merely to bid his friends good-night. While he was doing so, Mr. Fanthorp came in. Miss Irene seemed glad to see him, but he would not take a seat. "I wouldn't dare to say it, if the general had not stepped out of the room," he said, after a little conversation; "but, do you know, his excellency Old Ugly — I passed him just now — came to town expressly to call upon a certain young lady?"

"Please," Mr. Venable demanded, dreading to hear more, "tell me *now* why they give him such a name? I'm a new-comer, and I've heard it continually."

"Because," Miss Zenobia replied, "he is young and hand-some, and such a favorite among the people: it is a kind of pet name."

"Everybody of decided character in the State has his nickname," Mr. Fanthorp added, his own being Mr. Farce Fanthorp; "but," he continued with affected astonishment, "can I believe my ears? And *you* think he is handsome, Miss Zenobia? Well! It is all over!" And Miss Irene laughed, as her modest sister blushed and smiled.

"Let me show you how it will be," Mr. Fanthorp said; "only don't let Roland know;" and, going out into the hall, he pushed up his hair, arranged his necktie, and came in again. "Why, Mr. Venable," he exclaimed, personating the governor with wonderful fidelity, "glad to see you, glad to see you! — And Miss Irene Buttolph," and he went up to her also, and took her cordially yet deferentially by the hand. "We have had charming weather today. — And this is Miss Zenobia." Mimicking the governor in tone and manner, he halted as he approached the lady, and let his extended hand fall in a helpless way, as if embarrassed.

"Excuse me," he said: "you are very charming — the weather is, I mean — hum — haw — I ask your pardon" —

The mimicry of their late visitor was so good that Irene exclaimed with delight, and her sister laughed even while

she colored afresh. But at this moment Gen. Buttolph returned to the room, and, after saluting Mr. Fanthorp, began,
instead of sitting down, to walk to and fro across the room
in a restless way. Possibly Mr. Fanthorp may have observed
that the general glanced covertly at his watch once or twice,
as the lively conversation went on, for he soon after bade
them good-night, and withdrew; and Mr. Venable followed
his example, but not to sleep.

CHAPTER X.

MR. EZRA MICAJAH PARSONS BEGINS TO EXPLAIN HIS IDEAS TO MR. VENABLE.

I AM glad to see you," Mr. Ezra Micajah Parsons said to Mr. Venable, as that gentleman stepped upon the veranda of his house the morning after the events last recorded. "Walk in. How are you? Because I wanted to explain to you," his host proceeded rapidly and without further salutation, "my plan for the conversion of the Catholics of America. It is," he added, "like Columbus and his egg: nothing can be simpler when stated. All I ask is your attention;" and he arose, and stepped to a blackboard which took up one side of the room into which they had entered.

Mr. Parsons was long and lank and lean to a remarkable degree, reminding one of a greyhound even in the length of his nose. What little hair he had was white and disordered, the temples deeply sunken, as were his eyes, the forehead narrow but unusually high. His clothes were shabby and ill-fitting; and he had forgotten, in his haste, to take off the well-worn felt hat which he had merely knocked up from off his brow as he took a lump of chalk in his hand, the bared wrist adding to the appearance of unusual length in hand and fingers. Had his visitor known that his eccentric host was to rank, in the end, as one of the most successful inventors of the day, he would have listened to him more attentively. At that date, however, he, like every one else, regarded him as the most complete specimen he had ever met of a visionary; merely a masculine variety upon Mrs. Chaffingsby. Not an inhabitant of St. Jerome but knew him to be the most generous of men, as well as the most earnest of Christians: yet they were as unanimous in despairing of and laughing at him then as they were in forgetting and denying that they had ever done so, when his name had become a household word, and his income had reached a hundred thousand a year.

"We will suppose," said Mr. Parsons, "that there are five million Catholics in America," and he dashed down the numerals upon the board. "These have"—and three million was rapidly inscribed—"*that* many children! Very well. Now, a book for each child will cost twenty cents"—

Mr. Venable was far from being in a mood for Mr. Parsons; would not have come, in fact, if he had not engaged to do so. Being there, he gave himself up to the occasion, if only to escape from his own thoughts, and interrupted the other.

"I beg your pardon: a book?"

"Certainly. A book," the other replied, "containing the essential facts of history and the gospel, in the largest and clearest type, printed on linen so that they cannot be torn, brimful of pictures, strongly bound, with attractive covers. The children and parents will be as greedy for them as for cakes. Three million children at twenty cents each, sixty million cents," working it out on the board, "six hundred thousand dollars; say a million of dollars. Do you suppose that a single child so supplied would grow up a Catholic? In fifteen years—if you hesitate, say thirty years—Romanism would have become extinct, and at an expense of two or three millions at the outside. Could money be better invested? Surely the combined Christianity of the land could easily raise the means."

"Are you in serious earnest?" Mr. Venable asked.

"Certainly I am. Why not?" the other replied, turning with amazement, and without a particle of hesitation in his manner. "Surely it would be worth the money."

"My dear sir," his visitor said, "do you suppose the priests would allow it?"

"But if you *gave* the children the books, attractive books, mind, and *gave* them;" yet, as the other said it, he faltered, his eyes clouded, the chalk fell from his hand. It was but one of a hundred schemes, most of them worked out in accurate diagrams and conclusive numerals upon the same board, the feasible part of which was seen by him so vividly as to dazzle his mind to all the rest.

"Won't you allow me to see your place?" Mr. Venable hastened to say. "I have heard so much of it, and it is too fine a day to stay in doors."

"I'm not satisfied about that matter. Never mind, we'll talk of it again," said Mr. Parsons. "Come along. You are too abrupt in your contradictions for so young a man. However! That is my fig-orchard," he added as they walked rapidly out into the grounds. "The trees are bandaged in straw for fear of a norther. Those are my oranges. Yonder are the lemons. Wait a few weeks if you would see my place in its glory."

"And what is all this?" his friend asked as they passed an enormous iron kettle, surrounded by empty hogsheads and the wrecks of machinery.

"That was one of my ideas," Mr. Parsons explained, but without pausing. "Just then I was full of hydraulic pressure. I would put in water, half a hogshead of sugar, and a cart-load of fruit, figs say, into the kettle. Then, while hot, I would press the preserves into ten-pound canisters made very strong for the purpose. But I learned better. I never drop an idea except for a better one — never! So about those Papists. I'll pass the children, and aim for the priests. This is my banana-grove, under all these bundles of sacking.

It is against the storm of the Last Day, that the Great Husbandman wraps up our bodies under seas and mountains. Would you like me to explain it all to you?"

"Certainly. I will gladly listen," the other replied, wondering at an explanation of the resurrection from such a theologian. He stopped while his host cut a twig off a neighboring tree, and split it open, saying, —

"This is an almond-tree. Do you see how large the pith of the switch is? It is because the almond is a peach all run to stone. Now, if I take out this pith, and graft the twig, the fruit will lose the stone in favor of the pulp. You can do almost any thing with every thing. If you plan and think, and, as fast as you drop one thing, seize upon another. What I want to say is this : The world is changing. In the direction of condensing. All-work is done now in a hundredth part of the time by machinery. People have stopped writing long letters. You flash all you have to say condensed into one line, and by lightning. If I had an absent son, do you suppose I would write him pages of advice? Not at all. I would simply refer him to a chapter of the New Testament for his theory, and to the proverbs of Solomon for his practice. Even lovers write no poetry, nor any other stuff and nonsense, now. They condense all they have to say, I suppose, into a kiss ; that is, when they can get time to meet a moment. Time was when people would sit down at a table, and spend hours at a meal. Napoleon never took over twenty minutes to dinner : *I* am through in fifteen. People have almost lost the faculty of fooling away their time. That's past. Let me show you ;" and Mr. Parsons walked rapidly away, followed by his friend, to a sort of warehouse in one corner of his grounds. In the centre was a baker's oven, while all around were tables, and heaps of small boxes.

"We have stopped our works to see how we will sell," he said ; "but no sane man can doubt the result in this case.

What do you suppose that is?" taking up, as he spoke, what seemed to be a cracker, from a small pan on the table.

"A soda-cracker, of course," the other replied.

"No, sir. That is a spring chicken! One chicken to a cracker, as you call it; exactly twelve chickens to a pan. I boil the chicken in a vacuum, on the other side of the house, extract every atom of bone and fibre, leaving the essential chicken itself. The superfluous water is expelled by baking in a pan. What is left is intensely and exclusively *chicken*. Drop that cracker into a pot of boiling water, and it makes strong soup. And what do you think that is?" passing to another and larger set of pans, and taking up another fragment. "Bite it, and see. That is a turkey; a whole drove of turkeys in those pans. Now, what do you suppose is in this box?" Mr. Venable shook his head, with inquiring eyes. "A calf, and a fat one. In this larger box, all in cakes to be handy for use, is a beef. A pig is somehow as hard to catch," Mr. Parsons continued, "when dead as alive; but we have penned up, oily as they are, a whole barnyard of pigs in those boxes. I am the original inventor of Focussed Flesh; remember that! In a few years the armies and especially the navies of the world will be fed upon my food. It will be by reason of my invention that the North Pole and the South will be discovered. Why, sir, one small ship can carry in its hold, thus, whole herds of cattle as well as vast fields of vegetables."

Mr. Parsons straightened himself up as he said it, pushing back his shabby old hat from his forehead, his restless gray eyes fastened keenly upon the other from their sunken sockets.

"I am on the right track only," he added, — "after years of experiment. Have merely begun. I intend, if I don't break all to pieces, to condense every thing that people use. I mean to put a potato into a pill-box, a pumpkin into a tablespoon, the biggest sort of a watermelon into a saucer. Every thing hermetically sealed, of course. The Turks make acres of roses into attar of roses. I'm told you can put all the rose-fields of Syria into a demijohn. I intend to make attar of every thing ! — flowers of every sort, fish, vegetables. The day will come when a distiller will have learned from me to put a whole vineyard into one barrel. Look at nitro-glycerine. There you have tons of powder concentrated into an ounce. Eh? Why not? What do you think of it?" he demanded, as sharply excited, in his way, as was Mrs. Chaffingsby in hers; and for half an hour he continued to the same effect.

" It is all new to me," Mr. Venable said modestly, at last ; " but an idea has occurred to me."

" Let's have it," interrupted the other, " I'm steel. You may be flint. Out with your spark, if it *is* only a spark."

" I have to keep up with the news," his visitor said, entering into the mood of his host, " but I have no time to read a daily through. In order to get to my studies as soon as possible, I have formed the habit of running my eye down the head-lines, merely down the middle of each column at that. Now, how would it do, Mr. Parsons, to publish a daily of the size of your hand, head-lines and nothing else ? If you please, let us go to your blackboard, and I will explain. I do believe," he laughed to himself as he walked to the house, followed by his host, " that his mania is as catching as yellow-fever." And, arrived at the room in question, he laid aside his hat, rolled up his sleeves, wiped the Catholics out of existence from the board, and said to his host, —

" Your idea, Mr. Parsons, is condensation. When you feed a man, you intend leaving all unnecessary portions of his food in the slaughter-yard. Now, the details of the daily news are utterly unnecessary. It is like giving a man, with his steak, the horns, hide, and hoofs of the ox. With many sorts of news it is worse : it is as if you heaped his plate with the disgusting blood and bowels of his beef or pork.

Now, let us imagine a daily for the Union. No; call your daily 'The Globe,' and mean it. Let it give to-day all of yesterday's intelligence of and for the universe. The cables will enable it to do that. But, condensed. Allow me to illustrate;" and, half in jest, he made out a column of his daily, beginning at the top of the blackboard, and defining the proposed page with bold lines upon every side, as follows : —

THE GLOBE.

947 fires yesterday: accidental, 490; incendiary, 457.
Defaulters, 500: $2,396,072 stolen; 200 arrested.
Suicides, 450: love the cause, 156; rum, 294.
Failures, 325: assets, $8,956,372; liabilities, $20,746,932.
Murders, 504: money the cause, 102; rum, 402; caught,
*   75; proved, 49; hung, 3.*
People baptized, 1,800; disciplined, 176.
Marriages, 6,000; average age, 29.
Books published yesterday, 780.
Births in the world, 897,451.
Deaths in the world, 702,345.
Speeches made, 487: good ones, 80; bad, 407.
The joke of the world yesterday.

"By that last item," Mr. Venable explained, "I mean that the very cream of the fun of the planet during the day before should be concentrated into a line or two. The paper might have a dozen microscopic illustrations, too, — photographs of actual scenes, or of the leading character of the day to be looked at through a magnifying-glass. Excuse me," he added, laying down the chalk, brushing off his hands, and seating himself with a smile, "but I believe some day it will be done. If they were to apply the same condensation to encyclopædias and systems of theology, what

a blessing," he added, "it would be ! Why, sir, the poetry of
the race is tremendous in quantity, but all the lines in it
men care for are less than are the grains to the wheat-field.
When your vessel sailed to the Pole, it could carry the litera-
ture of the world in one bookcase, if it was duly concentrated. The ship might be locked up in the ice for twenty
years, and have all the civilization as well as the food of the
world in its hold, and plenty to spare."

"I don't know," Mr. Parsons said, "whether you are
joking or not. A young man ought to be very careful.
Begin," he added somewhat dryly, " by condensing your
sermons, Mr. Venable, as also your remarks in prayer-
meeting. Although," he said after a while, "there *may* be
something in your reckless suggestions."

"Thank you, sir," the other replied, badly hurt, but putting a smiling face upon it, for he was a thoroughly sensible
fellow. "You know I'm in the period of mere bloom yet,
like a peach-tree. I hope I will condense into fruit some
day. Besides, you know how it. is about Mr. Phip Quatty
on Wednesday nights."

"He is undoubtedly the best man," Mr. Parsons inter-
jected, " and the biggest fool, I ever knew." At which the
other could not keep from laughing. Only the day before,
Mr. Quatty had said the same of Mr. Parsons; for, of all
people alive, peculiar people are the most impatient of the
peculiarities of others. "Who wants to be told over and
over and yet over again," Mr. Parsons continued, "by Mr.
Quatty, that he was once an oysterman, and that the religious stranger said to him as he was dredging for oysters
—what was it?"

"Why, Mr. Parsons," the young minister said, with a
laugh, "you have heard him so often, too ! Gen. Buttolph insisted upon my taking up a great deal of the time at prayer-
meeting, so as to afford Mr. Quatty less chance to speak.
You know how you all rise and pray or sing or speak as
rapidly as possible, before he can slip in " —

At this moment, however, a bell was heard to ring ; and, with the sound, a lovely little girl of six years of age ran in, seized upon Mr. Parsons by his long legs, and endeavored to drag him away.

"Come to dinner, Ezra Micajah Papa," she said. "We've got a puddin' because Mr. Venable is here. Make haste, ma said, or she'd eat it all up." And their visitor did not wonder at the sudden change in the lank and dry old man as he took the laughing little Hebe into his arms.

"This is our little Alice," he said, evidently with a great deal more pride than in his inventions. "Our only one, — our owny, owny one ; " and he rubbed his sallow face against the fat and blooming cheek, while she laughed yet louder, tumbling his scanty hair about with her dumpling fingers. "And this is my second wife," he added, introducing his friend to a round and rosy-faced lady at the end of the table, after they had gone into the house and had sat down to dinner.

"Why will you always say I am your second wife?" the lady inquired laughingly, after the little girl had been adjusted in her high-chair, and blessing had been asked.

"Oh ! I am such a dry old stick," he said, as he proceeded to help Mr. Venable to soup. "I don't want people to think that you are old, Ally."

"There is small fear of that," their guest remarked, and very sincerely ; for the wife was full twenty years the younger, — still younger than that, in virtue of her particularly jovial appearance.

"I wouldn't do it, sir," she remonstrated with Mr. Venable, as the host held out the plate of soup. "I know it is polite in you, but I wouldn't ! "

"It is a fat hen which I condensed with my own hands not three months ago," Mr. Parsons persisted. "Put in plenty of pepper and salt and butter, sir, and I know you will like it. I always eat it ; more nutritive food never was eaten."

"It may be nourishing," Mrs. Parsons said, "but it is musty, Ezra: all the pepper and salt on the table can't hide that. Our little Owny here and I never touch it;" and the lady made a face, with a comical shudder of her plump shoulders. "We don't believe in his inventions, sir, — not one bit. Don't *do* it, Mr. Venable!"

But he did. The soup was, he said, after tasting it. "good soup, excellent soup." He "had never eaten better soup." The fact, however, was, that he "never was particularly partial to chicken-soup." It was "always prepared for sick people" where he had lived before. Notwithstanding which, and in deference to the inventor, he finished the bountiful plate, under the merry eyes of mother and daughter. There was nothing wrong about the article, except a hazy sort of doubt which seemed to rest, like a fog, upon the taste thereof. It seemed to be a small matter, partaking of the article when he would have much rather not; but it was good practice at what he knew must be the habit of his life, and that was never to allow what he personally liked or disliked to enter at all into the question of what he had to do.

"My husband is forever inventing," his wife added when the soup had been removed. "We have a table, the rim of which is as broad as a plate, and is fixed, while all the rest revolves. The dishes are placed on the central part, you observe, and go around at a push to whoever wants them. You have no idea, sir, the expense he went to in making and patenting it in time for our wedding. I had a good cry over it. There was a large company, and he had forgotten that you could not use a tablecloth on such a thing. I was too afraid of him then to say one word: I could only cry."

It was plain that the lady had lost her terror since then; for she kept up a laughing attack on her husband during the whole meal, warning her guest energetically against the hydraulic pressed preserves when they came on with the prophesied pudding. Mr. Parsons was used to the ridicule, and ate steadily and somewhat enormously, his long body bowed down over his plate, leaving the entertainment of his friend to his wife. It was very plain, however, to Mr. Venable, that any one else would laugh at the inventor at their peril if she was to know of it. Under all her merriment he saw with pleasure the devoted love of the mother, as well as of fat little Owny as they called her, for the gaunt old man.

"Don't misunderstand me, Mr. Venable," she said as they rose from table : "I do *not* believe in his inventions, — at least," she added, with an arch look at her husband, "not very much, — but I do believe in his motives. Mr. Parsons has no wish to make money, except to do good with it. He knows that very much is needed for Christian work ; and he is anxious to make, if he can, millions for that. I don't think, myself, he will do any thing but lose ; but I am only a woman, and I don't know. There's his terraqueous machine, for instance. Owny and I don't believe in it, not a mite ; but we do believe in Ezra Micajah Papa, —yes, we do believe in him with all our hearts," and she looked lovingly at him as she said it. "Take warning, Mr. Venable," she called after him as they left the room, "don't ride in it if he asks you. Beware !" The guest had thrown himself as far as he could into the occasion ; but the merry eyes and words and ringing laughter of Mrs. Parsons, as well as of Owny who was her duplicate in miniature, were the most delightful part of it all. It may have been the contrast of the mother and her child to the rapid and dry old man and his exceedingly dry desiccations in the warehouse ; but their visitor had never met any persons, who, in a purely flesh-and-blood way, seemed quite so full of the life and health and abounding joy of mere existence.

"I always take one hour after dinner," the lady said, following him to the door, "of good sleep. Mr. Parsons

never does.   He condenses his sleep, he says, into his six
hours of that much the sounder sleep at night.   But he does
as *he* pleases, and lets me do as *I* please.   Good-by, Mr.
Venable ; but remember, as you value your life, don't promise to go in his machine ! "

CHAPTER XI.

WE CONTINUE OUR ACQUAINTANCE WITH MR. EZRA MICAJAH
PARSONS, AND HIS OWNY.

"NO man respects women more than I do," the inventor remarked, as he led his guest from the dinner-table towards the building on the other side of his place, which held the terraqueous machine; "but no woman since creation ever invented any thing, and no female ever will. You have read of Palissy the potter. His wonderful discoveries were made after years of agony from the opposition of his wife. Mrs. Parsons is very different; but, being a woman, she can't appreciate such things."

Mr. Venable had lifted little Owny from her high-chair at the dinner-table when he arose; and it was under cover of such a shield upon his bosom as he walked that he replied, exhilarated by the mirth of Mrs. Parsons as well as by a hearty dinner, —

"That is what Mrs. Chaffingsby says of those who criticise her paintings, Mr. Parsons. She told me that it only awakened her pity. 'I feel,' she said when I was at her house, 'as a soaring angel feels if one of us could criticise its seraphic song. It would merely smile and sing. I often hear of their remarks,' she told me; 'and I simply pity them, and continue to paint.'" Mr. Venable would not have had such a sparkle of malicious fun in his eyes if he had known how hard he hit the lean, nervous, and excitable old inventor.

"Fiddlesticks, stuff, and nonsense!" he said, and vehemently. "I see that her husband has told her what I said the day we sailed to take our last soundings off Hacamac. She is crazy. Painting? pot-pie!" he added, with that nausea of disgust at the eccentricity of the lady which only one who is himself eccentric could feel. "I have no time for such folly. What I wished to say, Mr. Venable, was in reference to yourself. It is a critical time with you, sir," he began; and his guest saw that his host was irritated by what he had said, into speaking even more concisely than he had intended. "You see what a plain-spoken man I am," he went on. "In my inventions I succeed solely as I get at the exact facts of the thing. As sure as there is the least lie in my plans, whatever it is, the machine will not work: it hitches it, and drags it, and breaks every thing to pieces, — that lie does. You are very young, Mr. Venable, and flowery. We all know that you are perfectly sincere. But you know nothing except books. I had not supposed that even a girl could be so ignorant of human nature. You mean well; but you are not driving direct at any special thing or person in your preaching. What is the good of rambling over all creation, telling us about the blossoms, the brooks, the clouds, and the stars? It is a variety upon Dr. Burrows; but people cannot live on flowers. As sure as you live, you must come down to pork and greens. People must be fed. The sin and strain and suffering of life are steady and severe, and we must have food. And you must condense your food for us into enough on Sunday to last us through the week. You must excuse me; but I am an old man, and I try to be as practical with myself as the cogs and shafts of a mill. Give us what we *need!*"

"Certainly, Mr. Parsons," his companion said. "I am obliged to you. But you mentioned Dr. Burrows. What, between us, was the matter?"

"Yellow-fever. It was that which killed him."

" Why, he is living at Chemaraw," began the other.

"The Chemaraw people called him, because the St. Jerome people let him go," Mr. Parsons explained. " You have heard about the rivalry of the places before this. Both towns, by the by, are humbugs ; and Hacamac, as I've told you, is the only true site for a city in all this region. But, if ever a man was killed dead by the yellow-fever, Dr. Burrows is that man. He fled when the fever came ; and we had no use for him after that. Never mind him now. I am too busy to see you often, and I wanted to say this. We all like you ; but the tide is sure to turn."

" Excuse me," the other asked, with a sudden sinking at heart.

" The people went almost crazy about you at first," his dry old host continued, as they walked slowly along. "I never heard Miss Aurelia Jones quite so ardent in her praises before. The trouble about her is, that she is always in a blaze. She is not content with being a sincere and active Christian : there must be the blast and crackle and flames of a conflagration, or she thinks the last spark has gone out. I like enthusiasm ; but there is something too hot, too *fierce*, in such piety. There is too much fever in it for health : you feel all along that there is a strain the machinery cannot stand. Action is measured by re-action ; and Paul says, ' Let your moderation be known to all men.' There is too much of the mere woman in her religion ; and in Christ there is neither male nor female. But she is only a specimen. Now, in · good earnest, Mr. Venable, has she got beyond bookmarks yet ? Is it slippers by this time ? Perhaps she has got to a dressing-gown. It may be a horse next. Mind my words, sir, the day will come, when instead of replying to her notes, thanking her a thousand times, as you do now, you will be tempted at least to write back, ' My dear Miss Jones, please don't ! As you love me, I entreat you to let me alone. I am as grateful as a man can be, but would rather not.' Not that she is not "— and Mr. Parsons used the highest eulogium current in that region, singular as its form was —"a most an excellent woman ; only she is too warm and easy with her words, as she is with her tears. But we won't speak of her any more. When you preached about temperance, and Mr. Clarke poured his liquor in the gutter, and you baptized him, it had a wonderful influence. You are sincere : you are in dead earnest, Mr. Venable. But the time of giving you slippers and dressing-gowns will end. Dr. Burrows had his day of that. He was a larger man than you, older, more experienced, very able in argument ; but it all slackened and stopped in regard to him. It will with you. The large majority of our people are substantial and sensible. It is the few fussy ones that make all the enthusiasm at first, and do all the mischief at last. I wouldn't have any very intimate friends, if I were you. Don't look to, or lean too much upon, Gen. Buttolph. You think he is rich and generous, and has the highest opinion in the world of you. Don't be too certain. There are things you know nothing about yet ; yes, many things, and some very terrible things. And don't be afraid of Commodore Grandheur, nor other people I might tell you about. Up to the moment the crash came, Dr. Burrows was as profoundly ignorant of what everybody else, to the very children, were talking about, as if he were a baby, — a great big baby ; for the doctor was double your weight. When the time comes, if it does, and I will let you know, don't stop one instant : go, and go like a shot."

"I confess I was not prepared — I did not think "— said the other, sick to the heart, and endeavoring to hope it was but a part of Mr. Parsons's eccentricity. "What do you advise? You take me by surprise."

"I am terribly practical, you see," his friend said with a kindly glance at the paling face of his guest, — "too much so ; that is, I am more rapid than the rest. I always get to

a point on the common road long before other people, —
always. It is only a question of time. Slow and stupid as
people are, they get there too, sooner or later. You are full
of hope. I never met a man more ignorant of life, or quite
so full of enthusiasm, or blind belief in everybody. And
you may have a reserve power in you to drive you over the
bar, as the steamboat people say, when the tide leaves you
fast in the mud. All I say is, *Aim* at something ! — to convert sinners, to help Christians in their daily needs ; not
merely to instruct a congregation, or to please them. When
you let the people out from a sermon, chattering to each
other as they go, and delighted with themselves and you,
then you may be sure you have done them no good, only
harm instead. What you want to do is to make them forget
you in your message, and that message will disgust them with
themselves. Then never fear any living man or woman.
And the only way is, get away from all of us, from yourself
especially, by getting nearer to God, and holding tighter to
Christ, than you have ever done. Do that, and there is
nothing to discourage you. That is all. If there is any
thing more to say, when the time comes I will tell you.
This is the house where my terraqueous machine is kept.
You cannot see it yet, but I am making up a party. When
I am ready I'll let you know. If we do not have the grandest ride over this island ever known, perhaps over more
than the island, I am mistaken. My wife won't go, but I
intend taking my little Owny here ; " and the old father took
the little girl from the arms of Mr. Venable, in which she lay
sound asleep, her fat cheeks pillowed in a nest of her own
hair upon his bosom. " No one except my sworn workmen," the inventor added, looking at the closely boarded-up
building as a miser looks at his chest, " has seen it. The
papers have been full of it, but I keep blood-hounds in that
stable yonder, especially for reporters : they come prying
around, you see, at night. Next to the focussing of flesh,

I consider this *the* discovery, so far, of my life. In less than a month you shall ride in it yourself. It is the grandest thing " —

"Why, Ezra Micajah Papa!" exclaimed his small offspring, wakened up in the transfer from the one gentleman to the other, and specially bright after her nap. "My b'ack rooster c'owed so loud yesterday, I crep' in dare to see how many eggs he laid, — crep' in by a itty bitty hole. It's nuffin at last," said the spoiled beauty, in tones caught from her mother: "your 'chine is nuffin at all but one gate, big, old " —

At this juncture, her father pressed his faded cheek upon her rosy mouth, giving his long left hand in farewell to his guest. "Mrs. Chaffingsby?" he added. "Bah! Good-by. Fiddlesticks! Wait till you have ridden in it. And don't be offended at what I've said," with a cordial squeeze of the hand. "You are more sensible than I thought; and I am going to aim at the priests. Good-by!"

Mr. Venable put a pleasant face upon it, but he felt sore as from a beating. He walked wearily away. The re-action would come, he would brace himself after a day or two, and walk with head more erect, and with firmer step, but not yet. He went to bed early after reaching Gen. Buttolph's, but it was not to sleep. Prayer had no calming influence; for prayer was being answered in his case, as often happens, by process, — by process long and slow and very severe. We live as long as God; and his processes have the imperceptible curve of a circle which encloses eternity. Mr. Venable endeavored, as he lay in bed, to think his affairs thoroughly over.

Two months had passed since he, Hartman Venable, had stepped, so to speak, from the deck of the Nautilus upon that of the First Church of St. Jerome. It was a critical time indeed. He was coming to know that the peril as well as charm of his new home lay in its tropical character. The

excess of light and color and life, in sea and sky and luxuriant earth, was but a condition of quivering re-action from
an equal excess of storm and darkness and danger. He had
exulted in the sudden surge, as it were, since he came, of
a measure of soul in himself of which he had not hitherto
supposed himself possessed. But he was beginning to learn
that this electric condition of things was true, in all its degrees and varieties, of the blood and brain of all others with
him on the island.

"I wonder," he said to himself, waking suddenly out of
a light sleep, at last, in the dead hour of the night, "if there
is not something almost volcanic in the people as well as in
the soil, — something feverish, at least spasmodic, and liable
to sudden revulsions. Miss Aurelia Jones merely gives her
fervor the direction of an effusive piety. I am sincerely
grateful to her ; but I do wish, as Mr. Parsons said, that she
would not be so generous to me : that embroidered sermon-
cover is too fine, for instance. Mr. Parsons, and Mrs.
Chaffingsby, not to speak of Mr. Quatty, seem to be under
too tense a strain to keep it always up. And so am I. But
I don't know, at last. These people have been so for years.
Look at the variety of the cactus in every yard and prairie.
The queer plants seem like living snakes, almost venomous
in their thorns, twisting and writhing themselves as if in
convulsions of oddity as well as beauty. They say that three
of their purple pears will insure an ague. Their blooms seem
poisonous in the splendor of crimson and yellow. Clear
Grit, as they call him, does not seem like other children.
Look at the lizards flashing about, with preposterous horns
on their heads ! The very grass is sharp with spikes ; the
odd-looking fish rolled ashore by the waves startling you, if
you touch them, with their stings. Then those tarantulas !
who ever dreamed of spiders as big as a saucer, as hairy as
a bear, throwing themselves at you with red and clashing
jaws ? And the idea of a centipede armed in lapping coats

of mail, lovely as a fragment of rainbow, yet gripping your naked foot, and spurting deadly venom into your blood through its *legs !* Now, these things have lived here from creation. Mr. Farce Fanthorp has always been a mimic, I suppose. Commodore Grandheur would be a commodore anywhere. And why am I so nervous in regard to Miss Aurelia Jones, — Mr. Parsons only said about her what I had already thought, — the most fervent soul I ever knew outside of biography? There are people of marked character everywhere. It is because I have been cooped up in college hitherto, and am green and inexperienced. I think they will find that I can learn," he added coolly.

But at this point in his midnight reflections Mr. Venable laughed at his accident with the towel. In wiping his face one morning after washing, to his horror something had fastened upon his nose with a sharp pain. Seizing upon and dashing it on the floor, he saw it was a scorpion. A glance was enough to show him that it was an accurately scriptural scorpion, the picture of which he had often shuddered at in his Bible Dictionary. He blushed now to recall Irene Buttolph's paroxysms of mirth when he had gone down stairs. It was not worse than the sting of a wasp, at last; and he had arranged the order of his dying words !

Another mishap was too bad. A young girl had urged him one day to call and induce her mother to attend church. But the Providence which never sleeps had prompted him to take Mr. Nogens with him. The instant they entered the house, they saw their sad mistake ! The recoil of the slatternly harlot therein from them was as instinctive as theirs from her. Not a word was spoken; they were not in the door one minute; but the heart of the young man almost stood still with the extremity of his peril, and then leaped with energetic gratitude at having taken Mr. Nogens with him. He fancied that even the sallow, set face of that officer of his church had taken

a tinge of green as they walked rapidly away, not daring
to glance around for shame. Such a hair-breadth escape
surpassed all former experiences. He well knew that one
syllable of it, had he in his ignorance been there alone,
would have slain him as a minister, on the spot, and forever,
and like lightning.

"How could I tell," he said to Mr. Nogens, in the agony
of the moment, "who she was? She staid behind to converse with me after Sunday school. I saw that she was not
more than twelve years of age, a singularly intelligent child.
She was so deeply interested in the subject of religion, conversed so earnestly and with such sincerity too, that I never
dreamed of — of " — and it was all he could say. But, to
all he said in his excitement, Mr. Nogens replied, "Yes."
And the other blessed Mr. Nogens that he was Mr. Nogens ;
and, in an incidental way, he silently poured benedictions
upon the head of Mrs. Nogens, too, for being so deaf that
her husband, even if he had tried ever so hard, could never
make her understand about their blunder.

But at this juncture the fevered mind of the wakeful man
as he lay upon his bed chanced, in its tossings and turnings,
upon Mrs. Chaffingsby. The instant, however, that he entered in imagination her door, the absurd pictures upon the
walls were forgotten in the loveliness of Clara Chaffingsby.
And so he went over every curl of her hair, every curve of
her perfect face, and lay quiet in his restlessness while he
gazed again deeper down into her marvellous eyes. But
she had scarcely spoken, merely smiled ; and he reverted
suddenly to Zeo Buttolph, matronly to see at meal-times,
low-spoken and quiet. But between her and himself the
tall form of Gov. Magruder insisted upon interposing itself.
Very well. How beautiful was Clara Chaffingsby! how
brilliant and intellectual and well-read was Irene Buttolph!
And *she* saw the points of his sermons, — saw and appre-
ciated his beautiful ideas as swiftly as himself. Not as beau-

tiful, physically, as Clara; but what a charming frankness, what a bold yet beautiful outspokenness in regard to all that interested him most!—the face of Clara Chaffingsby coming and going through it all. But once more Zeo Buttolph came into his thoughts, and came like a Zenobia indeed, — came driving like a victorious empress over Irene and Clara and all the world, himself most of all.

"I will *try*," he said. "It is desperate odds against the governor and Col. Roland; but I will try, *must* try as I must breathe, if the universe is against me."

Suddenly Mr. Phip Quatty arose, unasked, in his meditations, — arose tall and sunburned, waved everybody aside, persisted in being heard. Mr. Venable thought of all that took place last Wednesday night at prayer-meeting, and of what was sure to take place next Wednesday evening,— thought of it, and laughed aloud; and as he laughed, young Plenty, to his astonishment, knocked, and came in with his coffee hot and fragrant, — the stalwart black man so much too big for a task such as that. It was time to get up.

CHAPTER XII.

MR. PHIP QUATTY FEELS IT TO BE HIS DUTY TO MAKE A FEW REMARKS.

IT was the Wednesday night following upon Mr. Venable's visit to Mr. Parsons's place. The large and handsomely furnished vestry of the First Church was rapidly filling for prayer-meeting. Before the new pastor came to St. Jerome the people would arrive as it suited them, up to the hour of closing; but their new minister let no man despise his youth in this, that, having given notice to that effect, he began the exercises to the instant, even if Commodore Thomas William Grandheur himself had not as yet come in. This promptness was resented at first; but when we come to see that an object, a man or any thing else, is iron and oak, we accept and yield to it as such. Mr. Venable had been sorely smitten by the plain talk of the inventor; it bruised and sickened him to the soul: but it did him good, and he was all the stronger for it.

"How profoundly ignorant I am of the hearts of these people!" he could not help saying to himself during the singing of the first hymn. "They seem so kind and polite. They sing heartily, and pray, some of them, fervently; yet some of these, I know, dislike me. I do not know who they are, how deep their aversion, nor how right, for that matter, they are in it; nor do I know how active and successful they may be in disaffecting the rest. I am sorry I came. I am *not* sorry I came! My Master placed me here. I dare say it would be the same in every charge. What is the sense of trying to look down into an abyss, trembling miserably, and exhausting myself with peering over the edge? I will do, day by day, the very best I know how, clinging as close as I can to " — and his voice rose in the hymn as strong and clear as that of Miss Aurelia Jones herself. And yet, through all the verses, had his heart put itself into words, the congregation would have been stupefied by hearing from him a solo somewhat intermittently to this effect: —

"There is the Commodore. How stout and erect he looks, settled down in his front seat! With his gold-headed cane between his knees, he fills, with his velvet waistcoat and watch-chain, the channel between me and the people, — a sort of dam to check the current from my heart. . . . May God forgive my wandering thoughts! . . . With what fervor Miss Aurelia Jones sings! How she fires all around! Yet how little I know of the instant in which her feelings may be reversed, and pour as ardently against me! I don't wonder people shrink and smile at each other as they sing. Yonder is Mr. Quatty. We will have to be *very* prompt to prevent. . . . Forgive my foolish fancies, but what a comfort it is to see Gen. Buttolph in his seat: he is so large and genial and firm! That is one substantial bulwark of things, at least. No Irene here to-night. Always at church, and appreciating my sermons so. I wish she would come to prayer-meeting, at least now and then. . . . What a regular attendant Miss Zeo is, though I wish she would say more about my sermons than she does! I wonder why she brings Grit with her: he always goes to sleep. . . . There is old Father Fethero, at last, behind his blue spectacles. What a pity a minister should retire from his ministry into the seclusion of such dismal despondency! It would have been so much better for him to have gone to heaven. But I dare say he would gladly have done so if he could. — Father Fethero, will you lead us in prayer?" This last, however, was said aloud.

Mr. Venable waits patiently as the person called upon coughs in response, slowly draws an enormous silk handkerchief from his pocket, blows his nose, coughs once more, and very deliberately arises. He is an old man : his hair, in which is a dying struggle between the original red and the white of years, is in strong contrast with his large blue spectacles, and face furrowed and beaten and burned into a permanent red by forty years of exposure. He wears a white neckerchief, somewhat yellow and frayed out ; and his black broadcloth is very sleek with wear, and quite shiny, especially at the knees. Whenever his name was mentioned at Gen. Buttolph's, Irene was sure to laugh, and say, " I plainly perceive a gloom ! " that being an expression often used by Father Fethero ; all his utterances, in fact, being but variations of that. He had entered upon his training for the ministry, as Mr. Venable had learned, very young, and had taken the complete number of years at college and seminary. No graduate had mastered more laboriously all the Greek, Hebrew, and theology, systematic, exegetic, polemic, patristic, didactic, homiletic, hermaneutic, and the rest. Yet Father Fethero had not enjoyed a successful ministry. People said he was as good a man as Mr. Nogens, better, if that were possible. No disciple since Paul had labored harder. For many and many a weary year, in the manifold changes of his life, he had ridden through river bottom and cypress swamp ; among the mountains or piney woods, prairies or post-oaks, as the case might be, to his " appointments " at mills and cross-roads, court-houses and school ; experiencing all weathers and housing, feeding and sleeping, known to men in that western region. The years of hard work, of small pay, of mortifications still more bitter, of little apparent success, which was bitterest of all by far, — all this had worn him out. His self-respect had been sorely tried under the heedless heels of man, and for so long. Starting out a learned man, he had been ground through a series of candidatings for vacant pulpits; which, like the revolutions of a steel mill, had taken off from him every kernel of originality, as the grain of corn is cut from the cob. Not a gesture, not a tone, not a phrase familiar to his lip and heart, not a kind of argument or form of persuasion, appeal or pathos, — in a word, not a peculiarity of the man, even those the most essential to his individuality, but had been hit, and severely, until he had at last given up himself in every point and long ago, as, in every square inch of his person, a dead failure. Although he had been compelled to take in that belief (that unbelief rather) in regard to himself, as by and in and at every pore of his skin, yet, with strange perversity, he could not but feel as if in some dim way, and against all the world, he was at last not as worthless as people supposed. Of his almost desperate desire to do good, he was sure. And ah! in what agonizing prayer, with strong crying and tears, he had lain whole days of fasting, long nights through of prayer, God knew, and he knew. That was his consolation, that God did know. He had about given up the struggle now. Through his blue spectacles he was looking to another world; and a goodly part of his anticipations of heaven lay in this, that the Master would there explain to him why, although he had loved that Master so well, and had tried so hard and so long to serve him, such small success had been granted him. And thus he was spending, with a widowed daughter in St. Jerome, the darkening evening of a day which had never been bright. It was by reason of all this that Mr. Venable treated the old man, to the astonishment of St. Jerome, which had so long regarded Father Fethero as an object of pitying amusement, with the tenderness of marked respect; always giving him the first place at prayer-meeting, as everywhere else, so far as was possible. It was the harder to do, as Father Fethero had been de-educated, so to speak, by the severe stress of his troublous life; had lost not only his Greek, Latin, and Hebrew, but a correct use of his English as well.

By reason of Mr. Venable's kindness, the prayer of the old man was not as mournful in its set phrases as it used to be. He stood with his brown and wrinkled hands clasped together, lifted up and being let fall in the swell and subsidence of his supplications; the tears trickling down, as from long use they very easily did, toward the close of his prayer; conscious, somehow, as he told over the sins and backslidings and sorrowful prospects of the world of Christians, and of those of the First Church in particular, that the heart of the minister at least was with his. The prayer was far too long. Mr. Venable winced at the speciality of the petitions, "For this our brother, so young and inexperienced and untried of affliction as yet;" but he imbued, as it were, all present with his own loving respect for the worn veteran.

"If, now, we can only manage Phip Quatty"— That was the thought of the pastor, as well as of every soul present, when old Father Fethero had safely landed, as was his wont, all there in heaven, and had ended his prayer. That was the hope of even Mr. Quatty himself.

In that, as in many a church, there were laymen, uneducated laymen too, who could speak, and did speak, at meetings, with a practical sense and power which made them of invaluable service. Heaven has in too many cases set the seal of its approval to the commission of such, to doubt their right and duty to speak,— a seal in many instances of success so broad and clearly cut, that none can hesitate as to whether or no their credentials have issued from the Head of the Church. But Mr. Quatty was, alas! an exception to this rule. He was no more an Eldad in the camp, or an inspired Medad, than he was a Moses. He had received, in reference to his speaking, many hints, strong and indignant remonstrances as well, and had come into the room resolved, as he always was at the outset, not to say a word. But the earnest deprecation of divine judgment on the part of Father Fethero, to say nothing of the singing, had greatly quickened him. In fact, Mr. Quatty's solemn promises to his wife on their way to church, in regard to "holding his tongue to-night," were but as those of a man liable to anger in regard to his wrath, or of a drunkard in relation to his temptations. No one could make a more deliberate, not to say desperate, resolve, than did Mr. Quatty.

"No, Sally, not one word!" he said to his wife. "Why, sir," he would often say to Capt. Chaffin or to Mr. Parsons, in reply to stringent suggestions on the part especially of the inventor, — "every Wednesday night, before I go to prayer-meeting, I kneel down in my little office there at my livery-stable, and ask God to help me hold my tongue. But the moment I get in the vestry! I suppose it is the lights, the room being crowded full of people; but I cannot help it! Some Scripture is read, somebody makes a remark; and, if any man would say what I want to have somebody say, do you think I would speak? not a bit of it. No, sir! It is not that I want to speak, — to please myself, you mind. The *duty* is so plain! I think of something pat to the purpose. It is something which ought to be said, must be said. It is wicked to leave a thing like that unsaid. Thank God, I've given up swearing; but this comes to my tongue then, a thousand times more natural than a curse ever did. It's no use: I'd speak if you held a derringer to my head."

It is the knowledge that Mr. Quatty lurks like a panther in the jungles of the back seats, with ever-increasing eagerness to speak, ready to spring upon the meeting and destroy it, for that time at least, which gives a certain nervousness to all present. There is no fear until after Mr. Venable has read Scripture, and made his ten minutes of explanation

and application. And they are safe during the hymn that
follows. But the last verse is sung with apprehension; and
there is a moment of relief as Capt. Chaffin, on the occasion of which we are speaking, says, "Let us pray," before
the last line is well ended. The chorister, who is also the
organist on Sundays, is ordinarily somewhat stolid. But he
has been reminded and urged, too often to fail; and, with
Capt. Chaffin's "Amen," he strikes a chord upon the melo-
deon, and all are safely launched into anôther hymn. The
only thing the people can blame Mr. Nogens for is, that,
knowing so well the circumstances of the case, he is not
more prompt in the prayer he makes next, and which, with
small variation, he has made for many years. Then Mr.
Clarke, the reformed liquor-seller, is sure to make a few
practical remarks, especially upon the danger of intemper-
ance. The chorister has his hands on the keys of the instrument. A familiar note sounds before Mr. Clarke has
well done; and the audience, becoming more interested as
the meeting proceeds, are beginning to forget Mr. Quatty
behind there.

The First Church has dozens of men in all degrees of
wealth, education, social position, and piety, who are able
to take part. They are trained to the emergency; and now
one and then another offers prayer or makes a brief remark.
The meeting deepens in interest. Good Mrs. Quatty, an
uneducated but sensible woman, tightens her hold upon her
husband's arm. For Mr. Quatty is chewing his tobacco
now as if it were good; shifting it from one side to the other
of his mouth, instead of letting his quid lie quietly in the
corner thereof. He spits more and more energetically and
frequently into the spittoon between his legs, shifting his feet
and hands. The hour draws near to close. It has been an
excellent meeting. Commodore Grandheur is actually rising
to sum up, as is his wont, and then make the closing prayer.
It is impossible, however, people fear, for a man of his weight

and dignity of bearing to be as rapid as he knows he should be.

Mr. Venable had observed Mrs. Chaffingsby in a front seat. He had noticed her the more, as she rarely attended; and he had been struck with this peculiarity in the little, pale-faced woman, that she seemed wholly uninterested in the services. In his solid way, her husband sings, listens, bows motionless during prayer; but his wife is nervous and restless. Mr. Venable is glancing at her while Commodore Grandheur is in the act of rising. As he looks, he sees her suddenly sink in a limp and helpless way into the corner of her seat, her head falling to one side as if she had been struck. But her pastor needs no explanation. Mr. Quatty can hold in no longer. He has broken from his wife's tightening hold; has been deaf to her earnest, "Phip, don't, don't!" and Commodore Grandheur is constrained to sink, even in the act of his preliminary "ahem," into his seat, for Mr. Quatty has the floor.

"Excuse me, brethren," he says, plump and positive. "We are about to close, but I cannot refrain from adding a few remarks. As you all may know, I was once an oyster-man. Yes, friends, little as you may think it, I made my living by dredging for oysters. Sometimes for clams. An oysterman! And if there ever was a cursing and swearing, yes, lying and almost stealing and murdering, scoundrel, your humble speaker was that man! One day a man happened along. I was an oysterman, remember. He said to me, 'Under all your rough ways I see that you, sir, are a gentleman and a scholar.' Which," Mr. Quatty added, as if that were apology enough for speaking, "which," with slow and deep emphasis, "I am *not!*"

It was sad; for the young people had their heads down upon the pews before them, laughing at the well-known words with which Mr. Quatty always began. Father Fethero had turned his blue spectacles sorrowfully toward the speaker.

Capt. Chaffin was openly fanning his wife, his arm around her drooping form. It was in vain that the chorister had struck a key when the commodore sank back into his seat ; for there was such force in the words, so evidently from the heart, of the tall, brown-visaged, thoroughly in earnest interrupter, that there was nothing to do but to listen. A thunder-storm would have seemed as irresistible ; and the one idea in every mind was, how to get out of the rain as soon as possible. But there is this to be said for honest as well as earnest Mr. Quatty. All his soul lay in the first outgush. The torrent rose rapidly in him, broke over all resolves, and poured itself out over demolished barriers, yet exhausted itself by its violence. The stranger who had so flatteringly entered into conversation with him had been some good Christian, whose acquaintance had resulted in Mr. Quatty's conversion. But somehow the narrator always slackened in speech as he proceeded, rambled more and more wildly, and finally sat down in confusion. Possibly the counter influences without him were too strong, for they were very strong. In any case, the conclusions of Mr. Quatty's remarks were by no means equal to the energy of their beginning. And that was his trouble : having not said, when he tried, all that he intended, there was nothing for him to do but to seize upon the earliest opportunity afterward, or make one, in which to do so.

"O Phip, Phip, Phip !" It was all his wife could say, and that was merely a groan, as they walked home.

"Couldn't help it, Sally," was his only consolation in reply.

Before pronouncing the benediction, notice was given, on this occasion by the pastor, that "the officers of the church will remain behind for the transaction of important business ; " and the congregation slowly departs, whispering, laughing, looking with curious eyes at the officials, who group themselves about the pastor.

"Ahem !" Commodore Grandheur begins, before the sexton can shut the doors upon the retiring people. "Ahem, brethren ! It was at my request the notice was given. You already know what is intended. It is insufferable ! It is disgraceful ! We have endured this thing until we have become the laughing-stock of the world, — of the city, I mean. Miserable man ! Wretched creature ! Intolerable nuisance ! As you observe, brethren," the commodore adds, his face pale with rage, grasping his cane as if it were a weapon, "I am perfectly calm. I remember where we are, and am entirely cool. But we cannot stand it ! For one, I will not ! No, *sir !*" He addresses himself to Mr. Nogens ; and that official closes his eyes, and purses his lips more and more tightly, his forefinger feeling for the curl on his forehead to be sure that his wig is safe, as the irate commodore waxes warmer and warmer, until, at the final burst of the other's wrath, his eyes and lips are drawn into knots ; and, when the denunciation is ended, he opens his eyes and mouth again, and says, "Yes." The rest of the officers laugh, and then look grave.

"What do you propose, sir?" the pastor asks seriously.

"Propose, sir? I demand the suspension, deposition, expulsion, of the man. Immediately, sir ! Upon the spot, sir !" The commodore says it angrily, his brown face all aglow in contrast with his white moustache, which bristles with indignation. "I do now demand his instant — excommunication !" and the word is emphasized with a thump on the floor with the cane, which startles the sexton in the vestibule, yawning, and wishing them to get done.

Whereupon follows a long discussion, in which amusement mingles on the part of the rest. When the subject is exhausted, Mr. Venable points out that certain forms of church-law have to be followed, and adds, " An idea has occurred to me. If Commodore Grandheur will kindly allow me, I am sure I can arrange the matter " —

"Sir! arrange the matter!" The commodore interrupts him and with violence. "What do you mean, sir? *Arrange!* I do not understand you, sir!"

The old gentleman is greatly excited. The veins upon his forehead are swollen. It is not merely his eyes which seem larger: his whole person has suddenly broadened as well as become taller. There is an uneasy feeling on the air. Here is a declaration of war. Mr. Nogens in his alarm looks, without being addressed, from face to face, and says, "Yes."

The pastor had never before been spoken to in such tones. On the instant he, too, is angry, — enraged, if the truth must be told. The officials wince, and let their eyes fall as they see how livid his face has become. His lips are suddenly so dry that he moistens them with his tongue before he can speak; his chin works, his hands are clenched.

"Brethren," he says at last, slowly and distinctly, "I mean no disrespect to any one. Mr. Quatty is a troublesome man in this one respect. In every other regard he is an excellent man and a devoted Christian. If you will allow me, as I said, to try, I think I can so arrange, yes, *arrange it*, as that you will have no more trouble. Will you suffer me to try?"

There is that in the manner which gives force to the words, and the meeting dissolves upon that basis. But as the commodore wheels and departs, more like a squadron than an individual, all feel that war impends indeed. Mr. Quatty may be silenced, but a more determined foe is in the field.

CHAPTER XIII.

MR. VENABLE SOARS AMONG THE STARS, WHILE ZEO BUTTOLPH DESCENDS IN QUITE ANOTHER DIRECTION.

IT is the Sunday afternoon following upon Mr. Quatty's remarks at prayer-meeting. Zeo Buttolph is alone in her room. She has not slept the night before ; and now sits beside her bed, upon which lies an open Bible. She has knelt in prayer, and risen weariedly, and knelt once more to pray more earnestly ; the tears trickling between the hands which are clasped over her face, as she leans her head upon the bedside. At last she gets up, bathes her hands and face slowly, arranges her disordered hair, sits down again, her Bible lying in her lap, her young head bowed down in tired and sorrowful thought. She is dark and grave, but the seriousness of her aspect is full as ever of sweetness. Under the anxiety, there is the calm and the purity of a settled purpose ; the shadows resting upon her are no more a part of herself than are those which an overhanging willow casts upon a stream, a portion of the stream. Even as she sits and thinks, her eye falls upon some passage in the open volume, and grows brighter as she reads. She lifts her face, and gazes upon a portrait of her mother, returning steadily its loving look. Some sudden hope slowly illumines her face. It is as if the wind had lifted the willows, letting the sun in upon the pure water ; and it is easy to see that brightness is the nature of the woman, shadow only the transient accident.

The cloud falls again as her sister breaks, laughing, into the room. On the instant you see, that, of the two, the elder is the least like their mother portrayed above them. It is the more singular, as, if you were to see the father and his two daughters together, you would observe that it is the younger who is most like the general also. In some subtle sense, Zeo is most like both father and mother; and that although the parents have not the least resemblance to each other.

"Oh, me, I feared so!" Irene exclaims at sight of her sister, and in tones of vexation.

"I cannot help it, Irene," the other says gently. "And I am glad you came in," she adds, with the accent of a child. "You are the elder. There are only us two. I do not want to trouble and tire you; but who else is there?"

"What good is it? What is the use?" the other adds pettishly. "Two girls like us!"

"But it is so bad, so terribly bad" — begins Zeo.

"That's the very reason," her sister breaks in passionately. "If it were not so terrible we might do something. As it is, we can do no more than if we were two flies. What is the use? I won't think about it at all. Hateful little wretch!"

"Grit is your brother, Irene," said the other, lifting her steady eyes to her sister. "Is it his fault, that, when mother died, he was given over to the negroes? Nothing could be more horrible; but it is only on the outside. It is as if he had fallen into the mire. But I know he can be made clean again. That is what the Bible is written to tell us about, you know."

"Such oaths!" said the other; "and," with a shudder, "he is like a young fiend when he flies into a passion. But I wouldn't mind it if he were not worse than that. I am astonished, Zeo," with a look of disgust, "that a modest girl like you will allow him to touch you. Loathsome little nuisance!"

" He is my brother," the other replied softly, " and your brother, Irene, — our only brother. Mother is dead, and I intend to do all I can."

" The idea," the other added indignantly, " of your trying to teach him music ! To think how I kissed him, and had him in my lap, when I first came home ! Faugh ! If I had known ! And you know all as well as I do, yet you let him sit with his cheek against yours while you try to teach him how to draw. The idea, too, of his learning French ! You ride with him ! I saw how you held his hand when you walked down the steps yesterday, after all that Aunt Plenty told you too. Cah ! " with an expression of deepest aversion. " I tell you, Zeo," her sister continued, turning to the mirror, and beginning to take down and brush out her hair, " I can hardly endure to touch you after you have been with him ! "

" It was not about Theodore I was thinking," began her younger sister.

" Zeo," broke in the other, whirling herself around, " you must not talk to me about *that!* I cannot endure it. I will not allow it. Grit is more than enough. So far as the money goes, I will do all I can. I am economizing. There are a hundred things that I need, need badly, and I am doing without until I am positively shabby. What did papa go into sugar-planting for, if it only breaks him? What does he stay in sugar for, if it is only worse year after year? And we are so young, — just beginning to enjoy life ! It is too, too bad ! " and her violence changed to passionate weeping.

" We are doing the best we can, Reny," said the other, after some silence, as quietly as before. " You are helping me, dear. You cannot tell how much we have saved since we came home and found out. Every day, though, I find things are worse than I had supposed. Why, Reny, only yesterday I went to papa, sat down by him with my sewing, told him I could bear any thing : all I wanted was to know. He told me, at last, that if all were sold, — this place, the sugar-plantation, and every one of the people too, — it would not pay what he owes."

"Yes ; and one good crop of sugar would more than make it all right ; and you know it, Zeo. What a poor faith you have in God !" was the reply.

"I was not thinking about that, Irene," her sister said, "not at all. We are doing all we can. I haven't told you about Mr. Parsons," she added, her face lighting up. "He almost ran over me, he was walking so fast, one day last week. Grit and I were taking a stroll along the beach. He was on his way to Hacamac, his wonderful city that is to be, at the other end of the island. As soon as he saw who it was, he turned and came back. What an odd, kind-hearted old man he is ! He stood there with his hat in his hand, the sea-breeze blowing his hair all about, and said he wanted to tell me that my father was the most awfully swindled man, swindled by the overseer up at the plantation, the most abominably cheated man, even for a sugar-planter. 'And one other thing,' he said, 'I want you to tell your father.'" But here Zeo smiled.

"Why, what was that ?" her sister demanded.

"'Do you know Farce Fanthorp?'" the other continued. "I said, 'Yes, sir.' — 'And what a perfect fool he is ?' I said nothing to that, and he went on : 'You tell the general from me, that, fool as Farce Fanthorp is, he is the very man for him.' I laughed, and asked him what he meant. 'If I were your father,' he said, 'I would have Fanthorp go up suddenly, — he is a splendid lawyer, you know, — and take a snap judgment upon that rascally overseer, look over his books, examine into his accounts. Farce Fanthorp is a fool,' he went on to say, 'and as perfect a fool as I know; but, if he was to take that plantation in hand, he could make it pay. Tell your father that,' he said. And I did tell him," Zeo added, her face all in a glow.

"What did papa say?" asked her sister, seating herself and greatly interested.

"He laughed," Zeo replied, "and said he had no doubt Mr. Parsons was right, and he would see Mr. Fanthorp. Papa told me that Mr. Parsons owns the plantation next to his, and has almost ruined it with his experiments; but when it is not his own business which is concerned, Mr. Parsons has the longest head of any man he knows. But I did not tell papa," Zeo added, "that Mr. Parsons said that he had known a good many sugar-planters, and my father was the laziest as well as the most gentlemanly of them all. 'Your father is so large and heavy,' he explained."

"Queer old creature!" Irene exclaimed; "and was that all he said?"

"Oh, no!" Zeo added with a laugh: "he shot off, putting on his hat as he went, only to take it off and come back again. 'The best thing you can do,' he said to me, the wind blowing and the surf rolling so high I could hardly hear him, 'is to marry your sister Irene to Farce Fanthorp.'" Zeo paused a little, maliciously.

"What an old goose!" said that sister, blushing.

"'Because,'" Zeo continued, — "I am only quoting Mr. Parsons, Irene, — 'because,' he said, 'Col. Roland never has married any lady, and never will.' No, hear me out," Zeo persisted; "'and because,' Mr. Parsons went on, 'I do *not* think she is a suitable match for Mr. Venable.'" And at this point the younger sister laughed merrily, re-acting from her anxiety before. But even as she laughed the young lady colored to think of something the eager old man had said, and which she did not care at all to repeat. It was this: "My dear Miss Buttolph, it is the talk of the island, that Gov. Magruder is desperately in love with you. He is so much in love, that he dares not visit you often. He comes down from his plantation expressly to do so, and then turns and goes back, afraid to call. Now, Old Ugly is a good

fellow, but if I were you"—   At that point, however, Miss
Zeo had bid him good-by.

"Perhaps," Irene continued with disdain, coloring as she
spoke, "Mr. Parsons invited you to ride in his machine
before he left you."

"Yes, he did," said the other, reflecting her sister's color
in her own face; "in his terraqueous machine, he called it.
He says that Mr. Venable — he evidently thinks a great deal
of him, dear — and you and I, Mr. Fanthorp and Col.
Roland, because he is an editor, are about all he intends to
have."

"Catch me!" the other added contemptuously. "He
condenses pigs and cabbages! They talk of Mr. Quatty
and of Mrs. Chaffingsby: he is the craziest of the three.
Wouldn't it be fun, Zeo, to see Mr. Fanthorp take him off?
only it is too easily done. And how that laughing young
wife of his ever came to marry such a queer old soul, is more
than I can understand. What a darling little girl they have,
too! They call her Owny, and she is a perfect beauty. But
I must leave you. Marry Mr. Venable, indeed!"

"Wait a moment, Reny," her sister said, as the other was
going out of the room; and her whole manner changed as
she said it.   •

"Oh, no, no, no, Zeo!" exclaimed Irene, looking with
dismay at her serious aspect. "Don't, don't! I cannot
endure it."

"Reny, I dare not put any thing in his brandy," Zeo said,
rising, and holding her sister firmly by the arm. "A wife
might do it, to make him sick and disgusted with it; but
I ought not. Yet something must be done. It is almost
every night now. All the negroes know it. O Reny! it is
terrible to see him lying there as if he were dead. And he
will die in one of — those — those — He is so heavy, you
know! If I only knew," the poor girl added, her hand upon
her head, "what to do! I cannot find one verse in Scrip-

ture as to what a child ought to do when a father does that."

"Let me go, Zeo; don't ask me," her sister said, as violent as before. "It makes me desperate. There is nothing we can do. We are only *girls !* Oh ! what did mamma die for?" and she gave way once more to weeping. She had a full measure of energy, bodily and intellectual, but in emergencies it was sure, like other tempests, to spend itself in rain ; abundance of force, but it exhausted itself in tears, and so dissipated itself into the dampened air. Not that her sister did not have her showers also ; but she was unlike Irene in this, that, the more she was aroused and driven toward her highest climax by circumstances, that much the less was she disposed to weeping. We know that Christ wept at Gethsemane ; but there is no record of a tear when he had reached Calvary. The women wept there ; but would they have wept if they could have done any thing else? So with Zeo. She had her December rains as well as her April tears ; but her soul allowed to her eyes merely its overflow. Unlike Irene, it was the surplus of her strength that went in that way, leaving the substance of it cleared for use. By the laws of her stronger nature, the more deeply she felt, the more was she impelled to act, not cry. Therefore her eyes were dry as she held Irene firmly, and said, —

"Sister, it is not only about this I wanted to speak : something must and shall be done about " —

Irene lifted her face, pale with the parching of sudden wrath, and said venomously, "Zeo, if that vile animal comes in my reach I will *kill* her !" and then gave way, with sobs and ejaculations, to tears, — tears, and nothing but copious tears, and so melted into utter weakness and worthlessness for all practical uses. To Zeo, it was like trying to lean upon water.

It was on this account, that, at midnight of the same Sunday, the poor girl had no wish for the presence of her sister,

as, fearing he might die, or she knew not what, she sat
beside her father lying upon the sofa in the dining-room,
drunk, and dead drunk !

Mr. Venable had preached a fine sermon that night, in
the hearing of the general and Irene, upon "the sweet
influences of the Pleiades;" proving quite conclusively, that
the influences referred to were the attraction which swung
the entire universe around a certain star in that constellation; and the discourse was garnished with all that poetry
afforded, as well as science. Miss Irene had expressed
herself rapturously about it, as they walked home together.

"It was excellent, admirable, very good indeed; did you
great credit, sir," the general remarked, when he bade
Mr. Venable good-night. "The constellation Pleiades, you
said," passing the key of his sideboard from hand to hand,
"and Alcyone is the star in it around which we revolve:
I must remember it. Excellent, very sublime ! Good-night,
good-night;" and in a short time thereafter his delighted
auditor had forgotten every thing in the depths of his drunk-
en stupor.

Usually there was not a more magnificent man to be
seen in St. Jerome : now he was only an enormous sot, his
large face purple, his clothing all awry, snoring discordantly,
an object of disgust amounting to terror. The servants
were asleep, only Grit and Zeo in the room. The two had
not gone to the night service. Zeo had read to her brother
from a Sunday-school book. So far as nine-tenths of the
Sunday-school library was concerned, the best celebration
for an anniversary would have been a bonfire of the books,
with the children rejoicing around. But Zeo had slipped in
a good deal here and there, as she read, trying to interest
and keep Grit awake. He was at the critical moment when
a cherub child becomes a lubberly boy; and with a woman's
keenest instincts, and subtlest devices of love, she was trying
to lay her grasp upon the very soul of her brother. He

was all she had left. And he was very wide awake now, standing beside Zeo, whose arm was around him as she sat beside her dead father. Dead, because Gen. Buttolph never drank except at home, at night, with the richest and best of liquors in unlimited quantity at hand; drank with enormous thirst; drank, with the immense inertia of his heavy build, like a mountain sliding into a bottomless sea, purely and exclusively for the drink's sake. Yes: no gentleman in the city was more sumptuously clad, more regularly in the hands of his barber, more genial, hospitable, liberal; and there he lay, a huge swine. There he lay, every ounce of his immense weight upon the heart of that one poor girl. And she has, unaided, to lift him in her frail arms back, if it be done at all, to all that he used to be. He has to be held from his downward descent, and lifted, when, by reason of that in him which was worse than drunkenness, she dared not think of her dead mother because of the new horror it awoke in her of the one she had to save.

While Zeo and her brother kept watch over their father, Mr. Venable, too, was awake up stairs.

"The church was crowded to-night," he soliloquized. "I am doing a grand work! Col. Roland asked for a copy of my sermon for his paper; and, when Miss Aurelia Jones came up to thank me, she burst into tears as she took hold of my hand, and could say nothing at last. But it was all as nothing to me, because *she* was not there. I did not understand what old Plenty said that morning about her, and I cannot comprehend why she did not go to church to-night. Can it be possible," he asked himself after a while, "that Gov. Magruder was in the city, and spent the evening with her? I never thought that *she* would entertain company upon Sunday. Perhaps," — and the dreadful suggestion smote him as worst of all, — "perhaps she is sceptical!" And it was little he slept that night.

CHAPTER XIV.

MR. VENABLE BECOMES BETTER ACQUAINTED WITH MRS. CHAFFINGSBY AND HER HOUSEHOLD.

EARLY the next morning after his wonderful sermon, Mr. Venable set out with Commodore Grandheur, Mr. Nogens, and other gentlemen connected with the First Church, to attend a conference of his denomination, at which would be decided the question of his acceptance of the pastorate of the church. It was a fatiguing journey; for the conference met at some distance away, at an inland town, and a good part of the travel was upon horseback, to which he was only of late becoming used; and it was several days after he came back before he felt disposed to much exercise.

"I landed on this island on the first day of January, and this is nearly the middle of March," he said one afternoon to himself, as he took, at last, a slow walk through the suburbs of St. Jerome. "It seems three years instead. I suppose it is because of my secluded life before; but it is as if I were living upon a fragment which had been smitten off from the earth, and was revolving more rapidly than the old world. I am so inexperienced, so ardent and impulsive, — the wonderful appetite and health I enjoy, — every thing is against me. The days were emptier when I was with men only. I wish I could strike Miss Irene and her lively talk, as well as this beautiful vision at Mrs. Chaf-

fingsby's, out of my life. I could give myself then more
completely to my work. But I cannot wish to strike *her* out.
How absurd and hopeless the idea of my competing with
Gov. Magruder ! — a David with such a Goliath ! " And he
was surprised, as he walked, to find himself at last in front
of Mrs. Chaffingsby's house. At the same moment Mrs.
Chaffingsby came out of the gate, dressed for walking.

" Mr. Venable ! " she exclaimed. " Is it possible ! I was
hastening to call upon you. There is a divinity in art, or
we should not have thus met. It decides me, decides me !
Wait a moment, sir : I wish to recover myself."

She was dressed in silk, with a good deal of lace and
jewelry about her neck. Under her bonnet, which was
adorned with artificial flowers, was a halo of small curls of
light hair, in which her face was set like that of a doll, rather
than even a child. Her eyes were large in proportion, blue
and singularly bright. She was in the act of opening her
parasol, when she came out ; but folded it now, and continued, after the other had replied· to her salutation, and
made all due inquiries in regard to the health of her family, —

" You remember, sir, that, as you left upon your last visit,
I was smitten by a sudden inspiration. I have had many ;
but this was the first of the kind. You will be astonished,
sir ! I venture to hope you will be more astonished than you
ever were in your life. My husband is violently opposed to
it ; but I have given it, I may say, an agony of consideration.
In fact, I may add, I have not eaten with appetite since, or
slept. I was hesitating even as I was going out of the gate ;
but your presence confirms me."

" I thank you, madam," the other replied.

" You *cannot* thank me until you know," she interrupted
him. " Mr. Parsons is an absurd inventor of impracticable
machines ; and he," she added, " speaks contemptuously of
my art, to my husband, who is associated with him at times.
He objects to what I now propose, possibly on the same

grounds with my husband, that I have confined myself hitherto to prophets, apostles, martyrs, angels, and the like. But I am determined, and since you came, to descend. 'Captain,' I said to my husband, 'I will delineate you as Jonah being hurled overboard.' — 'Paint away,' he said. 'But no,' I continued : 'I will paint a gorgeous banqueting-hall, and Gen. Buttolph shall sit to me as Belshazzar.' My husband became alarmed at that. But the inspiration which smote me at the close of your visit was that at which I was aiming ; and all this was but preliminary. When at last I mentioned this my original idea to my husband, he was arranging a compass ; and he dropped and broke it, swearing, I regret to say, at the same time. My husband glories in my art, sir," she said with pride ; "so much so, that, although he had suggested that I should recreate myself upon lesser subjects, he himself shrank when I proposed it."

" Proposed it?" the other repeated with a sinking heart.

" Say that this is the wilderness," the artist said, making a circle upon the boards of the gate at which they stood, with the end of her parasol. " *There* a Sadducee, and it shall be Mr. Parsons ; *here* a Pharisee ; on *this* spot, the coarse countenance of an Herodian, and for that I have thought of Mr. Quatty ; *here*," and she struck the centre of the gate with decision, "John the Baptist shall stand with the skin and leathern girdle ; and," she added, turning upon the other with enthusiasm, "*you* shall be John the Baptist."

" Pardon me : you must excuse me," Mr. Venable exclaimed with energy.

" You object to assuming so sacred a character? I had thought of that," she said with utter unconsciousness. " Very well.   Better still : I like few women, but I do sincerely love Miss Zenobia.   Abbreviations I abhor, and therefore will not mention her as Miss Zeo. The theme shall be the meeting of Jacob and Rachel at the well. She will make, with a jar on her head, an admirable Rachel ; and you shall be Jacob,—Jacob regarding her with the dawn upon your brow of a passionate love. Not one word," she continued breathlessly, "but please come in while the inspiration is upon me. If you will excuse me, I will hasten to my room, and get on my working apparel : I am not myself without it."

Mr. Venable had never been more perplexed, but resolved to escape in some way. He followed her to the door of the house, and lingered there while Mrs. Chaffingsby hurried in and up-stairs.

As he waited, puzzling his brains as to what to do, her daughter came along the hall within, and stood in the door. He had doubts, afterward, whether she could be as lovely as she had seemed the day he had come suddenly upon her beneath the Syrian Martha portrayed so savagely upon the kitchen walls. The face which smiled upon him as the door opened shamed him for having doubted. He looked steadily at the girl, so fair and fresh in the purity of her guileless bearing, in order that he might never waver again as to the possibility of such beauty off of canvas and out of marble. The only idea he had of her dress was that it was largely apron ; and of her hair, that it was not dressed for church, the girl having evidently come from domestic duties.

"Good-day, sir," she said, at once and without explanation : "he is asleep ;" and, although fully sixteen years old, it was somehow merely a child of six who smiled upon him.

"He? Who is he?" the visitor asked, surprised at her words, and entering, although his invitation to do so lay altogether in the manner of the other, whose wonderful blue eyes were fastened upon his with the full and steady look rather of a babe than of a child.

"Charlie," she replied. "He is a great deal of trouble ; but he is asleep in his chair. She is painting up-stairs. She is almost always painting. Do you like pictures?" she added, as Mr. Venable seated himself under the flying Judas in the parlor. "There are hundreds of people in this house; up in the attic too. She has put David on the wall of the observatory, where the flagstaff is. He is praying on top of his house, you know. Ananias and Sapphira are falling dead in our cook's room. You know the negroes tell such awful lies; but Aunt Lucy, our black woman, says she don't care. She is our cook, and sleeps there. She says when the owls cry all night, they say, 'Tu-who, tu-whit, tu-who-cooks-for-you-all!' The little maid telling Naaman to go to Elisha is on my wall. Every room is full of them. Whenever I open a door, they all stop throwing their arms about, and talking, until I go out. They stand stock-still, looking at me with their eyes." The young girl had not seated herself, but stood smiling and looking at her visitor steadily. Whatever loveliness there is of color and curve and tone of voice, possible to one of her sex, were certainly hers.

"Why, Miss Clara, you are as original as your mother," began Mr. Venable, wondering at her artlessness. At this instant, however, there was a rapid step along the hall, and Mrs. Chaffingsby came into the room in a brown and paint-bespattered dress, a palette in one hand, a brush in the other. There was an expression of terror in her face, as she saw Mr. Venable, that alarmed him.

She glanced from her visitor to her daughter, her hand upon her heart, evidently much agitated, and then motioned to the door, saying, "Charlie, Charlie!" as if it were all she could say.

"Please excuse me, madam," her visitor said, as the girl left the room. "You had said something about some intention. I will call again at another time. Allow me to say," he added, as he opened the door, "that I have rarely seen a young lady so capable of — of — Pardon me," he continued, "but I would think that, with a thorough education and travel and society, your daughter will make one of the most char — I mean remarkable" — He felt, as he spoke, that he had been guilty of some indiscretion. Mrs. Chaffingsby looked at him first in astonishment, then in wrath; then the poor little woman lifted her palette and brush before her face, and sank upon the sofa in a flood of tears. The next moment the young man found himself, after a hurried apology, walking rapidly away from the house, dazed, blaming himself severely, yet amazed as to the meaning of it all.

"That is what they told us there," he said to himself, of his seminary: "other men may escape, at least for a time; but the instant a minister sins, that instant he is smitten as by lightning,—by lightning accompanied by thunder enough to fasten the attention of the whole world.

"But what have I done? Can my honest affection for Miss Zeo be a sin for which I am to be punished? And why is she so silent?" and he worried himself as to that and Mrs. Chaffingsby, until he was wearied out, walking along the beach, in deep thought, for miles.

"What could have possessed Mrs. Chaf"—? He sat down at last, as he said it aloud, and watched the fiddler-crabs scurrying away. Then he got up from the hillock of sand, and stooped over one of the jelly-fishes washed ashore, and turned the transparent mass over and over, wondering how a living creature could exist with nothing resembling an organ of any sort. But it was only after he had tired himself down, and rested as upon the final basis of being the greatest blunderer living, that he turned his feet, in the growing darkness, toward home. The only hope left him was a steady purpose not to stay a fool, if God could show him how.

That very afternoon, he was being thoroughly discussed by others as well. The commodore had called at Gen. Buttolph's, and had met Miss Aurelia Jones there, who had been unusually fervent in her expressions of regard for their pastor. "Since he is not at home, I will leave a message for him with you," she said to Zeo, after some conversation. "There is a purse," she added, showing it to her, "which I worked with my own hands. It contains a little money. Tell Mr. Venable to apply it to any good cause he may know of.

"I like him," she added, "not as the people generally do. His sermons are very beautiful. He is faithful and devoted in his visiting among the poor and the sick. Nor is it because of his earnest supplications. It is the unworldliness, the glowing self-devotion, I appreciate!" and the lady clasped her gloved hands together as she sat, her black eyes suffused with tears, her face overflowing with feeling. "I know you people cannot appreciate such things," she added at last. "I fear you are altogether given up to the world. You will soon sicken of it, as I have done. Zeo is more thoughtful, even if she is so silent" —

"Is it possible, Miss Aurelia, that you do not know?" Irene interrupted her guest.

"I know that Commodore Grandheur would prefer an older and colder man," the lady continued, not regarding Irene, who had risen, and was standing before her. "You are of a more formal temperament, sir; you like more argument, more instruction, more deliberate and unimpassioned reasoning. But you are no fair specimen of the mass of our people," added Miss Jones, who did not fear the commodore at all, and who, in virtue of her wealth and position, never restrained her ardors for any one. "A church is not a man-of-war, commodore, as I have often told you. We are neither the passengers nor the crew of any thing of the kind."

"Miss Aurelia!" persisted Irene, stooping, as she stood before her, to touch that lady on the knee, "Miss Aurelia" —

"I have had but one opinion," said the gentleman appealed to, his two hands upon the top of his cane, which was between his knees as he sat. "Ours is the first church of St. Jerome. Dr. Burrows, whatever his weakness, was a man of great ability. We are not children. Neither are we all ladies. Emotion is unreliable, evanescent, without solidity. What we need," and the commodore's voice and manner were adjusted to his words, "is a man who is deep, powerful, experienced, regular, symmetrical. Would you believe, madam, that Mr. Venable almost defends Mr. Quatty in his insane course?"

"I myself told Mr. Venable all about Mr. Quatty," the lady said earnestly: "what a rough excellence he possesses; how he never allows a horse or buggy to go out of his stable upon Sunday, except when a steamship arrives, although that is the chief day for beach-driving. He will not let you have any thing, even for a funeral, on Sunday, unless you solemnly promise to return direct from the funeral, and not make a drive of it afterward. There is a sign," added Miss Jones, laughing, "in his stable, with letters six inches long. I did not believe it, and went there and hired a saddle-horse in order to see it myself. There it is.

> *No Swearing, Gambling, Bad Talk, nor*
> *Sabbath-Breaking, in this Concern.*
> *No sir-ree Bob!*

"Mr. Venable's plan," she added eagerly, "is to engage a public hall for Mr. Quatty, to give notice of it on Sunday, and let the man have a full opportunity to say what he has to say, once for all. I am like our pastor," she added. "I hate formalism, however respectable; and I *do* love to see earnest, energetic piety, however homely it may be. I had rather laugh at the one than weep over the other, myself," she concluded.

It was an old, old quarrel between Miss Aurelia and the commodore, dating from the days of Dr. Burrows, long before Mr. Venable. The two could not agree. And they could no more meet without contest than could ice and fire. As usual, the gentleman was indignant. He stiffened himself as he sat, took fresh hold upon his cane, cleared his throat to reply, but was interrupted.

"And now please listen to *me*," Irene said, still standing before her. "Do you know, Miss Aurelia, that Mr. Venable has fallen hopelessly in love?"

There was something unlike the usual audacity of the young lady, a laugh in her voice, but not in her eyes, as she spoke.

"Why, what do you mean, you foolish child?" asked the lady addressed, her face turning pale, her lips remaining apart, and as if suddenly dry, after she had spoken.

"I am not a child, nor foolish," the young woman replied, with some haughtiness, as she drew herself up. "Let me alone, Zeo," to her sister, who had placed herself beside her, a hand upon her arm. "I happen to know that Mr. Venable has a passionate admiration for — now, for *whom* do you suppose?" she added with bitter sarcasm. "For Clara Chaffin, or Chaffingsby, as her mother calls herself!" and the disgust upon the face of the one speaking was reflected, as soon as the astonishment had passed from their eyes, in the countenances of all present.

Except Zeo. "It is because he does not know. She *is* very beautiful, as we all know; the loveliest creature, poor, poor thing, I ever saw," she said. "He is ardent and impulsive, Miss Jones, very warm-hearted, and full of imagination." And Zeo was astonished at the eagerness of her own tones, as she thus defended the absent.

"I did not think any human being"— began the commodore, oblivious to the sudden and unusual earnestness with which Zeo spoke, flushing as she did so, lifting his cane, and letting it come down again with emphasis, in the silence which ensued. But his eye was arrested in the act, by the change in the face of Miss Aurelia, and he paused. She was, as we have said, an eager lady. Her face was a good face, full of kindliness; the black eyes quick to sympathize beneath their clusters of curls, her manner as effusive as it was ardent. The florid color was gone from her face; it was drawn and hard; her eyes had, on the instant, become as cold as those of a statue. At least Zeo was aware, too, that her jewelled hands, lying the moment before open in her lap, had suddenly clinched themselves. Zeo winced in sympathy with a cruel pain, which, she knew not why, had as suddenly wrung the heart of their visitor. All who knew Miss Aurelia, knew that her fervor was the desperate effort of her soul against experiences in her past life; experiences the bitterest a woman can know. All knew, in a vague way, that this was so; but none except the One to whom she had fled for help knew how much more deadly than death those agonies had been. The poor lady was almost as much amazed as Zeo was, at the anguish, as from a rude hand upon old scars, which Irene had inflicted. But she said nothing. It was certain that, from that moment, the feelings of the lady were reversed toward Mr. Venable, and as by the shock of an astonishment of which the suddenness equalled the bitterness. Yet it was only those of her own sex present who understood, absurd as it seemed in the case of a lady so much older than Mr. Venable, the secret of it all. And of the two sisters, Zeo alone knew that Miss Aurelia had been as unconscious of her interest in him — at least almost as unconscious — as any other.

"I do not wonder so much, at last," Commodore Grand-heur added after some silence; a revolution taking place in him also, by reason of what he saw in the face of his invariable opponent. "Our pastor is young and ardent. Let me tell you, ladies, — I did not intend to mention it," he slowly continued, — "on our way up country to the conference, at which the call to our church was placed in Mr. Venable's hands, — we came, Mr. Venable, three other gentlemen, and myself, to a part of the road which was overflowed from the late heavy rains. We were all on horseback. The bridges were washed away. There happened to be an old canoe on the roadside, but there seemed to be nothing to do but turn back and give up going. In this emergency Mr. Venable took off his outer clothing, and swam his own horse over, all our horses following in a string behind, we ourselves coming after in the canoe with our saddles. He had to swim along the windings of the road a long distance, and against a swift current. What I liked, ladies, was that he asked my opinion before he attempted it; and that he did it as if it were matter of course. Conference passed a vote of thanks to us, for it was very important we should be there. Mr. Venable," the old man continued slowly, more and more conscious, as he spoke, of the sudden chill in Miss Jones's manner, "is young, quite young. He is excitable, possibly extravagant. But he has noble qualities. Under suitable guidance there is the stuff of a man in him. I am free to say," the speaker continued, drawing, after some search, a document in an official envelope from a breast-pocket, "that I had with me this protest against his settling over the First Church. I intended to urge it upon conference. I did not present it, however. When I left the navy, ladies, I resolved never to use the peculiar dialect of the navy, profane or otherwise. I believe I have kept my resolve. And now," added the commodore, with great self-importance, as he arose, walked to the hearth, and threw the document into the fire, "I have made another resolve. I need not mention it. As Miss Zenobia has observed," he added as he took his leave, "there is really nothing whatever in the matter to which Miss Irene has alluded, — nothing whatever. We are agreed not to speak of it ; " and with special courtesy toward Miss Jones, he departed. Miss Aurelia left soon after.

"There is the money I spoke of for your guest," she said to Zeo as she emptied the coins out of the purse upon the mantle, and replaced it in her pocket. "Tell him it is for the miserable."

Her tones were as metallic as the sound of the gold upon the marble ; and the tears came into Zeo's eyes in sympathy with those, so much more bitter, which remained unshed in the heart of the other as she took her leave.

To the commodore, as to Miss Aurelia, the First Church was the one object in life, neither having any other employment. By the habit of years, the change in the lady necessitated a change toward Mr. Venable in the other ; and, for every reason, he was glad to make it. But the change in her was not to be measured by his, nor by any masculine measure whatever.

"Irene," Zeo said as soon as the company was gone, but with evident reluctance and not looking at her, " who told you that about Mr. Venable ? "

" Nobody ! There was not a word of truth in it," her sister said defiantly. " He told me that the poor girl was so beautiful, he wondered her mother did not make her a model, and persisted in changing the subject : that was all."

" O sister, how could you " —

" Hush, Zeo ! I only did it to tease that poor, or rather, that rich, old maid. Who," demanded Irene, " could have thought it would have hurt her so ? But I don't care. No, hush ! I won't listen to you ! I get so desperate over our troubles, I don't care what I do. It is none of your business. Yes," she added rapidly, and somewhat bitterly, "it *is* your business. You poor little thing, he is in love with *you !* Blushing, are you ? Yes, you know he is ! A clergyman should have more self-control when you are in the room — I *won't* stop! While he is pretending to listen to me, he is devouring you, miss, with his fine eyes; and when you are not there, he has so much work to do, he really cannot stay. I will tell the governor of it the next time he calls. You treacherous girl!" But Zeo had left the room.

CHAPTER XV.

DESCRIBING A WONDERFUL RIDE IN THE TERRAQUEOUS
MACHINE.

ONE night, about a week after the events recorded in the last chapter, a number of persons found themselves at the house of Mr. Parsons. They had been summoned by that gentleman himself, speeding after dark and in breathless haste from street to street. For months he had promised them a ride upon his terraqueous machine on its trial trip. Every soul had been told of it under seal of strictest secrecy: as a consequence of which, St. Jerome was thoroughly informed of the fact. Mr. Parsons's house was at some distance from town, however, near the sea-beach; and this rapid assembling under cover of night enabled the inventor to baffle the curiosity of the city. Col. Roland was of the party, note-book and freshly-sharpened pencil in his breast-pocket; and, with the dawn of day, the great motor was to be heralded, by his paper, to the world. All were in high spirits, laughing and talking as they stole in together like conspirators. Their host had enjoined silence; which, with the splendor of the clear and starlighted night, and the curiosity alternating with certainty of failure as to their ride, imparted by each one to every other as they trooped in, made it as noisy a gathering as could be imagined. The discoverer had ushered them in, meeting them, as they came, at his front gate, with many a " Hush, if you please.

Hush ! Hush ! " And all had arrived on foot, Mr. Parsons having promised to deliver each one at home at the end of the ride.

" Rome was betrayed by the cackling of geese," he said, with some vexation, as he stood among his noisy guests assembled at last in the room, his thin hair scattered on his head, his tall and gaunt frame taller and gaunter than ever, his eyes more sunken, his words more rapid. "*Do* hush, dear friends ! You will alarm the whole island ! " he entreated nervously.

" I beg your pardon, Mr. Parsons," said Mr. Venable, who was as much excited as any : " it was the geese *saved* Rome."

" And we are on a wild-goose affair, anyhow, you know," added Irene Buttolph ; and the chattering grew worse than before, Mr. Farce Fanthorp only more extravagant in his spirits than Col. Roland and the rest. Capt. Chaffin was the one alone who behaved himself in virtue of being always wooden, and even when under worse wind and flying froth than that. The sudden adventure of the hour had stirred the blood of Zeo too : her eyes sparkled, her cheeks glowed ; she tried to cast out of her mind her father, lying asleep at home. Grit had been sternly denied being present by the inventor, who had yielded to his entreaty, not until after the assurance of Zeo, that, if he could not come, she would not. As radiant as any there, the boy stood by his sister, full as a boy could hold of the fun of the hour.

" Now, friends," Mr. Parsons, who had been hurrying in and out of the room, said at last, "we are about to take the most rapid ride of our lives. I hope to make many miles an hour. Your nerves will be tested to the utmost. Food is necessary before we start. A little supper awaits you in the dining-room. Come at once ! " and the company followed him into the apartment, to find Mrs. Parsons at the head of the table, Owny at her side.

"Friends," began the inventor, after he had motioned them to their places at the abundant board, "there is not an article of food upon this table that is not of my own invention. Of some you have partaken before, with pleasure you said at the time. Some are wholly new to you. There are articles on this table, from which, if you knew what they were in their original condition, you would turn with loathing and horror. I have passed them, however, through certain processes by virtue of which they are delicious. Out of the offal of the kitchen and the streets, I have created, as our Maker does by his processes in nature, a food for the poor which will cost almost nothing. I have transmuted even the dirt itself into delicacies. Not one solitary article of this board, I repeat," he said, with outspread hands, "but is my own invention. — Mr. Venable, ask a blessing! — I had hoped," he added, holding the minister in abeyance for a moment with his extended hand, "to have had his Excellency Gov. Magruder with us. He promised when I told him Miss Zenobia was to take part. He is detained on his plantation. — Proceed, Mr. Venable."

It was some moments before that gentleman did so : the stifled mirth of Irene Buttolph and the rest, as well as his own, making it hard to do.

"And now, friends," Mrs. Parsons said from her end of the board, before he had well finished, "Mr. Parsons says eat ; but I say, as you value your lives, don't! We don't intend to, Owny here and I, — not a single bit!" and the laughing hostess, who had welcomed them as they entered, with a comical warning of uplifted hands and shaken head, joined in their mirth, the loudest of them all, certainly the plumpest and most jovial there.

"My Ezra Micajah Papa is good, but his dinner isn't good," little Owny announced at this moment ; put up to it, it is to be feared, by her mother. It's all "*harky!*" the little beauty added with emphasis, her rosy face screwed up into a disgust comical to see, amid peals of laughter. But the inventor was used to ridicule. Seated at his end of the table, his long body stooped over his plate, taking enormous mouthfuls, as is the habit of all men who are long and gaunt, after heaping, as was also his wont, the cup and platter of every one else with more than could be consumed, Mr. Parsons set them an example of appetite. Mr. Quatty was seated near by; but he was not used to being in company, and was largely taken up with the proper disposition of his legs and hands, to say nothing of his knife and fork, breaking a glass in his confusion, for he was, in addition, always restless when separated from his horses. The only one who emulated the host in appetite was Grit. Like all boys of his hearty age, he was always ready for food. Besides, it was a midnight picnic, with a suspicion of wickedness in it; and little he understood or cared for the originals out of which the inventor's chemistry had produced the pies, cakes, preserves, soups, tarts, and delicately-browned custards, before him. The fun of the company he enjoyed incidentally: to the eating he gave his serious attention.

"You'll *till* yourself, 'ittle boy," Owny, who was seated beside him, remarked, after watching, her blue eyes opened to their widest, the way in which Grit despatched his food. Her voice was drowned in the clatter of knives and plates, as well as of laughter. Not that any one except Grit and Mr. Parsons were eating especially. With unusual interest, each in every other, everybody at table was politely offering and urging the nearest delicacies upon all in reach, declining with thanks, and making but the faintest show of partaking, in their own case; the one who entered most heartily into the fun of the hour being the wife of the host.

"Take care, Col. Roland," she cried: "that butter is only lard churned in milk. — You had better not, Miss Zenobia: that nice-looking bread is chiefly bones ground fine. — Don't, Mr. Fanthorp, as you value your life: that bronze jelly is the horns and hoofs of oxen ; I saw him crush them myself. — I wouldn't, Mr. Venable," she continued, laughing until the tears ran down her full and rosy cheeks : "as sure as you live, those cakes were cut in those beautiful shapes out of the hides of the things he slaughtered ; he soaked them in acids, and then cooked them in sirup. — Grit, my dear, that brown powder on the custards is blood burned to a crisp and then pulverized." And, amid exclamations and screams of surprise, the hour passed. Fortunately Mr. Parsons ate as swiftly as he did every thing else.

"Hurry up, my son," he said to Grit, who was not quite done. "You are the most sensible one at the table. Put any thing you like in your pocket. But come, we must go. Our trip must be done before day. Now, friends," he added in a voice and manner which was becoming more excited as the event approached, leading his guests back into the parlor, waving and hurrying them on with both his long arms, "put on your things ; and, mind, I am skipper of this cruise. If any one here is not going to obey me, instantly and absolutely and to the end, let that person go home. All who will consent to that, let them," he added, as they stood ready around him, "follow me and Capt. Chaffin."

As Mr. Parsons and the captain disappeared, Mr. Quatty suddenly placed himself between the company about to follow him, and the door. The fact is, Mr. Quatty spent his waking hours upon the seat of some vehicle or other, driving from one horse to four, and usually at full speed, all the time ; and, where there was so much around him of life and motion, his fingers itched for the reins and the whip.

"Excuse me one moment," he said, awkwardly, but none the less blocking their way out ; "whoa ! I mean, hold on a little. This," he continued, his long, loose-jointed body hung to one side, to balance his arms extended on the other, in the direction of their departed host, "this, Mr. Parsons tells us, is the inauguration of what is to be a revolution in

travel ; a grand insurrection against horses, as I understand it.
I desire to make a few remarks, ahem ! before we start, you
see. I was at one time only an oysterman, although I sometimes dealt in clams. Having become a Christian, I wish to
benefit my fellow-men. So far as I can, I never let an opportunity pass so to do. Now, friends and fellow-country-
zens, — I mean fellow-city-mens, — never mind, you know
what I am driving at. Who knows," Mr. Quatty continued,
in the tones of an orator, " to what a smash-up we are pro-
ceeding? We may all end up in eternity. A few remarks " —

" Phip Quatty, you are a fool ! " Mr. Parsons said, suddenly appearing from behind him as he stood in the door.
" Come," thrusting him aside with anxious arm, " make
haste ! It is late ! "

" Take warning ! he wanted to take Owny, but I wouldn't
let her go ; and *I* won't. You'd better not : don't go ! "
Mrs. Parsons called to them as they trooped out, standing
in the doorway laughing, and holding Owny up in her vigorous arms. It was a pretty sight, the joyous woman and her
beautiful child, as the two filled the doorway, the parlor
lamps lighting them up from behind, and making the golden
hair of the child like an aureole about its head. The party,
as they followed Mr. Parsons, looked back, scolding the
wife merrily ; for all were in highest spirits. No one hesitated, however. While they had small faith in the Terraqueous Machine, all had perfect trust in the well-known goodness of the inventor. No fear of *his* leading them into
danger.

" Now," said that gentleman when he had led them across
the entire grounds, stumbling and tripping over kegs and all
sorts of machinery and implements, " now understand. This
is the door of the shop which holds my machine. Until I
have tried it, and find that it is free from all mistake, I intend
no soul of you shall see it. I have made mistakes before,

but I am pretty sure this time. You will enter a room. After I have locked you in, and the light out, I will open another door, and hand you up by a few steps into the machine. Your part of it is covered in like an omnibus. Sit down in it, and sit still. Ready?" And, after an assurance to that effect, the inventor did as he had said, helping each up, in the darkness, into a large vehicle of some sort, with a hand which each person wondered at as it held his or hers, it was so hot and hurried.

"All in?" he called, in an eager voice. "*Do* make haste. Laugh as much as you please, only hurry. Hurry! All in?"

Then, as the company adjusted themselves as well as they could in the midnight interior, upon cushioned seats, "Phip Quatty!" they heard their host call as he shut and locked the door. There was the tramp of horses; and then, "You are not a fool at all, oh, no!" Mr. Quatty was heard to exclaim, amid the jingling of harness and the backing of horses: "Oh, not a bit, certainly not; we'll see! G'lang!" and, with the crack of a whip, the vehicle rolled out, the passengers being at the hinder end thereof.

"Strike for the beach, Phip. All right, Chaffin?" Mr. Parsons, who seemed stationed upon the step outside the door which he had closed upon them, called out.

"Ay, ay!" Capt. Chaffin was heard to reply from the front.

"Then go ahead! I'll steer when we strike the beach. Drive ahead, Quatty!"

"I do not like this. I do not like this at all!" Irene Buttolph exclaimed.

"Why, Irene!" her sister was heard in reply. "It is only a wagon drawn by horses. How fast they go! Listen. We have got on the beach. Hear how their hoofs ring on it. And how the wind whistles, and the surf roars. It is only Mr. Parsons's joke. How fast we go!"

"That will do," they heard Mr. Parsons shout. "Chaffin! Now, Chaffin, now!" and a moment after, amid a good deal of thumping upon the roof of their conveyance, as well as of creaking and cracking, they heard the same voice, "Phip Quatty!" and in rapid, excited tones, not as easily heard now in the roar of the wind and sea, "Look out! you will be run down: cast off!" The same moment Mr. Quatty could be heard yelling to his horses, and cracking his whip. Somehow the sound of hoofs was now to one side; then the voice of their driver died instantly away behind them. But the vehicle kept on, — kept on at a speed which was evidently increasing, and so on and on, in the wondering silence of all, for a while. Possibly twenty minutes may have passed; but it seemed to the passengers more than that, all attempts at conversation or amusement being held in suspense by the novelty of their situation.

"Let me out!" shrieked Irene at last, evidently struggling with her sister. "I won't hush! We are going out to sea. Help! help! If there is a gentleman here, he will break open that door! Col. Roland! Mr. Fanthorp! Mr. Venable! Mr. Parsons! Stop! let me out!" and the excited girl screamed as if beside herself.

"We *can't* stop," Mr. Parsons shouted, opening a slide in the door, and putting in his head. "I solemnly assure you there is not the least danger. We could go to sea. I intend we shall go to sea. But not yet. Don't scream so: you distract my steering. It's all right," in jubilant tones, as he shut the slide again. No wonder: the vehicle seemed to be flying over the earth; the howling of the wind and the sea swelling the horror of the darkness to those within, and the screams of Irene, after some cessation, rang loud and louder.

"Why, Irene!" her brother was heard to yell, "Hold your tongue. It's the bulliest ride you ever had. Zeo ain't afraid. You hush!" The terrified girl, however, continued to scream, until Mr. Venable, despairing of influencing the exultant inventor, tried for Capt. Chaffin.

"Captain!" he called, rising and steadying himself with difficulty in the vehicle, which swayed from side to side in what seemed to be its terrific and ever-increasing speed.

"Ay, ay! What is it, Mr. Venable?" was the reply.

"A lady is frightened; hold up!"

"Don't do it: go on!" saluted the captain's ears at the same instant, from Mr. Parsons. There was an unloosening of something in front, a creaking, a crash upon the roof, and the conveyance slowly slacked its speed; and, Irene Buttolph diminishing her outcries accordingly, both the lady and the machine came to a stop finally at the same moment.

"Chaffin," shouted Mr. Parsons from his end, "you are discharged!"

"Discharge away!" was yelled in reply from the other. (The captain explained himself to Mr. Fanthorp, the next time he met him on the streets, to this effect:—

"I knew Mr. Parsons would be dreadfully mad at my stopping you all; but the way I put it up," he argued with his two thumbs point to point, "was this. Weemen are so deelicate! Suppose it had been my wife! I thought of that, and I shut down. I tell you, *we* are tough as you please: they ain't. Deelicate is not the word for it. They are what we will be if so be we ever get to heaven. Think so?" But this explanation was some days after.)

"The next time I go," exclaimed Mr. Parsons as he un-locked the door and let them out, "I'll pick my passengers a little better!" greatly enraged.

"But it is a lady, Mr. Parsons!" Mr. Venable explained: "besides, it is a glorious success!"

"That's a fact! But keep away from the front," the inventor added sternly. "Not a soul shall see. Get in again while Chaffin and I fix some way to get you back." For the passengers had got out into the moonlight, the mounds of sand washed up by the sea being on one side of them, the surf foaming to their feet on the other. " It's a shame, a burning shame," he added, as the party got in once more, out of the wind and flying spray. " I was going to steer you all out to sea, — at least, I was thinking of doing so ! "

" Thank you, Mr. Parsons," Col. Roland and Mr. Fanthorp said in a breath, " but this will do for the present."

The truth is, Irene Buttolph had only put into screams what all had more or less felt, as they soon agreed in the excited conversation which ensued. " But how are we to get home?" was the chorus with which it ended.

" Oh ! I fixed," the inventor said, somewhat angrily, " for Phip Quatty to follow with horses in case of accident. He'll be here in an hour — no, not for about two hours," he corrected himself with vindictive pleasure. " In ten minutes more we would have turned the end of the island, and had the smooth water of the bay. This isn't a *land* wagon only, it's a *Terraqueous* Machine," he said with emphasis : " what it has done on shore isn't a circumstance to what it can do on water. Afraid? Bah ! Fiddlesticks ! Stuff and nonsense ! Con-cern Chaffin ! " Mr. Parsons added. He was guarding his passengers lest they should get out and pry into the mysteries, at Capt. Chaffin's end of the machine, of his wonderful motor. Sitting within and near the half-shut door, Mr. Venable could not help hearing an additional sentence from the lips of the excited and exasperated inventor. It was but one sentence, and spoken in a lowered voice ; but a sentence or so, and yet the alarm of Irene Buttolph was pleasure compared to his feeling at the words he heard, — words which stunned him at first. And it was not for months afterward that they ceased to shock him as at first. These words, which nothing save the disappointment could have compelled from a man like Mr. Parsons, were merely, —

" Con-cern Chaffin ! One *would* suppose a crazy wife

and two idiots for children was enough, without a fool for a fourth!"

But Mr. Venable had no time to take in the full horror of the words then. It had been singularly warm for the season of the year, almost sultry, even in that climate. While the rest were conversing together in their confinement, Mr. Venable, feeling as if he must get away from them or suffocate, broke through Mr. Parsons's resisting hands, got out, and walked down to the edge of the inrolling surf. The sky was clear, and the sea was smooth under the mild air; a thousand stars sleeping upon its slow and oil-like swell and subsidence. Low down in the northern horizon, he observed a cloud, the only one in sight, small, but singularly black. But what arrested his attention was that the cloud was continually opening to show a heart of fire, and closing again; increasing very rapidly as he gazed, the alternate blackness and brightness growing more vivid. Although the atmosphere around him was perfectly still, there was a sound of roaring in the direction of the cloud; and as if in a moment it had rushed upon them with all its lightnings. Before the observer could hasten to the machine, the wind was howling in a hurricane; and as the cry, "A norther!" came from the lips of Mr. Parsons, an arctic winter seemed to have rushed in an instant into what had been almost summer weather.

"Hustle in, hustle in, Mr. Venable," the inventor said, as the rain mingled with hail came down in torrents. "Don't be screaming in that way, Miss Irene!" he had to say it at the top of his voice, the roaring of the tempest was such. "Stuff and nonsense! It is only a norther. I knew it was coming when we stopped, and ran the invention high up the bank, out of reach of the surf. You'll find plenty of wrappings under the cushions in there."

"But when are we to get home?" Mr. Venable, being nearest to the door, remonstrated.

"Home? Fiddlesticks!" replied the irritated inventor. "Mr. Quatty's coming with his horses, as I told you. All you have got to do is to do nothing.—Is that you, Quatty? Yes, here he is now. Hitch up, man, and get these troublesome people back."

But it was daybreak when, his invention hauled slowly along the beach and into its house again, Mr. Parsons handed them out of the machine and the building which concealed it.

"Run, every soul of you, to the house!" he said, "and you'll find my wife has something, I dare say, for you to eat, although you don't deserve it."

But better than Mrs. Parsons's hot and abundant breakfast, was the glee with which she and Owny welcomed them.

"Didn't I *tell* you so!" she said, radiant with triumph. "We believe, Owny and I, in Ezra Micajah Papa; but we don't believe in his inventions, not one bit! But sit down, sit down. This is a breakfast Owny and I invented: he had nothing to do with it."

*

CHAPTER XVI.

MR. VENABLE BEGINS TO BREAK HIS SHELL TOWARD ENTERING UPON A LARGER LIFE.

GEN. BUTTOLPH had put at the disposal of his guest a young and spirited horse; but one afternoon, when Mr. Venable wished to take a ride, young Plenty was absent, and he went into the stable to saddle the horse for himself. Behind it was an open shed, into which the April sun had been shining warmly; and, as he began to saddle his horse, he heard old Plenty's voice as the aged negro sunned himself therein. What he had gathered when he first listened to the soliloquy of the poor old soul had so distressed him that he had refrained afterward from giving ear to him whenever he heard him talking to himself about the grounds. Now, however, the tones of the negro were so peculiar that he stopped to listen as the other said, —

"I'll line it out, an' you sing:" and then in a high recitative, —

> "'When I can read my title clear
> To mansions in de skies'"—

and in a cracked and feeble voice he sung the words to a familiar tune, adding at the end, "Ef you can't sing up more peart dan dat, you lazy ole creeter, you better shet up. Now den," — in high recitative again, —

> "'I'll bid far'well to ebbry fear,
> An' wipe my weepin' eyes.'"

And yet again the weak and trembling voice of the solitary worshipper arose in song. There was such sincerity in
this prayer-meeting of which old Plenty was both congregation and leader, that the other listened to verse after verse
alternately lined out and sung. The old negro never failed
to rebuke himself between the lining-out and the singing;
but he was cruelly unjust, for he was evidently doing his best,
feeble as it was, every time.

"Now," he said at last, "I is goin' to try an' lead dis here
meetin' in prar; an' when I pray, what I want you to do is to
pray! Ef you can't sing," he added with sarcastic severity,
"try an' see, you mis'rable sinner, ef you can't pray anyhow.
Don't you go to lyin' to your Marster, makin' believe to pray
when you know you ain't prayin'.' "

But the listener made haste to leave; for, from the beginning, the supplicant made such importunate entreaties for
his "weeked mars general," for "dat highty-flighty Miss
Reny," that he wanted to hear no more; but, as he led his
horse out, he could not help hearing one thanksgiving, so
hearty was it, for "dat blessed angel sent to save dis house,
my Miss Zeo: you is mighty sensible to send her, Lord;"
and Mr. Venable rode away with food for reflection.

The April sun had gone behind clouds as he left the
grounds, and it was not of Zeo Buttolph that he was thinking.

"It was a terrible shock when I heard Mr. Parsons say
that of Clara Chaffingsby," he said to himself as he rode, unconsciously imitating the negro in his conference with himself, "to know that she is an "— But he could not repeat,
even to himself, such a word of one so beautiful.

"It is *I* who am the idiot," he thought. "I might have
known it a hundred times over from what people hinted to
me before I saw her; from her childish way when I did;"
and he was filled with self-contempt until a tender and loving pity instead, for the poor girl, flooded his heart. "By
the by," he soliloquized, "that must be the reason Miss Irene

has been so disdainful and sarcastic with me of late;" and he felt his cheeks burn.

Touching his horse with the spur, he galloped as if to escape from himself along the hard beach, not drawing rein until he was miles away from St. Jerome. On his left hand was the dreary expanse of sand, which composed the island: not a tree was in sight. Outside the suburbs of the city not a house was to be seen, great or small; nothing but the sandy surface heaped into hillocks or ridged into long lines as the withdrawing sea had left it, with here and there a pool of blackish water. A scanty tuft of grass appeared now and then, diversified with prickly pears, chapparal bushes, mesquite shrubs.

"The grass is coarse, and the miserable shrubs are black and contorted, from eternal wrestling with winds and water," he reflected as he rode. "They cling none the less to the sand, fighting desperately for dear life as if they thought life was worth it!"

The sea stretched out to the dim horizon on his right, but not a sail was in sight. A dull, leaden day rested upon it all, through which the sea-gulls flew heavily as if their wings were clogged; and he turned his horse at last, and rode slowly homeward.

"I thought Gen. Buttolph was one of the noblest as well as most genial of men," he said as his head fell upon his bosom. "For so many years I have been shut up to hard study and intense moral purpose, and how I relished, by way of variety, a man who seemed to take the world indolently. So splendid a specimen of flesh and blood was a relief to me after exclusive devotion to intellect and soul. I enjoyed such a vigorous instance of the present, after going back so unceasingly to the apostles, or forward to the Judgment Day. The persons and things I have studied about so long, glimmered like unreal ghosts in comparison with such a man. He seemed as generous as he was rich, so genial and chiv-

alrous too, and in such easy reach : it required no exertion
to believe in him.   And now?"

He recalled the stupor of his host during the first night
of the storm at sea, nor did he admire as much as before
the glowing cordiality of the general's face : a ruddy hue
may have other sources, he thought, than the heart, and purple is not always the emblem of a king.

He remembered times at table when the general and his
daughters seemed not as much inclined to talk as usual;
but he remembered that when Miss Irene was less brilliant
than common, her sister had taken more part in conversation ; a weight in what she said from her position, as really
the mistress of the house, at the end of the table, which had
made him eager for more acquaintance with her than had
seemed possible, she was generally so busy.

"I thought that poor idiot was beautiful," he said as he
rode along; "and she has beauty, but no mind.   And I admired Miss Irene for her talking, her singing, her laughter,
her accomplishments, her audacity ; but I wonder how much
heart she has."   For he had begun to be surprised that Miss
Irene should find so much pleasure in the company of Mr.
Fanthorp.   That gentleman, having of late taken the general's plantation in hand, was, on that account, very often at
the house.   He talked business with Gen. Buttolph, smok-
ing with him upon the veranda, of an evening; but he.
always came into the parlor before he left, and his coming
was the signal for an hour or two of mirth with whoever was
there, usually Miss Irene.   "I like fun as much as anybody," Mr. Venable continued his meditations; "and he is
a perfect mimic, and the most amusing of men.   Yet I
wonder Miss Irene doesn't get tired of it; but she does not.
I can hear her laughter after I have gone to bed."   The
beach was the only drive — and there is not a finer in the
world — of St. Jerome ; and many persons were out upon it
that afternoon, for the norther had been the expiring breath

of winter, and the weather was like that of summer. As he
rode homeward he lifted his hat to more than one party
meeting him on horseback and in carriages. Suddenly he
saw Col. Roland driving toward him in an open buggy with
a pair of blooded horses, Gov. Magruder seated beside him.
They were so absorbed, the colonel talking, the other listening, that they hardly looked at him in passing. By this
time he had learned enough to explain and confirm what he
had unintentionally overheard the night he stood at Gen.
Buttolph's gate.

"And here is this Roland," Mr. Venable said to himself
bitterly, "as polished a gentleman as one cares to see, a
genuine poet too; and, under it all, a scheming politician.
He is paying his court to Miss Irene, and he does it amazingly well. How jealous he is of Mr. Fanthorp! I wonder
if any woman can love a man whom she hears so unmercifully ridiculed and mimicked as he is by the other. But,"
Mr. Venable announced to himself, "I, for one, will not interfere. Whichever of the two wins her, can have her, so far
as I am concerned. But Gov. Magruder" —

A fierce jealousy of that dignitary arose on the instant in
his bosom.

"They barely condescended," he said, "to see me in
passing. The colonel is tutoring him, I dare say, for his visit
to Miss Zeo to-night; and what am *I* to them? to them?
What am I to Gen. Buttolph? to Farce Fanthorp? Good
heavens! what am I in any practical sense to anybody?
And how can I be any thing that is strong and manly to
her? It is disreputable here in the South not to go to some
church; and so they come and hear me when the weather
suits. Look here!" and he turned upon himself after the
example of old Plenty, "you simple soul, what change does
your poetizing in the pulpit work in these men, in anybody?
I am nothing to them at last, but a younger sort of Father
Fethero."

As the two gentlemen drove rapidly by, it had not been at the colonel, but at his companion sitting erect, handsome, attentive, beside him, that Mr. Venable had glanced. The governor was so rich, had such a position, such brilliant prospects, was so widely popular, was, above all, so certain to win Miss Zeo, that, as by an instinct of nature, it was a hungry glance he cast at him.

"Small wonder," he endeavored to console himself, "that he should seize so cordially upon every one, should listen so eagerly to everybody. It is the natural craving of emptiness ; but of an emptiness which no more retains than it returns any thing. Every thing he owns was bequeathed him ; and, apart from his father and Col. Roland, what is he?" But he envied him none the less, nor was it the first time substance has envied shadow, and influence affluence ; and yet even then the magnetism of the other had not changed from attraction to repulsion : for his life, Mr. Venable could not help liking the man. The repulsion was from himself instead, and somewhat as, when a man is dying, the soul repels from itself the dead body.

"As Heaven helps me," he said, "I will see if I cannot make myself felt !" and, spurring past Gen. Buttolph's house, he continued down the beach. Young Plenty had waited long and anxiously for him, when late that night he returned, and gave his horse up to him at the general's gate.

CHAPTER XVII.

HAVING REFERENCE TO A VARIETY OF PERSONS AND OF THINGS.

YOU must allow me, sir," Gen. Buttolph said to Mr. Venable one evening a few weeks after this, as he and his daughter Irene accompanied him home from prayer-meeting, " to congratulate you upon the vigor with which you have gone to work of late. Your sermons are exceedingly practical and excellent. I hope you will spare no one. I am glad, too, that you have established the Bethel for seamen, and that you have enlisted Zeo in your efforts for the poor and neglected children of our city. You are doing a good work, sir, a great work, sir! Do not overtask yourself. If you need money call on me, call on me."

"You know I rarely go to prayer-meeting: I'm afraid of that ridiculous Mr. Quatty," Irene Buttolph said to Mr. Venable, as they seated themselves in the parlor after they had got home; "but I'm glad I went. It was admirable! Where you described the old apostle in his prison at Rome, after so many years of hard work, — forsaken by Demas, — soon to be killed, it was grand! I could have cried; but I was expecting Phil Quatty to pop up every moment. Besides, just as I was about to cry I saw Mrs. Chaffingsby. Did you notice her, Mr. Venable? While the tears were running down her odd little face, she was looking up and about the ceiling and the walls, as if she were taking their measure for something. But I am in good earnest," the

young lady added as seriously as possible, "it was excellent!
—your remarks, I mean." For, after a period of coldness
amounting at times almost to rudeness toward her guest, the
young lady had re-acted into a measure of unusual friendli-
ness of late.

"It was most excellent," Gen. Buttolph added, taking,
as he said it, a key from his vest-pocket, "very good indeed.
I have always admired the devotion of that man to his Master. Paul was a large man, I am sure. Peter, I feel certain,
was a little fellow, a whipper-snapper sort of a person.
Your remarks were good, very good indeed;" and the general had arisen as he spoke, and was rubbing his upper lip
with the key, twisting it around with his forefinger through
the loop thereof, passing it from hand to hand. His younger
daughter said nothing. Her head was drooped as she sat;
but her eyes and her mind were upon her father at the
moment, rather than upon Paul or Peter.

"Thank you," said their pastor: "that is one reason why
I am glad, general, to accept your invitation, and spend a
few days with you at your plantation. I want to have Father
Fethero preach for me while I'm away."

"Father Fethero!" exclaimed Irene. "What, that hor-
rid old man? Why, Mr. Venable! The idea! Please don't.
Commodore Grandheur would have to be carried home from
church on a shutter. It would make even Mr. Nogens say
something."

"I consulted the commodore," Mr. Venable replied;
"and, although he was surprised at first, he cordially con-
sented. He has been exceedingly pleasant in his intercourse
with me of late. Mr. Nogens also: I asked him."

"The idea!" Irene persisted, her hands in the air.
"I can imagine that poor old soul rising in our pulpit, with
his red and white hair, his bronzy face, his blue spectacles,
his dingy white cravat, his shabby old— What did Mr.
Nogens say?"

"He said yes," Mr. Venable answered, with a smile. "And I am glad," he added gravely and warmly, "that I can show Father Fethero this mark of respect. · We were speaking of Paul," he continued ; "and here is a man who has worked just as hard, as long, and as single-heartedly too, as Paul, and for the same Master. He is old and poor. I am afraid he has fewer friends even than the apostle. With all my soul I honor him, respect him, love him, think myself unworthy to preach while he sits there so humbly Sunday after Sunday." As he said it he was aware that the other sister had lifted her head, and was looking at him with a new interest in her eyes, — a look which thrilled him with pleasure.

"You are right, perfectly right, entirely right," Gen. Buttolph added, walking about the room in a somewhat purposeless way, playing nervously with the key in his hand. " I honor you ; I mean, I honor him : that is, I honor you both. Isn't it rather late? We must not allow you to overtalk yourself, Mr. Venable ; and, young ladies, it is time you were in bed. I prefer Paul to Peter, myself ; " and, like his daughter Zeo in that, the mind of the general seemed to be in the key which he was passing eagerly from hand to hand. Had it been the costliest of jewels, the heart of the poor girl, from under her eyelids drooped again, could not have been fastened more eagerly upon it. No wonder! The young people were hardly out of the room, before the key was rattling in his eagerness against the keyhole of his sideboard in the dining-room adjoining. More like a tiger upon its prey than a human being, the general seized upon the heavy decanter of cut glass, did not take time for a goblet in his terrible thirst, placed the vessel to his greedy lips, and drank and drank, as if it were life and not death which he was drinking. And while he drank, Zeo, in her own room, with rapid hands had hastily changed her dress for the night. Then she knelt beside her bed in prayer.

It was more than the woman grasping the mantle of Christ;
for she was entreating for another, not herself, and for that
other under the curse of a malady the most hopeless of all.
As she prayed, she sank down from beside the bed, and
lay at last, with dishevelled hair, upon the floor. The
woman of Syrophenicia did not call to Christ so importunately; for this was no child for whom she prayed, but a
grown man, diseased and dying. Nor could any Mary of
them all have held so firmly to the feet of Jesus, since this
woman knew, unlike them, that he had not merely risen
from the dead, but had also ascended to heaven, — was not
a man merely, but likewise the Son of God. She had not
been to prayer-meeting that night, occupied in some way
with her brother at home; but ah, how she clung to God in
prayer now! Thoughts of her mother, in white, and singing
among the saints, were in her mind; but that mother could
not have sung to Christ there with such earnestness as this
daughter, in her night-clothing, besought him. There was
the difference, however, of utter weariness at length; and she
arose, and went into her sister's room. Irene was already
asleep. Zeo shrank from disturbing her, sleeping so sweetly,
her cheek in her hand. She stooped over her, and kissed
her. Her tears — she did not intend it — dropped upon her
sister's face. In a moment Irene was sitting up in bed,
alarmed, enraged, then weeping hysterically.

"O Zeo! why won't you let me alone?" she said. "If
you must kill yourself, do let me live! I know; but what
can I do? what can you do? It's night after night, night
after night! We've begged and implored him. I'm desperate. Go to bed."

"Irene, sister," Zeo began.

"You are losing your senses!" Irene continued, her
eyes suddenly becoming dry. "I tell you I cannot endure it. Zeo," she added fiercely, "I'm driven to desperation. The next time Col. Roland asks me, I'll say yes.

There is Mr. Fanthorp, too. He is full of his nonsense; but he is a splendid business man. See how he is managing papa's plantation. You said so yourself;" and, with a singular change in her passion, the girl laughed as hysterically as she had wept before. "Take the governor, Zeo: take him, — take him, and be done with it; and let us get away from papa. Nonsense!" she said, as her sister blushed, "I know what you are thinking about: he is no worse than men generally. Col. Roland has only asked me eleven times; and I'll take him at the dozenth. If you *will* talk!" she added.

"Reny, dear," her sister said, rising from the bed on which she had seated herself, "I felt so desolate, that was all. We can do nothing. Perhaps God can. Won't you pray to him too?"

"Zeo, you are a goose," the other replied, settling herself comfortably in bed: "you *have* lost your wits. The Nautilus spoiled you. You think it was your prayers, that trip, which kept the old boat from sinking. I wish it had sunk, with all my heart. I don't want to live. What can we do? Go to bed, and go to sleep. I'm too sleepy even to cry."

It was an hour after that, and Zeo was seated by her father, lying as usual on the sofa in the dining-room. The decanter lay broken upon the floor, her father snoring heavily in his drunken sleep. Zeo had loosened his neckcloth, and propped up the heavy head, as usual; and there she sat stupid with grief and weariness. The air was foul with the debauchery, so to speak, of the smell of liquor; it enclosed the girl as in its immorality, and she shuddered and shrank. At last she started, as the door slowly opened. It was Grit, his clothes only half on, his shoes in his hand, his hair, and his face as well, telling of the sleep from which he had just arisen.

"I was dead asleep," he said, "but you and sister talking

wakened me up. I tried to go to sleep, but I can't. I thought I'd steal down and stay with you." He said it in a common and even coarse way. Sentiment may be found in the bosoms of boys of a lighter build ; but Grit possessed no article of the kind. He was a bad boy, in virtue of a stronger will worse than even the negroes ; and not one of these knew him better than did, by this time, the pure young girl by whom he stood.

"Grit," she said at last, putting her arms around his waist as he fastened up his suspenders, "I never intend to call you Grit, again, as long as I live. You are my brother Theodore ; and you are all I have to lean on in this world. Grit," very wearily indeed, "do you believe in God?"

"I don't know nothing about God," he said, as he buttoned up his vest. "What do you girls suppose a fellow thinks about such stuff? But I tell you what it is, Zeo," he added, pushing her off a little, the better to complete his toilet, "tell you what it is, Zeo, I believe in *you*. And," he continued, "I am getting to believe in Mr. Venable. You know he never goes riding these days, nor fishing, but he wants me to go along. We race when we get out of sight, Zeo ; and you bet I beat him ! and he talks to me, tells me stories he has read somewhere ; the best fellow I know. I told you how he has me up in his room, and shows me every book he has that's got pictures in it, — hang them that haven't ! He plays checkers with me, and says he'll teach me chess. I like him. I say, look here ! is there any cake handy anywhere?"

The two must have been up late that night. The general, however, was looking about as well as usual the next morning, at breakfast.

"I wish, general," Mr. Venable said, in his ignorance, although not without his fears, as he rose from the table, "that I had your splendid constitution, you look so ruddy and strong. But I'm afraid Miss Zeo does not sleep well.

—You must have been dreaming of your many conquests, Miss Zeo. Commodore Grandheur admires you exceedingly. Mr. Parsons, too, told me last night after prayer-meeting, that you were the only sensible person in his machine the day we took that ride."

"And what about Old Ugly?" Irene asked slyly. " Don't blush so, Zeo. If the governor is successful, they need not call you Old Mrs. Ugly, you know."

" I fear," added Mr. Venable, eager to change the subject, "that Mr. Parsons thinks so highly of you because, unobserved of all of us, perhaps, you ate as heartily as Grit here, at the banquet Mr. Parsons gave us. By the by, he insists on our taking another ride when he has made some alteration in his invention. The next time it shall be, he says, by day. There must be something wonderful in it. He said we made twenty miles an hour. Miss Zeo, could I see you one moment?" he added.

"Secrets from me?" Irene called out after them, as they left the table. She was in radiant spirits, laughing and talking about their visit to the plantation, the magnolia-trees, the negroes, and the mocking-birds, from the moment blessing had been asked.

" I wanted to ask you "— the gentleman and lady said it in the same breath, each holding out to the other a little roll of money as they entered the hall, closing the breakfast-room door behind them.

"What *I* wished," the gentleman said, laughing, " was to beg you to take this money, and be so good as to get it, in some way, to Father Fethero's daughter."

" He does need a new suit badly. It was the very thing I was going to ask you to do. But, thank you, I will," Zeo added. " I had already talked with Miss Aurelia — she had spoken with me, I mean — about it. Thank you, I will attend to it to-day."

" I wonder what I have done," Mr. Venable said ruefully,

as he gave her the money and took his hat from the rack :
"Miss Aurelia is very cold toward me of late. I would
gladly apologize and correct it, if I knew. Can't you find
out, Miss Zeo?"

"I'll try: good-morning," and Zeo closed the door after
him with a smile. But why is it — oh, why? — that, in the
small affairs of life, a woman is sure to know all about a thing
when one of our pre-eminently superior sex, standing as
near the thing, whatever it is, as she, remains as ignorant as
a fool? It is not proper that a man, compared to any
woman, should seem like a donkey in contrast with an angel.
The man may not know he is an ass, but the woman does ;
and it makes her conceited, — spoils her for the service of
man.

In the climate of which we are speaking, twilight is a thing
unknown ; it is either day, or it is night. So of the seasons
of the year. Winter had gone as with a bound, and summer
had come without any transition of spring, as Mr. Venable
walked, that day, rapidly along toward Father Fethero's
humble home. Looking around, and observing no one in
sight, he whistled as he trod the green grass, looked upon
the blue sea, saw how rapidly the leaves were unfurling their
flags upon china-tree and oleander. Driving unpleasant
thoughts from his mind as by main force, he endeavored to
encourage himself, instead, as he went. There was, for instance, a deepening gravity in the manner of his host, which
he liked. The general was plainly becoming, under his min-
istrations, whatever old Plenty had said, more thoughtful. If
he were only prepared to speak in prayer-meeting, he would
be such an additional bulwark against Mr. Quatty, to say
nothing else. Mr. Venable resolved to urge his duty upon
him at the earliest opportunity.

The visitor lightened up Father Fethero's house im-
mensely that morning. It was a poor place, scantily furnished. The half-dozen grandchildren did not seem, some-

how, as happy as children should be, when the visitor went into the little garden in which their grandfather was busily at work with them. At sight of him, the little ones huddled together, as is the way with things that are feeble and frightened. The faces of all were timid, and yet too hard for children. Care and poverty had grimed itself into the grain of their skins, the glance of their eyes; there was that which was lank and hopeless in their very hair; and their grandfather was very rusty indeed. The straw hat on his head, as well as the foxy black suit he wore, should have been retired into the seclusion of the ash-barrel or the paper-mill years before.

"I don't know,—I do not know," Father Fethero said, when his young brother had told of his intended absence, and begged him to supply his pulpit. It was not so much that the old man was slowly thinking over the pile of yellow sermons in the hair trunk up-stairs, trying to recall any that would do; nor that afterward, as he leaned upon his spade, he went deliberately over, in his mind, his best suit as when he had examined it last Sunday morning. He could not recall the suitable sermon on the instant; and he remembered that the seams up the elbows of his coat were, even to his dimmed eyes, really—really— For years now, and to every proposition, he had always said at first, "I don't know,—I do not know." But then the other part of his ritual came in; and after a half-hour of talk, he said, "Well, brother, if it is so, I will stand in the gap. Yes, stand in the gap. I will stand in the gap." That matter being disposed of, the two leaned against the palings,—Mr. Venable having too much sense to go into the house at that hour of the morning,—and refreshed themselves with a little tough theology. And then Mr. Venable spoke with eagerness in regard to the new work upon which he had lately entered, and of his joyous hopes of success. But Father Fethero, though much brightened up by the visit, and the liberal compensation he was to receive, could not in conscience agree with the other.

"It may be so, may be so.   Young men are hopeful," he said at length; "but," with his sorrowful spectacles fastened upon the sea beyond, "I plainly perceive a gloom, brother Venable.   The god of this world, the power which now worketh in the children " —

"Is not half as strong as our God," the younger man interrupted heartily, but respectfully too. " Pardon me, Father Fethero, but I have a sermon to write.   I wish you would lend me one of yours."

Mr. Venable said it as he laughed and walked off.   He tried to get up his whistling again, but that which haunted him day and night would not be whistled off when he tried that once more.

"O God!" the man said to himself, with sudden violence, "what does he or I understand of theology or religion? What do we know, poor fools, about God?   Hers was such a beautiful face !   So pure !   Such perfect grace and charm ! Surely the angels have not eyes deeper or more lovely ! And is music so sweet as her voice?   I can never see such another.   It is impossible for such an ideal to be seen twice.   An idiot?   What can God mean by such a deed?" And he laid his hand upon his mouth to crush back the blasphemies which arose in his heart.   But summer, to him, had vanished as he strode along.   All that he could do was to hurl himself into his next sermon.   It should be on the mysterious doings of God.   He would try to convince others, perhaps he might convince himself.   Yet, strange to say, he had no sooner settled on a text than, as he walked away, Zeo Buttolph, in most illogical fashion, constituted all the consecutive heads thereof; and the application was, that in some way, some divine way, Providence would vindicate itself in regard to Clara Chaffingsby in the end, especially in regard to Zeo and himself.

In due time Father Fethero received, in a delicately-worded note from anonymous ladies, a good deal more than enough to get a superfine suit. It was handed respectfully to him over the fence, as he worked, by a negro whom he did not know, although the man, taking off his hat as he did so, — it was young Plenty, in fact, — evidently knew him. As Mr. Venable constantly said to himself, this negro resembled a statesman, if only in his gravity and silence; and a statesman could not have presented his credentials as ambassador to a king with more dignity. The note was weightier than is generally the case with communications bearing the spidery handwriting in which it was addressed. The old man read it doubtfully through his blue spectacles; but somehow they grew dim, and he tried to read it without his glasses. · Adjusting his spectacles again, he studied the writing, and then the coins of gold, as if the one had been a passage from his neglected Hebrew Bible, and the other specimens of the mintage of King David.

"No, my dear Jane," he said at last, after days of consultation with his widowed and sad-visaged daughter, " I will do as I said at first. The children must have shoes and many other things. Your dress is not suitable for a minister's daughter. No one would ever notice the pants. I will compromise, to please you, on the vest, if you select a cheap one. But a coat will do. I would prefer, in any case, to get into the pulpit before the mass of the congregation arrive. And I never like to go down from the pulpit until they are pretty much all gone. I have heard things which have hurt me when, after preaching, I have mingled with a retiring congregation. Their backs were toward me as they went. The pants are not at all needed. All that will be seen of me over the pulpit cushions will be the coat. No, Jane, no. But you may get me a new cravat. One will do. Can you recall, Jane, any one of my sermons which you would prefer I should preach? The people of

the First Church are critical to a sinful degree. Please
keep the children as quiet as you can to-day. I may have
to re-write my sermon. — Run out and play, little ones : summer has come." So saying, he went to his little room up-
stairs, and, placing an old Bible upon the one hide-bottomed
chair in the room, he knelt down upon a little spot already
worn white in the rag carpet thereby, intending to engage in
prayer in a certain set order of invocation, adoration, thanksgiving, confession, supplication. But his course was at last as
illogical as that of his visitor ; for, laying his old cheek
upon the book, he could only weep. He was merely a
homely old man, and very poor : yet who will undertake to
swear that the prophets and apostles were always as grand of
aspect as painters and sculptors would have us believe ?

.

CHAPTER XVIII.

IN WHICH WE DESCEND INTO THE CHEMISTRY OF ELOQUENCE,
AND LEARN HOW AN ORATION IS PREPARED.

A MORE sincere and every way excellent man than Mr.
Phip Quatty never lived, nor a more thoroughly uneducated one; and a more sensible man you never knew.
In the dialect of St. Jerome, "If ever a man had what you
may call good, strong, hard horse-sense, Quatty's your man."
As all admitted, however, there was that fatal exception which
was always stated in making out this verdict: the individual
in question "would speak." As has been already remarked,
there were many excellent private members in that, as there
are in every church, whose remarks at prayer-meetings met
with the cordial approval of all; but Mr. Quatty was an
oddity, a wholly exceptional case. Mr. Venable begged
him in private, and almost with tears in his eyes, — for it was
a very serious matter indeed, — not to make remarks, yet
entreated him in vain. Mr. Ezra Micajah Parsons had patented a variety of railway-brakes among other things; but
he failed ignominiously in devising any mode of stopping
Mr. Quatty, and never had Mr. Parsons given his mind more
vigorously to any thing. Mrs. Chaffingsby became herself
a picture of disgust in the framing of her pew "at meeting," whenever Mr. Quatty arose to speak. Mr. Parsons and
herself, as members of the same church with the offender,
had a strong aversion to his peculiarity. Commodore Grand-

heur had an alarming way of growing purple as to his face when angry, and bristling as to his heavy white moustache, and demonstrative as to his still heavier gold-headed cane. It was not every one who dared face the commodore when the veins about his bald head became blue and swollen. After every attempt of Mr. Phip Quatty to "make a few remarks" at any church-meeting, the commodore would roll down, so to speak, upon the culprit in a thunder-storm even more terrible than the one before ; and yet what good or evil did his almost apoplectic expostulations do? Not a bit. To Mr. Quatty, at least when the next opportunity to speak was come, the vehement denunciations were no more than the puffs of smoke from the cigar of the last passer-by. Mr. Quatty *would* speak.

It was very remarkable. Every Wednesday night he went from the livery-stable of which he was the energetic owner, to prayer-meeting, as fully resolved as any man could be, that he would not say a word. Alas ! the lights, the singing, the prayers, the reading by the pastor of some specially striking scripture, most of all, the exhortations of some brother present, would be sure to stir him up, and altogether beyond his own control ; and in spite of himself, as well as of all the world beside, speak he must, and would, and did.

He was, as has been described, a tall man, long, lean, sunburned by reason of unceasing exposure with his horses, which, by the by, were so many manias to him, only less than his speeches. Restless of eye, generous to an absurdity with his money, whoever wanted it, with a shrewd and kindly face, he had but one fault, — he would speak ! Nor was that a fault when you came to know the reason prompting the simple-hearted man : really it was an excellence instead.

The fact that Mr. Quatty was one of the shrewdest of men in every thing else caused this insanity of his to stand out in grotesque contrast upon the daily background of his otherwise uniform and vigorous common sense. Explanation is easy. He had heard a vast deal of oratory, often of an exceedingly florid kind, on Fourths of July, during political campaigns, on Masonic anniversaries, and the like; and whiskey could not have so intoxicated him. Not that the subject-matter of the eloquence was of the slightest interest to him. A breathless listener from first to last, by far the most excited hearer present, his one thought through all was, —

"Oh, if I could only get a show at this crowd in that way! Yes; and, if I could just get to going, I could pile on the agony higher than *you* are doing, you bet!"

In other words, to Mr. Quatty, public speaking meant declamation, and declamation meant something immeasurably more than ordinary language. What so poor and mean as the daily talk he held along the streets, now with this one man, and now with that! In contrast, what so glorious as for him to have to do with a thousand people at once, his talk swelling into a sort of thunder-storm proportionately! But Dr. Burrows, his previous pastor, had stimulated his hallucinations into almost madness. A very *ore rotundo* speaker Dr. Burrows was. Portly of person, powerful of voice, orbicular of gesture, the solemnity of his themes gave a sanction to his oratory which made it a matter of conscience, in addition to all else, that Mr. Quatty should imitate and surpass it. He would be more than President of the United States if he could present truth in that way, now sinking hand and voice into the still small whisper of thrilling appeal, and now — and this he liked best — crashing upon the people in thunder of righteous denunciation.

"Ah, me!" Mr. Quatty had many a time groaned to himself on leaving church, "if I could get up as high as the doctor did, I could have got up fifty times higher, and I could have come down upon those people a hundred times harder. You bet! No, not bet: it's Sunday, and it's a ser-

mon. But, oh, if I only had any sort of a show, — but one
fair chance, — just one ! "

And thus it came about that he arose one eventful day
at an unusually early hour. He had been very wakeful all
night, so that when his wife groaned as he got up, " O
Phip, Phip, I wouldn't if I was you ! " and her husband
replied, " Can't help it, Sally," it was but in continuation
of a conversation to a like effect which had been kept up
intermittently through the hours of darkness gone before.

Mrs. Quatty sat up in bed, arranged her hair a little,
rubbed her eyes, which had evidently been deprived of their
lawful rest, and made one last, despairing appeal, —

" Oh, how I do *wish* you wouldn't ! "

" Can't help it, Sally." The words were few ; but it was
in substance all Mr. Quatty ever said, in that connection, to
her or to any one else. They were few and final, because
they were the utterance to others of what was to the man
himself the decree of destiny, necessity, nature. *He* did
not desire to make remarks in meeting. A vast deal rather
would he listen, instead, to anybody else you might mention.
" There is nothing I have to do I hate more," he often said.
It was the grief of his life. " I would rather, any day, have
an overseer take a rawhide to me," he was continually observing. By an inscrutable doom, more perplexing and
painful to him than it could possibly be to any other, he
" had to speak," and that was all there was of it. Mr.
Quatty had never read of the Virgin at Delphi uttering
oracles sorely against her will, or he might have quoted that
precedent. As it was, his reply, as final in its tone as in all
else, so cool because concerning something in relation to
which all discussion was idle, — his reply expressed it all, —

" Can't help it, Sally."

The morning alluded to was that of the day upon which
it had been arranged by Mr. Quatty's pastor that he should
have a hall engaged for the purpose, and an entire evening

to and for himself. Then and there he was to make fully, finally, once and for all, the remarks which he had so often and faithfully tried to make in prayer-meetings and else-where, and tried in vain. Although the plan had been sug-gested by his pastor cautiously and with hesitation, lest it should hurt his parishioner's feelings, Mr. Quatty had con-sented to it promptly, cordially, almost rapturously. It was precisely the thing he had desired for years.

"I have never had any show, you see, sir," he explained to Mr. Venable at the end of their conversation. "People all around me are going to ruin; and even when you get such people into a meeting, somehow what is said does not hit a man of the crowd as a hammer hits a nail on the head. It may all be very good, but it is mighty misty and round-about. Somehow it don't hit so as to hurt, and people go away exactly as they came. That is the reason I get up. Something must be said. I would as lief have a hand chopped off as to have it to do; but if nobody else does it, I *must!*"

"But why not say it all," his friend asked, "to people in conversation? You have many wicked men coming into your stable every day, you tell me: why not seize an op-portunity then, and have a private talk? I find *I* can do more with a person in such conversation than I can from the pulpit." The other made prompt reply, —

"Because, being a minister, they don't interrupt, you see, any more then than when you are preaching. Talk? I try to do so every day of my life. But the fellow, whoever it is, will interrupt. He is sure to say, 'O Quatty! let me have a horse and buggy, and go;' or, 'Stuff, Quatty, nonsense! if you care so for my soul, why won't you let me have that ten dollars?' I *do* let them have the ten dollars, — fifty, for that matter," — Mr. Quatty added, "except when I know for dead certain it will go for whiskey or gambling or some-thing worse. No, sir! and twenty to one, as sure as I begin to talk, the man will say, 'Well, now, you have had *your* say, let *me* talk;' and then he will fly off with some joke or story, or start me talking horse-flesh. What I want, you see, is to get at people when I can say all I've got to say, without anybody putting in. My idea is to get a crowd to sit still as they do for you at church, and listen. Then I only want a good fair start, and I can always have that by beginning with my being an oysterman, and all I want is to get to going, you know! I have so much to say," he added with almost tears in his earnest eyes, "that if I get the hang of the thing, the swing of it, you know, the *rush* of the thing, you understand," with an illustrative gesture of both of his long arms, as if he were pushing some vehicle rapidly before him, " the gush and rush and roar of the thing, I could make a speech that would *tell*, — yes, sir-ee bob, tell like thunder!"

And now the morning of the day set for Mr. Quatty to speak had come. Full notice had been given in all the city papers, Col. Roland adding in his sheet a special editorial in reference to "Mr. Quatty, our well-known, estimable, and *enterprising* fellow-citizen," the subject of the commendation as ignorant as a lamb of the sarcasm of the colonel's Italics. Never had his many friends seemed so zealous in his affairs. Profane men and gamblers as many of them were, they had cheerfully contributed toward posters advertising the meeting in the hall, — posters exhausting the resources, both as to largest type and most vivid colors, of all the printing-offices in the city. No wonder Mr. Quatty was unable to sleep the night before. Nor is it to be wondered, that on rising, as we have said, he resisted his wife to the last as he put on his best clothes at once, so as to give his whole mind to the matter without the interruption of having to dress again at night. Immediately after breakfast he had his span of "crack" grays harnessed to his own private buggy, and drove off to the sea-beach to be by himself, and to think.

It was a morning bright, cool, crisp enough to inspire the

dullest man living. Mr. Quatty's soul was charged and surcharged with an abundance of things to say, — things to him of the highest conceivable beauty and sublimity, things which held and stirred his own heart beyond any thing else in the world. There was plenty to say, no fear of that; and no man could be in more vigorous, even rugged health: the blood coursing swiftly, that bracing morning, through his brain, enabling him to dare and to do every thing, as it did through his stomach, enabling him to digest every thing. As he struck the beach he shook the reins eagerly. " G'lang ! " he said to his grays; and as they sped along in the fringe of the surf, " That is it," he said aloud, " that's the way to get to going in my speech, — the way to get the rush of the thing. And now let me study."

But the orator found it almost impossible to do so: he could not help going over in mind his many past efforts and failures; then he pictured to himself the hall as it would be that night, the lights and the crowd, the deathlike stillness of attention, the deepening interest, the tears of all present as he proceeded, the applause when he should end, the congratulations of his friends, the notices in the papers next day; and more, far more than all, the good he would have done in general, and to certain specially " hard cases" who were sure to be in attendance. As his horses flew along the beach, their driver continually shaking the reins and urging them on in his eagerness, Mr. Quatty had never been so excited in his life.

" The morning I was to marry was not a circumstance to it," he said; "not even the day I joined the church. But look here, Quatty," he continued, " this isn't studying your speech. Hold up a moment," he said aloud, and he reined in his grays until they came to a stand : " let me imagine all the people there, still as mice, and attentive as you please. I wonder if the hall will be crowded. Perhaps some will have to sit on the platform : never mind. Whoa, hold up ! let me begin at the beginning."

Now, as we know, Mr. Quatty always began his remarks in public by telling of having once been an oysterman, and a rather disreputable one ; also of his having been rescued from his evil courses by the intervention of a stranger who had told him, somewhat singularly, that he perceived that he, Mr. Quatty, was a gentleman and a scholar. It is not improbable that Mr. Quatty had made a hundred efforts to speak, and every time he had begun with these facts ; but somehow he always broke down almost immediately after stating them, whereas he had always regarded them in theory as but the safe beginning of the rousing address he intended to make. " I was once," he now rehearsed, " an oysterman, that I've got pat ; then that man, and how I said that I was *not* a gentleman and a scholar, pat as you please. Now, here is just where I begin to break down : it's the weak place in the harness. I must have something strong to say exactly there. Can't you stop your stamping and pawing? Whoa, I say ! Let me see, let me see." At this juncture a sea-gull swooped by, and so near the heads of his pair, that, eager for the least pretext to do so, they started off on a run, jerking the reins out of their driver's hands. There was not much danger, seeing that the ocean was on one side of the beach, and that the sand was heaped up twenty feet high on the other. The horses, however, were, as well as their driver, full of life, and put such soul as they, too, possessed into their heels. Mr. Quatty had been run away with, who can say how many times? in his life, and was before long master again of the situation ; but when he had his horses standing still once more, and all in a foam, it was miles further along the beach, and all his preparations up to that point in his address had to be gone over again.

" Yah, you beauties ! " he said to his horses as they struggled once more against the long and sinewy arm which held them in : " you upset my speech, that is all. You would, would you? I only wish I may run away with that hall full of people to-night the same way. Yes; and I can do it if nobody interrupts. If I can get to going, that is all I ask; to get under a good head of steam, to get into the rush of the thing. Now, what next? Just at that weak place I'll have something as strong as I can fix it, smart and strong to keep me from stopping one moment. Let me see;" and he meditated deeply, with his head down, but with no result. "If you only *could* be still one moment!" he ejaculated to his animals. "It is that, it is the interruption, that halts me; and all I need is to get into a good headway. Let me see," and his eye fell on a crab burrowing in the heaped-up mounds of sand on his left. "Exactly!" he exclaimed: "yes, I see; I'll illustrate that way, how a fellow burrows in the dirt when he drinks and gambles, and such like. I can bring in the hard shell and the claws, as sure as you live. That's good: they'll understand *that!* Get up: I'll see something else;" and Mr. Quatty revolved his illustration over and over as his horses trotted rapidly along against a tight rein, the driver deep in thought.

Suddenly they shied to one side; and only by sheer strength could Mr. Quatty hold them in, rearing and plunging. Lying right across their way on the smooth hard beach, its head downward, and still tossed as to the matted hair by the receding tide, was the body of a drowned sailor. It had evidently been washed up by the heavy surf of the night before, and it was not the first time Mr. Quatty had come on such a sight along that beach: he held his struggling horses in as he considered matters. Life had long been extinct. The glazed eyes were staring at the sky; the brawny and tattooed breast was all bare to the day; the ineffectual arms, pictured over even to the tips of the fingers with anchors and crosses and hearts, were spread out in dumb appeal on either side, still being lifted and let fall by the ebb and flow of the retiring sea.

"Poor fellow; but you ain't the first," said Mr. Quatty,

"nor will you be the last. I'll drive right back, and send
out the coroner," and he turned his horses suddenly around.
"Hold up!" he exclaimed with excitement as he did so:
"it's a providence has pitched you into the very outset of my
speech. Why, it's the grandest sort of an idea! — A man,
dear friends," and Mr. Quatty transferred the reins from his
right hand to his left, and extended his long arm to an
imaginary audience, "a mortal man once as full of life and
deviltry, I dessay, as any of you, and now behold — Oh!
I have got the idea. I am sorry for you, but glad for my
speech. Yes," he added, shaking his fist at the buzzards
slowly circling round and round overhead, "I'll put *you* in
too. — Many and many a man of you," Mr. Quatty continued, returning to his audience with an inflation of his
voice into oratory, and a wave of his hand, "is a worse tur-
key-buzzard, a-circling and a-swooping every day round and
round many a poor sailor in our harbor! Oh, but I'll make
your feathers fly to-night!" Mr. Quatty added with another
shake of his fist, this time at those of whom the birds of
prey were but a type. "G'lang, boys!" he added to his
horse; and, as they gladly sped homeward, "I'll hold on to
what I've got, and go for the coroner. Get up, will you!"

It was dinner-time before he had despatched the legal officer and his jury in a wagon from his stable, — quite a jolly
set as they drove off. Through all these arrangements, as
well as during the hasty meal which followed, Mr. Quatty
clung closely to so much of his address as he had accumu-
lated thus far, his enthusiasm greatly quickened by the events
of the morning, as well as by the posters of the night's
meeting which he could not help seeing as they blazed upon
every wall. "O Phip, Phip, I would not!" his wife, holding
to his arm as he rose from the table, continued to urge.
"The people are only making game of you. Please don't!
The children have had ever so many fights with boys about it
to-day already, and you so sensible a man in every thing else:
don't make a fool of yourself, Phip, please don't."

" Sally," her husband said, " it's because you don't understand. Look here ! you think it will be only my having
been an oysterman. I tell you ! why, I've got plenty of
new ideas to-day, — splendid ideas ! all I want to do is to
do good, and you know it. Somebody *must* talk to these
people, and who else is even trying to? You might have
stopped me this morning, but I wouldn't give up making
that speech now for the best horse in America. Just you
wait," and he was gone : it was to get a fresh pair of horses,
and drive along the beach in the direction opposite to that
of the morning. " All I want is to have no interruptions.
Once let me get fairly to going," he said again, " and all the
fear is, I'll never be able to stop. An engine, let alone a
horse or a man, goes better after it gets warm to its work.
Let me see, oysterman — *not* gentleman and scholar — crabs
— buzzards — no, hold up, the dead man comes before that ;
and now, what after that? " Mr. Quatty reined in beside
the surf, and meditated, " Why, here's the sea, rolling and
rolling. — Whoa, hold up ! — And there is the blue sky too,
and plenty of stars ; yes," he continued with enthusiasm,
" and the wind too, blowing, blowing. — Can't you be still,
you fools? " to his impatient horses. " It's a splendid idea ; "
and, looking carefully around to be sure that nothing but sea
and sand were in sight, he stood up, for he was now using
an open wagon, and, holding his reins with one hand, he
extended the other.

" Fellow-citizens ! I am here to-night — never mind about
oysters — scholar — degraded vermin wallowing in the sand
— mud, I mean — worse than that, swooping down on car-
rion wings — *no!* why can't you remember to have the dead
man in first? — a something to swoop *on !* never mind,
that'll all come right when I get into the rush of speaking —
and, oh, friends ! the boundless booming sea, rolling in like
death, swallowing us all u ﹀ — that will be grand, you bet !
And ye tremendous winds " — Mr. Quatty here held the

reins firmly down under his foot, that he might use both hands, and continued, "You powerful breezes which sweep us all away, you — whoa, hold up ! can't you hold up, you brutes ! — and this superior sky a-bending down from up there — oh, I'll get that in, you bet ! As also those clouds, they are like our flimsy lives, you see. Ye float about, you melting and fluffy things — halloo, no, sir, fluffy won't do. Never mind, when I once get fairly a-going, those little things will fix themselves. And O ye — you — what else ? "

Mr. Quatty stood with extended arms, the honest soul of the man in his eyes and tones and long hands sweeping around him, in the bursts of his oratory, like a windmill. The livery-stable keeper was not insane. He was surrounded every day of his life by very bad men whom he was anxious to turn from their gambling and drinking and other desperate courses, in which some of them were being killed almost every week. He had an abundance to say. His imagined audience were people who never went into a church, "or, if they did go," Mr. Quatty repeated as so often before, "what good would it do them ? Preachers never say the sort of things such people need ; or, if they do, they never begin to say them half hard enough." If ever a soul was driven, and as by its own fulness, to express itself, that soul was Phip Quatty. He had a vast deal to say, and of more pressing importance than Demosthenes before him, competing with the sea-surf, ever dreamed of having : only the impediment in his case was worse than in that of the orator with the pebble in his mouth. Neither Whitefield, Chalmers, Spurgeon, nor the rest, had a larger or sincerer heart to do good ; nor did these know as much more as you might suppose of that which was of practical value to say. The trouble was, that somehow this lover of his kind had never been able to say out to people the much that, he felt as sure as he did of his own existence, he had to say. John Bunyan, the tinker, managed to write out his message to men ;

and Hans Sachs, the cobbler, succeeded in singing to the listening world what he had in his soul for them : all that Mr. Quatty wanted all along was a "fair show." He would have it for the first time in his life in the hall that night, and he would use it !

Standing erect in his vehicle, his foot firmly pressed upon the reins, he poured out for some time quite a torrent of exhortation, denunciation, and entreaty in rehearsal.

" Ye hard-headed and harder-hearted ones," he continued with increasing vehemence, and, in the earnestness of his appeal with both extended hands, forgetting the reins under his foot, "you miserable men soaking yourselves along our wharves with strychnine whiskey, awake, rouse out, get up ! " It was said with such emphasis that his horses mistook it for an address to them, and started forward with a bound. The impassioned orator fell back into his seat ; and when at last he had recovered the reins, he had his whole address to go over again from the first.

When Mr. Quatty went to the hall at night, he was exhausted as from the hardest day's work he had ever done. But his flagging spirits revived when he forced his way through the crowd, and stepped upon the platform. As he did so, a band of music struck up. It was a most gratifying surprise. The fact was, that the friends who had plastered every wall in St. Jerome with the flaming posters had also secured the best band in the city ; and it put its entire energy into Hail Columbia as soon as he had taken his seat. The attendance was enormous ; for it was a large hall, and every seat and standing-place was occupied. A doubt held the crowd as to the exact nature of the conduct to be pursued. Was it a show, with Mr. Quatty as clown? or was it indeed a religious service, with that gentleman as the speaker? The large audience, made up almost wholly of men, — chiefly of men never seen at church, — oscillated as upon an edge, somewhat more ready, however, to laugh than to weep ; but

every man present had the sincerest liking for the orator of
the hour.

"Now, Quatty," that gentleman kept saying to himself,
"you keep cool, hold a tight rein, don't get flurried : it's
only like driving a big team. Be slow and steady until you
get to going. As soon as you do get going, get fairly started,
get into a rush, you let yourself out. Never mind how long
you speak : you let her *go*, and somehow you'll come out
all right ! Don't forget, now. Oysterman — scholar — buzzards — no, crabs — you fool, it's the drowned man first —
all right — wind flowing forever and ev — no, sir, the sea
comes first, rolling and rolling — the splendid sun. The
sun? Oh, never mind, I'll get something to fix with that ; "
and under his anxious exterior Mr. Quatty conned his list
of ideas over and over again, until the brass-band had exhausted the national air. With the silence which followed,
the orator of the hour stepped forward to the front of the
platform. In the uncertainty as to whether it was a show or
a church, the audience sat still, ready for any thing. Now,
a little to one side in front of the platform was seated
Mr. Fanthorp, who was universally known, as has been said
before, by the cognomen of Farce Fanthorp by reason of
his unwearying fondness for "a little fun ; " a fondness which
he indulged by the equally unwearying manufacture of that
article when it was lacking ; the essence and success of his
jocularity consisting in the gravity of his countenance
through it all. Men began to laugh and to look out for a
joke at the very sight of the man ; but Mr. Quatty, although
he recognized him from the first as well as all along, was too
much absorbed in his speech to remember that it was Farce
Fanthorp. The moment the orator stepped forward, the
lawyer began, with eyes kindling with enthusiasm and with
the most serious of faces, to applaud ; and the entire audience
accepted the suggestion with enthusiastic delight. It was
some time before Mr. Quatty could get a hearing above the
pounding of feet and the clapping of hands.

"My friends," he began at last with extended hand, "your humble speaker was once an oysterman. You may be surprised, but so it is. I made my living by dredging for oysters " —

"Clams?"

The question was put by Mr. Fanthorp, from his seat among the people, in clear but respectful tones: evidently his only object was to know.

"Occasionally, yes, sir," Mr. Quatty replied, turning his honest face in the direction of the questioner. "Yes, fellow-citizens," he continued, again extending his oratorical hand: "little as you may think it, I was once nothing but an oysterman " —

"Crabs?"

Nothing could be more respectful than the question. The serious aspect of Mr. Fanthorp showed that his sole desire was to be thoroughly informed.

"Very rarely," the speaker replied, with the utmost candor. "But I haven't got to crabs yet. Once I was an oysterman, gentlemen," Mr. Quatty continued, again lifting his hand which he had let fall in replying to his questioner. "I am ashamed to say that I used to lie and even to steal " —

"How much?"

"It is impossible for me to state exactly," the orator continued in reply to the question, again letting his hand fall. "Also, I blush to say, I was in the habit of drinking. O friends! I used to keep a demijohn buried in the sand near by, and drink and drink almost to the destruction of my imperishable " —

"Rifle, or bald-face?"

"Rifle, bald-face, rum, gin, all sorts of liquors," Mr. Quatty hastened to say. "As bad a man I was as the best man here, I mean the very worst. And I used to quarrel and squabble and fight. One occasion I will never forget. I had had it rough-and-tumble with a gambler. We fought " —

"Fetch him?" the question was asked by some one in a distant part of the hall, who had taken his cue from Mr. Fanthorp, with grave uneasiness.

"No, sir! I'm glad to say I did *not* fetch him: I never used any thing but my fists. And, O my friends! it was a happy thing for me," the speaker continued, evidently with an effort, "when one day a stranger came along; I was dredging oysters in the flats: he stood looking on for a while, and we passed the compliments of the day. Says he at last, 'Sir, under your rude garb I see that you are a gentleman and a scholar;' which, my friends, I am *not!*"

Mr. Quatty seemed refreshed by the energy with which he said it, and still more by the applause with which the denial was received; and launched out with much vigor into a detail of the conversation which followed between the stranger and himself. "Yes, sir," he added at last, "that man was — was — I lack power to say — *what* that man was — I mean to me. O my fellow-citizens! to me he was" — and Mr. Quatty stood, overflowing with gratitude, his hands clasped together and lifted up, his eyes searching slowly over the audience as if for the strongest word to be had, "I wish I could say what he was: to me he was" —

"A peddler?"

The suggestion came very loud from the back of the hall.

"No, sir, not at all," the speaker said with entire frankness, but fallen suddenly from his fervor. "Not much, not at all; no, sir, he was nothing of the kind whatever!" but Mr. Quatty was compelled to give way for quite a time to the laughter and applause which followed. The trouble with the speaker was not in the interruptions alone, but that they constrained him to change, and so suddenly, from the inflated tones wherein, as he firmly believed, all oratory lay. There was a sudden resumption of the specie payment of ordinary language, which was very unpleasant. He was not the man, however, to yield as yet, especially as he had the leading incident of the morning's ride still in reserve ; and he made another and more earnest effort.

" My friends," he began again with outstretched arms, as the crowded room became comparatively quiet, " what is life ? It was this very day it happened. I was driving up the beach ; yes, this very day I beheld a fellow-creature lying all prostrate upon the cold, cold ground ! " Mr. Quatty had practised this part of his address, standing up in his vehicle, a good deal, and rallied his waning energies upon it. " A fellow-creature, a sailor like a good many of you, lying on the cold, wet beach ! One a few hours before," in slow and solemn tones, " as full of life as any one of you all, perhaps not a quarter as bad ; and there "— the orator added, recoiling as from the sight, and holding out a horror-stricken hand over the drowned man lying at his feet, " there he lay," in low, sepulchral tones : " yes, friends, there that sailor-man lay dead — dead " —

" Drunk ? "

The question was put by some one near the platform, and was unheard by the audience.

" No, sir, he was not *drunk!* " Mr. Quatty said it with such indignant energy as to bring down the house in peals of laughter.

" I had intended," the speaker continued, rising in his wrath above the uproar, and dropping all oratorical tone and gesture entirely, — " I *had* intended to make a good, long, rousing speech to you," he shouted with voice and manner exactly as when calling to his friends along the streets, or when the wharves were crowded on the arrival of a steamer. " If I could only have got a fair start, if I had only got to going, into the rush of the thing, I could have done it," he continued in his most natural manner. " You fellows need it ; if ever a set of men need it, you do ! I intended telling you about how you are like vermin burrowing in the sand, and like turkey-buzzards; was going to tell you about the rolling sea, and the rushing sky, — I mean wind, — but it does not matter now. If ever," the exasperated orator continued, shaking what looked very much like a fist at his audience, "if ever I make, or try to make, another speech — No, sir, I never will again as long as I live, so help me Heaven!" As he said it, Mr. Quatty turned to take his seat, surprised, even in his wrath, at the sudden silence, the slackening at least of their laughter, which had fallen on the people. It was explained when he saw that Mr. Venable had stepped upon the platform, and was standing at one side waiting for him to get through. By a mutual movement the two men shook cordial hands as if in ratification of the pledge just given; and the audience gave way to hearty and good-humored applause as well as laughter at the sight.

"Friends," Mr. Venable said, laughing, and holding up a hand for silence, "our esteemed fellow-citizen is greatly obliged to you for your attendance here to-night. We all know Mr. Quatty, and we all like him. Why, only this very day I heard of a generous act of his to a poor widow with a large and needy family;" and Mr. Quatty's pastor proceeded to tell of it. And that suggested another deed of kindness on the part of the ex-speaker to some one else, even more liberal; and that, another still. By virtue of the simple narration of the facts, the audience were laughing and in tears alternately.

"Now, we all know," Mr. Venable said at last, "that for one real, sterling, honest man who *does* what is generous and noble, there are a thousand who can make speeches glibly enough. It is the *man* we respect, not the flippant talker. You all know what Burns says;" and Mr. Venable, who had the lines at his tongue's end, repeated the whole poem, "A man's a man for a' that," with all his energy and pathos. As he sat down, Mr. Fanthorp sprang upon the platform, and proposed three cheers for Mr. Quatty. They were given with a will, the audience rising to do so more effectively; and then, to the music of the Star-Spangled Banner performed with unusual power by the band in attendance, the large congregation slowly dispersed, quite a number lingering behind to shake Mr. Quatty cordially by the hand.

Although that gentleman never again tried to speak in public, as an orator at least, somehow he felt that he had made a grand success of it in his last attempt to do so.

CHAPTER XIX.

A NIGHT ON BOARD THE BAYOU-BOAT.

GEN. BUTTOLPH, his daughters and their brother Grit, Mr. Venable, and Mr. Fanthorp, stood upon the deck of the bayou-boat Magnolia a few days after Mr. Quatty's oratorical effort. The sun was slowly sinking into the sea as they thus set out upon their visit to the general's plantation. Of all of them Mr. Venable was most eager to go. Since he had come to St. Jerome, and of late especially, he had done the hardest work he had ever attempted ; and he enjoyed a change.

"How are you, sir?" he said to Mr. Quatty, who came on board to bid him good-by. "Yonder is the old Nautilus."

"Yes, she keeps afloat still," Mr. Quatty said. "Sea-going men say the Flying Dutchman is not to be mentioned alongside her. Bets run ten to one every trip, against her coming again next time. Why, sir," Phip Quatty continued, "there's sporting men that go on her as a regular thing, betting heavy odds against surviving. Life-preservers thrown in, too, at their own risk. That boat is a sort of roulette ball, if you understand gambling, sir, — a something always on the move, and sure to go down next time. I gambled like sixty when I was an oysterman, and it takes all the religion I have to keep from betting on her. But there's your bell. I'll remind them to remember you Wednesday night at prayer-meeting ;" and Mr. Quatty parted from his friend with the usual cordial grasp of his hand. There was a sort of physical magnetism which drew the two together, — a supply and demand, each of what he did not himself possess in the other, which made the man of horses love his pastor only less than his own wife, while the scholarly minister preferred Mr. Quatty decidedly to Commodore Grandheur, Mr. Nogens, Col. Roland, and a dozen beside.

Next to Mr. Quatty, Mr. Venable liked Capt. Chaffin and Mr. Parsons. As to Mr. Fanthorp, very rarely indeed did he go to church. If he did so more of late than formerly, it was because of Miss Irene. To Mr. Venable, after his long and steady work in his study, as well as among the poor and suffering, the jocose lawyer was of medicinal value as an alterative. He deplored the fact that the other was as destitute of the religious faculty as Charlie Chaffingsby of intellect; and yet, after his own long-continued devotion to things spiritual, there was in Mr. Fanthorp the variety at least of a fiddle after the solemn thunders of an organ, and he was glad that he was to accompany them.

As the Magnolia steamed away from the wharf, Mr. Fanthorp beckoned him to go with him down stairs.

" I want you to see," he said.

" To see what? " the other asked, on his guard against some practical joke; but following him down and toward the rear of the vessel. " There ! " Mr. Fanthorp said; and he pointed to the mulatto woman, Iphigenia, seated on the deck near the furnace-wood, a bright-colored handkerchief tied about her head, her hands lying listlessly in her lap, her complexion like a film of ashes over a coal of fire.

" What of her? " he asked; adding, " that is only Iphigenia. She belongs to the general. He bought her when he was on after his daughters. She came over with us in the Nautilus. What about her? " with a smile ready upon his lips for Mr. Fanthorp's joke, whatever it might be.

" She is going with us to the plantation," the other said, looking steadily in Mr. Venable's eyes.

"Well, what of that?" the other demanded.

Mr. Fanthorp rubbed his hand impatiently over his chin, looking at the other with curiosity, and added, —

"What do you think of Gen. Buttolph?"

"Gen. Buttolph! Why do you ask? I think what we all think," Mr. Venable said, — "that he is as liberal as he is wealthy; a warm-hearted, noble-minded, excellent man in every sense of the word. An indulgent father, possibly an indolent man: you know how large and heavy he is." Yet his heart sank within him as he said it; for the words of old Plenty, as well as certain things he had seen of late, had filled him with painful doubt.

Mr. Fanthorp had ceased rubbing his chin, and, with his hand arrested in the act, was looking at him with his eyes drawn together as if he were near-sighted and wished to make sure that the other meant what he said.

"Well!" he remarked at last. And then, "You will excuse me, sir, but " — and he uttered an oath, with deliberate intention, as if before the judge on the bench. As they walked away, he stopped and held the other a moment by the arm.

"I have heard of the heavenly innocence of you preachers," Mr. Fanthorp said, as he released his arm. "Lamb-like! Well, may I be " — and with a silent gesture he gravely consigned himself to perdition. "Why, how," he added, turning almost fiercely upon the other, "do you hope to grapple with and lift men out of their boots, and whirl them around in their tracks, and yet remain as ignorant of the people next you as a baby? No wonder you rove among the flowers and purling brooks: sheep always do. I like you, sir," the swarthy little man said, "but you are as utterly ignorant of men as — as Capt. Chaffin's Clara! Excuse me!" and he was gone.

Mr. Venable would have been less surprised, if the words had not found instant confirmation in himself. "But is it

my fault," he said to himself as he went up-stairs again,
"when intimate friends in the church, the very officers
appointed to aid me in my work, never tell me? People
always show at their best before me, as if I were a lady.
Where do I ever see them except in church, or parlor, or
when they are sick or dying? The instant I come near
them, they put on, from head to foot, their Sunday-go-to-
meeting manners. Their very smiles and tones are sab-
batical with *me*. As Heaven helps me," he added, "I will
try hereafter to know people. They cannot be harder than
Hebrew or Greek. But there's the gong for supper;" for
he was glad to escape from further thought just then.

The supper-gong! Ever since he reached St. Jerome he
had heard of the suppers of the Magnolia. Mr. Fanthorp
had already pointed out to him among the passengers this
old judge, and that venerable and fat major, and the other
colonel, as people who, having nothing in particular to do,
lived on the boat, journeying up and down almost every trip
expressly to eat those celebrated suppers. Nor did he wonder when he assisted them on that occasion. It evidently
was an occasion. The negro waiters — from the head steward, stationed as high-priest at the separate table upon which
every dish was placed before it was served, down to the
least yellow boy — showed by the solemnity of their aspect
how portentous was the feast. There was no hurry here;
nor was there any confusion or mistake as to seats, any
more than at church. People expectantly waited the signal, lingering near their chairs at the table, peeping out of
their staterooms on either side. Not one but was comfortably located at the board before the gong had ceased its
thunder. A sumptuous repast it was. If any thing could
have been added — as to quantity, variety, quality, cookery,
— Mr. Venable, at least, could not imagine it.

But he had no appetite, none the less, and withdrew to
the "guards" outside the cabin as soon as he could. Sit-

ting thereupon in his arm-chair, he was conscious, as night fell, that Mr. Fanthorp was beside him, cigar in mouth. The boat was steaming steadily up the bay. Nothing but the sea was in sight, except low-lying reefs of sand in the distance toward the north. Even the volatile lawyer appeared to be subdued by the silence which was part of the sluggishness of the scene surrounding them. But Mr. Fanthorp was not one to remain long silent.

"I wanted to apologize for my profanity," he said at last; "but, frankly, I could not help it. You should not astonish a man so, Mr. Venable. Before a lady *and* a clergyman, swearing is improper. May I ask you another question?" he added, after quite a silence. "Do you know Gov. Magruder, who sat beside Miss Zeo at table?"

"Yes, sir. I was introduced to him at Gen. Buttolph's house," Mr. Venable said, with some reserve of manner. "A very handsome man he is; and wealthy, I am told."

"He has not been at the general's often?" the other asked.

"I really cannot say. He calls when he comes down from his plantation. His visits are usually in the morning, when I am at my studies. He has . dined there several times. They have often spoken of him. His popular manners were the only special impression he made on me. Why do you ask?"

"I wanted to justify my profanity," Mr. Fanthorp said, "by showing you, Mr. Venable, how astonishingly ignorant —I mean innocent—beg pardon—you are. This trip was arranged, sir, with reference to the matter. Gov. Magruder and Miss Zeo Buttolph are to be married in the spring. His plantation joins the general's. It is a splendid match. Miss Zeo has solidity and thorough excellence, as well as beauty; but Miss Irene—will you allow me to ask what you think of her?" Mr. Fanthorp little knew how terribly his news smote upon the heart of the other; but he mastered himself, and replied, —

"I think what everybody thinks. She is a very intelligent and brilliant woman. I have rarely known one of more original and independent opinions."

"What a fine performer she is!" the other remarked, "and it seems to me as if she had read every thing. I dare say at home, you know, out of company, she is very affectionate. A devoted daughter and sister?" Mr. Fanthorp rather asked it than gave it as his own opinion, somewhat anxiously too, and examined the face of his friend keenly under cover of his cigar-smoke as he said it. Mr. Venable assented, but did not seem disposed to pursue the subject.

"He was the grandest rascal!" Mr. Fanthorp added irrelevantly, after a long silence. "Do you know that scoundrel has gouged — I suppose you know what *that* means? — the general out of thousands of dollars? A scoundrel is invariably a fool. Although," he added with sudden drollery of manner, "a fool is not necessarily a scoundrel; now is he, sir?" He asked it very innocently, but the other colored and remained silent. This was *Farce* Fanthorp, he remembered.

"Of whom are you speaking?" he said at last.

"Gen. Buttolph's overseer. I thought you knew," the other replied, opening wide his eyes. "It was extremely reprehensible," he continued solemnly; and Mr. Venable felt rather than saw that his companion had fallen into his old trick of mimicking the one he conversed with. "I refer to the overseer. I speak with regret of the procedure adopted to make him disgorge. I am a saint, and would do nothing illegal for the world. I am exceedingly careful to know nothing whatever about it, as a saint: as an ordinary individual, I am aware that he is held in the hands of Judge Lynch until he settles up. The peculiarity of that court, beloved brethren, lies in this," Mr. Fanthorp added, as if from the pulpit, "that no lawyer is allowed, nor, alas! is the gospel or *habeas corpus* recognized. Yes, we are in the bayou at last." He added this in his own manner, his cigar being struck from his mouth, as he spoke, by the leafy bough of a tree upon the bank.

Sure enough, they had left the open bay, and had entered by this time what seemed to be a mere ditch, barely wide enough for the steamer to make its way amid the overhanging forest. There was water enough between the steep banks to float a man-of-war; but the bayou coiled and turned on itself, so that the night was spent, as the vessel steamed slowly along, in a series of bumps, now on one side and then on the other; now a shock as the bow ran into the bank, and then a jar more violent as the stern crashed against a tree, the steamer going ahead and backing, with the almost continuous brushing of the boughs of dense foliage upon sides and roof.

"You get splendid shots at alligators if you stand on the bow," Mr. Fanthorp said. "Look here!" As he spoke, he seized with a quick grasp a projecting bough, broke it off, and handed it to his friend. It was a magnolia-branch, laden with the glossy leaves and superb flowers of that tree. The air had long been burdened by the overpowering perfume; and, as the boat urged its way along, the banks in an arm's length on either side seemed a wall of magnolia leaves and flowers, towering up and meeting overhead. It was an experience to the new-comer as if out of the Arabian Nights.

All the more so, as Mr. Fanthorp took occasion, as they sat, to reveal to him pretty much every thing concerning which he had been almost guiltily ignorant. The lawyer kept back nothing, — the desperate condition of the general's finances, and the control Zeo had assumed, since her return, of the household economy; the "devil of a chap" Grit had been, as Mr. Fanthorp phrased it, and the influence she had secured over him. Nearly everybody, he said, knew of her father's secret drinking; but the lawyer had contrived in some way to learn of his daughter's determined efforts to save him, and imparted all he knew; while the boat pursued its way.

"As to that other matter," he continued, lighting another cigar, "that, of course! I don't look at it as you do. But Col. Roland is a wire-working rascal, and the governor is a first-class fool; and their plans are something worth talking about," and he did so at length.

"It happens very well," he added at last. "Old Ugly is rich, and it will be a help to her father. She will make him a good wife. The governor has been a great scamp: but he is desperately in love with her. It is the first time he ever did really love a woman. It is all settled; they will be married; you will get a big fee, Mr. Venable, — in gold, sir! I'm willing. But that rascal Roland is trying to marry Miss Irene: I'll break his neck first! Did she tell you about the ridiculous verses she got? No? That's a wonder. You see, I wrote them in his style, and in his hand, signed his name to them, and sent them to her, — best thing I ever did. If you will excuse me, I'll see if I can't find her somewhere; and if you'll sail in and cut Magruder out, Mr. Venable, I'll remember you in my will: merely for the devilment of it, you know. You'll find them on the guards."

Once or twice after that, Mr. Venable tried to join the ladies. It was in vain. Mr. Fanthorp had possession now of, and was laughing with, Irene at the piano; and he blundered next, it was so dark, against Gov. Magruder shielding Miss Zeo upon the guards against the sweeping foliage, as he made a desperate effort to converse with her. As to Gen. Buttolph, taking advantage of the way in which the governor had drawn off his daughter, he had immediately after supper locked himself up in his stateroom.

Mr. Venable did not enter his room that night, although he wanted to be alone; Grit kept him close company during most of it, as he wandered about the boat. At last they stood together at the stern. With a firm grasp upon Grit (who had become greatly attached to him), lest he should fall overboard, he wondered at the way in which, as they advanced, the dense foliage and the denser darkness closed upon them behind. Then, inducing his companion to go to bed, he climbed upon the top of the vessel, and lay upon his back watching the volumes of smoke and sparks rolling above him from the chimneys, grasping at the magnolia leaves and flowers meeting overhead, and almost touching his face as he lay. The pulsation of the engines as they compelled the vessel on its course, and the sharp cough of the escape-pipes, made a sort of rhythm, the boat jarring now upon one side and then upon the other, now at the stem, and then at the stern, as it forced its way along.

"I never loved a woman in my life," he communed with himself, "until I knew her, and I began to do that from the moment I saw her. She drew me to her by her silent and beautiful strength. If the governor has a power of attraction, why should not she have, and as much stronger than his as it is purer? Gov. Magruder!"

When the family had come aboard the Magnolia, he had stepped forward to help her up the gangway; but that gentleman had interposed in a nervous manner. "Excuse me, Mr. Venable," he had said very politely: "you must let *me* do that, you know!"

"No wonder she prefers him," he groaned now: "he is so light-hearted, so free from care! It is a relaxation to hear him laugh. He must be a relief to her under the strain of her duty. But I can't help it. I must go on loving her, as I must go on hoping. Her sister has intellect; but her beauty is deeper still, of the heart, of the soul. Her smiles are more than her sister's laughter, the little she says than all Irene's sparkling talk. To think I should have lived in their house so long, and have learned only of late what it was in her which attracted and held me even when I understood it as little as I did!

"Gov. Magruder, I have no more intention," he said at last, and getting upon his feet as he said it, "of giving her up to you, your Excellency, than I have of giving up my life." And, going to the bow of the boat, he stood for hours looking forward upon what seemed an impenetrable barrier barring them back. Behind him as he stood, and projecting from the deck on either side, were iron baskets filled with blazing pine-knots : yet even when the light from these was re-enforced by that of the furnace-doors thrown open, the lurid glare played upon what appeared to be a compact wall of earth and forest. Apparently it was madness to press on.

"And yet," he said, "we *do* force our way through it. My path is more hopelessly shut to me : none the less, I also will press steadily on."

CHAPTER XX.

IN WHICH IT IS SHOWN THAT ALL THINGS AT A SUGAR-PLAN-
TATION ARE NOT NECESSARILY SWEET.

EARLY in the morning the Magnolia landed the party at
Gen. Buttolph's plantation, and passed on to Chemaraw, the city higher up the bayou which was the rival of St.
Jerome.   The house was a huge two-storied wooden building,
standing a hundred yards back from the high bluff, and surrounded on all sides by an ample porch.   It had not been
painted for a long time, and presented a mournful appearance, overhung as it was also with gigantic live-oaks
bearded with gray and patriarchal moss.   In front and on
either side had been flower-beds ; but the only growths
remaining were masses of bear-grass, rows of bristling bay-
onet-plants, and every variety of the cactus, as well as the
invariable oleanders, ailanthus, and china-trees.   Behind the
mansion, and a quarter of a mile away across the level fields,
were the negro-quarters, a village of log cabins in rows ; behind them the vast shed-like structure and towering chimneys
of the sugar-mills ; the dense foliage of a cypress-swamp making, in the distance, a background for it all.   Although Mr.
Venable was of Southern birth, this was his first visit to a
sugar-plantation ; and, fresh from the excessive activities of a
colder climate, there was something not unpleasing to him
in the air of languor and neglect, in the drowsiness and mel-
ancholy even, which rested upon the whole scene.

But his attention was diverted from this. As soon as the party came together about the breakfast-table, it was plain that something of importance was on hand.

An assumption of indifference upon the part of most of those present was proof of that. Gen. Buttolph, however, in cordial good-fellowship with every one, exerted himself beyond his wont to entertain Gov. Magruder, who seemed least at his ease of all. Almost wholly uneducated, leaving all the governing to Col. Roland, his Excellency had been simply the best fellow going, himself the jolliest of the jolly crowd which constituted the majority of the Legislature, when it was in session. Mr. Venable had never envied any one, not the grandest preacher he had ever heard, as much as he did this florid-faced, black-bearded, warm-handed man, whose sympathetic eyes seemed so deeply interested in you and in all you said.

"Ah, if I had that magnetic power over men when out of the pulpit," he had remarked to himself, the more he saw of him, "what I said in it would have tenfold force." But this envied man was shy and silent at breakfast, blundering and awkward, on which account Irene Buttolph responded the more eagerly to the witticisms of Mr. Fanthorp. Her younger sister held, as usual, the head of the table opposite her father. "The halo," Mr. Venable thought, "which Mrs. Chaffingsby has painted, as if their hair was on fire, about the heads of her characters, is not a myth. This quiet girl wields such an influence, that even when she is most passive its atmosphere is about her. His Excellency is little more than a sort of perfectly good-humored leopard, and he has an animal instinct of her strength: her eyes embarrass him as those of a human being do even a lion. But how will that help me?"

He could not but notice the plainness of her dress in contrast with that of her sister. There was a home charm to him in certain cuffs about her wrists, as she handed the coffee ; in a species of snowy frill around her neck ; in the way in which her face, sweet yet serious, was framed, so to speak, in her plaited hair.

Grit hastened through his breakfast, and asked her permission to go to the mill, which Zeo granted on certain conditions.

" The idea," Irene exclaimed, " of his asking anybody ! I believe that you have absolutely bewitched that boy, Zeo. He seems to have put his soul into your hands. He follows you about, and minds you, more like a dog than a boy." All that Zeo said in return — but it was not said aloud — was, " O God, give me my father too ! I hardly hoped that God could give Grit to me, he was so bad. Now that he has, I know he will give me my father, — I know it, I know it ;" and she was literally as happy as a queen, because she was one.

" They don't want us," Mr. Fanthorp said, as he and Mr. Venable strolled out of the house after breakfast. " The governor makes his formal proposition to-day. Any one could tell that by the way he made a fool of himself just now. That is the strangest thing about Magruder : he is the life and soul of a crowd until he gets on the stump. Once up to make a speech, he hums and haws and blunders and breaks down : he is worse at it than Phip Quatty. He knew enough, at last, never to try again. The governor is a splendid fellow ; but," added the lawyer in his droll manner, " bless my soul, humph, ah !

" Dearly beloved brethren," Mr. Fanthorp continued, with an oratorical outspreading of his hands to an astonished group of negro children in shirts and nothing else, before whom he paused as they lounged along, " our friend the ex-executive is rich, in fact, he owns boat-loads of you ; and he is the jolliest fellow breathing. But I must not, beloved, can not, will not, soil the snowy purity of — I look deeper than your linen — your souls, by intimating wherein that individual is a sinner. The congregation is dismissed with an urgent request to wash itself. Amen. Get out, you little rascals!" with a sudden spring among his dusky audience, which scattered them with streaming shirt-tails to the winds.

"You will excuse my taking you off," he began.

"It was not a bit like me," Mr. Venable said indignantly.

"You think not? Well, never mind; but I have two excellent reasons for being in spirits to-day. One reason lies that way:" the lawyer said it with a backward gesture of his head to the house they were leaving. "The other reason lies yonder," pointing toward the swamp bounding the plantation in the rear.

"Did you ever read of Antigone?" his companion asked, after a while, as they walked over the fields which were being ploughed by gangs of negroes.

"Aunt Tiggony? A relative of yours? Oh! you mean some black aunty," Mr. Fanthorp said, with serious and respectful manner. "Have I? Of course I did," he said, growing serious by ceasing to be solemn. "At college," he added. "Yes, Miss Zeo is that. But the marble grandeur of the Greek girl leading about her miserable father, blind and doomed, lay in her doing so not alone merely, but in defiance of her gods. Medea, Alcestis, Electra, and the rest are not to be compared to her."

"I am glad," the other said eagerly, "to know that you are a scholar. Except Col. Roland, you are the first I have met; and he is so — so " —

"Perfectly a fool," Mr. Fanthorp supplemented. "To think of a fellow at his years — two hundred and fifty at least — sending bouquets and verses and making love to young girls! That man," the lawyer added, "is the most beautiful, yes, and powerful writer in the State. He does very well in a parlor; and yet he could not get a vote for a State office, to save his life. The people have as little use for him as they have for that silk-weed;" and he pointed to the plant so named, which was waving its glossy and abundant silk streamers about the decaying stumps and fallen logs near by; nothing more beautiful or more useless.

"What I wanted to say," his companion added, "was that the Greek Cordelia — for the Antigone is that — is too marble-like. I can imagine a woman, and a very young woman, as much superior to Antigone as Christianity is to Paganism. Imagine a mere girl caring in her loving weakness for the *soul* of her wretched father, too, trying to save him from deadlier foes than those of Œdipus " —

"Excuse me," Mr. Fanthorp interrupted; "but bother Antigone, and, if they will allow me," lifting his hat to them in their absence, "the ladies also! This, you see, is the mill. It is nothing but a warehouse with tall chimneys, huge kettles, furnaces, iron pipes, and the like. Yonder is the press. That heap of white stuff is what is left of the *Begasse*, the sugar-canes with the juice crushed out; they burn it for fuel, you know. — Hallo, Plenty, come here!"

They had entered the mill, and Mr. Venable recognized young Plenty as he now approached them, his old grandfather tottering behind him, feebler than ever.

"When the general — it was Miss Zeo's doing — put this plantation in my hands," Mr. Fanthorp explained, "I accepted it on condition he gave me young Plenty as foreman. He manages, and goes and comes between here and St. Jerome. Have they got through, boy?" he asked significantly. But the old negro had put himself between his stalwart grandson and the speaker, and replied promptly, —

"Hush up, child! You hold your tongue! Lemme talk to the gentleman. — Ah, dat's a missable business, Mars Fanthorp. No, sah; I wouldn't let him cowhide dat man. I wouldn't let him, nebber, sah, nebber!" and the old soul, his trembling hand on his son's broad and naked shoulder, drew himself up with a sort of decayed dignity, holding his white head as erect as he could.

"They wanted *him* to do it? That's too bad. — But, you

old ghost, you bothersome old codger," the lawyer added, "what business is it of yours?"

"I is from Firginny, sah. Dis poor boy was only born in St. Jerome."

"Look here," the lawyer said to Mr. Venable, "do you see this great, strapping boy? He manages the two hundred hands on this place. See what a head he has. Forty years old he is too. — I say, *you!*" he added, turning suddenly upon the man, "why do you let the old fellow follow you about — I know he only does it before the white folks — as if you were a baby? What do you *mean?*" he asked, with an accent like the crack of a whip.

"Lor, massa!" replied the younger negro, confronting the lawyer, with a smile all over his face, "my Lor, massa, as if you don't understand. He is my *gran'fader!*"

"Go to thunder!" Mr. Fanthorp said; and, turning away as he gave a key to the man who had spoken, he added, "No spirits, Plenty (there's the smoke-house key); but you may cut as much tobacco for you both as you like, a hogshead if you want, when I am gone. — This way, Mr. Venable." So saying, his friend led his companion into the other half of the huge warehouse. "Be careful," he said; for there was no floor, the visitors having to step from joist to joist upon which scores of hogsheads of sugar were standing, molasses dripping from each into a dirty lake of the same below. "That is the sugar," he added. "This, when it has gone through its chemistry, and been ladled into barrels, is the sirup, and that is all. It does not look very nice, and rats, mice, cockroaches, and yellow-jackets don't improve it: anyhow, there is a mint of money in it, I tell you. Now, I've got to go with Plenty here, and see to things. If you want to learn a page in human nature"—

"Excuse me," the other said to his quick-motioned, mercurial companion, "but what was it the old man would not allow the other to do? Whip somebody, was it not?"

"Whip somebody?" the lawyer exclaimed, with wide-open eyes. "Whip! Bless me, whom? I haven't the slightest idea. What a remarkable mistake! But if you would like to understand human nature — do you see that belt of live-oak?" pointing to the cypress-swamp which bounded the sugar-field. "Go down there. You are not armed? Oh, of course not! But, remember distinctly, I don't know any thing about any thing in the world. Good-by. Take care of yourself. I can't be always with you;" this last being the formula of parting current among jocose people just then and there.

It was half an hour's walk, a tiresome one, over the newly-ploughed ground and growing cane ; but Mr. Venable was not sorry to be alone. His meditations were perplexing enough ; and he was glad to have them scattered, as he walked, by a sudden peal of laughter from the wood, toward which he had now drawn near, — the laughter of a crowd.

Halting a while, and then getting within the curtain of hanging live-oak limbs draped with heavy moss, he came on a sight which held him to the spot with horror. Twenty men or more were seated or standing around a poor wretch, whose face was from him, whose only clothing was his trousers, and whose hands were tied behind him. It was the overseer of whom Mr. Fanthorp had spoken ; and the men composed the court of Judge Lynch, who was represented by a white-headed old reprobate seated upon what appeared to be a pile of dirty boxes. The man had been beaten severely, but this had failed to draw any confession from him. A rope was around his neck, the other end passed over the limb of a live-oak overhead, and held in the hands of some of the men. By drawing him up until almost strangled, and then lowering him, they had extorted from the miserable man, and box by box, the hiding-place of his plunder, which year after year he had buried in the neighborhood of the spot upon which he was being tortured; for, with criminal indolence, the general had long given over the plantation and its crops into his hands.

The intruder only saw a victim in the grasp of his cruel enemies. One moment of horror, and then he was amazed at the fury, as of a tiger, in him. At a bound this wild beast suddenly born within him carried him among the men.

"You scoundrels," he found himself saying, his lips parched, his wild hands clutching at the ropes which held the prisoner, "how dare you!" Every man had sprung to his feet, no man without a rifle or revolver. There was a moment's pause, while, still plucking at the ropes, he looked at them with desperate face and as if in a dream. The men were not regarding him so much as glancing over his head and beyond for those who might be following. Then, to his astonishment, there was a sudden, unanimous, and hearty burst of laughter. He could see that every man of the rough set of poor whites (for he knew they were that at a glance) had sheathed his revolver again, or lowered his gun, and was laughing with a sense of amusement too evidently heart-felt not to be genuine.

"My friend," the intruder said, somewhat dampened as well as bewildered, "who — why — what" — and he laid his hand upon the naked shoulders of the victim from behind.

"Oh, get out! Go along with you!" the man yelled, with a curse, snarling at him over his shoulder, and giving a vicious kick at him backward. "If you had come before, it would 'a' been some good! Now," with a frightful oath, "get out!" Upon which there was another storm of laughter, which, it seemed to the new-comer, could have been heard for miles.

"And now, boys," said the grizzly-headed old rascal who seemed to be the leader, wiping the tears of mirth from his eyes, "to conclude this here camp-meeting with a benediction, this here honorable Court orders that the pris'ner be packed off on the Nautilus on her next trip."

"On the *what!*" roared the man. There was a horror in his tones, a genuineness in his dismay, which brought down the audience in another peal of laughter.

"Gentlemen," Judge Lynch said, when the fun had slackened, "this overseer has had his voice, plenty of it, and mighty loud it was, in these here proceedings. No man wants *his* views about that old and highly-respected boat. We've had to scare that money out of him, inch by inch to the spot where he hid it, and dollar by dollar then. But we've got it about all;" and, to indicate the whereabouts of the money, as he spoke he rose up and sat down again with emphasis on the heap of boxes upon which he had been seated, and which from their muddy appearance had evidently been just dug up out of the earth. "Thousings on thousings in here he had chiselled Gen. Buttolph out of, going on for six years now, besides his other rascalities you hearn him confess. Mind, the general don't know, and Lawyer Fanthorp 'specially is not to know, any thing of all this. Bundle him off until the committee can start. 'Nuf said. If the prisoner will sing a hymn we'll be dismissed."

It was near dinner-time before Mr. Venable, hunting everywhere for the lawyer, succeeded in finding him upon the other side of the plantation. "It is so very much the easiest way," that gentleman replied, at the close of their conversation. "Of course I never dreamed of such an outrage, knew nothing about it whatever; but it saved years of time, years on years of lawsuits, and one never gets the money then. I tell you it was a *haul*," he added. "I had no idea he had gone into the general to that extent;" for Mr. Venable had found the lawyer, when he did find him at last, in conference with the leader of the lynchers. "This sugar-making is all gambling, any way," he added. "However, we've saved the general this time, anyhow. But, bless you," with the face of a sabbath-school scholar, "I knew nothing about it!"

CHAPTER XXI.

MR. VENABLE VIOLATES THE PROPRIETIES.

AS the successful manager of Gen. Buttolph's plantation, Mr. Farce Fanthorp felt himself justified in the enjoyment of unlimited fun among the whites, as he did of unbounded energy among the blacks. In his own estimation, at least, his business qualification gave weight and authority to his humor, as it certainly did a new license to his audacity.

"As sure as you live," he remarked to Mr. Venable, the day after the lynching, "Roland will come up from St. Jerome very soon. He has become so used to controlling Old Ugly, and Old Ugly has become so used to being controlled, that, especially at this crisis, they cannot live apart. How I hate him!"

True enough, the colonel did arrive two days later, bringing with him quite an odor of civilization in his toilet, his poetry, and his devotion to the ladies. The instinctive aversion between the lawyer and himself was intensified by their rivalry in reference to Miss Irene. While the colonel defended himself with contempt as with a shield, his enemy resorted to his "buffoonery," as the other styled it, as naturally as a wild-cat does to its claws or a fox to its cunning.

It was in vain that Col. Roland endeavored to make himself heard at the dinner-table. He had begun, for instance, to speak of the hardness of the times, of the expedients to which men had to resort in business, when his adversary broke in, —

"You are right, Roland, finance is the most intricate of sciences. A few weeks ago I had given so largely to charitable objects as to be sadly reduced. I could not help myself from the public treasury as you could do, Roland. I will tell you what I did do;" and with a grave face Mr. Fanthorp detailed at length how, when he had applied to his father in a distant State by letter for aid, and had been refused, he wrote to him in a feigned hand and over another name a full account of his own death. In affecting terms he told him of the brilliant promise of his son, of the universal estimation in which he was held, of his last and fatal illness, of his dying messages, of the funeral, when St. Jerome in tears followed him to the grave: he detailed seriously and at length.

"In a postscript I incidentally mentioned," he added, " that friends had been to some expense, but that I would not press the subject upon the afflicted father. By return mail I received a handsome check from " —

"I do not see, sir," Mr. Venable said, not sharing the laughter which followed by reason of the narrator's manner of telling the story, "how you could so wantonly distress your father."

"It did *not* distress him. The check was my only comfort," Mr Fanthorp replied with a sad face, "when I saw how cheerfully my venerated father sent it."

He had told the truth: every one knew it was but one of many freaks of the kind. But Mr. Venable was glad to catch the eye of Miss Zeo at the moment, and to know that she found as little fun in the trick as he did; and the conversation changed.

For a day or two the gentlemen rambled over the plantation, hunting in the swamp, lounging about the mills, — all except Col. Roland, who devoted himself to the sisters.

Mr. Venable found himself watching the governor closely. The ex-magistrate was evidently very much in love with his charming hostess, but it was not in her company that he enjoyed himself most. He was always eager, instead, to get out of doors ; and with a cigar in his mouth, walking about among the negroes, leaning against a fence chatting with his friends, he was an excellent listener, himself full of anecdote of his experiences in city and country : a better companion could not be desired. The instant the cigar was thrown away, however, and he entered the presence of the ladies, the light died from his fine eyes, the laughter from his lip : it was as if he were in church or in the presence of the dead. Possibly Col. Roland had tutored him too much.

"Don't be a fool, Magruder," the colonel said to him at every opportunity. "You blush and stammer so that no modest woman can persist in talking to you, man."

"Look here, Roland," the other always replied, "you know how I've lived all my life on my place, among my negroes. And you know whether I am popular with those chaps in the Legislature, among people generally. But the moment you box me up in a parlor with such a lady as that ! I ain't afraid; but don't you suppose I know what a scamp " —

"Don't be a booby, or a baby, Magruder," was the text from which his Mentor discoursed to him continually.

One day the question came up at table, as to what was the noblest virtue ; and as the conclusion was reached by Mr. Fanthorp, who did most of the talking, that it was courage, Miss Zeo said, —

"Grit, my brother Theodore I mean, told me, as we sat down, of a cowardly thing. I do not think my father knows of it. Some low characters tied up our overseer, he says, and whipped him terribly. It was an outrage," she added with glowing cheeks : "it was a mean and dastardly thing.

— Mr. Fanthorp," she said in such tones as to arrest every ear, " have you heard of this?"

" The overseer ! Whip an overseer? No, Miss Zeo," Mr. Fanthorp said with apparent astonishment. " I knew that he had left; but whip a white man? It is impossible ! — I hope," he said to his host, " that you will allow me to search the matter out. Whip a white man ! It is the first I have heard of it."

" I am astonished at you, Zeo," her sister said. " Let us talk about something else. — Well, Mr. Venable, what do *you* think is the noblest virtue?"

" Truth, Miss Irene," he said, " *truth!* " He was aware that the emphasis in his tones and face added force to his reply. " Nobody has been whipped," Gen. Buttolph said, in the awkward silence which followed. " The scoundrel Zeo speaks of had swindled me. Fanthorp found it out, made the fellow disgorge, and he has fled : that is all. — You are right, Mr. Venable : a liar is a coward. Have some more venison." But that gentleman was aware thereafter of a curious coldness toward him, on the part of Miss Irene again, as once before ; as well as of an increased cordiality upon the part of Col. Roland and Gov. Magruder. To his gratification, Miss Zeo directed her conversation to him during the rest of the meal. But Mr. Fanthorp never was more at his ease ; and when they went into the parlor he favored them, Miss Irene accompanying him upon the piano, with several of his most amusing songs.

When Mr. Venable first arrived in St. Jerome, he was pale and thin from years of seclusion — as has been said — and hard study; but all that was gone. Like a plant removed from a winter cellar into midsummer sunshine, he had developed in health and strength until he hardly knew himself in his glass, and his difficulty now was to hold himself in due bounds. The last afternoon of their stay on the plantation, the party were seated under the live-oaks, some playing chess upon a rustic table, the rest conversing, when Col. Roland remarked, that, with the permission of their host, a basket of choice champagne had been sent him by that morning's boat from St. Jerome. He had been able to show one of the custom-house officers a little political favor, and this was the result.

"I wonder if it is the *only* result?" Mr. Fanthorp soliloquized aloud, in a thoughtful manner, stroking his chin as he did so; but Zeo had uttered an exclamation at the mention of the wine, and Mr. Venable caught the look of distress in her eyes. " Gov. Magruder was about telling us of his accident," Col. Roland said; " and his mention of whiskey as a remedy for the bite of a snake reminded me of the wine. Go on, governor, go on: the wine can wait."

In much briefer fashion than if the ladies had been absent, the governor told of being bitten, and healed in the way spoken of. Next Gen. Buttolph narrated the sufferings of one of his brothers, who had also been bitten. He had often told the story: it had been a tragic event, and he related it with great feeling, for, there being no remedy in reach, his brother had expired in agony.

"It was terrible," Col. Roland said, as he ended; " but suppose we have some of that champagne, general?" and the hamper was brought out and opened.

" Your story reminds me," Mr. Venable said, " of another event, so terrible that I never like to mention it, and it was of my only brother; " and, as the wine was poured out, he proceeded to speak of his brother, his appearance, his talent, his noble qualities. The grief of his life came back afresh upon him, as he told of the honors taken by this brother, who was many years his senior, when at college; of the pride of his parents in him. Under other circumstances he would not have alluded to the matter; but with Miss Zeo watching her father covertly under her drooped lids, he went into details of his last hours, and even of the death of his broken-hearted mother, and afterward of his father, in consequence. His father had been ruined in money matters also by the death of his gifted son; for after that he gave up in despair all effort as well as all hope.

The soul of the narrator was in his words, his own eyes also were moist : he could not restrain himself. An unopened bottle stood at his elbow; and to one side of him was an artificial mound of stones, upon the summit of which grew a flowering cactus. Among the stones he had observed one of the huge ammonites, common to that region, — a petrified shell larger than a dinner-plate, and very heavy. As he closed his narrative, yielding to the impulse, he said to Col. Roland, —

"May I have this bottle, sir?"

"Certainly," the other replied with surprise.

"You spoke of the bite of a rattlesnake, general," he added, "and of your brother's death. It was this reptile, sir, *this !* which killed my brother and my parents;" as he said it he arose, tossed the bottle to the earth on one side ; and, as if it were a venomous serpent, he crushed it to atoms under the ammonite. It was done in an instant, and with an intensity of feeling which thrilled every one.

"I trust you will excuse me," he said, quieting himself as he took his seat; "I never told the story before : but the impulse was too strong to be resisted," and he hastened, as soon as possible, to change the conversation. Not even Mr. Fanthorp proposed to open another bottle; and when Mr. Venable glanced at Miss Zeo she seemed to be awaiting his eyes, and, although he had not thought of her while speaking, the look in hers was more to him than any wine could have been.

There seemed something opportune when, soon after, a peal of thunder warned them to seek the house, and the sultry day culminated in a down-pour of rain. The ladies hastened to their apartments, their father suggesting that the rest should smoke their cigars in the billiard-room of the rambling old mansion.

An hour after, Mr. Fanthorp loitered into the parlor at · the other end of the house, where Mr. Venable was seated reading.

"Look here, Mr. Venable," he said to him, "do you know you called me a liar at the dinner-table?"

The other laid aside his book, and arose. "You know the facts of the case," he said coolly.

"And meant I was a coward?"

"Precisely," his companion assented.

"And in the presence of ladies?"

"Yes, sir."

"I declare," the lawyer said in a thoughtful manner, "I never was more perplexed what to do. If it were Roland or Magruder I would know, of course. You are a minister, you see: it is that has kept me bothering over it so long. How would it do for you to make an apology at table?"

"It would not do at all." Mr. Venable could not refrain from laughing as he said it, the other was so sincerely perplexed.

"I had thought," the lawyer said, looking up at the other, who stood tall and vigorous before him, "of taking this secluded opportunity of slapping you."

"You can try it," Mr. Venable said, with good-humor, but closing his right hand as he did so.

"I never *was* so perplexed," said his whimsical antagonist. "Can't you advise a fellow?"

But there was a sound of steps at this moment; and the two men, themselves hidden by the curtains, glanced out upon the back porch. It was Irene and her sister; Irene laughing and talking eagerly after a little nap in her room.

Suddenly, as the two men looked out, themselves unobserved, they saw that her eye fell upon Iphigenia, stealing
through the rain ; and Mr. Venable was rooted to the spot
with amazement.   With eyes and face blazing with wrath,
she sprang, at the sight, from the porch, and smote the
girl furiously in the face with her open palms, hissing at her
and spitting upon her in the extremity of her fury, and then
bursting, as she stood over the cowering wretch, into an
agony of weeping.   The gentlemen hastened to drop the
curtain, and conceal themselves ; but not until they caught
sight of Zeo, her firm grasp on the arm of her sister, her
face set and stern but very calm in comparison.   She was
pointing toward the negro-quarters, and she was saying
something as she stooped over the girl.   The crouching
creature lifted her face toward her young mistress.   All the
burning coal, so to speak, had gone out into the ashes of
her face, and her eyes, large and wondering like those of a
doe, were fastened upon those of the younger sister.   Then,
with her head held down, and as if obeying a command,
she ran with naked feet through the rain, and disappeared.

"What a splendid woman she is !" Mr. Fanthorp said,
and in a low tone, as they drew back.   "Beautiful is no
word for it.   It was grand.   A perfect picture !   I wouldn't
have missed it for a pretty ! "

"It is a revelation — like that of the angel at the sepulchre," his companion said, in a lower tone.

"Revelation?   Sepulchre?" exclaimed Mr. Fanthorp.
"Not a bit of it.   She was like a tigress.   I wouldn't have
cared if she had killed that girl."   As he said it he seemed
suddenly struck by something he saw in the face of the
other ; and, looking at him more curiously, the color came
so much more into Mr. Venable's face, that at last Mr.
Fanthorp smote his hand upon his thigh, and indulged in a
long whistle.   "I *thought* so ! " he said.   "Well, if that is

the case I *am* revenged! Gov. Magruder will do it for me. I am sorry for you, sir; for," he added, holding out his hand, "I like your pluck. She is worth your trying. Go ahead!"

"Thank you; I intend to," Mr. Venable said gravely, and left the room.

CHAPTER XXII.

ILLUSTRATING THE FACT THAT NATURE ABHORS A VACUUM.

AT the dawn of the day that Gen. Buttolph and his party left St. Jerome for the plantation, Commodore Grandheur awoke in a restless frame of mind.   After shaving, dressing, and breakfasting, with rigorous reference to the clock, he locked himself into his study, as was his invariable rule, for exactly one hour of reading the Scriptures and prayer.   That accomplished, he stood for some time looking at his well-stocked library.   On retiring from the navy, and when furnishing his house abundantly in every other respect, he had obtained also as complete a supply of books as any man could desire, and it had been his purpose to find in reading a large part of his long-looked-for happiness; yet somehow he hardly ever opened a book, the very supply seeming to dismay his appetite.   On this occasion, as so often before, he turned away from his library, and tried to amuse himself in a weary fashion for a while with a large globe, revolving it this way and that, his compasses in hand, for the purpose of getting, for the thousandth time, certain distances thereupon.   But this also was wearisome, and he made a visit to the room devoted to curiosities.   It was a collection which would have enraptured any stranger, but its owner was familiar with it to disgust.   He glanced with weariness over the seashells and marine monsters stuffed or in jars.   Every fish had its mouth distended, and he never failed to sympathize

with and imitate their universal yawn. The models of his
favorite ships, too, he had studied so very often. What did
he care for the weapons and dresses, the feathers and pipes,
displayed there from many an island of savages? No engi-
neer could have desired a handsomer assortment of model
torpedoes, to say nothing of improvements in cannon and
capstans of his own devising; yet these merely aroused in
him afresh the old anger at the stupidity of the War Depart-
ment in refusing to adopt certain suggestions which even a
fool could have seen would revolutionize warfare. There
was one case of rosewood and plate glass particularly dear
to him, and he turned to it as a last resort; but there was
not a particle of pleasure for him to-day in the gingerbread
decorations and orders therein displayed, and which Congress had allowed him to accept from certain foreign poten-
tates, great and small. Nor was there, when he stood before
the cabinet displaying them, a spark of satisfaction even in
the medals granted him by Congress for heroic deeds : they
might have been hard-tack, instead of gold and silver, so
dry and innutritious to-day were their disks to his hunger.

And the gallant old soul *was* hungry this morning — rest-
lessly, desperately, almost despairingly hungry — for something, he knew not what. His parlors were as tiresome to
him when he threw open the blinds and took a survey of
carpets and mirrors, marbles and pictures. Except when he
had the Sunday-school teachers to tea, what did he want
with all that furniture? and when he had them to tea, some
one of them was so certain to differ with him — Miss Aurelia Jones in particular — that it always destroyed for the
hour his very ownership in the house. There was nothing
left but to take a round of the garden and lawn, but he
could make nothing of it all but trees and grass. His
blooded cows might get good out of it, but he could not.
Twice a year he turned his Sunday school loose upon his
grounds, with plenty of dinner and swings thrown in; but

the rapturous children were not here to-day, and they were
as indispensable to his enjoyment of his property as spoons
and knives and forks are to a feast. His acres were the
envy of the city; but, had they been painted as a landscape
npon the bottom of his tobacco-box, they would have afforded him as much pleasure, and as little.

There was but one last resort, — the observatory on the
top of his house.

"If I were sick," he said to himself as he climbed up stairs,
"I could take salts; but I never was quite so well in my
life. I can't imagine any thing to eat or drink or wear that
I want. And one cannot compel his Sunday school to meet
except on Sunday. So far as people are concerned, what
good is there in talking to them in the streets or in their
houses? Either they have nothing worth hearing to say, or
they are eternally airing some absurd ideas of their own.
Miss Aurelia Jones, for instance. I can see her this moment
with her black eyes and her ringlets. She knows that she is
the only woman living that ventures to differ from me; and,
having nothing else to do, half the pleasure of Sunday school
to her is in defying me. It is as necessary to a woman of
her temperament as mustard is to beef. Well, what is there
to see here?" And having reached his observatory, after
getting over the perspiring and panting inevitable to a man
of his portly build and irascible nature, he proceeded, quad-
rant in hand, to take his exact bearings. He had done it
very, very often before; and, as his house had not sailed
anywhere since he was there last, the process and result
were too easy and too certain to do him any good. Then
he levelled his glass, and slowly swept the city and island
and sea round and round: yet that wide field did not yield
him a grain of harvest. As he snapped the slides of the
glass to, he thought of getting out his charts down in his
study, and sailing over again his whole series of voyages.
"But I've gone over it so often," he said, "that I can do it

as well up here, and without the charts; and I don't want to."

He had never been so miserable. Moreover, he knew well enough that as he grew older it would be worse. One would hardly have recognized him as he stood there on the summit of his house and his wealth and all, the world having nothing more to give him than he already possessed. The world? the universe for that matter; for in Scripture and church and prayer he had ranged over and gathered to himself all that lay outside the world too. Even Mr. Nogens would have exclaimed aloud, had he seen the commodore. His hands had fallen to his sides, his head upon his bosom, his white moustache drooped, his bronzed face was almost ghastly, the portly figure seemed wilted and shrivelled into sudden age. It was by an effort that he at last roused himself to say one word; but he said it without any special interest, —

"Becalmed !"

Nothing to say, to think, to do, to feel. Nowhere to go, nothing to look forward to. He went slowly down to his study, and opened, unconscious that he did so, his big Bible at the lesson for his school the coming Sunday. The first verse called to mind a preposterous opinion Miss Aurelia Jones had advanced in relation thereto at their last teachers' meeting. But as he meditated a wholly different train of thought seemed to enter his mind. Slowly, but very steadily, his head rose as he sat in reflective attitude, the color came back to his face, the stiffness to his white moustache, the light to his eyes, the portliness to his body. As if some great tide had turned within him from its lowest ebb, and was lifting him by its irresistible flood, he seemed to rise and freshen and brighten, until at last the incoming ocean fairly lifted him to his feet. He stood erect, looking into the air as if from his quarter-deck over wide seas, his gaze concentrating itself as if upon the vessel of an enemy bearing down upon him. At last it was as if the foe had climbed up his bulwarks, and were bearding him upon his very post as commander. He looked with rising wrath as if into the eyes of an insolent invader; and, with clenching hand, he said aloud, —

"No, madam, never!"

But the incoming flood of the future had not as yet reached its high-water mark, if the confusion of metaphor may be allowed. He stood for some time as if unable to resist. Then, as he still reflected, he slowly let his right hand be lifted by the advancing tide high over his head, to bring it down suddenly with clenched fist upon the Bible, and a violent exclamation, —

"Bearings at last!"

In an hour's time he came out of his front door dressed as for church. The servants watched him with amazement as he passed out and down the steps of his veranda, and crunched his determined way along the shell-walk and out of the gate, his cane tightly grasped, his head unusually erect, the gravest resolve in his eyes.

This atmosphere of ours conveys from person to person more than touch or sound, light or smell, and things which it, or the ether in it, conveys also from soul to soul are powerful in proportion as they are subtle. That very morning Miss Aurelia Jones had awakened in a frame of feeling unlike that of the commodore merely in this, that it was one of yet more profound discontent. Strange to say, she was as much more dissatisfied as she was richer than the other. The fact that her grounds and house were larger and finer and better-kept but increased the weariness which — but by no means for the first time — they awoke in her this magnetic morning. ·

"I must be getting bilious," she said to herself at the very hour the commodore was wandering disconsolately about in the wilderness of his museum. "There is no more sewing to be done. It is no use to sweep and scour and dust when I've seen to it that every room and chair and curtain and pane of glass is as clean as work can make it. Unless I want to leave nothing of my silver, there is no use in having it rubbed again. If Bob has left a weed in the garden, I couldn't find it this morning. The whole house has just been painted and papered. There's no church until next Sunday. The sewing-society and the parochial school, teachers' meeting and prayer-meeting, won't come before their time. Oh, bother!"

Miss Aurelia had already looked over her jewels that very morning as she sat in bed unwilling to rise. It was impossible for any woman to give more than an hour to brushing her hair, especially when she had given the same length of time to putting it up the night before. She tried the pier-glass in the parlor once more. Hair, eyes, the effect of poising her spirited and handsome head this way and that, the adjustment and re-adjustment of ribbon and frill, of necklace and breastpin, cannot be gone over, even by a woman with nothing else to do, more than a hundred times in one morning without weariness.

"There's no new drive," she lamented as she continued to survey herself in the glass. "There is not a soul but is owing me a call. All yesterday I was shopping until I am sick of the sight of silk and lace. I believe my Christian character is suffering seriously from the way I frequent the stores. I wish somebody would call, or die, or do *something!* What a stupid world it is!" and the solitary woman wandered aimlessly about her house. Once she called in two of her negro-women, and, seating herself in the middle of a room, made them bring and range her Saratoga trunks about her, with the view of surrounding herself with a chaos of dresses, purely for the purpose of putting each back again. But she merely locked them again immediately. "Carry them back," she said to the women. "I believe you look so discontented," she added, "because you know I was going to give you dresses, as I always do. The more you have, the more you don't care for any thing, ungrateful creatures ! Hold your tongues ! What you need, both of you, is to be field-hands again, a sharp overseer at your heels, with nothing but hard work and pork and grits."

Then their mistress made up her mind. Going down into her little library, she seated herself at a special secretary, unlocked the outer doors thereof, and held the keys in hand as she ran her eyes over the range of drawers revealed inside. Her past life lay waiting the unlocking in those drawers, — a drawer for each separate period. Letters, read and reread, were in them ; locks of hair ; fragments of ribbon understood by no one else ; miniatures and daguerrotypes ; jewelry not worth sixpence to look at ; bunches of withered flowers, and the like. Her face had grown hard and pale as she sat, the key in her hand, which was hovering about, undecided which of the receptacles to unlock. Suddenly she let her hand fall. "No, I can't do it !" she communed with herself. "I have exhausted my emotions long ago. They do me no good unless to make me cry, and I'm too tired to cry. No, no : it is the only place left me, and I will go there."

Locking the secretary, she went wearily up-stairs again into a little room opening into her bed-chamber. There was nothing in it beyond a chair, a table with a Bible on it, and a cushion on which to kneel, — nothing else, unless it were a small picture on the wall, apparently the likeness of some young man who could not have been regarded by his friends as handsome. And yet the poor lady, as if from force of habit, fastened a tired look upon it as she sank into the seat, and opened the book upon the table beside her. She read, or tried to read, for some time, then knelt, but rose again very soon.

"It is dreadful," she said to herself as she sat down, al-

most fretfully, again; "but there doesn't seem to be any
thing here for me, either. There is nothing to ask for, that
I know. It is like trying " — she shuddered as she thought
it — " to gossip with — with — God ! I don't suppose people even in heaven are allowed to do that. God forgive
my irreverence ! The Bible seems to say that they are busy
as they can be all the time in heaven also. One must have
an appetite before one can relish even the bread of life ;
and to have an appetite, one must be hard at work. I'm
hunting all the time for work, but there is so little to do !
I wish it were time for calling in the people to prayers down
stairs. If some beggar would only come ! It would be
a round sum to him if any agent were to happen in for any
society. If one only knew of a scalded child, or of a
woman whose husband beat her ! I would give fifty dollars
for a blind old woman to read to, — yes, or a hundred for
a poor girl that would let me teach her to read or to make
wax-flowers. And it is getting worse and worse with me
every day. I wish somebody would swindle me out of my
money, or set fire to the house, or charge me with stealing
something in the stores. Oh, me !"

For a long time she sat in her chair, her head upon her
bosom, thinking, thinking, thinking. But it could not have
been wholesome thought. Once she rose, and stood looking, another Mariana in her moated grange, out of the
window. She might as well have been looking at a stone
wall, for any thing she saw of interest. All that she did
note were her carriage and horses waiting, according to her
orders, at the gate ; and she commanded them away as if it
were an importunate tramp. Then, after walking hither and
thither like a caged lynx, she sank into a seat. As she sat,
her hands clenched, her eyes grew dry and bright, her
face hard and white and cold. At last she rose, shut her
Bible with a slam, left the little room as if finding it too
small to hold her, and walked up and down her chamber

with rapid steps and flaming glances. Her Sunday-school
class would not have known her. She raised her hands to
wring them, winding the fingers of the one in the other, and
when they fell to her side they were clenched. The curls
upon either side of her face suddenly seemed frivolous in
connection with the violence of her aspect; it was like ringlets adown the cheeks of Bellona. And terrible words broke
from her lips, — invective, reproach, scorn, despair, — the
very suppression of speech adding to its intensity and bitterness.

"And to think," she said in a fierce whisper, "that the
wickedest wretch living is not as miserable as I am! And
yet I have tried so hard to be good and to do good all my
life!"

As she walked, like a tigress now, from one end of the
room to the other, her eyes caught sight of her face in a
looking-glass, and she stopped terrified at her appearance.
An instant more, and she had fallen on the floor in an agony
of repentance, crying, pleading for pardon, weeping as it
were her soul away. Utterly exhausted, she rose at last,
bathed her face long and carefully, and arranged her hair.
The next moment she sank once more on her knees in her
little room, very calm and quiet. "Whatever is thy will,
O Heaven!" was all she said.

As she rose, the front gate opened and shut. Very languidly she looked out of the window. When she saw who
it was, there was first an exclamation of anger, then her
face relaxed into a smile, then she was laughing with sincerity and girl-like sense of the fun of it all. At a glance
she saw that it was not so much the visitor as it was a great
event which had arrived; and in the instant she recognized and accepted it.

"Very well," she replied when one of the women announced a visitor. "Tell him I will be down in a few minutes." But her visitor had to wait. Never had Miss Aurelia

Jones made a more elaborate toilet; and when at last she did go down, her face was the brightest and most beautiful thing about her. It would be wrong to liken so thoroughly excellent a woman to a barren and burned-out satellite as the moon, although Miss Aurelia had undoubtedly had her volcanic experiences as well as that orb: yet the moon itself did not wax and wane through greater variations of light and shadow than did she.

To the commodore her curls had never seemed so natural, her eyes so bright in their beady blackness, her face more effusive with the cordial welcome which gave such warmth to her hand as she held it out on entering.

"I am so glad you called this beautiful day, sir," she began at once. "I wanted," with a charming smile, "to say how wrong I was as to that cubit measure we were discussing."

"That is one reason, Miss Aurelia," the visitor hastened to say, "I called. I insisted, you remember, that a cubit is eighteen inches. On reflection, I am inclined to think you were right as to its being twenty-one inches instead. I have gone accurately over the chart of the tabernacle. It is absurd, when I come to think of it, that the house of worship for the millions led out by Moses was only forty-five by fifteen feet. Your cubit is undoubtedly the correct measure, and even that leaves the tabernacle extremely small."

"It is very kind of you to think so," she hastened almost impatiently to say; "but every respectable commentator adopts your idea of the cubit, — eighteen inches, sir, eighteen. And I wanted to say how ashamed I am that I was so impulsive and heated when we discussed it. People who are in the wrong always are vexed, you know."

"In that case I certainly was the one in error," the commodore said with energy. "I am always too positive, madam. The habit was formed on shipboard, where I had to be peremptory, as you are aware. I have never differed with you, Miss Jones, that I had not reason to regret it afterward."

"Please don't allude to it, commodore," the lady interrupted.

Now, Miss Jones had been painfully careful hitherto not to give that gentleman his title. She refrained from doing so, because she knew that he decidedly preferred it. By styling him *sir* instead, as a rule, — by speaking to and of him in moments of serious difference as *Mr.* Grandheur, even, — she had intended him distinctly to understand, that, whoever else in St. Jerome was afraid of him, she was not. In no way could she have hauled down her flag, too, to-day more entirely, and at the same time with more womanly grace, than in thus giving him, and as a matter of course, his rightful title. The sweetness to her visitor of such a sugar-plum was simply ridiculous, but in some respects the gallant old soul was the tiniest of babes.

"And while we are upon the subject, commodore," she continued in her eager way, "I want to acknowledge my error in regard to the talents."

"Not at all, madam," the other said, bringing his gold-headed cane down with quite a thump on the carpet, as he sat with it between his knees. "It was *I* who was mistaken. A silver talent could never have been sixteen hundred and ten dollars, as I asserted, any more than a talent of gold was merely twenty-seven thousand three hundred and seventy-five dollars. You were right, madam, — right!"

"Oh, no, commodore, — no, no! You know," the lady said, sweetly referring to a mite of a memorandum-book in her portemonnaie, "that I said a talent of silver amounted to two thousand two hundred and fifty dollars. Absurd! that would make a talent of gold no less than thirty-six thousand dollars. I am heartily ashamed of taking such ground. In that case, the temple of Solomon cost between eight and nine hundred millions of dollars. How absurd ! My position was positively wicked. Mr. Fanthorp is a scoffer, and he seized upon my estimate as proof that the Bible is false. You cannot tell, commodore, how sincerely I regret it.

"Please let me say one thing more, and then we will never allude to the subject again," she added softly and with lowered eyes. "We have often differed, — very often, I fear, — and the influence of this was bad upon the Sunday-school children, to say nothing of the teachers. I blame myself severely. But — no, let me say it all, please," she added as he made an effort to interrupt her. "One moment. You know me well. I am, I fear, of an ardent and impulsive nature, far too much so : I am so self-willed. It is my misfortune to be my own mistress, and — oh, you know " —

The visitor understood very well that she referred to her wealth, which, as everybody agreed, did somewhat spoil Miss Aurelia, as, alas ! whom does it not spoil? In all that she said, however, she remained a lady. No man knew that better than did her guest. He had but to presume upon any thing said by her, and those lowered eyes would be lifted with a flash which would have riven the commodore, stout as he was. They knew each other : from long and close association each knew the other perfectly well. Too long had they labored together in the same church for this not to be the case. All along they had quarrelled because each was so determined, as well as independent. But of late they had come to be aware that, in fact, each was, instead, unspeakably dependent upon the other, — a conclusion, which gave a converging direction to the determination steadily forming in the bosoms of both. He had come to know that his lonely life was intolerable already, and that it would become more so with every fleeting day. This being so, he knew of no other lady so well qualified, on the whole, to relieve his otherwise desperate estate. Possibly the same reflection was true on her part toward him, except that his opinions had been slowly forming, while hers had come, as a woman's best resolves always do, in the fateful instant she had seen him enter her front gate that morning.

There was, under all his concessions to the lady, the steady resolve, that, as captain of the ship, he must and would rule in the event of marriage. On her side there was almost an eagerness to be ruled. It was a welcome rest after years of strife against circumstances, and was in the last hour re-action from the violence into which that strife with the inevitable had culminated at the very moment its remedy was approaching her house in the boots of the commodore.

One thing surprised and delighted them both, and that was the degree in which they felt themselves entirely at home, each with the other. The spirits of the gentleman rose higher as he felt himself advancing to conquest; for a love of rule had grown with his growth, exactly as a passion for drink or for gambling might have done. Not a syllable had as yet been ventured by him in that direction, and yet the lady faced and accepted what she felt to be a certainty; and her increasing satisfaction showed itself in the deepening quietness of her manner, — a quietness which explained itself to her as she sat. Amazing to say, her surrender was, she well knew, but the path toward such a supremacy in the end over this grand old foe of hers as she had never dreamed of. She almost pitied him, knowing how unconsciously he was passing into her hands, to be as completely ruled as ever a husband was in this world, — a world from the primeval constitution of which, and by some astounding oversight, the salique law has been wholly omitted.

"There is another thing, commodore," she said at last, and after a good deal of conversation, — "a matter in which you were right. I allude to it with reluctance : your original opposition, I mean, to our pastor, Mr. Venable. You know how delighted *I* was. I overrate everybody, exactly as I did the cubits and the talents : it is my impulsive nature. I am afraid I made myself too active, I am so enthusiastic, you know."

"Pardon me, madam, — not at all. It but illustrates," the other hastened to say, greatly struck by it, " how much your excellent judgment was superior to my own. As you will recall, I had taken my stand in opposition before I knew him, and I would therefore have disliked him whatever he had proved to be. It was sheer prejudice in me, — prejudice ! It has been my business in life, madam, to know my subordinates, in order to wield them in cases of sudden emergency. I am compelled to know them thoroughly, and I have come to know Mr. Venable. You must pardon me," her visitor said with dignity, " if I do most heartily appeal to your first impression of the gentleman, venturing to differ from you now as I do from myself then. I very highly prize our pastor. He is young, but he has the elements of sterling manhood. I speak so warmly because I confess, as I have come to know him, it has touched me to the soul to see how profound is his dissatisfaction with himself. A man, Miss Jones, may — please do not misunderstand me — may throw himself — I speak with all reverence — too prostrate even at the feet of God ! In a certain sense, I mean."

"Did you ever think of Daniel?" she said. "I mean when he had his vision of God beside the river. He fell flat on his face ; but his visitor would not speak to him while in that attitude, and made him arise. And when Daniel got up, but remained upon his hands and knees, the command was, 'Stand upon thy feet,' before God would confer with him. I like a man," the lady added with energy, " to *be* a man, — to be humble, but to be a *man !* "

The commodore flushed with pleasure as he exclaimed,

"I heartily agree with you, Miss Aurelia. And I thank you
for your admirable illustration from Scripture. When I was
going with my fleet into a storm or into a battle, I first
asked aid of Heaven. I asked it importunately, I hope;
but, having done so, I handled my ships myself. In a certain sense, I stood upon my quarter-deck in God's place.
Look at poor old Father Fethero, madam. The whole
tendency of our times is to lower and weaken the manhood of the ministry. A man must be a captain of his ship,
whatever the craft be, if he is to bring it into harbor. I
agree with you most heartily;" and he sat up in his chair
more erect than before, a gallant old soul as you could wish
to see, — sat up strong and commanding for an instant. The
next, shifting his cane from hand to hand as he sat, his large
figure-head of a face grew pale and then purple. In vain he
attempted to put on the port of a commander as he goes
into action, and at conscious disadvantage he began:
"Ahem! Miss Aurelia Jones, I wished" —

"Oh! by the by — pardon me, commodore," the lady
said hastily, but with ease, because entirely mistress of the
situation, and rising as she spoke, — "there are some
improvements I have planned upon my place. I am always
mistaking. Please oblige me with your excellent judgment;" and, so saying, she led her visitor, nothing loath,
out of her parlor and into the grounds.

CHAPTER XXIII.

THE EBBING SEA REVEALS SOMEWHAT OF THAT WHICH IT HIDES.

WITH August came the yearly repainting and repairing of Gen. Buttolph's mansion in St. Jerome; and Mr. Venable aceepted an often-repeated invitation of Mr. Parsons to make his house, at least for a while, his home.

Mr. Parsons was too much absorbed in his manifold inventions to pay attention to his pastor beyond the usual courtesies of a host; the more especially as Mrs. Parsons, overflowing with health and spirits, and sympathizing with the young man, exerted herself beyond her warm-hearted wont to make him feel at home. As to little Owny, she forsook father and mother to cleave to their guest; living, almost, in Mr. Venable's study, if not in his arms. He was by no means the enthusiastic person he had been, and for so long after his arrival. What was this wonderful island at last, but a reef of sand? The eternal sea, almost on a level with it all around, was wearisome; the heat of midsummer so oppressive that he was fain to sleep these hot nights upon the floor of the veranda, an umbrella up over him to keep off the brilliant light of the moon. And then the mosquitoes were so maddening, whenever a land-breeze blew, as to irritate him beyond endurance. Worse than all, the summer had poured a stupidity as into the arteries of his church. Not only was the attendance thereupon small, — at prayer-meeting exceedingly small, — but he could no more arouse himself than he could the people.

The unceasing unbelief of Mrs. Parsons and Owny in the inventor's ideas, their perpetual ridicule and laughter, amused their guest; but he was more interested in the loving devotion, none the less, of the blooming wife and her rosy little duplicate, to the gaunt and hollow-eyed old man, so eager and headlong in pursuit of bubbles which always broke as he grasped them.

"If I miss it in one thing I will hit it in another," Mr. Parsons said one morning at breakfast when his wife had been unmerciful in the long list she gave Mr. Venable of her husband's inventions, each of which had been, in its turn, so certain to succeed. "Ezra Micajah Papa is made of India-rubber," she replied: "when he falls hardest he bounces highest. Look at that ˏ ridiculous terraqueous machine."

"It is bound to succeed; yes, to succeed gloriously," her husband interrupted. "I am going to give you all another ride, sir. I am perfecting the wheels. Next time we will go faster, and not only by land."

"Will you take to the air?" his wife asked, laughing.

"Not with this machine. But I will one day; and," he added, "I will call it the terra-aërial-aqueous machine. Laugh away. — Hold your mug, Owny;" and seizing upon the pitcher of milk, he was, after looking thoughtfully into it, complying with a request of the child for more.

"O Ezra Micajah Papa!" the little one exclaimed, and with good reason. Her father had poured half a gallon instead of a half-pint, overflowing the mug. In hastily setting down the pitcher it had upset upon the pones of corn-bread, deluging the table.

"Stuff an' nonsense! Fiddlesticks!" the child cried, while the good wife, without a shadow upon her clear, healthful face, broke into a merriment which it was better than breakfast to hear. "What is the matter?" she called after her husband, as he got up hurriedly from the table, upsetting his chair, and nearly pulling the cloth off the board.

"An idea strikes me!" It was all he said as he disappeared. And it *was* an idea, if gold is the weight and measure thereof. The blow of that thought smote in the end from the lean and rocky old man a stream deeper and broader, and to flow considerably farther, than that flood of milk, — a stream upon whose tide, if the figure may be pressed, there sailed to him at last his ship of money, in good earnest, bringing to him at least one hundred thousand dollars a year.

But none at table knew it then; and Mr. Venable was glad to get away from it all as from another of the innumerable annoyances of the wearisome time.

"I am utterly disgusted," he found himself saying an hour later to Father Fethero, upon whom he had called as a desperate alternative. He had found the old minister working as usual in the garden of the poor place he called his home; and they had seated themselves, it was so hot, upon empty vinegar-kegs of which the children had made a playhouse under the china-tree in the corner of the ground.

"The people seem to have taken an aversion to me," he said in the distress of his soul. "Few except the members come to hear me. Almost no one attends prayer-meeting. I argue and persuade and entreat with all the soul I possess, and in vain. And I try to instruct in the doctrines and duties, yet is it water on rock. I make the most earnest effort to prepare sermons. They seem to me so interesting and striking; but no one cares to listen to them. It is terrible. I have no appetite. I cannot sleep at night. It may surprise you that I should speak so plainly, Father Fethero; but I know you will not mention it. And you are an experienced minister. I must have some one to advise with. And look at it, sir," he added almost bitterly: "here are a dozen churches, fully equipped, yet wickedness has become

so rampant that the people have had to organize a vigilance
committee.   It began, you know, with the lynching of Gen.
Buttolph's overseer ; and they have had to pack off a score
of scoundrels upon the Nautilus, — gamblers, swindlers, mur-
derers.   Is not the gospel in our hands a dead failure?
For one, I am disgusted with myself!" and his whole aspect
confirmed the fact.

This was but a small portion of what he said.   He knew
that he would regret next day having said any thing ; but he
had endured so long, he was desperate.   Besides, he sincerely
loved the worn-out old veteran, and he believed that Father
Fethero had come to like him.   And so he had.   But Father
Fethero had been Father Fethero for too many tough and
terrible years, to be any other than Father Fethero still.

"I don't know, I do not know," he said at last, and after
the other was entirely through.   "Ahem ! yes.   You are
grievously distressed.   I do not wonder at it.   For one, I
am astonished it is not worse.   When there is too great a
gush at first, you are sure to give out and dry up the sooner.
I said to my daughter, when they made such a to-do over
you at your coming, ' Jane, this cannot last.'   You have come
to me, and I will stand in the gap.   That is, so far as I can
I will stand in the gap; yes, stand in the gap.   But I must
be honest.   All I have to go by is my own experience.   For
fifty years no man could have toiled harder than I did.   I
am not saying I have had no seasons of refreshing from the
presence of the Lord.   But I have had a hard time, my
young brother, — a very hard time.   I have been strongly
tempted to regard him as a hard master.   On horseback and
often on foot: Paul did that, you know, to Assos.   Winter,
summer, wet, dry, cold, hot, all seasons, I have forded
creeks, swum streams, struggled through bogs, slept out in
the woods ; tried to do so on prairies, but could not by reason
of the howling, night long, of the wolves."   It was plain that
Father Fethero would take a good long time in which to tell,

in his slow way, of his sorrows; and the younger of the two adjusted himself by a severe effort to listen. From past experience he knew that the other was wearisome, to a young man full of his own trials, intolerably wearisome.

"Yes, yes: if any man ought to know, I do. Very often have I preached on an empty stomach. And all along," the old man added, fastening his mournful gaze through his spectacles on the face of his friend, "I did so sincerely desiring to know nothing but Him crucified. Once, after preaching and pastoral visiting among a people, — it was in the Hawley Post Oaks, I remember, for a whole year, — I happened to overhear their leading men say they would gladly double my salary if I would not preach at all. On another occasion, — it was at Limestone Court House, — I received one day what was all the compensation I got for months of severe labor. On this wise it was: At the house where I always staid Sunday nights, I had an attack of dysentery, and they gave me a phial of paregoric to take to my room. Monday morning as I was leaving, I handed the phial to the lady; and she said, 'You may have it, brother Fethero: *you* may keep it.' I put it into my saddle-bags; and *that*," Father Fethero added without a suspicion of humor in his manner, "was all I got for preaching at Limestone Ridge."

The old man rested both of his yellow and wrinkled hands, one on the other, on the top of his spade, for he had arisen; changed his weight, as he did in the pulpit, from one foot to the other; and after some silent meditation, he cleared his throat with peculiar pulpit clearance, and continued, "You are young, I am old: that is the only difference between us. I could preach when I was your age as much wood, hay, and stubble as you: and thought it gold, silver, precious stones, as much as you do. Look at me;" and the old man, with his wrinkled hands extended on either side, made appeal to himself, so rusty and patched in his working-suit, — such a weather-beaten laborer, from the tips of his broad-toed boots to the top of his old hat of black straw. " I tell you, my young brother," he added, " it is a sin, an awful sin ; but I am tempted at times. The silver and the gold are His, and it is paid out to me, his hardworked old servant, in pennies so few, so pitiful — May God forgive me ! " the old man added, the tears flowing unchecked from under the rims of his glasses. " If I could but have won more souls, I wouldn't care for the dollars. No : welcome poverty, if I only could know I had won a multitude of souls — !

" At many and many an appointment," Father Fethero continued, " I have gone into the church or schoolhouse with crowds on crowds of men gathered together because it was a Sunday and a bright day, standing about outside, whittling sticks and talking, not more than a dozen or two of the old stand-bys in to hear me preach. How full I was of the blessed gospel ! my soul running over with the good tidings, and not a sinner inside to hear it ; the people as clean out of my reach as if they were in Jericho. Poor sermons ! God only knows the difference it makes in a sermon to have nobody, almost, to hear it. Paul couldn't preach then. Suppose I never was a man of talent: I wanted to do good. They say this and that man ought never to have gone into the ministry. I have had ungodly men tell me I ought never to have left the plough. Wasn't it Providence? Is it only talent that is blessed? God forgive my wicked unbelief ! I know there remaineth a rest. As to your case," he added after composing himself a little, " I must honestly say that I plainly perceive a gloom. I fear things will be worse and worse. If people shouldn't continue to like you " —

" Let any one give me the least hint," said the other hotly, " and I resign instantly ! "

" I don't know. I do not know," Father Fethero made grave reply. " It is giving up a salary. You will not find it easy to get another charge, as I know from my own bitter experience. Yet," he continued, his blue spectacles full upon the other, "it may come to that. All I can say," he closed as they parted at last, "is what the aged Paul said to Timothy: Endure hardness as a good soldier."

The warrior in this instance, however, retreated as from a defeat.

"What did I go to him for?" he demanded of himself, after an hour's walk upon the beach. "That is part of my weakness;" and he strolled languidly along, heedless of the surf often dashing over his feet. As he neared the house of Gen. Buttolph, he came upon Grit, who was digging, in sheer summer idleness, a fiddler-crab out of the sand to see it fight. It was a relief to sit down beside the boy upon the clean sand. After the sorrowful old age of Father Fethero, the mere youth of the boy was a pleasant variety. "I am so glad, Grit," he said, after a good deal of talk about the bathing, fishing, boating, and the like, "that you are growing to be so good a boy. I hope you are not sorry I came."

"Oh! it wasn't you," his companion said with a boy's frankness. "It's Zeo. I can't stand preaching, you see. A fellow will go to sleep. Oh! as to that, yes, I was a hard case, a regular rip. What can you expect when a fellow's mother is dead, and there's nothing but the negroes? Irene only stopped her ears, and ran. She said I was a perfect nuisance, a detestable wretch. That's all she said. The best *she* can do is to scold like thunder, or to cry like sixty. Now, there's Zeo" —

"Hush, Grit," his companion said: "we must not talk about family matters. But," he added as the boy worried the crab which was standing up on its hind claws and clashing at the stick with its pincers, "I would like," he continued after a longer silence, "to know how your sister got you to — to" —

"Stop being such a scamp," Grit said promptly. "Oh! well, she loved me, and she wasn't afraid of me — not one bit. I have gone at her with a hatchet, and she never so much as winked. But it wasn't that, you'd better believe," he added, after a pause.

" Well, if it is not improper for you to say? " asked Mr. Venable.

" If I didn't curse and swear a few ! but," added the boy, " I said things worse than that for a white girl to hear, you know. Oh, but I was a rip ! The thing is, I was afraid of her. I used to peep of nights through the key-hole. My ! how she used to kneel and pray " —

" Hush ! never mind," began the other.

" And when she came at me, her eyes so fixed and steady and loving ; I tell you," he continued, " it wasn't because she seemed as big then as a barn, and as strong as a horse. What it was is, I was afraid, — afraid somehow : oh ! I don't know ; a sort of something with her, and more than her ; and a kind of something in me too. "Look here, Mr. Venable, you used to look at her so I thought," planting his unconscious dagger in the heart of the other, " that *you* were going to court her. But Zeo is going to marry Old Ugly, the governor, you know ; a splendid chap. Look at that," producing a pocket-knife : " ten blades, a corkscrew, a walnut-picker, and a pair of pincers. He gave it. That's the kind of a brother-in-law, you bet ! And I'm going to live with them. With Irene? I guess not.

" I say, Mr. Venable," he called after the other, "will you marry Zeo and the governor? You'd better : there'll be lots of cake."

But this last information was lost upon the other, as he strode away down the beach ; nor did he look up until smitten by a whiff of foul smell off the flats, from which the tide had gone out.

" Yes," he said, as he looked, but without stopping, over the slimy expanse of green mire, " I suppose it is a good thing to have the tide go out in me, until I know how much

mud and offal, what a rottenness of dead things and detestable stenches, there are in my inmost heart. All the processes
of God are to make the sea ebb out for that. Yes; and to
make it flow in again afterward, when the lowest ebb is
reached. Grit is right, — his sister, I mean. When we are
desperate in regard to any thing, the instant we find that
we cannot do it ourselves, that instant we begin to try to get
God to do it for us." He walked the more rapidly until he
reached his room at Mr. Parsons's. Once there he locked
himself in; nor did all the entreaties first, and then the
wrath, of Owny outside, avail to secure her an entrance for
the rest of that day.

CHAPTER XXIV.

THE TIDE BEGINS TO RETURN AGAIN.

MR. VENABLE arose early next morning, saddled a young horse assigned him by Mr. Parsons, and rode down the beach. All that his horse had learned so far was to stand still, or to go as if destruction were at its heels; and the air was all the fresher by reason of the rate at which they went. There was a pleasure, too, in being the first person along the surf that morning, a subtle gratification such as one takes in unfolding a daily damp from the press, in cutting the pages of a book just published, in playing with a child having the dewy charm upon its brow of laughing little Owny, — the delight of getting back to Eden and the beginning of things. The swift speed over the wet sand and along the lines of bubbles left by the retreating waves was as near that of flight through the air as one can attain, and it was long before he could draw rein. When he did, it was to dismount, fasten his horse to a drifted log, throw off his clothes, and plunge into the sea. It seemed to be as illimitable as the atmosphere, and more palpable to his enjoyment; and he surrendered himself to the billows as he had done to his horse. The difficulty with him in bathing was now, as it always had been, to come out again; and it was not until the sun, peering above the level sand, had fairly detached itself from the horizon, that he consented to enter with it upon the duty of the day by dressing and galloping back. Even then it was a shame to carry so keen an appetite to Mrs. Parsons's breakfast-table ; and he paused before he entered the house, under the fig-trees, to eat a few of the blue and purple figs which covered the grass, trembling in luscious ripeness upon the low branches, to fall thither in a moment.

"When I was at the North," he said as he ate, " men and women were as hard to win as the hickory-nut or chestnut in its burr : here they drop into any honest and cordial hand as easily as " — and he touched and received into his palm a plump fig — " this fruit. Except Commodore Grandheur, and he is yielding at last. But ah ! will not the governor find it so with Miss Zeo? Yet, as I took oath when I first awoke, to-day I will *not* think of her ! Till I die I will not despair ; but, please Heaven, there is another than she to be won first."

After breakfast, he refreshed himself further by kissing little Owny upon her rosy cheeks ; and, obtaining a solemn promise from her that she would not hammer with her fists upon his door till dinner-time, he hastened to his room. He had already prepared a specially elaborate discourse for Sunday. Tearing this to pieces as a good beginning, and taking a suitable text, he leaned back in his chair, planted Gen. Buttolph in imagination before him, and proceeded to say to him, as distinctly and as directly as it could be done without giving offence, precisely what he thought of him, and of the inevitable result to which that genial individual was hastening.

The next day was Sunday. There were fewer at church than he had feared. But he was strangely indifferent to this ; as much so as an arrow is to the air when sufficient aim and impulse has been given to it. With a subtle avoidance of offending any one, which was part of his power, he merely said over again in his sermon to the portly general sitting in front, as well as to every person there, according to

his besetting sin, what as to guilt and danger that individual
was saying to himself already ; and so ended.   He did not
need that any one should inform him as to the effect ; for he
knew that people assure each other only where matters are
so uncertain as to need assurance.

"My wife," Capt. Chaffin lingered after service to say
to him, "has something she is dying to tell you.   Weemen
are deelicate," continued the mariner, in a troubled way.
"All I ask is, when she does tell you — and she may never
do it — please say nothing about it till you've seen me first.
She is so very small a craft, carries so few tons and so much
engine, draws so little water for the size of her soul, — oh !
you know what I mean, sir, — that I am always afraid —
afraid " —

"She has already spoken to me," the other said, not
thrown from his certainty of results by an interruption even
of such a sort.   "I thanked her heartily, but I have not
done enough to have my portrait painted yet.   Please excuse me to her, captain, and say " —

"It isn't that, it isn't that," the husband broke in.   "You
never fear !   A grander idea has driven that clean out.   It
is, I do suppose," he said, eagerly yet watching the face of
the other with an almost pitiful anxiety, "the grandest, the
very grandest idea, a woman ever had !   You have no no-
tion, sir, *how* grand it is !   It will strike you at first like " —
with the same covert scrutiny of the face of the other, as if
for a suspicious smile — "like a squall !   But what I want
to say is — is — it must be weathered like a squall, too.
Don't you say yes, I mean, until you see me ; and don't tell
anybody about it.   You won't, will you ? "

"Certainly not," Mr. Venable said without a gleam of
amusement in his countenance.   "I understand perfectly,"
he added, with grave respect.

The face of the captain was rigid, and more of the hue
of walnut than before.   It was the increasing wear and

tear, as of salt seas and hard storms, beginning to leave deeper marks in the honest wood of which he seemed, more than ever, to be made. There was a hesitation and yet an enthusiasm, a dignity and yet a shamefacedness, in his assertions about his gifted wife, which had always touched the other to the soul.

"It is the case of young Plenty and old Plenty over again," he thought, as he walked home. "I wonder how much lying such love can excuse. Two idiot children, Mr. Parsons said, and a crazy wife? If the captain *is* a fool for a fourth, Heaven ranks such folly above the highest wisdom. O Love, Love, you are indeed — God!"

Owing to the scant attendance at evening services at that season of the year, notice had been given that there would be a conference meeting at night instead of sermon, to be held in the vestry instead of the church proper. When Mr. Venable arrived at the usual hour, he was surprised to find the room crowded, although individuals and numbers had both ceased to have the weight with him, somehow, they had possessed till that day. He imagined that Miss Aurelia Jones bowed as she passed him, as he was pausing a moment with Commodore Grandheur in the vestibule, less coldly than of late. Certainly the commodore was cordial enough. "I was just saying to Mr. Nogens," he remarked, "that you showed excellent sense in your way of silencing Mr. Quatty — by that plan of the hall. We will not be troubled with *him* any more."

There seemed to be deeper feeling than usual in the meeting which ensued. Mrs. Chaffingsby even ventured to join in the singing in her thin treble. It was plain from Father Fethero's prayer, that he had repented of his discouraging words, it was so hopeful in comparison to any thing before. There had been one or two deaths in the church, and the pastor dwelt with special solemnity upon the uncertainty of life. No one cared even to see whether Mr. Quatty was

present. As the service drew to a close, it became more
solemn with every hymn and prayer. Commodore Grandheur had never spoken with such weight. The grief of those
who had lost their relatives was contagious, and many were
weeping. As Mr. Parsons seated himself after one of his
rapid prayers, a voice from the back seat said, and very
gravely, —

"Let us pray. — Thou knowest, O Lord," it continued,
"that we are but for an hour. The wickedest men of this
wicked region had been packed off, thou knowest, upon
that steamship. Has not thy servant heard, as he came here
to-night, that the Nautilus has at last gone down at sea,
every soul lost? Dreadfully not ready! Surely our life is
vain" — and the supplication proceeded in language of
even thrilling power and pathos.

It was wonderful. So unlike were the tones, words, entire
manner of Mr. Quatty, — who had never led in prayer
before, — to any thing previously heard from his lips, that
people were some time in satisfying themselves — peeping,
in some cases, through their hands held over their faces —
that it was the man ; but there was neither indignation nor
amusement by the time they were sure. A better prayer had
never been put up. The words were homely, but the honest and sincere heart palpitated in every syllable. Every
eye was moist when he sat down. The special importunity
of Mr. Quatty was for a deeper and more general interest in
religion ; and all agreed that the new interest which followed
dated from that hour.

Among the unusual events, Miss Irene had attended the
meeting, bringing Mr. Fanthorp with her. Gov. Magruder
had dropped in at the close to escort Miss Zeo home,
although the fact that it was Sunday diminished to a fearful
degree the topics upon which that statesman could converse.
Even the presence of the man he most dreaded did not
turn the minister from his aim, nor slacken his impulse : he

and Gen. Buttolph walked silently together through the night. As they neared the general's house, the younger of the two proposed that they should stroll on toward the surf before the general went in; and the impulse upon his part was in close sympathy with the yielding upon the part of the other.

Gen. Buttolph was a magnificent person to look at. Reputed the wealthiest planter of that region, always handsomely if carelessly dressed, generous and hospitable, there was a certain Assyrian assumption in him which made people yield even where he was too indolent to command, possibly unconscious of any desire to that effect. And yet he was at last merely an overgrown boy. All that Grit was when Zeo returned from school, he was, save upon a larger and more decorous scale; as reckless beneath all the proprieties as he. When the two men had reached the seashore he turned and said, " Do you know, sir, that you have done a perilous thing to-day? "

" I do," Mr. Venable replied gravely.

" It is the first time any man has dared to attempt it, sir," he added.

" Is it? I can only say, sir," the other remarked respectfully but earnestly, "that I would have done it long ago, had I known. I had no wish to offend you, general, but I am in St. Jerome to do what I tried to do to-day."

Some storm had hurled a timber like a javelin into the beach near them; and the general laid one hand upon the projecting end, and, while the minister was sure of nothing beyond his duty to the slave of appetite before him, extended the other to him in the moonlight, saying, " I honor you, sir! You are right! My father had certain habits, as did my brothers. His death, their death, was a relief to us. I have been going the same way, have been transmitting our family curse to Grit. Zeo has long entreated me, but you have brought matters to-day to a conclusion. I thank you, sir, but it is not to you I yield : it is to my dead wife and to Zeo ; " and to the astonishment of his companion the voice of the other faltered, broke ; and there followed such a conversation between the two as rarely befalls, and when it does admits of no third party. Except that he was himself no Daniel, it was to Mr. Venable like the downfall before him of a king of Babylon. "Good-night," Gen. Buttolph said to him at last; "but remember, sir, I do not bind myself beyond the end of this year. By that time I will be able to judge, but not beyond then. Good-night, sir, I must go in : I wish to see my daughter."

CHAPTER XXV.

IN WHICH PEOPLE OF DIVERSE KINDS ARE NOT MORE MIXED
UP THAN THEY OFTEN ARE IN THIS TANGLED LIFE.

MISS ZEO was so long in leaving the church on the
Sunday morning following upon this, that Mr. Venable
could not help, as he came down the pulpit-steps after service, saying a word to her. She raised her eyes to his, her
soul in them, gave him her hand, said, " I thank you, sir," in
a low voice, and hastened down the aisle to join her father.
It took but a moment, it gave him a thrill of pleasure; yet
she would hardly have had the heart to do it if she had
known what mortal pain, too, it was to him.

"How can I endure," he groaned to himself, "to see
her the wife of another?" So far as he knew, her marriage
with Gov. Magruder was settled. The papers throughout
the State were filled with intimations of his election to the
United States Senate before long, some allusion to a bride
always accompanying them; and the derisive congratulations
upon his reform from his bachelor ways were numerous.
The pressure of her hand, the gratitude of her eyes, these
were to Mr. Venable like the light from the bayou-boat
upon the forest ahead : they merely showed how impenetrable was his path. "But," he thought, " I can but make an
effort to advance steadily day by day. It is all I *can* do."

The next day Grit hailed him as he was walking to the
post-office.

" I say, Mr. Venable, Zeo's got that key," the boy said, as he walked beside him.

" Key? " his companion asked.

" Don't pretend you don't know, Mr. Venable : pa's key, the key of the sideboard where the decanter is," Grit explained. " She's got it on a ribbon around her neck. I saw it one night when I was kneeling by her to say my prayers, and I twitched it out. Oh, but pa he gets restless about bedtime ! He misses it awfully. Zeo she sings and plays for him, reads to him, tells him all the funny things she can think of. She beats Irene at that, because, you see, I help her. Oh, but Zeo is good as wheat ! One night " —

But his companion would not allow him to say more. He was glad of this confirmation of his hopes, it thrilled him to hear the name even of the daughter ; but his thoughts turned again, after parting with Grit, to the extra services upon which his church was now entered. These continued during several weeks ; the interest spread to other churches ; and in the end quite a number were added to the First Church as the result.

One day toward the close of these special services, Mr. Parsons asked Mr. Venable at dinner to call at Gen. Buttolph's, and beg Miss Zeo not to be late on the ground for the trial trip of his greatly-improved terraqueous machine, his invitation having been already accepted.

" Be sure and don't forget," Mrs. Parsons added, but in such a way as to bring the blood to the face of her guest.

" I love Miss Zeo too," little Owny said, in the pause which followed ; for she seemed in this, as in every thing else, to get as much now as before her birth, soul as well as body, from her mother. Whatever Mrs. Parsons thought and felt, Owny did too, and at the same instant. " That's all the cause why I go to Sunny school," the child added, " to be her 'ittle girl. She is *my* one. Div her a tiss, Mr.

Venny, and tell her Owny sent it." But all that the mother said in parting with him when he left, soon after dinner, was, "I would call, if I were you," and with such a serious face that he walked away, his heart beating as if in fever — in fever, and aware that the finger of this female practitioner was upon his pulse.

But he did not go in when he got to the general's mansion. He had not been there for many weeks; and the same pretence of the repairs going on was rendered now, as he stood hat in hand on the veranda.

"Tell Mr. Parsons that I'll not be there, for one," Irene said. "I think it is shameful, Mr. Venable. Just as the religious interest is decreasing, too!" for, after vehemently refusing to attend church at all when the revival had begun, she had yielded to it as violently at last. Miss Aurelia Jones herself was not as faithful in her attendance, or as fervid, apparently, in her devotions.

"Mr. Parsons is compelled to act at once in order to secure his patent," Mr. Venable explained. "The party will be small. I have come to know Mr. Parsons," he added; "and the sole purpose of the man in his desperate efforts *is* to be able to give, — to give millions if he can. Of all men, he has the deepest conviction that it is nothing less than millions will do to spread the gospel;" and it was said earnestly. But the speaker seemed embarrassed, and anxious to get away; the more so, as there was a change in Miss Zeo standing there. It was a certain something in her which he felt rather than saw, much less understood. She appeared to be no longer the girl, firm and steady and strong, whom she had been. Her sister seemed, since he had last conversed with them, to have become her superior, certainly for the first time. There was no such weakness as downcast eyes and drooping manner and hesitating speech in the elder of the two.

"She is overcome," the visitor said to himself, "as we all

are, by the sultry season; and how sorely she is overtasked! the dead weight of her father has been, at least, so long upon her heart! A boy from the sheep-folds slew Goliath with his sling, and was done with it; but this girl had to grasp her giant, and to lift him clean off the earth, has had to stand night and day, her Goliath held alive and struggling in the air, and against an appetite dragging at him as steadily as gravitation."

Such was his thought; and he was in a hurry to leave his message, and be gone. Had she met him with the serene front, with the dark eyes full of silent power, as or old, it would have been different; but she seemed to-day so womanly in her weakness, was so humble and without self-reliance, that he was bewildered, and he hastened to speak of the church-work in which they had all been engaged. There was the Bethel for seamen, which was in such a thriving condition in the market-house. "Commodore Grandheur is in charge," he explained. "The sight of the blue shirts and glazed hats assembled before him made him a little too much as if upon the quarter-deck again at first: he was ordering them to repent and be Christians as if it were to hoist anchor or reef sail. There was a mutiny; but his own good sense, as well as Capt. Chaffin, came to his assistance. And only think, ladies," Mr. Venable went on rapidly, "Mr. Quatty has never informed a soul, since the interest began, that he was once an oysterman. He is at every meeting, is an incessant worker among the roughs of the city, lets no man have a horse or buggy from his stable without a tract and a word of exhortation; but in meetings all he has to say is not to man, but to Heaven. I believe his prayers are as effective with God as with man. My impression is," he added with a smile, "that Heaven likes just such men: it is he who is Peter over again without the denying of his Master. I like Mr. Quatty heartily. And look at Father Fethero: he has laid off his gloom with his glasses. Did you ever see such a transformation? he is whole years younger. I understand better than ever the change Heaven can make in us."

"And what does Mr. Nogens say?" Zeo ventured.

"Oh! he merely says, 'Yes,'" Mr. Venable replied; "but he says it more earnestly; and he rubs his hands together in saying it, as if he were intending after a while to say something besides. What I am glad of," he added gravely, "is the *depth* of feeling, the seriousness which seems to rest on all. We preachers thought the power was to be in our sermons; but these last weeks I see, for one, that the strong wind which changes the world is something more than the breath, in any shape, from my lips."

"You preach a thousand times better than you did before," Irene remarked impulsively.

"Thank you; but if I do," said the other with kindling eyes, "it is because I have stopped preaching. I never before knew there was so much wheat and honey, gold, silver, and precious stones, in Scripture, and in the very words of Scripture. All I do is to show others the richness I find there; and it has a value and a simplicity I never knew before. I come every day upon some verse which satisfies one as gold does debt: it suits hunger and thirst like bread and water; ånd I try to give it as I get it. I cannot say *how* beautiful and valuable it all seems to me. But I must go."

"Tell Mr. Parsons I won't come. And you can't know, Mr. Venable," Irene added, "how hard I am trying with Mr. Fanthorp, to make him good, I mean; but he has a worse devil than any the Bible talks about, — a laughing-devil. He won't be serious one instant; and he makes me laugh too. I bite my lips, and clench my hands, but it is no use. You need not look so wise, sir: there's not a particle of truth in it. Farce Fanthorp, indeed! I am as fond of fun as any one, but I hope to look higher than Mr..Fanthorp for a husband. No, sir," she added with energy, — "not if I know myself. I would not allude to the matter, but," with great dignity, " I know it is generally reported, and I want to deny it. The idea ! " — " Good-by, ladies," their visitor said, again going. " Here's Zeo," the impetuous young lady add- ed. — " I know Mr. Fanthorp manages pa's plantation. Pa says he and young Plenty do it splendidly. Perhaps so ; but he cannot manage *me !* Now, if you were to talk about the governor ! I believe you are afraid of Zeo, Mr. Venable : I am not. And I do believe she is afraid of you : I am not, one bit. What is the reason," she went on, thinking aloud, and not for the first time in her life, " that you two seem to have such an aversion to each other? You might at least be friends. *I* like you, Mr. Venable," she said, " not as much as Miss Aurelia Jones does, I mean did. Yes," she added, " only less than I do Col. Roland. Wait a moment " — But their visitor, laughing, and lifting his hat, ran down the steps of the veranda, and was gone, sorry and glad that he staid so long.

He slackened his pace after he had got out of sight. It was late in September. The heat was heavier even than it was hot. He took off his hat, and stood still, looking around while he wiped his forehead. In the slumberous silence he could hear the monotone of the surf, sounding once so wildly to him as out of Story and Song, but subsided now into one of the commonplaces of life. The sky was cloudless, as usual, but not clear. It was as if its deep blue had settled down upon the sand and sea much more closely. The ole- ander and china trees were motionless in every leaf as if waiting. The romance still lingered to him in the orchards of lemon and orange ; but they were all adust and dry, the vast leaves of the banana-plants hanging in yellow shreds about the arch of their stems. He had ceased long ago to notice specially the swift-jacks, or their less brilliant relatives the horned frogs, flitting about in the prickly grass, or darting across the white dust or brown sand of the streets. But now he saw many of them lying panting, with outstretched legs and open mouths, on the wayside. It was as if something were impending. The air seemed to be heavy with doom; and he said to himself, "I have ten minutes to spare. Yonder is Mr. Nogens's house. I'll make Mrs. Nogens hear this time, if I die for it."

After leaving Mr. Nogens's house, as he turned a corner on his way back to Mr. Parsons's place he came upon Miss Zeo on her road thither.

"I have just made a call upon Mrs. Nogens," he explained; and, in order to conceal his satisfaction, "it was literally a call, — as loud a call as I could. After all, I fear she did not hear a word. She is so willing to hear, so anxious to hear, that I'm afraid she says she hears when she don't, smiling and nodding her head."

"I'm obliged to go to Mr. Parsons," his companion hastened to explain, "because he said that he would not give another picayune for Father Fethero if I didn't. Grit went on before me, he was so impatient. — How are you, Clara?"

This was said, as they passed along the paling of Capt. Chaffin's grounds, to the captain's daughter, who was leaning against it from within, her face pressed like a caged creature against the fence.

"There are thousands on thousands of people in there," she said, putting a hand between the palings to be shaken. "I am so tired of them! and ma will keep on making more. Stop a moment. You can talk. They never do, — not to me."

"Are all well?" Zeo replied kindly, endeavoring to pass.

"Charlie is. He sleeps and eats. When I go by them at night," she continued, laying hold upon Zeo's shoulder, "with a candle, they waver and wink. But they don't in the day. They are all throwing their hands about, running as hard as they can, quarrelling and carrying on, until I get

in the room, you see. The moment I open the door, they
stand stock still, holding their breath till I get by. I tell
you, but they all go at it again when I'm out. I listen at
the keyhole, and peep. Sometimes I creep up, and open
the door sudden. But they are too smart. I catch them
all in a tremble, but they are stock still again. Charlie
laughs: he doesn't care. I do. There are too many of
us to be in one house this hot time. They crowd one so!
Sometimes I can hardly breathe. Kiss me good-by." As
the poor girl said it, she stood up on the lower bar of the
fence, and leaned over her beautiful face, holding with both
hands to the pointed pickets.

"That I will," said Zeo tenderly, one hand upon either
cheek of the other as she did so once and again; and the
faces of the two, brought into such contrast, thrilled the
looker-on like strange music. The one face exquisitely fair,
the other dark and sweet, — the hair of the one hanging
down in loose abundance as she bent over the fence, a mere
child without a thought or care; the other younger, yet so
many ages older, the shadow as well as the strength of her
life in her eyes, and upon her lips and brow.

"Good-by, lady. — And won't you kiss me too?" the girl
added, still holding on to the paling, and bending over
toward the gentleman, her full child's eyes on his, her child's
mouth held up like little Owny at home. "They are so
high up I can't reach them, and they won't stoop down. I
want to love somebody. Kiss me, please."

"Kiss her, Mr. Venable," Zeo said, as he stood irresolute.
He did so, the tears in his eyes. With the pressure of his
lips upon the rosy mouth held out to him, he passed on
with his companion.

Nothing was said; for they were behind time with Mr.
Parsons, as he was prompt to tell them upon their arrival.

"There is no hiding any thing now," he was explaining,
when they joined the friends assembled in the parlor.

"This is by broad day, and in an open car. — Humph! is that you, Miss Irene?" he added, as that lady came in accompanied by Mr. Fanthorp. "I hoped you were not coming. We don't want any more screaming at nothing, and such fiddlesticks."

"I said I would not go," she replied; "but here is poor Mr. Fanthorp: he came and begged me to go and take care of him. I'm not afraid."

"Don't go," Mrs. Parsons said, standing among the party, with Owny — both of them rosier than ever — clinging to her dress. "Don't go, Commodore Grandheur. — Be persuaded, Miss Aurelia," she said; for these two had taken the place of Capt. Chaffin and Mr. Quatty, who had refused to be present. "You know I warned you all before. Owny and I are too sensible." And she continued her warnings, laughing and shaking hands in farewell.

"No, I won't tiss you," Owny said, shaking a coquettish head at Col. Roland. "Dere's too much folks to tiss. — Mr. Venny, you may tiss me for dem all," she proposed. To the surprise of the child's mother, as well as Owny, that gentleman did not seem to hear: the kiss of poor Clara was too fresh upon his lips; and Zeo did so instead.

"No concealment, you see," the inventor said, as he led his company out of the grounds and over the sands, to a large open wagon standing on the beach. "It is nothing at all but a car, with, as you observe, a mast in front. The wind is fair and strong, and all I have to do is to hoist this square sail, as we did the other trip. Vehicles have been made," he added, as he assisted his friends to seats, "to be driven by the wind over flat plains. This will be a wonderful mode of travel over the broad prairies of our State. Old Ugly intends to urge my invention upon his friends in the Legislature. But there are rivers to be crossed inland, as well as arms of the sea along the coast. This machine utterly fails if it will not do for water as well. It is a terra-

queous machine, — for land *and* water. Some day I may
adapt it to the air. So far, it succeeds only on earth, and
possibly, for I am not too sure, on the sea. — Not there,
Mr. Venable," he added, as that gentleman climbed in.
"You are the youngest and smartest. Take that front seat,
and haul up the sail. The pulleys are my patent, and work
as easy as eating. I will stand behind here, and steer. All
right ! The glory of this discovery lies in the wheels. If you
lean over and look, you will see they are really screws also,
something like those of a propeller. Of course we go slowly at first," he continued, standing up, lean and long, upon
a step in the rear, his bony grasp upon the helm which
governed the steering-wheel. "Now, we don't want any
nonsense or fiddlesticks, no screaming or jumping out," he
said, as the vehicle, yielding to the wind, began to move
slowly along upon the hard wet sand, in the fringe of the
lapping sea. "I'll take care, if you don't mind me, that
you have something to scream for when you can't jump
out. Hold tight ! "

A strong wind was blowing up the beach. The large sail
filled, the mast creaked and bent, the vehicle, moving more
and more rapidly, at last fairly flew before the gale ; the inventor holding his hat on with one hand, the other hand on
the helm, his hungry eyes fastened eagerly upon the way
they went, as they tore along.

CHAPTER XXVI.

IN WHICH TRAGEDY AND COMEDY ARE NOT BLENDED MORE
THAN THEY ARE APT TO BE EVERYWHERE.

THREE o'clock in the afternoon; a beautiful day,
and the wind blowing strong from the north-east."
Col. Roland read it aloud from his note-book. The spirits
of the passengers rose as the vehicle flew more and more
rapidly along. Mr. Parsons had taken a liking to Grit in
consequence of his hearty appreciation, on the previous
occasion, of his delicacies; and the wild enjoyment of the
boy now was but little in advance of that of the rest. Mr.
Fanthorp never had been as droll; and it was remembered,
ah, how well! afterward, that they were all in a singularly
good humor. Jokes were laughed at, although no one
waited to hear them out. Conundrums were accepted as
admirable, apart from their answers. Puns and personalities,
and laughter at every thing and at nothing, seemed infectious.
Miss Aurelia Jones, now as always dressed in silk, was effusive beyond her wont. Commodore Grandheur beside her
was not at all on his guard against her any longer. All there
yielded to the excitement of the hour as to a needed diver-
sion from more important matters. The commodore un-
bent and laughed as if the sea-salt which had lain so long a
sediment in his veins had been thoroughly aroused again.
But the gayety of all, as they secretly acknowledged to themselves at the time, was too violent, was unnatural.

"We may be lords of nature," Mr. Venable said, standing in front, although nobody heeded him; "but we are nothing at last except straws before a blast: we are ourselves — see how we are driven along ! — as much a part only of nature as so many bubbles."

Little he understood that the jests and replies, flying so fast between the passengers, were but another kind from the electric flashes when a storm is coming on; the last outside, the other within, and heralding a tempest then impending, alas ! in contrast with which every disaster experienced before was but a trifle deserving laughter.

All agreed afterward that Mr. Parsons must have been borne by the contagion of the hour beyond the bounds of sanity. He was so long and lean and restless that his wife had often said to him, "You are, my dear Ezra Micajah, a living barometer." One thing was sure : the soul of the eager man, like the quicksilver in the barometer, rose and fell, and too exclusively for health, in one narrow channel. Through years of derision upon the part of the press, as well as of all his friends, — for enemies he had none, — his Terraqueous Machine had been, among many other projects, the hope of his life. The unanimous opposition had merely banked his mind in, and compelled it along that single current, the swifter for being so narrow. He had counted upon making a great speed on this trial trip, but he had not calculated upon the excess thereof under the rising gale. Worst of all, he had not ciphered out the force of the excitement upon himself.

In the very rush of his machine, — his hand on the helm, his eye upon the beach extending before him, — the enthusiastic visionary was standing also before his blackboard, the chalk between his finger and thumb, going over the old, old figures : —

"A million at least. One thousand is as much as a country church ought to cost — for steeples are fiddlesticks, so that this machine, if it succeeds, will put up one thousand churches. Say missionaries instead, — that is one thousand men at work from California as a centre, upon the Old World as well as the New. Or, say it is Bibles: fifty cents apiece is enough; I'll print 'em myself, — two millions of Bibles! The machine is for *water* as well as land. I'll do it! Yes, the millennium will take millions to bring about. I'll do it, if they *do* squall! but I will only run in a very few feet." But even then he would not have done it, had not Mr. Fanthorp repeatedly exclaimed, —

"Don't be afraid, Mr. Parsons!" by no means intending what followed.

The beach ran along the seaward side; broad, smooth, and hard for many a mile, ending with the point of the island. There the sea gave place to the sluggish water lying between the island and the mainland, the beach degenerating into deep sand. It was as they flew, the wind whistling about their ears, toward this critical point, that the sense of the inventor broke down (Mr. Fanthorp partly responsible therefor), and was ground to dust under his swift wheels. He had threatened to give them something to scream for, without seriously intending it. But the turning-point had been reached. Mr. Fanthorp, standing in the car, was, after calling out to the inventor, taking off Gov. Magruder at the time he made one of his well-known failures in stump-speaking. Col. Roland was indignantly denying that it was in the least like, laughing none the less beyond his usual refined habit. Miss Aurelia Jones was holding of necessity to the commodore, who was soothing as well as he could her anxieties, which were more for her costly dress than for herself. Irene was crying to Mr. Venable not to drop the sail. On the instant, without his fully intending it, and by the merest bend of Mr. Parsons's hand to the left, the vehicle drove under full speed into the water.

So sudden was it, and unexpected, that there was an

instant's silence of utter astonishment. "Don't touch the sail!" shouted the inventor, above the piercing screams of both Irene and Zeo as well as Miss Aurelia. Mr. Venable let the sail fall.

"Sit still, no danger!" yelled Mr. Parsons. "Concern you, sir! Fiddlesticks! Still, sit still!"

But there was a rush to the landward side of the vehicle. More slowly than could have been believed, for it floated high and dry above the smooth water into which it had been driven, the car turned over, and all its living load were struggling in the sea. It was not fifty feet from shore, and the depth of the shelving sand was not enough to drown; but the confusion was what might have been expected. With wonderful presence of mind, Col. Roland, his hand firmly pressed upon the note-book in his breast-pocket, leaped as far as possible from the others, thinking, in the very act of doing so, what a thrilling account he would give of it all in his paper. By reason of his thoughtfulness, he was soon ashore, and contented himself with advising his friends from thence what to do, if he could but have made himself heard in the confusion of the moment. Grit, with the agility of a boy who had spent the whole summer in the surf, off and on, had been the first ashore; but he had gone in again, after a glance around, and was now swimming about, looking for Zeo, and keeping himself carefully aloof from every other. Commodore Grandheur's gold-headed cane had been, as usual, between his knees as he sat; and, in the act of snatching after it, he seized upon Miss Aurelia Jones instead, who laid vigorous hands upon him in turn. There were several moments, which seemed hours, of gurgling cries and intermittent screams, splashing about in the water, and importunate and incoherent appeals to God and to man; then a laborious crawling up the shelving shore, and a grasping at each other of those who emerged, weighed down under the load of their dripping attire. After that there was an eager wiping of the water, as well as the streaming hair, from their eyes, and an anxious examination, on the part of each, as to who the other was. All the party were there.

No! The shrieks of Irene rang upon the air. It so happened that Mr. Fanthorp and herself had come out of the water where the sand of the surf had given place to the mire of the slimy bay; and, crawling up and falling down in it as they emerged, both of them were bemuddied beyond recognition. The earliest use Irene had of her breath, after wiping the mire off her mouth and eyes, was to fall into convulsions of laughter at Mr. Fanthorp; to be changed the next moment into screams and shrieks, for her sister was not there. Nor was Mr. Venable. The hysterical girl seized upon Mr. Fanthorp, and almost hurled him into the water, exclaiming, —

"You are a coward, sir. Go in and get Zeo, or — ah, you know what I will do!" The men needed no appeals, but rushed into the sea, up to their chins, shouting and calling, Irene going up and down the beach, as well as her heavy clothes would allow, wringing her hands and screaming as if bereft of her senses. Yet once again her cries changed into peals of laughter; and she went up the way along which they had come, and into the surf, rolling in heavily before the wind. She had seen Mr. Venable struggling up, and continually falling down in the waves, her sister lying as if dead in his arms. In her insane eagerness she fell against the gentleman, knocking him and his burden over, Grit zealously aiding him up again.

"Go away," Mr. Venable shouted: "do you wish to kill her? Let me get out!" The tones were such as he had never before used to any one, much less to a lady; and, Irene silently following as he bore her sister high up on the beach, he laid her down upon her face, and, directing what the ladies were to do to revive her, he labored in silence but with trembling hands with them, Grit beside her.

"Where is Mr. Parsons?" Col. Roland suddenly asked, in the confusion which ensued.

"Drowned, I do most sincerely hope!" Irene said as she plucked at her sister's neck, unlacing and tremblingly obeying directions also. "He richly deserves it!" she added.

"Ha! yonder he is," said the old naval officer, turning away with the other gentlemen as the ladies partially disrobed the prostrate girl; and, following the direction of his hand, sure enough, there was the inventor astride the top of his capsized car, busily at work doing something.

"Ahoy!" shouted the commodore; "can you make it?" his hands hollowed on either side of his mouth.

"Don't want to make it!" Mr. Parsons yelled in return. "It can't sink. Part of the invention! There was no danger. What did you make such fools of yourselves for? There was no danger. I told you the wheels are *screws!*" in great wrath. "There is an attachment to work them. The sail would have driven them. Con-cern you for dropping it!"

"Can we do any thing for you?" Col. Roland called, as the inventor slowly drifted before the wind.

"No!" Mr. Parsons roared in reply. "You have done mischief enough. I'm better without you;" and his lank body was clearly outlined against the sky beyond him, tugging and toiling at something as he floated off.

But the attention of all was fastened upon Zeo. The commodore had left with the ladies a flask of brandy he had brought, and, after directing them for a time impatiently from a distance, exclaimed at last, "What folly! I'm old enough to be her grandfather," and joined in their labors with such skill and energy that in a little while the rescued girl was able to sit up on the sand. When this point had been reached, it was Mr. Venable who held her up while the rest consulted as to how they were to get home. With her earliest breath she had to refuse her brother, who begged to be allowed to swim off to Mr. Parsons and share his fortunes. It took, however, but a breath; for the boy submitted, eager as he had been, at a word.

"We must be twenty miles away," remarked Mr. Fanthorp. As he said it Irene broke into peal on peal of laughter. Evidently Mr. Fanthorp was the object; but it was equally plain that there was a cause 'for it beyond his exceedingly bemired condition.

"We might as well walk, however slowly," Mr. Venable said, when at last Zeo was able to start. "I can support Miss Zeo easily. This is only a September gale, but she is wet, and may get chilled. You will be glad to hear that I engaged Mr. Quatty to bring an ambulance in case of accident; Miss Zeo — I mean the ladies — being with us. Listen!"

But no one could hear any thing, as they very slowly walked along, Mr. Venable supporting Miss Zeo on his arm; nothing, at least, beyond the roaring of the surf and the gale.

"Allow me to relieve you," Col. Roland said after they had gone a few hundred yards.

"No, sir, thank you: I'm not at all tired," Mr. Venable replied, the freshest person there, to judge by the cheerful energy of his tones. But Zeo settled the matter as he spoke, and kept bravely up with them, by resting her other hand upon the stout shoulder of her brother walking beside her; the whole adventure being, in his often-expressed opinion, the "bulliest fun" he had ever known. But Grit did not enjoy it all quite as much as did Mr. Venable.

"It's an ill wind which blows nobody any good," Mr. Fanthorp said, as they struggled on against the weather. "We are being dried rapidly, anyhow."

"O Mr. Fanthorp! it's *too* ridiculous," Irene said, going off again into a burst of amusement; but it was not at what he had said, and ever and anon the same thing would occur. Evidently there was some hidden cause for her mirth. It must have been, at last, more than an hour that the wrecked party had struggled along; Mr. Fanthorp seemed singularly daunted; and Col. Roland had repeatedly observed that if they caught him in such another expedition he "would know it;" when, before they were aware, Mr. Quatty had driven up, and had leaped from the front seat of his ambulance to the ground, four horses blowing beside him with the speed at which they had been driven.

"But, halloo! where is Mr. Parsons?" Mr. Quatty asked at last, amid the congratulations and exclamations that followed.

"Why, don't you know?" said Mr. Fanthorp, with an effort, as if in great surprise. "My dear sir! It was a contrivance to go through the air as well. We got out. If you look you can see him. Yonder!" and he pointed heavenward. "See? Just yonder, by the edge of that cloud. Ha! he is taking a bite — look — out of a patent biscuit. See?" Mr. Fanthorp was elated, as all were, by Mr. Quatty's coming; but that gentleman, instead of looking in the direction of Mr. Fanthorp's lifted arm, put his head on one side, screwed up his right eye, and looked with considerable curiosity on his informant instead.

"Very good," he said at last. "Capt. Chaffin's cruising off there in his yacht somewhere: he wanted to see the machine when it got to the end of the island. He'll pick him up if he should come down. Get in, folks. There's a big basket of supper my wife put up. She is a sensible creature. So are horses, too. You see it was a smarter than Mr. Parsons invented them. Now," turning their heads city-ward, "just see how these horses will go when they know they are going home. The ox knoweth his owner, and a horse his master's crib. G'lang!" Certainly the steeds in question, the pride of Mr. Quatty's establishment, did go along the smooth hard beach in a way that justified his commendation. Meanwhile the spirits of all within the ambulance had risen amazingly. Neither Zeo nor Mr. Venable, who sat beside her, had much to say, and Mr. Fanthorp was not as droll as he often was ; but the rest made up for them as they discussed Mr. Parsons, as well as the contents of the abundant basket. Miss Aurelia Jones's silks were utterly ruined, and her curls disgracefully disordered, but the youngest of cavaliers could not have been more attentive to her than was the commodore ; and she seemed in brilliant spirits all the more, accepting like a schoolgirl the fun, which, by reason of their new relations, was aimed at the commodore, also terribly bedraggled, and herself. But it was, and they congratulated themselves upon it, long after dark before Mr. Quatty put out each of the party at his or her house.

Except Mr. Fanthorp. He alighted at Gen. Buttolph's, and, refusing to go in, detained Irene, laughing and struggling to get away from him, on the veranda.

"You know I did, sir," she said, as her sister went in. "I can tell you every word you said ! every single syllable, as you clutched after me, and bobbed under and came up. A *man*, and not able to swim ! What if I was the tallest ? The water was not much over your head, if you had only struck bottom and stood up, as I did. A woman, too ! Oh, but won't they laugh at you ! It will be in every paper in the State. You've made fun of so many people, you'll have no peace again as long as you live."

"But listen to me a moment," Mr. Fanthorp begged. He was plainly in earnest. Like all practical jokers, he was the most sensitive of men to being himself made fun of. If it were reported that a lady had saved his life, it would be his ruin ; and no one knew it quite so well as himself. "Do listen," he said. He was caked from head to foot with the wind-dried mire, but his anxiety was evident through it all.

"No, sir. And I will not keep it either. It is the best joke I ever heard ! O Miss Irene, save me ! save me !" the young lady exclaimed, mimicking his tones, though in a lower voice. "The only thing for you to do," she added, "is to hurry back to the beach, and drown yourself in good earnest."

"It is not that," the lawyer said, driven to desperation. "Miss Irene, I admire and love you. You have supposed me to be joking. I swear to you I am in dead earnest. You are, under your exterior of mud, the most splendid woman I ever — Please listen. Hold on! Don't go. I love you with all my soul. Please be my wife. You think I'm a coward, do you! I'll show you;" and the shrewd practitioner threw his arms around the lady in the darkness, and kissed her vigorously. It was a *ressort dernier*, and therefore desperate.

CHAPTER XXVII.

WITH THE YEAR THE NEW WORLD ALSO OF OUR COLUMBUS HASTENS TO ITS ENDING.

THE afternoon following upon the day of their ride, Mr. Venable called at Gen. Buttolph's. The house and grounds had undergone a complete renovation. He could not but observe, during his rapid visit of the day before, the freshness of the white paint, and the coolness of the brilliant green, making the hospitable mansion with its wide welcome of verandas and Venetian blinds a picture, amid its abundant shrubbery, in harmony with the white and green, too, of the island, and the deep blue of sea and sky to the utmost horizon. He had not entered the house on his previous call; and was refreshed, as he did so now, with the reproduction of the vivid colors of nature in the fresh papering and sumptuous furniture. Zeo came into the parlor almost immediately on his arrival, and there was a newness of beauty in her for which the house and island and ocean and heaven seemed an insufficient framing. He would have scouted the idea of having any illusions in regard to her, such as young Plenty had in reference to his grandfather, or such as Capt. Chaffin entertained concerning his gifted wife; yet he differed from these merely in having a more insane idea still in his valuation of this young girl. She was beautiful, but his estimate was not so much of her loveliness as of her intrinsic and immeasurable value in a deeper sense.

It was that which made her, every thing about her, seem in such exquisite taste; the splendor to him of her modest eyes, when they were raised for a moment to his, lying in their being but revelations of the world within. He had been uneasy as to her health after their adventures of the day before; but that was gone without a question asked, in view of the color coming and going in the olive of her complexion.

"Have you heard?" The words, however, broke at the same instant from the lips of both as they met. Terrible words! Wherever any two met in the city, and soon it would be the same over the whole State, a like demand was on every tongue.

"Mrs. Parsons is sick," he said, declining a chair in his uneasiness. "She says it is nothing but a cold. Owny has it too, for that matter. They were waiting up last night for Mr. Parsons. It is nothing, nothing at all."

"Has she headache, and pain ' the back?" began Zeo, with terror in her eyes.

"I believe so; and nausea too, I think; but," he added, "it is merely a cold. She gives little Owny medicine, but will take none herself. She refuses to lie down. When I left her she was teasing her husband unmercifully. Capt. Chaffin did pick him up, sure enough. You never saw such a change in a man, Miss Zeo. She and Owny were laughing at him about his machine. They were in high spirits; and he was standing there, when I left, by the blackboard, seeming as if he had been petrified. I was really alarmed. With his hollow eyes and high, narrow forehead, he looked like a statue in bronze; and he was holding his child in his arms, with such tearless love for it and his laughing wife as no words can express. It was like a tableau."

"Oh, poor, poor Mr. Parsons! that is because he knows so well!" it was all that Zeo said, melting, to the astonishment of her companion, into tears. "And dear, dear little Owny! Do you not know?" she asked as she wept.

" I know that the yellow-fever has arrived," he began.

" Mrs. Parsons has the worst form. It is those of her full health," Zeo said, " who are first struck. They are always the ones too who persist, as the phrase is, in footing it through the attack, refusing to take medicine, never lying down, in overflowing spirits to the end. I thought of it yesterday when we were so wild with our ride. We have seen it all before. O Mr. Venable ! " she said, raising her eyes full of tears to his, " it is something worse than you can imagine. The yellow-fever ! "

But at this moment Mr. Fanthorp entered ; and, a little while after, Irene, white and nervous. " Isn't it awful, terrible ! " she exclaimed : " we are all going on the next bayou-boat. — Be sure and be ready," she added, turning to Mr. Fanthorp, who was standing hat in hand ; but, while she spoke, her fears gave place, as she looked at him, to a smile, and then to laughter, while he let fall his eyes and stood with a deprecatory manner. Her amusement, seeing that, was as soon gone as her fears. She arose from her seat, and, going over to him, gave him her hand in a way which conveyed the impression of something more than mere frankness. During the rest of his stay there was a gentleness on her part, and deference to Mr. Fanthorp, which struck the other gentleman, even in that anxious moment. He looked at Miss Zeo ; but that lady lowered her eyes with a rising color in her cheeks, and, notwithstanding her tears, a demure smile on her lips.

" Zeo," her sister said, a little sharply, " I wish *I* knew any thing to laugh at. Yellow-fever ! and all our packing to do ! Do you know that two-thirds and more of St. Jerome will have left in a week, Mr. Venable? That's the advantage of you bachelors. You will snatch up a valise, and be gone in ten minutes. Papa is at the wharf ; but please go, Mr. Fanthorp, and get our tickets. You know there will be thousands crowding the office, and you have so much more impudence than papa or anybody else. Get a ticket for Mr. Venable too," and she followed the lawyer out into the hall to give some directions; for he meekly obeyed.

"You know," Irene, conscious of detection, shot back that Parthian arrow in going out, " how agonizingly his Excellency our beloved governor will await us up the country. Hurry, Zeo."

" I must not stop your packing, and I must get back to Mr. Parsons's immediately," Mr. Venable said, moving to the door. "If I should not see you again"— and he held out his hand to the lady in parting. But she did not arise from her seat. She had ceased weeping, and sat as if almost unconscious of his presence.

"Yes," she said at last and very softly, "we are all going to Sulphur St. Jerome, the Springs you know, till it is all over. We sent Grit down to the boat this morning. There will be happy days again."

" I have no doubt of it," the other said as heartily as he could. "But not for me. I mean, not for me in St. Jerome. I ought to tell you, Miss Zeo," he said with some difficulty, as she lifted her eyes in astonishment to his, " I have never whispered a word about it to any one, nor do I intend to do so yet, but I intend leaving the island. The church is too old for me, or I am too young for it. I want a new enterprise in a fresh field. My mind has been slowly coming to that, and the thing is settled. Of course I greatly regret "—

"Then you leave immediately?" There was a sudden coldness in the manner of the other as she asked it, the tears gone from her eyes.

" Is it possible? After knowing me for nearly a year? Can you imagine such a thing of me?" Mr. Venable said, after a silence; and her color came under the mortification expressed in his tones. "Such an idea never entered my mind. I would be the basest of cowards if I did. Like every other minister, I suppose, on the island, I intend to stay and do what I can. It is after the fever is gone, and the scattered church is back again, that I intend to leave. I did not think that was a question."

"You are unacclimated, Mr. Venable," the other said, in stronger tones. "If the fever is as it was the last time, the probabilities are," and her eyes fell, "that you will die."

"If the certainties were — I am ashamed to say any thing, Miss Zeo, which sounds so much like boasting," her companion checked himself. "·When I was invited here, I took yellow-fever into the calculation. And do you know," he added with grave but brightening eyes, "that it is no merit in me at all? One takes a pleasure in it, like going into battle or into a storm. I believe, Miss Zeo, you, too, enjoyed those days on the Nautilus. May Heaven bless you!" he said, with a sudden change in the direction of his excitement. "Good-by."

"I wanted — wanted," she said, rising at last, standing before him, and looking steadily in his eyes, with a measure of control over herself which mastered him also, "to thank you, sir, — to thank you for my father as well as for life!" If the quivering of the lips could have been under perfect constraint, she would have succeeded. But it began there, and it was too swift, too deep for her : it was stronger than her strength. She had begun with being Zenobia, Queen of Palmyra, but she ended with being merely Zeo. Possibly she had been too severely tried the day before, and for so long.

"It is I who have to thank you," he said, continuing to hold her hand, when, being a clergyman, he should have shaken and dropped it, — "to thank you, as to yourself at least, for giving me the chance. It was hardly in drowning water, you know. Why," he added, "it was, at last, only a few feet from shore. There was no romance in it at all. Thank *you*, with all my heart. Good-by!" He shook hands, and went out like an apostle, — went out to turn and come back again like the weakest of men.

"Miss Zeo," he said, "you know it already, and what is the use of my saying it? Ever since I came to understand you, I have loved you, and would give my life for you" —

"Would you believe it!" Irene interrupted at this juncture, rushing in, "a negro came to Mr. Fanthorp on the steps as he was leaving, to say that Col. Roland is down, and ever so many more. Oh, is it not terrible! Yellow-fever! Just to think! — I beg your pardon, Mr. Venable, but we *must* pack up. Good-by till we meet you on the bayou-boat. — Come, Zeo." There was a new authority as well as gentleness in the volubility of the lively young lady. Their visitor connected it in a vague way with the unwonted aspect of Mr. Fanthorp; but there was nothing to do but to go.

As he walked rapidly back to Mr. Parsons's, he saw loaded wagons, crowded carriages, people hurrying little children along in groups, negroes with wheelbarrows or bending under great bundles: the whole town seemed out and hastening toward the wharves. For days after that the city papers indignantly denied the fact, but all knew that their old and terrible foe was upon them. The day was the more beautiful in this, that its cloudless blue seemed somehow, as has been said, to have closed in upon the island more nearly; the sea also girding it in with a deeper azure. It had rained during the night, and yesterday's gale had slackened into a softer wind, in which every plant and flower seemed fresher and more fragrant. The sand along the broad streets was as clean, beneath the oleander and Pride of India trees, as the washing of last night's rain and the eternal seas, as well as the bleaching of the sun, could make it. For months before, all that soap and scrubbing, white-washing, and every disinfectant could do, had been done in anticipation. There was not a rotting banana or an ill odor in the lowest alley. No vessel, so far as the most rigid watch could detect, had brought pestilence as passenger. But the disease had come none the less; the island was like a steamship which had struck a hidden rock in the deepest purity of the smoothest seas, the suddenness thereof being the worst part of the shock. It was not, the young man noticed, as in the days of the overflow when he first arrived. That was an open, honest affair of bellowing thunder, raging wind, inrushing ocean, — elements which every child, to say nothing of the seamen, had known and faced all its life. But the fever was a deadlier disaster, a something silent, unseen, impalpable, infernal: the doctors understood as little about it, the type it would take, the remedy it would obey, as the youngest. St. Jerome had looked upon the overflow as a tremendous joke; an hilarious and generous goodfellowship accompanied it. But there was no smile upon any face now, and almost every person was wolfishly for himself. The fugitives were liberal enough with their money when safe from harm up the country, those who devoted themselves upon the plague-stricken spot heroic enough afterward; but all that was afterward, indeed, not now.

When the minister went down to the wharf to see his friends off, it was difficult at first to detect them amid the multitudes with which the bayou-boat was crowded. Getting up upon a timber, he saw them at last grouped together upon the guards of the vessel. The bell had been ringing for some time, but it seemed to be impossible to draw in the plank upon which people were crowding on board in the terror of flight. Suddenly a cry rang from the centre of the throng upon the wharf, and it was scattered apart as by the force of an explosion. The pestilence had pursued the flying multitudes to the water's edge, smiting down a large and apparently vigorous man in the act of pressing his way on board. The vessel seemed itself to recoil, the crowd half on and half off the deck being parted in the middle, as it drew away from the wharf with an escape of steam from its pipes which sounded like a scream of terror; two or three persons falling into the sea to be fished out again with what seemed to Mr. Venable hysterical peals of laughter.

As the boat backed farther away it rounded toward its course; and he looked up and saw Gen. Buttolph and Mr. Fanthorp waving their hats to him in adieu, Irene calling something which he could not hear, as she flourished her handkerchief. The others were to him as nothing, however, his attention being riveted upon Zeo, who stood silent and still beside her father. As he lifted his hat she extended her hand to him, but it was her face at the instant which struck itself like a medallion into his memory. As he walked slowly homeward he took that with him. Whatever was to befall him, forevermore nothing could come between him and that beloved face.

He was bewildered when he sat at supper with the family that night. Surely Miss Zeo was mistaken. Mrs. Parsons, pouring out the tea and coffee, had never seemed quite so well, nor had little Owny in her high-chair beside her been more blooming. Considering the arrival of the fever at the island, the mirth, however, of the mother and the child was somewhat out of place.

"But I never could see any use in grieving over what cannot be helped," Mrs. Parsons said. "It is the people who fear the fever most, who are sure to take it. Do look at Ezra Micajah Papa! You ought not to have run your machine into the water. It is that which makes you as grave as an owl. I told you so. I'm so glad Owny and I are well and strong!—We will have you to nurse, Mr. Venable, since you are resolved to stay. It must have been the funniest thing, your upset in the water;" and she laughed and rattled on even more than usual. The brilliant eyes of mother and child, the glory of their seeming health in cheek and spirits, was terrible to see. It was impossible, however, not to laugh, Mrs. Parsons was so amusing, little Owny was so smart as well as sweet.

"Div *dis* hug and *dis* tiss to Miss Zeo, Mr. Venny, nex' time you sees her," the little darling said when that gentleman took her for a moment from her father, "'cause she dot so wet. I'm her 'ittle girl, and your 'ittle girl, and Ezra Micajah Papa's. I'm Dod's own 'ittle bit of Owny, too! Take me out, Mr. Venny: I want to have a womp with you out-doors. — Dood-by, folkses!" her chubby hands dancing in the air, her fat and rosy face against her favorite's cheek, her golden hair about her shoulders, the very double of her mother, who was laughing and throwing kisses to her.

Tuesday was the day of the ride; Wednesday they were smitten; Friday they were dead, — mother and child, one in this as in all else. Why tell of the increasing gayety until it consumed itself in its own fires? In vain the fragments of ice continually swallowed as the only medicine: they seemed to be but as so many living coals of fire instead to the raging fever. And why detail the increasing agony in back and shoulders, the nausea, the reddening eyes, the orange lines tinging first the eyes and then saturating and swallowing up the whole body as with a sunset of ghastly saffron, the vomit as of coffee-grounds? Then death, and a death over which there can be not one moment of idle lamenting. Is not the rapid decay of fruit always according to the exuberant ripeness just before? For God's sake, hasten to hide the dead out of sight!

That was the beginning. The tears of even the desolated inventor were dried up as by the simoom of the fever now raging with ever-increasing fury and breadth of sweep. Very soon three-fourths of the population had fled. Not a soul was left in the lately crowded city but such as poverty or duty held there. Mr. Venable was glad that there was too much to do for him to stop and think. In a week his horror was gone. There was no time for such weakness. Until he was himself struck down, nothing now but a work vastly more Christian than preaching. Church and sabbath were for the time abolished; and St. Jerome had to fall back upon the religion of which church and sabbath, scriptures, sacraments, revival, are nothing whatever, and worse than nothing, if they are not but merely its outer and temporary channels, —had to revert to the religion which precedes, as it will eternally survive, these transient agencies thereof. Visiting the sick, burying the dead, caring for the destitute survivors, — work was the duty until he should himself die; steady, unceasing work. In a little while he adjusted himself to it as if it had been his life for years.

"John Howard had not an atom of sentiment," he would often say to himself as he toiled with the noble association bearing that name, "any more than I. That is a luxury for the people that are up the country, and it will keep for us till afterward. Just now, as Mr. Parsons would say, sentiment is fiddlesticks."

CHAPTER XXVIII.

IN WHICH THE MIDNIGHT DARKENS TOWARD DAWN.

NOW, why do you suppose — why?" It was Mr. Parsons who asked it of his guest. The inventor was standing at his blackboard, chalk in hand. When Mr. Venable had first known him he was old and lean, rapid in talk and walk, and very dry; yet, while the sirocco of the pestilence had scorched him until he seemed to be many years older, leaner, dryer, than before, it had ripened him into a greater sweetness. Long ago Mr. Venable had found out that the visionary schemes of his host, manifold, and perpetually changing, were merely the froth made by the current, and by the very rapidity of the current of his purpose, a current as deep and strong as it was swift.

"Why?" his friend answered him, "excuse me, why *what?*"

"There is a reason at the root of every thing," Mr. Parsons said, — "a reason which *is* its root. If I can find the precise acid, I can also find the exact alkali to counteract it. The fever ravaged New York in 1822: why has it not been there since? It devastates tropical America and Africa: why not India and China? There is a *why* for its appearance in Vera Cruz and Panama, and never in Bombay or Calcutta. Why do Spaniards, Italians, French get well, and Irish, Germans, and Scotch almost always die? The doctors squabble as to whether cathartics, stimulants, or ice applied within and without, is best or worst. Frost kills the fever instantly. Now," Mr. Parsons went on, sketching his plan upon the board, "why not make a room, say, like that, — a room which is also a refrigerator? Put your patient from the outset in a New England, in an arctic zone of ice. I have got my machine-shop boarded up, and with double walls. If I can get ether enough, I will clap you in with the first symptom, and try the freezing process."

"Thank you," his friend said, "but not yet I hope. How many weeks is it, Mr. Parsons? For the first two or three I was in a rush of excitement. Then I was so tired out that I worked and walked mechanically, as I have been told that soldiers have been known to march sleeping. I have got into the third stage. The yellow-fever seems to us all as if it were the natural order of things, — matter of course, — as if it always had raged and always would. But how desolate it is!" he added, rising and standing beside his friend, who was making calculations upon his board. "St. Jerome is more terrible to me than the cemetery. I go through whole streets without seeing a soul. The houses are all shut up, and seem suddenly dilapidated. Besides the wagons carrying the dead, and the handful of hacks following them, I have not seen a vehicle for years, it seems to me. I sometimes wonder if people are laughing anywhere in the world. You never see a child. The babies all died during the first week. There must be something, Mr. Parsons," he added, "which makes the grass grow that much the faster as the people die. Everywhere oleanders are forcing themselves up between the bricks and flag-stones of what used to be the busiest streets. And how sepulchral the sea looks! We would not miss the steamers and ships if there were any sail-boats. The water laps sluggishly against the rotting wharves, as if it were that of a dead sea which never had borne a boat, and never would. There is such a dead halt! It is as if the old serpent himself had

coiled his slimy strength around the island, holding it perfectly still, and all the air is his venomous breath. Night
before last I dreamed that you had bored an artesian well
in your yard many miles deep, had filled it with nitro-
glycerine, and were in the act of firing it off in order to blow
the globe to atoms, when in trying to stop you I awoke.
And so again last night I started from a deep sleep, Mr. Parsons, and it was to me as if the whole universe were standing
stock still. There was not a stir, not a sound. Sea, sky,
earth, air, myself — all seemed to me to be dead. I know I
ought not to yield to it; but for an hour I lay motionless as
a stone, and St. Jerome and all we knew and loved here,
church and friends, were to me as much gone, and for ever
and ever, as the cities and people before the flood. Worse;
for a terrible time Christianity was dead, too! its graces
and good works, its saints and martyrs, its very God. It
was terrible!"

"It was fiddlesticks. Ether would cost," his friend said,
summing up the results on his board, "two bits an ounce.
Now it would take, say, one dozen ounces to freeze you
down to, say, 30° or 40° — I mean, to keep you for a week
as if under a white frost. Twelve twenty-fives is three dollars. Very well, let us grant that four thousand people are
left in St. Jerome. If we had the refrigerators ready I could
lock up every soul in a temporary winter with twelve thousand dollars worth of ether. I will go right away and con-
sult the Howard Association. Since the doctors fail, somebody must contrive something. Come, let us go."

There certainly was no inducement to stay behind. Every
negro on the place had died; and, there being no one to
work, the house and workshops, warehouses and grounds,
had fallen into woeful neglect. Here, as everywhere, the
great tide of human life which had ceased from the animal
kingdom seemed, as Mr. Venable said, to have found channels for itself in the vegetable; and, in the soft, moist, still,

and almost sultry weather, fig-trees and bananas, orange, lemon, and locust, as well as the oleander and china trees, were flourishing in licentious disorder as well as riotous exuberance. Especially did the ill-smelling ailanthus run riot, as if it found a fattening in the atmosphere, foul with disease, beyond that of the sandy soil.

Mr. Parsons would talk of nothing, as they walked along, but ether and the best modes of evaporating it; and it was a relief to his companion to excuse himself as having to visit Father Fethero.

"Bless me!" Mr. Parsons said. "I thought he was dead long ago. Poor old soul! Tell him from me that the most sensible thing he can do is to go to heaven. Get your dinner somewhere, Mr. Venable: you know we have nobody to cook it but ourselves. I wonder," the inventor added, halted by the sudden thought, "if the fever can penetrate those boxes. If it can get at my condensed vegetables and Focussed Flesh, it will be dreadful. There are twenty thousand dollars worth. I will pack them in that refrigerator as soon as I get back. I will leave space for you." And the grim humor of the old man was not peculiar to himself. As by a re-action from the horrors of the time, every one said the most amusing things he could, even in the act of handling the dying and the dead. But the mirth was confined to the saying of witty things: people had almost lost the faculty of laughing. "The brain acts," Mr. Venable said to himself in parting from his friend, "when the muscles refuse to do so. I suppose this is why whiskey affects these miserable topers as it does. They do not laugh nor fight now. Baser passions, the sedimental mud and vilest dregs of the soul, are stirred instead. Surely it is as if the Devil were in the whiskey as in the air. If the stealing were all," he added to himself; "but"—and he shuddered as he remembered the awful desecration of the dead by wretches fired with the madness of an hour when the dividing line between the worlds was vanishing, and the powers of the pit came as well as went freely over demolished barriers.

"Thank God!" he said as he opened and entered Father Fethero's front door without knocking, "that the walls between earth and heaven also are obliterated. How are you to-day, Father Fethero?"

It had always been a poor place; but the poverty had become squalid now. The widowed daughter of the old man had died at the outbreak of the pestilence; having, as Mr. Parsons had remarked at the time, "the good sense to take all her children with her." The garden was a mass of weeds. Here, as elsewhere over the city, the paling and fences had been more or less torn down by those who needed fuel and could get it nowhere else. Mr. Venable had often seen wretched women doing it, as well as pallid and miserable children, the men of the house being dead or assisting in regard to the sick and the dying. So far from blaming them, he had torn away many a heavy armful himself, from garden and front yard, and borne it to their houses for trembling women or for puny girls. As to carrying buckets of water, he was as zealous with that as with lifting the dead into the hearse and lowering them into the grave. But oh, the weariness of travelling over and over again that road to the cemetery! He had come to know every winding and turning of the well-worn road, every tree and hillock, almost every weed and pebble, he had gone over it to and fro so often.

"How are you, Father Fethero?" He had fallen into a mechanical cheerfulness of voice and manner; and he knew how the sick man was. With small variation, it was the same set of symptoms over again in every case.

"Such deadly nausea," the old man replied. "Such a burning in the stomach! The pain in the front of my head is terrible, — worse than in my back; and then the weight on me! How am I? I don't know. I do not know. I plainly perceive a — yes, a — gloom."

No wonder! His face was flushed and swollen, and with an aspect of distress seen in no other disease unless it be hydrophobia. The eyes were red as coals of fire, the breath slow and irregular, the skin hot, dry, harsh. Mr. Venable felt the pulse : it was at a hundred and fifty, the heart pumping as in a sinking ship. The protruded tongue was red at the edges ; in the eyes the first faint flush, amid the scarlet, of the ghastly yellow.

"Mr. Quatty was with you, I suppose, during the night, and Capt. Chaffin before him?" the visitor asked.

"Were they?" the sick man said, his face like that of some coin from which the lines by long use are almost worn out. "Somebody was here. Yes: one tried to cheer me up by telling about the grand pictures somebody painted. The other, — yes, it was Mr. Quatty : he told me all over again about his having risen from being an oysterman, and told me that so I might from my sickness ; but he prayed for me afterward. The night was a year long at least. I don't know ; I do not know."

"Are you willing to go, dear sir?" his friend asked.

"I am very willing," Father Fethero said, in broken sentences. "One would like more ground. Two feet is not enough for a grave. I know they come to water ; but I saw the foot of a man when I was there Friday. No, it was a woman. I got a shovel, and covered it up. What I can do, I always try to do. Stand in the gap, that's what I try hard to do — in the gap ; yes, stand in the gap " — very wearily.

"I know that my Redeemer liveth," began his friend.

"Most assuredly," the old man, seeming so very, very old and poor and utterly worn out, interrupted the other, his horny hand held up. "Yes, I know that he lives ; and I know that he has stood on the earth. Yes, and I know that in my flesh I shall see God. Mine eyes shall behold him, and not another's. Yes. But I'm not going to tell lies with my last breath. I cannot say, I will *not* assert " — it was said with the utmost energy of the failing man — "that I ever have seen him yet. No, nor that I understand him now in that matter ; no, not one bit ! I will, you know, but not yet ; no, sir. If you had known how hard I have worked ! I have walked and ridden, ah, yes, ridden and walked ; prayed and preached, preached and prayed ; wept and besought, besought and wept. I will be told in heaven, you observe. But I do not know now. It wasn't money I wanted. When I tried so hard it was for souls. If the Master — had only — given a poor — toiling — servant," he spoke with great difficulty now, struggling to get breath, his hand rising and falling as when he led in public prayer, "could — have given his poor soldier a few souls — now — and then " —

"Dear Father Fethero, listen ; " and, with his hand on the arm of the other, his visitor slowly repeated the Twenty-third Psalm.

"Ah, yes, yes ! " said the sick man before he was well through, "but never tell a lie, my young brother. The green pastures are no more in the wilderness than the still water : it is on the other side of Jordan." He spoke with revived energy. " Not but that I've had a little taste now and then. But it was honey from the rock ; honey, more like, out of some lion I had to rend if I wasn't Samson. I've had a hard life as a general thing, a mighty hard time. Crucified with Him ! Yes, and the crucifixion isn't done until you are dead. Very well. Now I ask," and the sick man argued the point with his forefingers point to point as from the pulpit, " if the crucifixion of Christ was an atonement full and sufficient, why must I be crucified too ? Heh ? All three are alike crucified, the penitent thief and impenitent thief, every one of us, as well as Christ ; crucified we are, every man of us, and to death. I tell you," he said in the delirious energy of his disease, " the Lord Jesus is not the weak and womanish person people think he is in and out of the pulpit. Thou shall rule them with a rod of iron ! He is a *master*. He is a great king. He is the terrible Jehovah " —

" Dear Father Fethero," entreated his friend.

" For years on years — I have been going over it all night," the other went on, not regarding him, — " I prayed and toiled and wept. It was not money. With strong crying and tears — souls, it was *souls*, I wanted. And he was as a rock to my entreaty. Say I was not talented, say I was dull and tedious, say I had such a shabby coat and face too. I suppose so, but what I wanted, was desperate for, was souls, — the conversion of perishing souls. Jane — not the Jane that died when the fever came — Jane's mother. My wife. People said she was my better sense. Well, why was she taken, then ? It was hard enough on me before. I tell you," the old man said, lifting himself up with terrible eyes, " he has been a hard, hard, *hard* Master to me ! "

" We thank thee, O God," the other said, in tones low and steady and strong, his eyes closed to shut out the sight as he knelt, "we do heartily thank thee that Jesus died for us. But we bless thee that we also die ; that we are crucified with Christ, crucified in the body of sin. We bless thee that, even as Jesus was, so are we arrested, scourged, mocked, spitted on, held fast on our cross ; and we do praise thee that thus not we, but our sins, are killed. We bless thee that scourge and nails are ours also " —

" And," interrupted the other, his clasped hands feebly rising and falling in the accents of supplication, "we do magnify thee that thou dost no more hear our cries in our Gethsemane than thou didst the agony of thine only Son. Sin has got to go ! We do indeed drink of thy cup. Not my will, but thine, be done. Amen."

His pulse had become more frequent, yet feeble ; the

deadly sunset was spreading its yellow hues over face and neck and hands. There was the calmness, at last, of peace upon the toil-worn countenance. He held the hand of his friend in his as he said it, his whole aspect so serene that his companion smiled at the contradiction in his words.

"I can't lie, my young brother. It would be playing the part of Ananias to pretend to any raptures. That was never my gift from God. My life has been a hard, a very hard life, that's the fact; but not as much so as His. Something awful in sin, my brethren, since God had to endure. God, you see, as well as you and I! We will have it explained hereafter. I am not happy. I never was. I plainly perceive a gloom. But I do see light beyond it. He loves me, but he is keeping it for me — there. I couldn't understand. Not to save my life I couldn't. I can't now. But I always loved him. I haven't done any thing for him, but I tried to as hard as I knew how. It's all right; I mean, it *will be* all right."

Then came the change which, by this time, the one watching at his side knew so well. It was with difficulty, that, supporting the head of the dying man with one arm, Mr. Venable endeavored to wipe away from the struggling lips the dark froth which was the corruption of death already doing its work within. Father Fethero put him aside with violence, his eyes looking straight before him.

"Get out of my way, will you?" he said, with irritation. "Go to one side, children. Mary, Henry, Jane — all of you! Why, wife Jane! Don't you see how you stop me, Jane? Out of the way, out of the way, all of you!" He said it with a gesture of both extended arms, like that of a man in swimming. "Not now. Wait! Wait! In one moment!" as if he were pressing his way through a thronging crowd. "Get out of the way, all of you! I want to get to Him. I want to ask Him" —

As the young man withdrew his arm, and let the head of

the departed saint rest upon his pillow, though the words were through his own lips, they came as from another, speaking by him : "Blessed are the dead which die in the Lord, that they may rest from their labors ; and their works do follow them."

CHAPTER XXIX.

SULPHUR ST. JEROME, AND WHAT HAPPENED THERE.

WHEN Gen. Buttolph fled from the island, he had taken his family some hundreds of miles into the upland interior of the State, to a spot famous for its medicinal springs. Quite a village had sprung up there of log cabins, clapboard shanties, and tents inhabited mainly by refugees from the fever; and in one of the more substantial of these temporary homes the general was living with his household. For more than fifty miles southward, and stretching indefinitely northward, the rolling prairies were almost unsettled as yet, deer, antelope, wolves, and bears being the only inhabitants except when the region was raided upon by savages from the wilder wilderness farther north and west.

Some weeks after flying from the pestilence, Mr. Fanthorp was out upon a hunting expedition a score of miles from Sulphur St. Jerome, as the encampment of the refugees was called, accompanied by Gov. Magruder. They had slept one night under the open sky, a blanket beneath them, their heads upon their saddles, the eyes of each being protected from the brilliant light of the moon by his broadbrimmed felt hat placed over his face.

"Look at that tarantula, governor," Mr. Fanthorp exclaimed as he arose in the morning, and shook an enormous spider off his blanket. "It must have been next my jugular vein all night. If it had bitten me "—and he indulged in a good deal of fun, while he rolled up and strapped together his blankets, as to his weeping creditors and their vain search after his assets, since a bite would have been death.

"Hang it, Farce, don't make such a to-do! A quart of whiskey would have cured "—the other began, and then arose slowly and cautiously from the camp-fire over which he had been boiling coffee in a tin cup. "Yes; but we've drunk up the whiskey. What is it?" his companion asked, for his friend, with his head upon one side, his right hand held up in a warning manner, was apparently listening as if to something in the distance.

"Indians?" Mr. Fanthorp again asked, grasping his rifle which lay at his feet.

As he spoke the other made a clutch at his trousers just above the knee, and, holding the handful of cloth as far off as he could from his flesh, he cried,—

"Quick, Fanthorp! cut it out. Centipede!"

The knife was mislaid, of course: it always is in cases of emergency, as Mr. Fanthorp, rushing about here and there among their "traps," explained with many an oath, urging his friend meanwhile to "hold on!" As soon as it was found, Mr. Fanthorp, having sharpened its twelve inches of steel upon his boot, proceeded with rapid but artistic care to cut away from the leg of the other the handful of clothing. As he did so the governor threw it upon the ground. Sure enough it was a centipede, with its coats of mediæval armor, and its multitudinous legs. The lawyer lifted the tin cup from the coals, inserted his knife under the reptile as it lay, and dropped it, coiling itself upon the blade and biting at it, into the centre of the fire.

"A tarantula," he added as he replaced the cup over its expiring agonies, "is bad enough. But a centipede!—You can take my hat, Magruder. I see you, but can go no better. My vermin is to yours what a cat is to a tiger: a tarantula, when no whiskey is to be had, is death ; but a centipede is death and perdition ! "

His companion drank his coffee, and ate his pork and corn-pone, in comparative silence. Nor did he return to the subject until they neared Sulphur St. Jerome toward night, each with a deer strapped across his horse behind him.

"Fanthorp," he said at last, "do you know I wouldn't have cared a cent if that thing had stuck every leg it had into me ? "

"What are you up to, governor ? I have been wondering," his friend replied, "that you have not laughed at my jokes. You haven't heard a word I said. What is the matter ? "

"Farce Fanthorp," he replied after some silence, "I don't believe you ever had a serious thought in your life ; and you'd be the last man living I would talk to if you were not going to marry her sister. Ride slower : my trousers are cut up too bad for us to get in before dark."

"Well, what is it ? " the other asked when nothing had been said for some time.

"You know what a man I have been, Fanthorp," the governor began reluctantly.

"Well, what then ? " the other asked.

"This, sir," he continued : "knowing what I've been, knowing that everybody who sees us together, she and I, knows what I've been, I swear to you I can't talk to her, to save my life. Don't I know how pure and beautiful and good she is ? Every time I dare to try and talk to her, I could spit in my own face. I am a scoundrel, but I can't play the hypocrite, Fanthorp ; " and the other drew his horse to a halt as he said it : " I *can't* and I *won't !* "

"Won't what ? " his friend asked anxiously, for he had much at stake.

"I wish the centipede had killed me as dead as a hammer. Look here, Fanthorp," the executive of the past and

the senator of the future added, "every time I see her I
feel as if I could crawl. I am trying to steal her, because
she is so ignorant of me. It is as if I were sneaking into a
man's tent, and trying to steal his money while he is asleep;
the meanest scoundrel and liar that ever lived! I am a
gentleman, sir," shouted the man, "if I *am* a scamp; and I
won't, and I'll be cursed if I do!"

Now, as a lawyer, Mr. Fanthorp would have argued the
point for argument sake. Moreover, he had indulged in no
scruples in his own case. Above all, it was essential to his
interests that the governor should become his brother-in-law.
Hating Col. Roland as he did, he intended, in virtue of
such an alliance, to oust the colonel from his guardianship
of the governor. Surer revenge than that he could not
desire.

"Only let me see this popular fool safely married to Zeo,"
he said to himself as often before while the other was talking,
"and myself to her sister, my fortune is made. With him
in the senate, there is hardly any thing in the State, or perhaps in the federal gift, but I can get; there's the St. Jerome
custom-house, the post-office at least. Roland never had
any trouble making him do any thing *he* wanted!"

"Let's ride on, Magruder," he said to him soothingly, and
added, "the fact is, confess, man, you care nothing for Miss
Buttolph; why not say so at once, and be done with it?"

"You are a liar, sir!" His companion said it in the lowest of tones, shifting the reins of his horse as he did so to
his left hand, his right going instinctively to the revolver in
his belt; for such language was not often used with impu-
nity in that region. Grasping that to be prepared for whatever might result, he deliberately repeated, —

"You are a liar, sir, and you know it!" and then added
in a way which left no doubt of his sincerity, —

"Not *love* her! Look here, you! I love her as no
woman ever *was* loved before! You know how I've been

raised on my plantation ; and I never knew, how could I know? what love was until I met her. Here I've been these months, and the more I see of her the worse it is. The longer I know her, the harder it comes to talk to her. Not love her ! "

"And yet you don't want to marry her," the other said, swarthier than ever with his anger, but controlling himself for a purpose.

" Marry her ! " the governor replied with suppressed fury, " marry her ! as if she would marry such a fellow as I am ! *Can't* you understand, it's because I love her that I do not dare to ask her to have me ! "

There was a vehement sincerity in the man, which staggered the lawyer. But Mr. Fanthorp was a lawyer whose client had every thing at stake ; and that client was himself. As they rode slowly along, once more he beat his brains as to what to say, and added at last, —

" Look here, Magruder, do you know that Mr. Venable is dead in love with her? You are going to let him cut you out, are you? "

" Venable ! " The governor repeated the name in a stupid way. Like an Andalusian bull, which comes suddenly upon a man standing before it in the ring apparently unarmed, his surprise allowed no room for animosity. " Venable? He's a splendid fellow ; but I'm not afraid," he said simply, while the other remarked to himself, " They call Charlie Chaffingsby an idiot. Great heavens ! he is a Solomon compared to this one.

" Gov. Magruder," he continued aloud and with all gravity, " I am glad I have to do with a man of your intelligence "—

" Hang intelligence ! No, Farce Fanthorp, no," the statesman replied, confronting him with the same honesty of aspect. " That is in Roland's line. It won't work."

" Hear me out, sir ; " the attorney emphasized the request

with an oath. "What I was going to say is, that I appeal
to you as to a man of honor. Here you have been waiting
upon Miss Buttolph for months, in the presence, sir, of all
St. Jerome. With the eyes of the whole State upon you,
sir, you have led the lady, above all, to believe that you
intended to ask her to be your wife; and am I to understand that you contemplate so dishonorable a thing"—and
the astonishment of the lawyer was exceeded only by his
disgust—"as to fly the track? It is impossible! *You* do
such a thing?"

His companion looked at him blankly at first, then stroked
his beard with a thoughtful countenance; then, as the light
came into his eyes, he held out his hand to the other in a
burst of pleasure, and cried, "I had not thought of that! I
always told Roland I was too great a scamp; but he led
me on, and now I am in honor bound as you say. That's a
fact: she ought not to accept such a fellow; but I can
try, you know; she may: who can tell?" The face of the
man was as full of delight as that of a boy; and, it being
now quite dark, the two rode into camp in excellent humor,
the governor often repeating, "I'm bound to do it, that's a
fact."

The next morning, as Zeo Buttolph sat with her sister
under the live-oak which overhung their cabin, Irene said
to her,—

"Wasn't the letter pa handed you just now from St.
Jerome, Zeo?"

"Yes;" and, as her sister said it, her eyes were full in
those of Irene, who seemed unusually petulant.

"It was very imprudent. Don't you know the infection
may be carried in paper? Suppose you should catch the
disease? Do you think I would stay and nurse you? I
would not do it! I would run away! O Zeo, Zeo!" she
added with indignation. And she may have been right;
for, judging by the color in her sister's face, there had been

fever in the letter, which she had read over more than once.

"Tell me one thing, Zeo, for there's no good in arguing with you: are you," Irene demanded, "going to answer it?"

"No;" and it was said with such smiling composure, that her sister smote her hands together, and then kissed her with sudden affection; adding, as she lifted her head, "you are right, Zeo! and yonder is the governor getting off his horse to come here. I do hope he will be brave enough *this* time. Good-by, you darling! Help him as much as you can."

As she disappeared in the cabin, the gentleman approached. He was dressed with care. His superfine broadcloth fitted him admirably, his linen was of the whitest and finest; his barber had done the little nature had left undone in his black hair and silken beard. But he seemed painfully awkward as he drew near: his cordial eyes were troubled, his manner was that of a big schoolboy on his way to receive a well-deserved chastisement.

"Good-morning, Miss Zeo," he said as he stood before her, hat in hand. "I hope you liked the venison I sent. Excuse me, I cannot," he continued rapidly and as if afraid to stop, as she arose and offered him the camp-stool vacated by Irene. "I am leaving for good this morning, and I merely called to say good-by. And I wished to say, Miss Zeo, what I've been trying to say for months, that—that"—The young girl looked up at her tall and pleasant-faced lover with interest. The man was desperate; the perspiration stood upon his forehead, his face was white and set. If he had been going into battle he could not have been so nervous or determined as he added, "that—that I—love you with all my heart and soul, madam—I mean miss; and I beg you to be my wife. I *do* love you," he said with a thrill of honest energy, "but, no, no, please don't, don't say one word! not yet"—

"Gov. Magruder," the young lady replied, with great dignity as well as modesty, "I thank you. If you will allow me "—

But the other, although with all deference, would not suffer her to continue.

"No, no, Miss Buttolph. Pardon my rudeness," he said, "but I cannot bear to have you say any thing now. Please think it over. I will see you in St. Jerome. I assure you of my deepest respect as well as affection; but I cannot take your answer now,—really *cannot!* I will write. Pardon me, but let me hope," he added, with the anxiety of a boy and the embarrassment of a girl: "you will understand it—your excellent sense— Good-afternoon;" and with a hurried bow he hastened away. In a moment after he had mounted his horse in charge of a negro at a little distance; and the sound of his departing hoofs was drowned in the laughter of Irene, who had heard it all, as she ran out of the cabin to kiss and tease her sister.

"Good-afternoon! when it isn't ten o'clock in the morning. I wish Mr. Fanthorp had been here to have seen it," she said. "Accept my congratulations, Mrs. Gov. Magruder. When do you leave for Washington? And as sure as you live, Zeo, he is so popular that Mr. Fanthorp and Col. Roland between them will make him President yet: see if they don't!" And Irene threw her arms about her sister, crying as well as laughing in her excitement.

CHAPTER XXX.

MR. VENABLE IS RE-ENFORCED.

OCTOBER and November were gone at last. They departed laden with hundreds of souls; for never had the yellow-fever raged as terribly before in St. Jerome. But the death-rate had fallen to a dozen a day, then to six or eight, lately to two or three. It was not that the malaria was exhausted, but that its material had been used up; the fever was slackening its fires for lack of fuel. The labors of the young pastor and his associates, for he was but one of a band of heroes, slowly diminished. With more sleep and increasing appetite, his spirits revived, — began, in fact, as the days of rest came on, to be as fresh as ever. He thanked God for the tide of life beginning again to rise within him, conscious that he was as much the creature of its ebb and flow as any bubble lifted and lowered again upon the sea round about him.

He was not surprised when he was summoned one day to Capt. Chaffin's house; but he blamed himself for not feeling more sadness when he stood there beside the dead. It was Clara, and she lay in her own room as if sleeping sweetly. The little Israelitish maid was portrayed upon the wall over her head; a very little maid indeed in comparison with the mighty Naaman whose leprous condition was frightful to see, and whom she was in the act of urging, with violence, to seek the prophet. The visitor could smile

as he saw it; for there was nothing to distress him in the
little damsel of the better Artist lying beneath.   It was
one of the few instances in which the disease had not
stained the dead with its horrible yellow, and no dream of
genius carved in purest marble could have been so beautiful.
He had no feeling of regret, the reverse instead, as he tried
to photograph upon his mind with steady and almost critical gaze the arch of the brows, the delicacy of forehead
and nostril, the curve of cheek and chin, the Cupid's own
bow of the mouth, the sculptured perfection of the hands
clasped on the bosom.   He had but the moment, as of
photographing, in which to do it; for the body, more per-
ishable than the white roses lying upon its bosom, must be
hastened out of sight.   "We can safely leave her to the loving Hand which made her," he said.   "He who formed her
from the dust to be so lovely, will raise her again in the
perfection of an intellect in keeping with a form so fair."
Beside himself no one was present but the father, his face
sad but not bitter, his aspect breathing of patient sub-
mission only.   Mr. Quatty had his hearse at the door; but
there was no one to tend his horses, standing with drooping
heads, worn out with funerals, and he waited outside until
the brief services were over.   Then Mr. Venable took his
place while Mr. Quatty and the father brought down the
coffin, and placed it in the hearse.   Mr. Quatty was the most
sympathetic of men; but he had little to say to Capt. Chaffin, who rode beside him as they drove down the only street
in which the grass was kept under, that which led to the
cemetery; emotion was exhausted for the present.   The idiot
brother laughed loud and long, when, idling at the gate in
vigorous health, rosy and fat, he saw the coffin placed in
the hearse; but no one thought even of wondering why the
one was taken and the other left: they were too tired; and
that question also would keep until afterward.   There is no
one else to watch with Mrs. Chaffingsby, and Mr. Venable

goes back and to her room until her husband returns. He is hardly aware of the Judith pictured upon the wall, holding the head of Holofernes over that of the artist lying beneath. He is barely conscious that it is a portentous Judith, which dwarfs the meagre creator thereof into a mere mite, for he had no idea before how very small and frail she was. The fever is raging at its hottest in her. Her eyes are as coals of fire; her tongue is tremulous with the fierceness of the heat; her wasted arms, the white sleeves falling away like films of ashes from them, rise and flicker, and fall and rise again, as if they were the very flames which consumed her. She will not pause for Scripture or prayer, much less for conversation, but talks incessantly.

"You put me out dreadfully that day," she said before he had taken his seat. "I had my plan all ready. It was to cover the walls of our church as they do in Italy with the saints. I wanted to tell you. You didn't know about Clara. All the world knew. I wanted to tell you my plan, but you struck me with that, and drove it out of me. But it came again afterward. It was so cruel, when I was trying to get used to Clara! You didn't tell him, captain? No, I ought not to have told *you* my plan. You could not understand. We could " —

At this moment the door behind Mr. Venable opened softly. "Come in, my dear," the dying woman exclaimed, with uninterrupted tongue: "you will make a better Madonna than a Rachel; you are dark and deep like her. You know something great, and you keep silence " —

He had watched over too many a raving sufferer of late to be easily moved; yet, as Mrs. Chaffingsby talked on, he turned, and, to his horror more even than surprise, he saw it was Zeo Buttolph.

"Miss Zeo!" he exclaimed, started to his feet. "Are you mad? Pardon me, but go quick!" As he said it, he tried to shut the door upon her, pushing her out; but she was as determined as he, and pressed her way in.

" I am acclimated," she said : " I got back yesterday ; and
Mr. Parsons passed our house just now to say that there was
no woman to be had here. I will stay," she added, laying
aside her bonnet and shawl. " My dear madam, please " —
and she held up a quieting hand.

" I am not a dear madam," the poor, weazen-faced little
artist said with dignity. " I will be one of the old masters ;
old mistresses, I mean ; but that is *too* absurd. You two
go together in a picture, whatever it is. But I had a grander
idea then about you. It was such a glorious idea ; and,
like all glorious things, so exceedingly simple," she added,
sobering down for a moment as into the artlessness of a
child. " You see, I took the measures with my eye at
prayer-meeting and church. You soothe me, my child, and
nothing could be simpler," with a girl-like laugh. " I will
begin at the vestibule down in the basement, where we have
prayer-meetings. As a beginning, I will paint chaos on the
wall, outside the inner door, you know. You have no idea,"
— another laugh — " what a splendid chaos I could paint."

" My dear Mrs. Chaffingsby," Mr. Venable began.

" It is useless," said his companion : " better not repress
her " —

" Repress !" the sick woman interrupted with shrill sarcasm. "You have no right to prevent me, captain. It is
not my soul, as you try to make yourself think : it is Charles
and Clara. It kills me. I must get away from them, or go
mad. You make believe you are such a block you don't
know. Oh, yes ! then Adam, as you go in the door of
the basement on one hand ; Eve, you know, on the other.
There is plenty of room upon the walls all around for the
Old Testament people, up to Malachi. I will paint him
on the ceiling of the basement, pointing upward to the New
Testament in the church above. A picture, he said, must
be a pyramid. I can get in a good deal of the New Testament in the church. The Revelation on the ceiling, of

course, and everybody in it pointing, with a sweet smile, upward — to heaven, you know. That will be the apex. Oh, it will be perfectly glorious ! I tell you, captain, I will go at it right away. The negroes are all dead, but you can watch Clara and Charles until I am done. Let me alone ! "

The poor woman struggled to rise. It was more than Mr. Venable could do to hold her down in bed : Zeo had to come to his assistance.

"You shall not prevent me," she exclaimed, struggling with an almost superhuman strength. " I have at last a conception of Christ ! I never dared to put his face on canvas before ! I can do it now ! He is here ! *He sits to me himself !* " But, as she strove to break from the restraining hands, the re-action came. With the inky foam to her writhing lips, she sank back upon her bed, sobbing like an exhausted babe. Then with eyes as peaceful as those of an infant, she clasps her feeble hands, and joins in with low and half-uttered words as her pastor whispered the consolations of the gospel, and uttered a brief prayer, Zeo kneeling by him. When her husband returns, it is to prepare the dead for burial, Zeo helping him. He does it with face so set that he is not himself conscious of the tears which trickle and fall. That brown and rudely-carved face has endured many a sea, but his tears are drops of the saltest brine it has ever known ; a something in the affection of this man for his little wife, which gave to all who saw it a new conception of love.

It takes few words to tell Mr. Venable, when they walk away together, how Zeo Buttolph happens to have returned. She and her father were acclimated. The fever, too, was regarded as over. Her father had resolved to return. She could not keep him away any longer. " I could not let him be here alone," she added, and her companion understood it all.

It was almost startling to himself, the way in which his

spirits rose again as they walked along in the open air, laughing and talking as they went. He felt almost extravagantly
elated. "We are through our severe trial at last," he explained to her.

"I am glad to find you looking so well," she said. "We
have heard of your heroism, of your devotion. You cannot
tell, sir" — she began, but completed the sentence by lifting
her eyes, and looking for a moment steadily in his.

"I was but one of many others," he said, the re-action
going on so rapidly that his heart bounded within him. "It
has seemed ages since we parted," he continued, "but we
are nearly through;" and his face brightened, his eyes
sparkled. "There is but one thing now"—

"But I haven't told you about our friends," she interrupted, with rising color, as she proceeded to do so with
a degree of eagerness unusual to her. Commodore
Grandheur and Miss Aurelia Jones had spent the season
together up the country, and were really and truly to be
married. The same was true of her sister and Mr. Fanthorp. Both couples were waiting their return to the island,
to have Mr. Venable perform the ceremony. "You have
no idea," she added, "how Irene tyrannizes over Mr. Fanthorp, nor how submissive Miss Aurelia is to the commodore. It is amusing."

There was a good deal of conversation as they walked the
grass-grown streets, and passed the deserted houses; but
there was an emptiness in all they said, that which interested them most being held in reserve. He told her of his
plans. He was firmly fixed in the purpose he had formed
before she left. The capital of the State was a noble field
of labor. As soon as the church people returned, he would
resign, go up to that important centre, and organize a church.
He would build it up from the foundation. He was full of
his scheme.

"It has been a terrible time," he said at last; "but do

you know, in a certain sense and all along, I never was hap-
pier?" He laughed and talked on, and was so much in
earnest, he did not see a sudden change in her face. From
the first she had been looking at him with covert but lingering eyes; but now as they drew near her home she glanced
at him once and again, and then turned deadly pale. After
they parted at her father's gate, she stood for a time holding
firmly by it, her face drawn and almost desperate. When
she entered the house it was to go direct to her room, and
lock the door behind her.

Mr. Venable was smitten with the fever: his wild spirits
had left no doubt in her of that; and he reached Mr. Parsons's house only to fall. His duty had raised him out of
all thought or care for himself, had kept him going as by
its increasing lift and pressure. In relaxing it had left him
prostrate. The storm had passed; but he lay helpless as in
the trough of a sea which still rolls after the tempest is gone.
Capt. Chaffin and Mr. Quatty aided Mr. Parsons in nursing
him; and they could have nothing but fear for the result.

Besides him, Gen. Buttolph had to be nursed. His
placid obstinacy had always been the curse of his character. An unusually plump infant from his birth, the general
had, alas! never ceased in many senses to be but an infant;
and in returning too soon to the city, he had, as in every
thing else, yielded at last as to his own avoirdupois.

The talk with Mr. Venable upon the beach that night had
been the slow result on the inert man of the long-continued influence upon him of Zeo. Even then his promise
ended with the year. It was because she had been with him
at Sulphur St. Jerome, that he had remained, so to speak,
indolently firm. As the close of the year drew nigh, the
habits of a lifetime asserted themselves with increasing appetite. He grew restless; and, one morning, leaving his
daughters and Grit to follow in the care of Mr. Fanthorp,
he had suddenly left for St. Jerome, in order to be at least

upon the spot where he could indulge when his time of ab-
stinence was out. Zeo, however, had seized the opportunity
of acquaintances returning; and leaving her sister weeping
and remonstrating, to follow at her leisure, she had hastened
homeward but a few hours after her father. He had not
broken his promise; but his portly habit and his years of
indulgence had made him as resinous to the fever as pine
is to fire. Almost immediately upon her return with Mr.
Venable to the house from Mrs. Chaffingsby's bedside, she
was summoned to the dining-room to find him lying upon
the sofa. Although he had not drank a drop, he had, the
key being in her possession, broken open the sideboard, and
placed the decanter upon its marble top, where he could at
least see it, and was lying unconscious, struck down by the
pestilence. They did not remove him; and the sofa was
but as a funeral pyre. In a few hours the greedy flames had
consumed him; and no one contradicted Mr. Parsons, who
had hurried there for a moment from beside Mr. Venable,
when, as emphatic as ever, but in a low tone that Zeo might
not hear, he said, —

"He has been a slave so long: it is best as it is, best at
least for her."

When the first blow of her father's illness smote Zeo, she
felt sure of one thing. During the weeks of darkness and
prostration which followed, she felt it only the more certainly; it wrought itself into the rhythm of her beating heart,
it spanned like a rainbow her fast-falling tears, — the commendation of the Master in regard to a woman and never
yet of a man, "She hath done what she could."

CHAPTER XXXI.

IN WHICH IS ENDED WHAT IT IS HOPED THE READER MAY
CONSENT TO SAY HAS BEEN A YEAR WORTH LIVING.

WE weary in these pages of the pestilence, as men
wearied of it then.

December was at last rolling away, and the scattered population of St. Jerome began to return. The freshness of the
crape upon the hats of the men, and the mourning apparel
of the women, as the city slowly filled up, told always and
everywhere of the dead ; the absence of it was itself the
mark in any one of the alien and the stranger. Old neigh-
bors stopped each other along the streets, and shook hands
sorrowfully together at front gates, comparing experiences.
Yet it seemed with no one as when death has stricken its
victim singly. There was the sublimity of a great catastro-
phe in the loss of each : affliction weighed less upon the
survivors, because its general load was borne upon the
shoulders of so many, individual grief being soothed in the
air of universal sympathy. There was no outcry of anguish,
no violent weeping, seeing that the whole atmosphere was a
mist of tears ; and that also would lift and pass away in due
time, personal grief hiding itself more every day in silent
homes, then drawing itself deeper still into hearts of bereave-
ment. As the days fled, the world came rolling back.
There were vessels at the wharves, vehicles along the streets,
new faces in shop and store, in the market and counting-

room and warehouse. Everybody was coming back, and going to work again with double energy to make up for lost time. Very soon the schools and churches would fill up; the cotton-compresses and brokers' offices, the theatres and billiard-saloons, the auction-rooms, drinking-establishments, cigar-shops, gambling-hells, and places worse still, would be in even fuller operation than before the pestilence. Boys quarrelled and turned somersaults along the sidewalks; negroes shouted to each other, and argued with obstinate mules, upon the wharves, as if refreshed after rest. The tide of life was coming in more bountiful and brilliant, and salt with all variety, than ever before; and speedily the last traces of its awful ebb, the long wrinkles it had left, the ridges in the sand which were the graves of the dead, would be covered up as by the ocean. In a little while, "the fever" would be talked about as a something which befell long ago. The houses and palings would be repainted, the grounds restored, the exuberant overgrowth of vegetation pruned down, and everybody come to wear as cheerful a face as possible. Before long, no man would be so disloyal as to hint or even believe that the fever had been so disastrous as had been represented; and many would be ready to swear that it never could or would come again, world without end, for ever and evermore, amen.

No two men could be more unlike, in a bodily sense especially, than Gen. Buttolph and Mr. Venable. For that reason, the fever which flashed up again its dying fires in consuming the one had spared the other.

Sunday, the last day of the year, had arrived. Mr. Venable was still pale and weak; but every hour since the white frost had silvered the graves of the crowded cemetery, he had grown stronger. He was able to sit up at last in Mr. Parsons's parlor, and had been telling his host of his intention of resigning his charge, and of organizing a church elsewhere, as soon as he could get away.

"I want a new field," he said, "because I intend to be a new man. To do the work of the grander days before us, a man must be — the strain is so much greater — a stronger man than ever. As soon as possible I will be off. I must go, as you once told me, like a shot."

"Fiddlesticks!" Mr. Parsons replied. "We will let you do no such thing. I am alone in the world now, and you do nothing without *my* permission! Do you suppose we would have had the fever, had people settled Hacamac instead of this wretched end of the island? Never. I never mistake."

"The terraqueous machine?" suggested the other with a smile.

"It was a success, sir! If you foolish people could have had the sense to sit still," the inventor said almost angrily, "it would not have upset. If you hadn't dropped the sail, we would have gone out upon the water beautifully, sir, beautifully! But, as I told you before, I have hit upon the thing at last, at last;" and he rubbed his hands together with quiet assurance. Well he might. The idea had come to him, as has been recorded, in the act of pouring out milk for Owny; and, applying the principle of condensation, he had since then perfected his invention. In a word, he had, in good earnest, made his great discovery, which was to net him his hundred thousand a year, as the reader would agree if that invention might be named here. "No, sir," Mr. Parsons added: "I am very rich henceforth, am that much more positive; and you shall do nothing except as I say. Yonder comes Miss Zeo again, and it is the most sensible thing she could do. Don't talk too much: I must go."

It was by no means the first call she had made since Mr. Venable began to get well. To judge by the manner of their meeting now, what had passed between them before must have been satisfactory to both.

"I can hardly believe it," he said at last, as she stood beside him in her mourning, grave and strong. "The gov-

ernor is so handsome and rich, so popular, has such a future
before him, is so — so magnetic."

For of course he knew how, in addition to writing again
and again, as he had told her he should, the governor had
sent Col. Roland, who had just recovered up the country
from the fever, as an ambassador; how her sister's wrath
and tears had each in turn been poured upon her, while Mr.
Fanthorp's ridicule and mimicry of himself had exhausted
their utmost powers toward the same end.

"I like him," Zeo replied, "sincerely, and told him so
yesterday when he came. He is generous and warm-hearted, but, apart from Col. Roland, nothing more. The strain
upon me before was too great. No: it is I who am too
weak. Unless I had loved him, I dared not risk it!"

For a moment she was silent, for the governor's visit had
been one of the most painful experiences of her life; and
her eyes filled with tears as she remembered how in his
eagerness all embarrassment had been forgotten as he plead
his own cause with the eloquence of intense feeling, in the
knowledge that it was the last effort he could make to win
her. Then she added thoughtfully, as she seated herself
beside her lover, and yielded her hand to his, "I can dare
every thing where I love; and of you," she laughed with
brightening color, "I have hopes;" but she would not have
indulged him with such a loving look in return for his, had
he not been still weak from his sickness.

"You are an angel!" he exclaimed.

"No: I am only a woman, not even a heroine," she said.
"Irene has all the romance; and I am afraid," she said
modestly and in a lower voice, "that all I know is to try
and trust."

"Thank God, Zeo!" he said, his face full of gladness,
"thank God most of all for such weakness: it is thus you
are most truly a woman. You are not Mrs. Chaffingsby's
Martha or Judith; but you are all I can wish. I could not

have imagined an improvement in you the first day I saw you; but," he added with enthusiasm, "you have no idea how you are changed, you darling."

"Do you remember," Zeo said softly, "that magnificent day after the storm, — the first day of the year, I mean, on board the Nautilus, the day we landed?"

"It was the brightest day of my life," her lover said; "but to-day, and after the tempest of the fever, is far brighter, and the pain of the year has been better to us than the pleasure. Mr. Parsons could state it all upon his blackboard, and give you the exact result of loss and gain. I cannot; but I know that to me it has been a wonderful year — a year brimming full and running over. This new year, Zeo, will be better still, because I will have you." Her eyes were drooped; but she lifted them wholly at one with him as he said, and drew her to his heart as he did so, 'But the old year has been to both of us, has it not, Zeo, a year worth living?"

Franklin Press: Rand, Avery, & Co., Boston.